Rog
Rogan, Barbara.
Hindsight : a novel of
    the class of 1972 $ 24.00

Also by Barbara Rogan

Suspicion
Rowing in Eden
A Heartbeat Away
Saving Grace
Café Nevo
Changing States

HINDSIGHT

A Novel of the Class of 1972

Barbara Rogan

Simon & Schuster
New York London Toronto Sydney Singapore

SIMON & SCHUSTER
Rockefeller Center
1230 Avenue of the Americas
New York, NY 10020

For information regarding special discounts for bulk purchases,
please contact Simon & Schuster Special Sales at
1-800-456-6798 or business@simonandschuster.com

Manufactured in the United States of America
10 9 8 7 6 5 4 3 2 1

Library of Congress Cataloging-in-Publication Data
  Rogan, Barbara.
    Hindsight : a novel of the class of 1972 / Barbara Rogan.
      p.   cm.
    1. Class reunions—Fiction. I. Title.
  PS3568.O377 H5   2003
  813'.54—dc21   2002036637

ISBN 0-7432-0599-5

This book is for my Westbury friends, and in memory of
Harvey Oxenhorn and Jay Goldman.
Dedicated also to Dr. Ari Ezratty, brilliant cardiologist and
mensch; and his colleagues, the dedicated professionals of
St. Francis Hospital.

acknowledgments

If I ever committed murder, the last man I'd want on my trail would be Detective Sergeant Bob Doyle of the Suffolk County Police. Fortunately we met under happier circumstances. I'm grateful for his generous help with this book, and to Bob Baumann for introducing us.

MOMA's Georgia O'Keeffe exhibition is imaginary, but the quote ascribed to O'Keeffe is not. It came from *O'Keeffe,* by Britta Benke, Taschen Verlag, 1994.

Thanks to Bill Strodthoff, who not only taught me everything I know about car repair shops but also kept my car running in the process.

Rob Byrnes, a sysop on Compuserve's political forum, was most helpful, as were many of the kind souls who frequent the writers' forum.

Thanks to Joy Harris, Laurie Bernstein, and Ben Kadishson for their comments on the first draft of this book, and to Marysue Rucci for smart, sensitive editing.

And finally, I'm grateful to my family for their unfailing patience, support, and tolerance for fast food.

"It is the future we must look to," said Constance. "It is useless to pursue the past."

"It is needless," said Audrey. "It will pursue us."

Ivy Compton-Burnett,
A Father and His Fate

HINDSIGHT

prologue
June 1972

In the beginning was the dress, and the dress was beautiful: a shimmering concoction of black and silver, strapless, formfitting, the sexiest item Willa Scott had ever owned in all her seventeen years, thanks to Angel, who'd taken her shopping and made her buy it. She'd had to smuggle it out of the house and change in the car, but it was worth it if only for the expression in their eyes as they looked up from the rocks and saw her coming. Patrick and Angel were there, Vinny, Travis, Shake, and Nancy. Two missing: Jeremiah, who wasn't expected, and Caleb, who was. Patrick untangled himself from Angel and rose from the rocks, lurching toward her like a marionette. "Jesus Christ, girl, are you *trying* to break my heart?" She laughed and offered him her cheek. His lips brushed her neck instead, descended to her bare shoulder, and remained there until she gently pushed him away. There was beer on his breath but he wasn't drunk yet.

A hot afternoon, late in June, sun streaming down on Beacon Hill. Unencumbered by houses or roads, its crest reachable only by a footpath that wove through dense, fragrant mats of low-growing juniper, the hill was their private spot, their place to hang out after and, often, during school. An outcropping of rocks overlooked the high school football field. Other kids knew about Beacon Hill, but they didn't go there without an invitation, and few were forthcoming.

Below them, on the field, Willa saw parents and teachers gathering. "Where's Caleb?" she asked.

"Who cares?" Patrick's arms enfolded her. "I'm here, you're here . . ."

"And I'm here, or did you forget?" said a sultry voice. Angelica Busky—Angel, they called her—pinched his ear between two scarlet-tipped fingers. "Down, boy," she said. Patrick obeyed meekly, and Angel turned to Willa. "Foxy!" She unstrapped the camera attached to her wrist and snapped Willa's picture.

"Look who's talking," Willa said, for Angel had somehow poured her bounteous self into a ruby-red flamenco dress, flared at the thigh and cut to flaunt the famed Angelic bosom.

Angel shimmied and the boys on the rocks let out a collective moan. She thrust her camera at Patrick. "Take us both."

He staggered, clutching his chest. "You have no idea how long I've waited to hear those words."

"Our *picture*, wiseass. Like you could handle the two of us!" She flung her arm around Willa's shoulders; Willa stiffened for a moment before encircling Angel's waist. If ever there was a time to let bygones be bygones, surely this was it. They vamped for the camera and for the boys, well aware of the pleasing contrast they presented: Angel of the wild red hair, green eyes, and voluptuous body; Willa tall and slender, with dark blue eyes and golden hair that flowed like honey over her shoulders.

The others, too, had dressed for the occasion. Shake—John Shaker—and Nancy Weston were dressed alike as usual, in matching white bell-bottom pantsuits. Her hand was in his hip pocket, his in hers. Travis Fleck, in a sports coat and tie but no shirt, clambered monkeylike over the rocks and, under the cover of a congratulatory hug, rubbed his tall skinny self up against Willa. She shoved him off. Willa was no prude, no matter what Angel thought, and never minded the occasional friendly squeeze or hug; but Travis was always so sneaky about it. Vinny, looking after Caleb's interests as usual, shambled over and removed Travis by his scraggly ponytail. He offered Willa a joint.

"Those your graduation duds?" she asked, accepting a light. Vinny wore jeans and a tie-dyed Grateful Dead T-shirt with the left sleeve rolled up to hold his Camels and reveal a pumped bicep.

"Hey," he said defensively. "It's a new shirt. Where the hell's Caleb?"

"Dunno. I thought he'd be here."

"They're starting," called Patrick, and they joined him on the rocks to watch their class graduate without them. Two by two, they marched onto the field, the class of '72, ushered in by the high school band. As strains of music wafted upward, Willa glanced at Shake, who played first sax. He was watching the band with an unguarded, forlorn look that disappeared the moment he caught her watching. "Man," he said, flashing his dimples, "look at those turkeys. Best part of busting outta this joint is never having to wear that fuckin' band uniform again."

"Fuckin' A, man," said Nancy, his loyal acolyte. Angel and Willa exchanged glances, allies still when it came to Nancy. Girl-friends came and went, but Angel and Willa were the only girls who belonged in their own right: a crucial difference, in their eyes.

"Nah," Patrick said. "Best part's never having to deal with that asshole Grievely again." It was Donald Grievely, Millbrook High's principal, who had barred Patrick from the graduation ceremony, ostensibly for his little prank with the audiovisual projector—a cut from *Deep Throat* spliced into a ninth-grade sex-education filmstrip—but actually because Grievely had been spoiling for one last shot at busting his balls. Of course once Patrick was banned, his friends were bound to boycott. All or none, that's how it was for them, with Jeremiah as usual the exception.

"Hell yeah," Vinny said, "but I gotta tell ya, my mother was pissed. She was looking forward to seeing me graduate."

Patrick peered up at him through a shock of black hair. "What you talking about, man? They were never gonna let you graduate."

"So? *She* didn't know that."

Travis laughed, spraying beer through the gap between his front teeth. "Your mom didn't notice you were failing every sub-ject?"

"Fuck you, man." Vinny stepped back from the spray. "You think it's easy flunkin' all your subjects?"

"Quit yer bragging," Angel said. "You passed shop."

"Couldn't help it, could I? I'm just too good with my hands." He reached for Angel, who evaded him easily and went to sit with Patrick. Willa peered down the hill. Where *was* Caleb, anyway?

"They should've given you a special award," Travis said, "for the lowest GPA in school history. You should've been the counter-valedictorian." A joke, but he kept his distance. Vinny was the reason no one ever messed with them or invaded the hill, his friendship their collective umbrella; but it barely stretched to cover Travis Fleck, designated hanger-on and purveyor of essen-tial substances.

"The retrotorian," Willa offered. "You could've made a speech like Jeremiah, only everything he says, you say the opposite."

Vinny struck a valedictory pose. "Ladies and gentlemen, teachers, parents, and fellow students, fuck you all very much for coming."

Below him on the field, Jeremiah Wright was striking a similar pose at the podium. When Patrick had gotten banned from graduation, Jeremiah pled his case to the principal and, when that failed, gamely offered to join the boycott. He knew, of course, that they wouldn't let him, and they knew he knew, but he'd done the right thing by offering and they accepted that, as they accepted and forgave so much for Jeremiah. He was the valedictorian of their class; he had earned the right to speak for all of them, the bad boys and girls on the hill as well as the good ones below.

They nestled in among the boulders and listened in a haze of weed, the sweet hot whisper of summer on their necks, freedom's nectar on their lips. But the same breeze that so faithfully delivered the scent of juniper from the hillside scattered Jeremiah's words like dandelion seeds. Only a few reached them, high on their hill. *Future. Promise. Never forget.* At the end of the speech, he turned their way and raised his arm in a closed-fist salute: for Jeremiah, a gesture of the utmost defiance. Patrick leaped to his feet and waved back, and the others followed. The seated graduates, following this exchange, spotted them now for the first time, silhouetted against the setting sun. A murmur ran through their ranks; a few brave souls cheered, while, scrunched in his seat on the makeshift podium, the principal fumed. Willa threw kisses, Angel snapped pictures, and the boys saluted their classmates with beer cans.

A rare moment, charged with magic; even as it unfolded Willa knew that it would stay with her forever. All that was missing was Caleb, and suddenly he was there, striding gracefully up the crest of the hill, tall and lean, in a white shirt and khaki trousers, a headful of amber curls. He walked straight to Willa and kissed her on the lips, a long, soulful kiss. Now Willa's happiness was complete. She looked at Angel from the shelter of Caleb's arms and when their eyes met, she smiled triumphantly.

The others reacted to Caleb's arrival as they always did, by grouping themselves around him. If Jeremiah was the star atop their Christmas tree, Caleb was the trunk that held them all together. And he'd come bearing gifts, two bottles of champagne and a bag of clear plastic cups. Vinny uncorked the first bottle with a pop that could be heard down on the field. They drank to each other, to good times and undying friendship, to the past and the future. They finished one bottle and opened the next; they drank and grew merry, while below them on the field, the ceremony droned toward an end. Patrick turned on his radio and "Sympathy for the Devil" drew them to their feet. They began to dance. Willa danced with every one of the boys, each dance a good-bye, because tomorrow, much against her will, she was leaving on a summer-long trip to France. The boys were going on a cross-country jaunt in the '57 Chevy that Vinny and Patrick had spent two years rebuilding. Willa had begged her parents to let her go with them, but of course they couldn't wait to tear her away from her friends—as if physical separation could make a difference to what they meant to each other. Her only consolation was that Angel wasn't going either.

After dark, Jeremiah turned up with another bottle of champagne. They danced on. The hill was lit by a full moon and the gentle strobe of fireflies. Willa tried to save the slow dances for Caleb, but Patrick claimed one and would not be denied. Patrick was wiry and strong, not much taller than Willa. He held her close and it was obvious what he was feeling.

"Willa," he said, slurring slightly. "I've failed, Willa."

"How have you failed?"

"The one thing I promised myself I'd do during high school, the thing I wanted most, I didn't get."

"Oh, really? What's that?" They'd been flirting forever, she and Patrick; only this time, he wasn't playing.

His arms tightened around her, hands splayed across her back. He kissed the hollow behind her ear, heedless. "I think you know."

Angel was dancing with Jeremiah. Jeremiah was talking earnestly, but Angel wasn't listening; she was staring at Willa, who felt the heat of that scorching gaze. If Patrick made a fool of himself tonight, Angel would blame her; she would think it revenge. "Come on, Patch," Willa murmured, removing an exploratory hand from her ass. "I thought we were past this."

"How could we get past what we've never gone through?"—a pretty nifty notion for someone as drunk as he was acting.

"Have you forgotten Caleb and Angel?" Willa said.

"This is bigger than all of us," he said. It *felt* bigger, she thought, suppressing a giggle. Angel said he was hung like a bull, and she ought to know. Patrick's hand dipped downward once again, and suddenly Caleb was there with Angel at his side. "Wrong girl, pal," he said, not unkindly, and extricated Willa from Patrick's grasp. With the ease of long practice, Angel latched on to Patrick and bore him away.

When they could dance no more, they flung themselves onto the rocks to catch their breath. An outsider, had one been present, might have been reminded of seal pups exhausted from playing in the surf. Jeremiah opened the last bottle of champagne and poured it ceremoniously, serving the girls first. "Here's to the three most beautiful women at Millbrook High. Ladies, it's been a privilege."

Then Angel stood and raised her glass. She was a sight to see, a flame on the hill topped by a blazing cloud of hair and a pale face awash in moonlight. "I have a toast," she said with a faint, inward smile, looking from one face to another. "Here's to doing the right thing."

There was a moment of silence. Willa was struck by the oddity of such a toast from Angel, who prided herself on never doing the right thing. She glanced at Caleb, but his face was turned aside.

Jeremiah was the first to speak. "Here's to knowing what that is," he said, and their laughter dissipated the tension that had sprung up from nowhere. Angel sat back down beside Patrick, who put his arm around her. Shake produced his harmonica and started playing a blues tune, sweet and sad; and Angel, recognizing the song, joined in.

> "'Frankie and Johnny were lovers
> O Lordy, how they could love
> They swore t' be true to each other
> Just as true as the stars above
> He was her man but he done her wrong.'"

Angel had a husky, tuneful, been-there-done-that sort of voice informed by her idol, Janis Joplin. Shake's harmonica alone was pleasure enough; many of Willa's finest moments had been played out to its music. But combined with Angel's voice, the classic folk ballad of unfaithful lovers brought tears to her eyes. Never again, for as long as she lived, would she hear that song without remembering this night. When the last notes died out, there came a silence, and in the silence an acknowledgment that this was how it had to end. For end it must, their time together, this private good-bye. June nights were chilly in the hills of northern Westchester. Other parties beckoned, other people; and there were couples among them who craved a private hour in between.

"All good things come to an end," Jeremiah said. "So they say; and I'm beginning to see it's true."

"This isn't the end," Angel said. "It's the beginning."

"It's the end of the first stage and the start of the second," Caleb said. "We build on this. What we have together, no one can take away. This is the foundation." He raised his glass. "To all of us, till death do us part."

"To us," they echoed. It was the signal they'd been waiting for. One last round of hugs and farewells as they gathered their belongings and then someone—later on, no one would ever agree on who it was—someone said, "Let's make a vow: Twenty years from today, wherever we are, whatever we're doing, we meet again, right here on Beacon Hill."

Given the prevailing state of maudlin drunkenness, this was a proposition that could not fail to persuade. And so it was solemnly resolved and sworn to over a layering of hands, Vinny's proposal for a blood oath having been overruled by Jeremiah, who wanted none of his blood: Come what may, come heaven or hell, they would all meet again in twenty years.

1

January 1992

They offered to send a car. Willa refused; she hated being driven. The people sent to fetch her inevitably took upon themselves her entertainment through chatter, which in turn obliged her to hold up her end just when she felt least sociable. Far better to make her own way in peace. That afternoon, she drove to the station and took the Metro-North from Chappaqua into Grand Central station. Mid-December, and already it was snowing; all the more reason to be glad she wasn't driving. There were delays, and the ride took fifty minutes, which she spent working on her speech. Despairing over it, really, reading it again and again with growing horror. It was the same talk she'd given last year when her book had come out in hardcover, but now every line reeked of irony.

Willa knew she shouldn't be doing this. She wasn't ready; it was too soon. But Judy Trumpledore had gotten on her case—*Do you good; about time you got off your butt*—and it was pointless arguing with Judy. It wasn't that she didn't know the meaning of the word "no"—she was an editor, after all—it was that she tended not to hear it.

In Ardsley, a man entered the train and sat beside her, though there were plenty of empty seats available. Wall Street type, presently morphing from lean and hungry to fat and smug; married, without a doubt. Willa looked him square in the face. "I wouldn't sit there if I were you."

This remark seemed to encourage rather than deter him. "Why not?" he asked, flashing dimples that, amortized over a lifetime, must have been worth a thousand lays.

"They say it's not contagious, but who the hell knows?"

She got her seat back. Returned to her speech, slashing and cutting. Too bad she couldn't cut it all. Be calm, she ordered herself, and obediently took a few deep breaths. Leaning her head against the cold glass, she repeated Judy's words like a mantra: "Never underestimate the human capacity for self-absorption." Willa's story was four months old, longer than the memory span of the average New Yorker.

At Grand Central she took the number 4 downtown express to

Union Square. It was Willa's conviction that no one could say he knew a city who did not know its underground. She saw the subway as the city's circulatory system, its veins and arteries; the passengers as platelets. She took pride in her ability (the product of a good memory and a misspent youth) to navigate the subways, which she continued to do long after the need was gone. Simon had hated it. "My clients ride the subway," he would say, as if that in itself were sufficient reason for his wife to avoid it. Willa had spared his feelings by not telling him.

She emerged from the subway into a blast of cold air and a dazzle of white. A thin blanket of snow covered Union Square, and more was falling: thick, slow flakes that landed on her eyelashes and the hair that streamed out from under her brimmed hat. No one's going to come out in this, she thought, and her spirits lifted.

The signing was at a small, independent bookstore called Illuminations, a popular spot for Village residents as well as NYU students, among whom, according to Judy, a Compton-Burnett cult had blossomed. Turning a corner onto East Fourteenth Street, Willa was confronted by a plate-glass window full of her books, not just the new one but the two earlier biographies as well, dozens of copies in hardcover and paperback, along with a blowup of the cover of her latest, *Family Secrets: The Poison Pen Novels of Ivy Compton-Burnett*. Beside it was also a poster-size portrait of the book's author.

Willa cringed at the photo and tugged the brim of her hat down over her face. That god-awful glam shot. Judy had made her do it. The only good thing about it was that it looked nothing like her, so no one ever recognized her from her jacket picture. They'd posed her to look like the heroine of some soppy romance: standing barefoot on a windswept jetty, long dress blowing, hair tousled, nothing but sky and sea behind her. Simon had loved it; so he'd said. Kept a framed copy on his desk, faced outward. Simon had been very supportive of her career. Whenever they went out, he'd introduce her as "my wife, the authoress." Writer, she'd told him, again and again. Author if you must. "Authoress" is patronizing and archaic. And he'd promise to remember, but the next time he introduced her, he'd say it again: my wife, the authoress.

Judy was standing just inside the revolving door, peering out with a worried look. When she spotted Willa, her face lit up and she waved. Willa stepped into the revolving door. As it opened into the store, she heard a babble of voices and glimpsed a dense knot of people milling about with wineglasses in their hands. Panic seized her; she kept turning and emerged back on the sidewalk.

Judy followed her out. "What are you, nuts? It's freezing out here."

"I can't do it, Judy."

Judith Trumpledore, publisher of Trumpledore Books, an imprint of HarperCollins, was a short woman, expensively dressed, with a figure that at their age bespoke considerable effort. She had wavy black hair, sharp features, intelligent gray eyes, and a nanny-like certitude. "Sure you can," she said, seizing Willa's arm with a grip of iron. "It's like riding a bike. Where'd you come from, anyway? I didn't see a taxi."

"I took the subway to Union Square. You don't understand: The speech is a disaster."

"The subway? Jesus, Willa, I said we'd send a car."

"What's the big deal? We always used to." Back when they were roommates, she meant, before Willa's marriage and Judy's ascension up the ranks; back when they were both newly minted editorial assistants at Harrow Books.

"And Nathan's was our favorite restaurant. That was then, this is now." Judy was still holding Willa's arm, as if afraid she would bolt.

Willa stared through the plate glass at the crowd inside. There must have been fifty customers in the store, which made no sense at all. Through pure luck, which occasionally runs good as well as bad, the publication of *Family Secrets* had coincided with a reissuing of several of Compton-Burnett's out-of-print novels; consequently her own book had been widely and generously reviewed. Nevertheless, literary biographies are hardly the sort of books that attract crowds; there couldn't be this many people in New York who'd even read Ivy Compton-Burnett, much less a book about her. "Who are they all?" she asked.

"Friends, fans, a bunch from NYU. I told you, Compton-Burnett's hot."

"Did you publicize this thing?"

Judy laughed at her accusatory tone. "Guilty. We ran an ad in the *Times* and sent invitations to some friends of yours. This may come as a shock, my dear, but most writers like publicity. They have the odd notion that it sells books."

"It's not that I'm not grateful. It's just—"

"Enough, Willa. Let's go. Chin up, chest out, march."

Inside, someone took her coat, and someone else produced a glass of wine. Judy hovered by her side, but by now there was no need; Willa had made the switch to full authorial mode. Many faces were familiar: there were colleagues of Simon, as well as people from Harrow Books, where she'd worked, and Harper-Collins, where her books had been published. Some of them had been to the funeral; none of them had seen her since. "How *are* you?" they all asked. There was concern but also, unmistakably, curiosity. Willa hid behind a Plexiglas smile and moved quickly from one to another.

Manny Schultz, her literary agent, emerged from the crowd to envelop her in a massive bear hug. He smelled of wool and snow and pipe tobacco. Willa was amazed to see him. Publicity was the publisher's concern, and Manny made a point of never going to his authors' appearances. "If I crave pontification," he would say, "I'll listen to the pope."

"What are you doing here?" she said.

"If Mohammed won't come to the mountain, the mountain must go to Mohammed. You owe me a book, my sweet, and I will have it."

"You should twirl your mustache when you say that."

"I don't have a mustache."

"Then you should cultivate one."

He smiled but stayed the course. "Are you working?"

"Of course." She looked past his shoulder at the rear of the shop, where a podium and some thirty chairs had been set up. Most of these were taken; booksellers were hastily adding more. "Excuse me, Manny, I think they're ready for me. You played me," she said in a different voice to Judy as they moved off. "It's a goddamn coming-out party."

"You had to come out sometime," said Judy, practical as always. "*Are* you working?"

"I meant to slink out. This is a freak show."

"It's a show of friendship and support. Why look a gift horse in the mouth?"

"I've never understood that expression. If someone gave me a horse, first thing I'd do would be to check its teeth."

"You've been reading too much Compton-Burnett," Judy said, and handed her over to the owner of the store, a tall, thin, flustered man whose name Willa had missed.

She sat in the front row, smiling politely throughout his introduction, as if he were speaking of someone else. The usual inaccuracies, things puffed up to sound so much grander than they were. "Formerly an editor at Harrow Books, Ms. Scott began her series of remarkable literary biographies when she moved to the country. Publishing's loss was literature's gain." Assistant editor was as far as she'd gotten, one step above entry level for well-brought-up girls with Ivy League credentials. She'd been noticed, though, given books to edit, and slated for promotion until her pregnancy grew evident; and that was the end of that. Publishing, it was often said, is a great field for women; childless women is what they meant, though that usually went unsaid. Judy Trumpledore stayed single and chose her lovers judiciously. She got a promotion; Willa got a baby shower.

Her salary was a pittance and likely to remain so. Simon's practice was thriving, and ever since she'd gotten pregnant he'd been agitating to leave the city. Growing up in suburbia, Willa had vowed never to return. But she never went back to Harrow after her maternity leave, and six months after Chloe was born, they moved into their first house, a small Victorian in Chappaqua, a twenty-minute drive from where Willa had grown up.

A burst of applause; she'd missed her cue. The owner looked at her expectantly. Willa rose and made her way to the podium. She adjusted the mike, opened her folder, and raised her eyes to the audience. Every seat was taken, and there were people standing on the edges and half hidden among the stacks. A sea of faces, familiar and half familiar, studied her through eyes opaque with hidden thoughts, dense with speculation. Willa's poise shattered; suddenly she could not bear to be looked at in this knowing way. Then Judy caught her eye, and something in her look reminded Willa of who she was and made it possible to begin.

"Ivy Compton-Burnett took to novel writing relatively late in life, at the age of forty, when she burst forth onto a stage dominated by contemporaries such as Virginia Woolf and Anthony Powell. Critics were astounded by her work, scandalized, enthralled. 'Aeschylus, transposed into the key of Jane Austen,' the London *Times* wrote. She was compared to a surgeon, her novels to scalpels, but in fact her method was more akin to vivisection than to surgery. Compton-Burnett sliced into living families and laid them bare; they, like severed worms still ignorant of their plight, continued to go about their business while the writer went about hers.

"Her specimens were upper-class Elizabethan families of the utmost outward gentility, but what she exhumed from beneath that surface gentility would bring a blush to the cheeks of Harold Robbins. Incest, adultery, blackmail, matricide, patricide, infanticide—everything, practically, but genocide. Events on a large scale didn't interest Compton-Burnett, who lived through two world wars without ever feeling the need to incorporate them into her fiction. Or not directly, at least. She was interested in power, without a doubt; totalitarian power and its various abuses were her life's study. But she was drawn to work on small, exquisite canvasses."

She paused for a sip of water. The next page was full of angry blue slashes. Already Willa had strayed into dangerous waters. Somewhere out there Simon's colleagues were sitting, two of his partners and his secretary. Faithful Minty, who must have known: How dare she show her face?

"Her view of human nature was not benign. Compton-Burnett believed that most of us would succumb to strong temptation, that many did, and that the great majority got away with it. 'There are signs that strange things happen,' she told one interviewer, 'though they do not emerge. . . . We know much less of each other than we think.'"

Willa soldiered on, somehow got through it. The audience was kind, the Q and A that followed blessedly brief. The usual questions: "How do you choose your subjects?" ("I don't; they choose me.")

"How many hours a day do you write?" ("Since both my editor and agent are here today, I'd have to say between twelve and fourteen.") And so on. Then it was all over but the book signing. Willa sat behind an oak table piled high with copies of *Family Secrets*. Beside her, a young bookseller asked names and opened books for her to sign. Willa used a simple blue Bic. The gold Cartier pen Simon had given her on the occasion of her first book signing was at home in its box. Someday she would give it to Chloe.

Simon's secretary, Minty, third in line, fixed her with a wet-eyed look that brought out the beagle in her long, lugubrious face. "Willa, my dear."

"Hello, Minty," Willa said, briskly yet with an air of having only just remembered her name. Minty got not only a signature but also an inscription, a quote from Compton-Burnett: "'It is better to talk honestly.'"

She signed the next book, and the next. After a while she stopped looking up. "Who would you like it signed to?" she heard the bookseller ask for the twentieth time.

A man's voice replied, a voice so tantalizingly familiar that a chill ran through her. "To the fool on the hill," the voice said. Willa looked up. The man before her was a stranger until he smiled; the moment she saw that cocky smile, she knew him. "Patrick," she cried, thrusting out her hand; the table was between them.

"Hello, Willa. Lovely as ever, I see."

He was older, of course, and better dressed than she'd ever known him to be, in a tweed jacket, sweater, and khakis. Fine lines radiated from the corners of his eyes, but the eyes themselves were unchanged, full of mischief. His hair was shorter but still dark, with the same stray forelock slanted across his forehead.

"This is a surprise," she said, and felt herself blush. He laughed, and her numbed heart contracted in a spasm of yearning for the old Patrick, the old Beacon Hill gang. More than friends, they were the gold standard against which all subsequent friendships had been gauged and found wanting.

He'd wanted to surprise her, he said. He'd planned it that way. "From the moment I saw the ad in the *Times*, I anticipated this meeting."

"What if I hadn't known you?"

"Impossible," he replied with perfect confidence.

"It's been a long time."

"You proved me right yourself. And people don't change that much."

No, she thought, we just get to know them better. So Compton-Burnett said, in one of the passages Willa had blue-lined in her speech: "Familiarity breeds contempt, and ought to breed it. It is through familiarity that we get to know each other."

The people behind Patrick were growing restless. The little bookseller placed an open book before her, and Willa bent to the task. "To Patrick," she wrote, "nobody's fool." That part was easy, but how to sign it? *Love?* For a man she hadn't seen in ages, had never even known as a man, but only as a charming, feckless boy? *Fondly?* That was cold. Finally she signed it "Your Willa," and felt the blood rush to her cheeks as she held it out to him.

But instead of taking the book, he grasped her wrist. His hand was warm, or hers cold. "I'm taking you out after this." Although it was a statement, not an invitation, something in his look as he waited for her answer recalled her old power over him.

Willa glanced aside. Judy and Manny were beside the podium, heads canted together, talking intently. They meant to take her somewhere and double-team her. She turned back to Patrick, who had not budged, though the line exerted its pressure.

"I'd like that," she said.

2

He didn't ask where she wanted to go but led the way briskly to a little basement joint off Thirteenth Street, improbably named El Cantino Szechuan. A sign in the window touted "the world's finest Cuban-Chinese cuisine."

"Only in New York," Willa said as she picked her way down the steps to the entrance.

"I wandered in here my first night back," Patrick said. "Best grub I've had in years, plus they let me run a tab. I love saying, 'Put it on my tab,' don't you? It's like ordering a martini shaken, not stirred, or walking into Rick's and saying, 'Play it again, Sam,' which, as a matter of fact, no one actually says in the movie. I eat here every night."

"The same restaurant every day?"

"Sometimes twice a day. I am nothing if not loyal. Besides, Consuela here has adopted me, haven't you, *Mamacita*?"

The large, dour woman behind the counter simpered and turned girlish in his presence. "*Hola,* Professor," she greeted him, ignoring Willa. She led them past a long bar to a booth in the rear of the restaurant, which was larger than it looked from outside but sparsely populated; the only other diners at the moment were a party of three, two young men and a teenage girl trying hard to look older. Scenic posters of China were hung haphazardly along the walls. The subdued lighting surely owed more to economy than any attempt at atmosphere. Patrick ordered wine and waved away the menu. *"Estamos en tus manos, Mamacita."*

Then they were alone. Patrick looked at Willa and she looked back, each marking the passage of time in the other's face. It was strange to see a face at once so familiar and so changed. Though she could still see the boy in him, Patrick had acquired a man's opacity. He looked solid, successful; he'd grown into his self-confidence. She was glad to see him, but there was something sad about it, too, like meeting Peter Pan all grown up. As for herself, she was grateful for the dim lighting.

"Feels like old times, doesn't it?" he said. "Or like a wrinkle in time."

She smiled at the reference. The book of that title by

Madeleine L'Engle was one of many finds they'd shared with one another. Each of them had had a passion. Books had been hers, movies his. "It does," she said. "So much so, I keep waiting for the others to arrive. What are you doing here?"

"Teaching film at NYU. Just started in September."

"So you *are* a professor!"

He laughed at the look on her face. "Don't blame you for being surprised. I'm amazed myself. I keep waiting to be unmasked."

"How did it happen?"

"Pretty much by accident. College suited me. Didn't want to leave so I kept on going. Ran out of degrees after a while, and found myself unexpectedly employable."

Willa's parents used to call him a bum and a hoodlum. One day, they'd predicted, he'd be parking her car, if not stealing it. Now she regretted that they weren't on better terms; she'd have enjoyed calling them up and gloating.

"I wasn't surprised by what you do," she said, "only that it's such a perfect fit. Life rarely works out that way."

"Yours has," he said.

She stared at him. Was he mocking her, the life she'd settled for: truncated yearnings in a *Town & Country* setting?

"I mean," his voice less certain, "you always wanted to be a writer."

"I wanted to write novels. Instead I write about novelists."

"A fine distinction."

"No," Willa said, "a salient one."

"Are you married?"

"Widowed."

He blinked. "I'm sorry."

"I have a daughter. Chloe's almost fifteen."

"Fifteen," he said, in a reminiscing tone. "Driving all the boys crazy, if she's anything like her mother."

"She's not, thank God. How about you? Wife, kids?"

"No kids. Married, sort of."

A flat silence followed. A world of heartbreak in those words: not hers this time, some other poor sap of a woman. "Sort of." Was that what Simon used to say when asked?

"She teaches at UCLA," Patrick said. "Wonderful woman.

Hates New York as much as I hate L.A. We're like Woody Allen and Diane Keaton, geographically incompatible."

Willa nodded but said nothing. There was an element of judgment to the silence. For the first time, she had looked at Patrick through grown-up eyes and found him wanting.

He seemed familiar with the look. "I saw this T-shirt the other day," he said. "It read, 'If a man speaks in the forest and no woman hears, is he still wrong?'"

Willa laughed. Let him keep his secrets, she thought. They weren't kids anymore, to spill out their hearts to each other. As she had no intention of expanding on her own situation, she had no right to pry into his. "Do you like teaching?"

"I do, actually. I seem driven to fulminate, as you may recall. I'm sure I talked your ear off, back in the days."

"You introduced us to some of the best films ever made. Bergman, Malle, Truffaut . . ."

"Ah yes. *Jules and Jim.*"

"My favorite."

"Of course. It was our story."

She stared. "What do you mean?"

"Best friends in love with the same girl—sound familiar?"

"Sure. It's an old story; Truffaut didn't invent it."

"You broke my heart, you know," he said, so simply and matter-of-factly that Willa could not believe or even pretend to believe he was joking.

She said, "You were crazy about Angel."

"Apples and oranges," he said with a shrug.

Men. She turned away. Across the room, one of the boys was kissing the girl, while the other, believing himself unobserved, watched with a complicated blend of vicarious satisfaction, frustration, and longing.

"Dumplings," a voice said. Consuela balanced a tray on one massive hip as she transferred dishes to the table. "Refried rice and beans. Beef with peppers, very hot. Watch out."

Willa, who for months had been eating dutifully but without appetite, was assaulted by an aroma so deliciously earthy that her mouth began to water. She filled her plate and Patrick filled his, and they ate in the most comfortable silence she'd shared in ages. No need to make conversation; it was only Patrick, after all, spouting his usual line of nonsense. Because surely it *was* nonsense. They'd been friends, close friends, nothing more. They'd flirted, but so what? If they'd given academic credit for flirting, Patrick would have made valedictorian in place of Jeremiah.

When her plate was empty, she leaned back and smiled. "Was I right?" Patrick asked, refilling her wineglass.

"You were. Excellent grub; thank you."

"Don't say that. It makes me feel you're about to leave."

"I do have a train to catch."

He started to speak and stopped. Their eyes held. His were free of guile. *We're adults now,* they said; *we can do what we want.* But he had no idea what she wanted.

She excused herself and went to the ladies' room. Tiny, two stalls and a single basin. The girl from the other table was there before her, fixing her makeup in the cracked mirror above the sink. Behind the bright red lipstick and thick mascara was the soft, unformed face of a child. This girl couldn't be much older than Chloe. Willa had a sudden impulse to speak to her, warn her. *Careful,* she wanted to say. *They seem so sweet, but they'll break your heart.* She waited for their eyes to meet, but, though the room was so small they had to squeeze past each other, the girl never looked at Willa. Too old, too worn, a nonperson to this child.

When she returned to the table, the plates had been cleared and Patrick was drinking a cup of coffee. There was one for her as well, covered with a saucer to keep it hot. A small gesture of consideration; it was a measure of Willa's instability that she needed to blink back tears. Simon used to do that. Every Sunday morning she'd wake to the smell of coffee, his and hers. And by the time they got around to drinking . . . but she wouldn't think about that now, or ever.

She took a sip, the strong black brew as bracing as a slap on the cheek.

"Regular okay?" Patrick asked. "We're not at the decaf stage yet, are we?"

"Not quite." Willa glanced at her watch. She'd already missed the nine-fifteen. Didn't matter; Chloe was spending the night with a friend, and the trains ran every hour.

Eventually the conversation turned to the old Beacon Hill crowd. Willa's parents had sold their house and moved to Palm Beach during her freshman year in college; between obligatory visits to them and her deepening involvement with Simon, Willa had gradually lost touch with her old friends. Patrick hadn't spoken to any of them in years but knew more than she did. Jeremiah was a lawyer in Washington, he told her, and Vinny owned a garage somewhere in the Bronx. Shake had married Nancy shortly after high school and last Patrick heard he was playing in a band down in Maryland. Neither of them knew what had become of Travis Fleck. That left Caleb and Angel, but where those names should have arisen, there came instead a hole in the conversation. What cause Patrick had for discomfort, Willa did not know; she had her own. Her parting from Caleb had been bitter. And from Angel there had been no parting, no good-byes, bitter or otherwise. They had quarreled; there had been a rupture, followed by a long, unbroken silence.

She asked finally—how could she not?—"What about Angel?"

"I've no idea. I haven't seen or heard from her since high school."

"Neither have I," Willa said. They stared at each other in disbelief. "How is that possible?"

Patrick shrugged. "She ran away that summer, and as far as I know, she never went back."

"I know she ran away, I heard about it when I got back. But she'd run away before, and she always went home eventually."

"Not this time. She wouldn't have dared."

"Why not?"

"Smashed up her old man's car, didn't she?"

It came back to her then, the story she'd heard when she returned from France. A week or so after graduation, Angel had fought with her father, stolen his keys, and smashed up his car on her way out of town. The cops had found the car, but no sign of Angel, who was presumed, by the lack of blood, to have walked away from the crash and hitched a ride. But was that a reason to break forever from the only parent she had?

"Busky loved that car," Patrick said. "It's the only thing he did love. He'd have killed her."

"But then why not get in touch with you, with us?"

He scowled into his empty cup. "For years, every time the phone rang, I expected to hear her voice. Never happened. But I thought for sure she'd reach out to you, sooner or later."

"She never did. I tried to reach her for a while, but at some point I stopped." That point was right around the time that Simon came into her life; Willa had gone from hoping Angel would visit to dreading it. "I figured if she wanted to see me, she knew where I was. We'd had that fight, you know, at the end of high school. And I guess she never forgave me."

"I seem to remember that you were the offended party."

Willa bit her lip. "Offended" wasn't quite the word. She'd been stunned. How could you? she'd asked over and over, until Angel finally exploded. "Why are you making such a big fucking deal of it? Haven't you learned anything these past two years? You might be smart in the classroom, girl, but in real life you're a fucking moron!"

"I was," she said. "But she was angry at me, too, for making such a fuss."

Patrick frowned. "Angel had a temper, God knows. But it wasn't like her to hold a grudge."

"Maybe she just gave up on me." Even now it hurt to say it. A lot of staying power in old wounds.

Then Consuela returned with a pot of coffee. There was a silence, not quite as easy as the ones they'd shared before. "What about Caleb?" Willa said at last. "Are you in touch with him?"

"He dropped me years ago," Patrick said indifferently, but with a faint aroma of old bitterness.

Willa was amazed. Although she herself had moved on, she'd retained a notion in the back of her mind of her old friends going on as before, together. Logically, it was no surprise that after twenty years *(Is it really twenty years?)* they had drifted apart. Still, she would have expected some of those relationships to have endured; Caleb and Patrick's in particular, for they'd been the closest of friends from kindergarten through high school. "What could have happened?"

"Ask him," Patrick said with a shrug. "Last time I saw Caleb was his mother's funeral. My mom phoned to tell me she'd died. I took the red-eye from L.A. to be there. Shake came, too; skipped a gig to make it. Caleb never spoke to us. No, I lie: He said one sentence, 'Thanks for coming.' Then he shakes our hands like we're strangers and turns to the next guy in line."

He was good at that, she remembered. The last she'd seen of Caleb was his back. Junior year, he'd hitchhiked all the way from Miami after receiving her letter; made it to the campus by ten o'clock the next morning. Willa was crossing the quad with Simon when she saw Caleb striding toward her, the edges of his long coat flapping like wings. People made way for him. Willa dropped Simon's hand and waited.

Caleb halted in front of her. The sun had bleached his hair and darkened his face. Caleb didn't spare a glance for Simon, though he must have known who he was. Her letter was in his hand. He wadded it up and tossed it at her face.

Simon sucked in his breath and stepped up. Willa grabbed his arm. "No—this is between us."

"What the fuck, Willa," Caleb said. "You can't do this."

"She already has," said Simon, who'd never met Caleb, his absentee rival.

Caleb kept his eyes on Willa's face. "Fuck off, man."

"No, you fuck off," Simon said. "You got your walking papers."

Caleb finally looked at him, a measuring look followed by a smile Willa knew all too well. The two men were about the same size, Caleb a bit taller, Simon a bit heavier; to look at, they were evenly matched. But she'd seen Caleb in action and knew what would happen if they fought. Simon's humiliation would make for an unpropitious start to their impending marriage.

She pushed between them. "Let me talk to him," she said to Simon. "He has a right to hear it from me." He didn't like it but she insisted. Simon backed off far enough to give them some privacy but remained, watching Caleb's every move. Willa led Caleb to a bench out of the flow of pedestrian traffic. She sat down; he stayed on his feet, pacing before her.

"What did you expect?" she said. "You didn't want to be with me yourself, but you can't stand it that I've found someone else."

"I didn't want to be with you?" he said furiously. "I worked my ass off for you! Everything I did, I did for you."

"Spring break you went to Mexico. Last summer you didn't

even bother to call. You left me hanging. What were you thinking? Did you suppose I'd wait forever, play Penelope to your
what's-his-face?"

"We had an understanding. What difference does it make if
we're apart or together? We belong to each other; we're two
halves of a whole."

"Meaning you get to do whatever you want for as long as you
want, while I sit at home knitting stockings."

"You want to fuck some asshole lawyer, go right ahead. It's not
like I've been a monk all this time. All I'm saying is don't forget
where you belong."

Over his shoulder she saw Simon watching them. The contrast
could not have been more striking: Caleb in sandals and dreadlocks,
his only concession to the northern winter the floppy black overcoat
that looked like a castoff from a Marx Brothers movie, slung over a
body so tense it vibrated; and beyond him, in the background,
Simon, impeccable in his Burberry coat, hair slicked back, as solid
and powerful as the ivy-covered buildings around him.

And the only thing they had in common was the conviction
that they alone knew what was best for Willa.

Willa stood at a crossroads and she knew it. She saw two
paths, one marked "Simon," the other "Caleb." (There was a
third, but it was overgrown and neglected and she didn't notice it
at the time.) Of the two paths she did perceive, the choice was
obvious. If being with Caleb had been like shooting the rapids or
riding out a tempest on a raft, being with Simon was clear sailing
over moonlit seas, secure in her captain and her craft.

"I'll always remember us," she said. "You made me what I am.
But I'm marrying Simon."

"Marriage," he sneered. "Is that all you want? A husband, two-
point-five kids, and a house in the suburbs? Your mother's life,
that's enough for you?"

"I want a man who's with me in more than spirit."

"What if I said I'd marry you?"

"I'd say you were a day late and a dollar short."

He sucked in his breath, stood and stared. Willa held his gaze.
Then, without another word, Caleb turned and walked away.
With every step, his shoulders unfurled, his back straightened,

his head rose. Women looked at him as he passed and he returned their looks. Before he was halfway across the quad she knew he had already put her out of his mind. She watched until he disappeared from sight. He didn't look back.

So Caleb had walked away from Patrick, too. In an impulse of sympathy, Willa reached across the table and touched the back of his hand. Patrick misunderstood the gesture; his hand turned and captured hers.

It was awkward. She didn't want to hurt his feelings by pulling away, but she didn't want to hold his hand, either. Then Patrick, with a rueful laugh, raised her hand to his lips, kissed it, and let it go.

"So they're both gone," Willa said. "Maybe they're together." She meant it as a joke, didn't expect his stricken look, still less the pang in her own heart.

Old betrayals never die. They just hunker down, like cancer cells waiting to recur.

"Unlikely," Patrick said. "But we'll find out soon enough, won't we?"

"How's that?"

"You know."

And the astonishing thing was that she did. All evening long she'd waited for him to bring up their pact, and now he had. *Twenty years from today*, they'd said, *wherever we are, whatever we're doing*. In June it would be twenty years exactly. "Will they remember?" she wondered.

"We did," he said.

"But will they come?"

"Of course. Come hell or high water, we said; dead or alive."

"We were wrecked."

"We were always wrecked," Patrick said serenely. "They'll come."

3

"Why a widow?" Patrick asked. "Why a ghost?" No one answered. He gazed out at a class full of blank faces and eyes that slid away like minnows at his approach. How many of them had even watched the film he'd assigned? Half, maybe. The trouble with teaching a course like "Film and Society" was that it tended to attract a lot of non-film students looking for an easy way to fill their humanities requirement.

"Think about it," he said. "Unlike real life, the world within a film is deterministic. There's a reason for everything; nothing happens by chance. *The Ghost and Mrs. Muir* is a love story, one of the greatest in film history. Why construct a love story around a widow and a ghost?"

Still no takers. He picked out a kid in the back whose name he happened to remember. "Cruishank?"

"Don't ask me, man," Cruishank said, playing to his buddies. "It's a chick flick; ask a chick."

"That is so sexist," said the girl beside him. "I can't believe you actually said that."

While they argued, Patrick sat back and zoned out for a moment. He was whipped. No sleep last night, too stirred up over meeting Willa, who had changed, but not in any way that helped him. He'd deliberately arrived late to avoid running into her; his first sight came as she climbed the steps to the podium, dressed in a fitted gray suit with a slit skirt and a belted V-neck jacket with no blouse. At that moment, Patrick had nearly lost his nerve. She looked like money and ice to him. If he hadn't known her, he would have been smitten, but he'd have done his admiring from afar. Tough to approach, would have been his thought, and expensive to maintain. Women like her weren't interested in men like him.

But he *did* know her; he knew her well. Old running mates, partners in truancy. Somewhere along the line she'd acquired the self-possessed, touch-me-not air of a grown woman. But whoever said that no man is a hero to his high school classmates might have added the corollary that no woman is unattainable.

He forced his attention back to the classroom, where the girl next to Cruishank was presenting her own theory of the movie as a feminist parable. "When Mrs. Muir first meets the captain, she totally defers to him. Even though he's dead and she's alive, he's still The Man. I mean, come on, the movie literally shows her taking dictation. But as she gets out into the world, she starts gaining a sense of her own power, till finally she realizes that she doesn't need a man at all . . . at which point the captain gracefully recedes into the twilight."

"But he comes back," Patrick said. "In the very last scene, as she's dying, he comes back for her. How does that fit into your interpretation?" From the corner of his eye, he saw a hand waving. The student's name was Stacey but Patrick thought of her as Lolita; she had the face of a child and the body of a woman, clad today in a tight pink sweater and a leather skirt the size of a man's handkerchief. There was a butterfly tattooed on her right thigh, but Patrick, who'd been down that road before, kept his eyes on her face. He prided himself on never making the same mistake twice. Why bother, when there were so many new ones to be made?

"Yes, Stacey?"

"I don't buy the feminist angle. To me, this is a story about a love that transcends even the greatest of barriers, death. And the last scene is the payoff for the whole movie; it's what validates her choice."

"So why a widow?" Patrick asked. "Why a ghost? Bear in mind that this picture was released in 1942."

"World War Two. Men going off to war, women staying behind, both wanting reassurance that whatever happens, love endures."

"Give me a break," the feminist said. "You can't love a ghost."

"Mrs. Muir did."

"That's a fantasy. In real life, trust me, shit happens and people move on."

"But do we?" Patrick asked. "Do we move on, do we forget? Young love, the first kiss, the first embrace: Do we ever forget those things? Or do they endure?" Talking more to himself than to them, for they'd hardly had time to forget; thinking of Angel, a double first for him: first kiss, first fuck. Could he forget her?

He'd been trying for years, with fair success till Willa stirred the pot. Dangerous to exhume old ghosts. Willa, too, had been a first: his first unrequited love, creator of the synapse that linked love and grief. Forget her? Not a chance. Though his wives would surely disagree, Patrick considered himself a man of uncommon faithfulness; not in the dreary, technical sense of the word, but rather in that his affections, once bestowed, were bestowed forever.

After class, he ran up two flights of stairs to his office. He made a habit of running up the stairs; apart from the aerobic benefit, it got him away from any students who might be tempted to detain him. The door was unlocked, so he wasn't surprised to find Barney at his desk, drinking coffee and grading papers. Patrick considered himself lucky in his office mate. Barney Glass, whose course on gay and lesbian themes in film was known to politically incorrect students as "Fag Flicks," was a companionable, laid-back guy with a backhanded skill at departmental politics.

"Morning, sunshine," Barney said, as Patrick helped himself to a cup of coffee from the pot on the filing cabinet. "We're up bright and early."

"I had a class. What's your excuse?"

"Exams. And no, I couldn't work at home. Frank has the world's worst cold, and you know what a bitch he is when he's sick."

Patrick settled himself at his desk, facing Barney's. "Some wife you are."

"In sickness and in health, darling. Crankiness is another matter."

"Please don't call me darling."

"Too faggy?"

"Too L.A." Patrick tipped his chair back and propped his heels on the desk. He ran his hands through already disheveled hair.

"How'd it go last night?" Barney asked, with an air of remembering. "Did you see her?"

"Oh yeah, I saw her."

"And? How'd she look?"

"Different."

"Frumpish?"

Patrick laughed wryly. "Hot."

"Married?"

"Widowed."

"Uh-oh," Barney drawled. "I smell trouble."

"No trouble," Patrick said, though he wouldn't have bet a nickel on it.

"Old girlfriend, hot, bereft, and in need of consolation. This by you is no trouble?"

"She wasn't my girlfriend."

Barney threw up his hands. "Worse yet! She's the one who got away."

Patrick didn't answer. It was true that there was something unfinished in his relationship with Willa, a jagged edge. She was a piece of shrapnel lodged too close to his heart to remove.

4

Somewhere between the produce and the meat sections, Chloe disappeared. Willa turned from examining roaster hens to find her shopping cart beside her but her daughter missing. She didn't worry at first. Saturday morning, the supermarket packed—Chloe must have spotted some friends and wandered off to talk. Willa placed the chicken in her cart and turned down the rice aisle. Wild rice, roast chicken, and a salad: nothing fancy, nothing like the meals she used to prepare when Simon's clients and colleagues came to dinner, but it would do for a guest who had foisted himself upon her. He was up visiting his old aunt, Patrick had said on the phone. Could he come see her, maybe take her and her daughter out to dinner? "Eat here instead," she'd heard herself say, regretting the invitation even as it issued forth; but what choice did he give her? He'd already taken her out once.

Finessed by her own politeness . . . her own conformity.

She turned the cart toward the frozen foods, keeping her eyes to herself. Wendell's Supermarket served as town center in their little village. You never knew who you might bump into, or what they might say, or how they might look. There's a fine line between sympathy and pity, and Willa's neighbors were prone to transgress. After Simon's death and all that followed upon it, she had avoided the danger altogether by ordering her groceries over the phone and having them delivered. Gradually she noticed that Chloe had begun finding excuses to hang around the kitchen on delivery days. Wendell's driver was a good-looking kid of eighteen or nineteen, with spiky blond hair, a gold hoop earring, and dark, sultry eyes. Chloe said he was a drummer with a band that played at local sweet sixteens; Roy Bliss was his name. Two weeks ago, Willa happened to glance out her bedroom window to find Wendell's red van still in her driveway, some fifteen minutes after she'd tipped the driver and shown him out. Coatless, hugging herself against the cold in her little Gap sweater, Chloe was leaning against the driver's-side door, talking to Drummer Boy.

After that, when Willa needed groceries, she fetched them herself.

Where *was* the girl? As the first prickles of trepidation percolated up her spine, Willa set out with her cart on a methodical
circuit of the store. It wasn't like Chloe to wander off like this, at
least not lately. Since Simon's death, Chloe had turned into
Willa's shadow. When she wasn't in school or at chorus, she was
home, trailing Willa from room to room, watching her with an
attentiveness that bordered on distrust. Willa chafed under the
weight of that insistent gaze, but how could she blame the girl?
Chloe had every reason for fear. In Willa's experience, the only
people who believed lightning never strikes twice were those
who'd never been struck.

She finished her tour. The supermarket was full of kids, none
of them Chloe. Abandoning the cart, she searched again, more
thoroughly this time. When at last she was certain her daughter
wasn't in the store, her very first thought was to call Simon; she
went so far as to look around for a phone before reality returned.
It wasn't the first time she'd forgotten. Death may be the ultimate
finality, but its assimilation, she was discovering, was a slow,
repetitive process.

Anger was all that held panic at bay, so Willa stoked it. *Where
the hell is she? How dare she?* Striding toward the courtesy booth,
nearly hidden behind stacks of Christmas remainders, she
pushed to the front of the line. The woman in the booth gave her
a reproving look.

"My daughter is missing," Willa declared. It sounded ridiculous, melodramatic. "I can't find my daughter," she amended.

"Have you looked for her?"

"What do you think I am, a moron?"

The woman stared. Willa was a second away from grabbing
hair when a hand gripped her arm. She turned and looked into
the face of Isabel Rapaport, the mother of Chloe's friend Lauren.
"I just saw her," Isabel said, her plump, kind face creased with
concern. "She's right outside."

Willa turned toward the plate-glass windows. Chloe was in
plain sight, standing with a group of kids in the parking lot.

"Are you okay?" Isabel asked softly.

"Apart from feeling like a fool, you mean? Fine, thanks." Willa
walked away stiffly, conscious of being watched, knowing what

would be said as soon as she was out of earshot. Damn Chloe! By tomorrow, it would be all over town. *Guess who lost it in Wendell's?*

She stepped outside. The sky was gray and smelled like snow. Chloe was talking to a tall boy with spiky blond hair: Roy Bliss. He gave her all his attention, and though he didn't touch her, Willa could see him wanting to. He whispered something in her ear and she laughed, not the bubbly eruption Willa knew so well, but a deeper, breathier laugh.

Driving the boys crazy, if she's anything like her mother.

Oh, Chloe.

They faced off from opposite sides of a kitchen island covered with grocery bags. "Because he's way too old for you, that's why," Willa said, with all the firmness she could muster. Simon had always played tough cop to her good cop, and since his death there'd been no need for any cop, Chloe having been scared into unwonted docility.

"It's just a party, for Chrissake! Besides, he's only eighteen."

"And you're fourteen."

"Almost fifteen. Hardly a kid."

"Hardly an adult. Which he is; and guys his age—"

"—want only one thing," Chloe finished mockingly.

Willa kept herself from flinching. It was true: She could have been channeling her own mother just then. From the time Willa took up with Caleb until the day she left home, it had been one long battle. "Boys like that want only one thing" was her mother's war song, to which Willa would respond with a mute gaze of pity and contempt. Clearly the poor woman had no concept of true love, hence no way to comprehend the bond between Willa and Caleb, soul mates who shared each other's every thought and emotion. How could a mind so mired in convention and middle-class propriety possibly understand the wonder of them?

When she fell in love with Caleb, Willa had been scarcely older than Chloe was now. The thought came as a shock. She studied her daughter, making an effort to see her as she was, not as she had been. At five-five, Chloe was nearly as tall as Willa. Short blond hair framed a face dominated by Simon's gray eyes. There

was a coltish gawkiness to her body, but already it was more
womanly than childlike.

Chloe returned her gaze defiantly. How to bridge the gap?
Willa wondered. How to speak so as to be heard? "It's not the
only thing," she said. "Boys also want love and security and intimacy, all the things girls want. But the main thing they want, the
one thing they want more than anything else, is sex. They can't
help it. It's hardwired into their system."

"That is so pathetic. Can't you see what you're doing? Just
because you had . . . just because your marriage . . ." Chloe sputtered to a halt.

Willa carried a carton of eggs over to the refrigerator and
transferred the eggs with shaking hands. What Chloe knew about
her parents' marriage and her father's death was a mystery to
Willa, who preferred to keep it that way. She crushed the empty
carton, tossed it in the garbage, and turned to her daughter. "We
are not talking about my marriage."

"Oh no?" Chloe's color was high, her breathing ragged. "You
judge everyone by *him*."

"I'm not judging anyone. I'm simply informing you that a man
of eighteen and a girl of fourteen are in different stages of life,
and those stages are not compatible."

Chloe stalked to the door, then turned around. Willa was waiting. Simon used to say that Chloe learned to talk for the sole purpose of having the last word.

"You just don't get it," Chloe said loftily. "You haven't got a
clue."

Patrick arrived bearing gifts: wine and flowers, red roses and
baby's breath. Willa kept a wary eye on her daughter, but Chloe
shook hands nicely and went off to look for a vase.

"Beautiful," Patrick said, looking after her while Willa hung
his coat. "Like mother, like daughter."

"Still blessed with the gift of gab, I see," Willa said, not without fondness. Though she had resented his intrusion, it had
turned out to be providential; tonight any buffer between her and
her daughter would have been welcome. She led him down the
center hall, past the living room, past the dining room where the

huge oak table was set for three, toward the den in the back of the house. She walked quickly, embarrassed in his presence by the size of the house, the formality of the rooms. Simon had chosen the decorator (to spare her the bother, he'd said), approved the scheme, and selected the furnishings, of which Willa had often felt herself a part. He had been proud of their house, and first-time visitors were invariably offered a tour. But Willa didn't offer one to Patrick.

After Simon's death, she'd thought of selling. She would be sorry to give up her study, the one room in the house that was altogether hers. Set in the rear of the house, it had terra-cotta floors and large east windows that overlooked the flower garden she'd planned and planted herself. But without Simon and his penchant for grand entertaining, the house was far too big; she and Chloe rattled around in it. The upkeep was enormous, the heating bill alone a monthly trauma as regular as her period.

The village was full of charming, smaller homes; she and Chloe could have had their pick. Several times, sitting with her daughter through the endless evenings, Willa had nearly suggested it; but each time she'd refrained. The child had just lost her father; it would have been too cruel to take away her home as well.

These days they spent most of their time in the den, watching TV, working jigsaw puzzles, even eating their meals on trays in front of the fire. The room had a vaulted, beamed ceiling, large windows, and French doors that led to the deck. The stone fireplace was flanked by two bookshelves, which held their favorite books, and the mantelpiece was pleasantly cluttered with framed photographs. The room was furnished with a hodgepodge of old but comfortable pieces, mismatched sofas, armchairs, and occasional tables that Simon's decorator had banished from the rest of the house.

With the fire lit, the room smelled like an autumn bonfire. Willa walked over to a small bar in the corner and looked at Patrick. "What can I get you? We have all the essentials."

"Would beer be too crass?"

"For you? No."

He grinned his old familiar grin. She poured him a beer and

herself a glass of the wine he'd brought, a sweetish Moselle. Patrick strolled around the room, pausing to examine the framed photographs on the mantelpiece. "Your husband?" he asked, indicating one of Simon and Chloe in ski gear, taken last winter in Aspen.

Willa nodded. If it were up to her, she'd have put all his pictures away. She kept them out for Chloe.

"Good-looking guy."

"Yes."

Patrick looked at her, waiting for more, but no more came. He moved over to the table holding their latest jigsaw puzzle. It was two-thirds done, a French harbor scene with a bustling waterfront in the foreground and a pair of high-masted ships in the bay. "Wow. Who's responsible for this?"

"Oh, we've gotten into jigsaws lately, Chloe and I. Someone gave us one right after the funeral. Seemed an odd gift at the time, but in fact it was a clever one. You'd be amazed how much time you can kill on a thousand-piece puzzle."

His eyes were like black ferrets, burrowing into her head. "How long ago—"

"Four and a half months." The half slipped out, to her surprise; she hadn't thought she was still keeping track of weeks.

"Sorry, Willa. I didn't realize it was so recent. How did he . . . ?"

"Heart attack."

"So young!" He came and sat beside her. For a moment, they just looked at each other. Once again, Willa had to absorb the change in him. When she wasn't looking right at him, when they spoke on the phone, it was the cheeky boy of sixteen she envisioned, not this opaque, weathered man, this intimate stranger.

"You have a beautiful home," he said. "Somehow I never pictured you in a house like this."

"Where did you picture me? In a garret somewhere, scribbling away?" It cost her something, to say this with a smile.

"Something like that."

"Are you disappointed?"

"No. It suits you."

"I'd hate to think so," Willa said. He looked at her and did not speak.

* * *

Over dinner, Patrick told stories. Expurgated versions, to be sure, stripped of any hint of drugs, drink, or truancy. Nevertheless Chloe was amazed and disbelieving. "Mom did *that*?"

He told the career day story. It was 1971, the war in Vietnam still raging. Mr. Grievely, the high school principal, was an ex-marine who thought a stint in the military was just the ticket to turn a punk into a man. Under cover of a job fair, he'd invited army recruiters to the school.

Word got out, and the Beacon Hill kids held a war council of their own. In an effort to attract more students, a number of carnival games were to be among the exhibition booths, each game to be run by a different school club. Vinny went to a meeting of the astronomy club, during which the astronomers decided to turn their booth over to Vinny and his friends.

"Just like that?" Chloe interrupted. High school was her turf, after all, and she knew how things worked. "They just *give* you their booth."

Patrick smiled. "Our Vinny was a persuasive lad."

Chloe snorted. There were guys like that at her school, too, and they weren't on the debate team.

The booth was supposed to be a bean-bag toss with cardboard ducks as targets, Patrick went on. The Beacon Hill kids swapped air rifles for bean bags and head shots of Vietnamese babies for cardboard ducks. They hung a sign: "Shoot a Gook: 25¢ a Pop," and blasted a tape of "The Ballad of the Green Berets."

Willa did her best to keep a straight face, but laughter leaked out the corners of her mouth. "Oh my God. Remember Grievely's face when he saw us?"

Patrick guffawed. "I thought he was gonna blow an artery. I was hoping."

Chloe was impressed despite herself. "What'd they do to you?"

"Nothing much," he said. "Suspension."

She looked at her mother. "*You* were suspended?"

"You're shocking her," Willa said. "She only knows me in PTA mode."

"I'm not shocked. Girls just want to have fun: Right, Mom?"

"Don't go there," Willa murmured, but her wayward daughter, with a sly look, turned back to their guest.

"Sounds like you guys were pretty tight."

"Tightness itself," he boasted.

"You had fun, too, right? It wasn't all protests and politics; you had parties and hung out and stuff?"

"Fun was our specialty."

"And my mother was how old?"

Sensing a trap, Patrick looked to Willa.

"Time for dessert," she said. "Chloe, would you clear?"

"Sorry about that," Patrick said later.

Willa looked up from the fireplace, where she'd knelt to feed the fire. "Not your fault. You were bushwhacked."

"Clever little bugger, isn't she?"

She brushed off her hands, took her drink from the mantelpiece, and curled in the corner of a sofa. He sat beside her, not too close.

"It's strange," she said, "to have a daughter practically the same age we were when we were doing that stuff. You see things from a different perspective."

"I'm sure you do." He watched her with soft, patient eyes. Though he sat a foot away and kept his hands in plain sight, Willa felt him a little too close for comfort. When they were kids, she and Angel had been the only girls of equal standing in the group. The boys had spoken freely in front of them; they'd speculated, fantasized, and bragged. Thus Willa, though an only child, had the advantage of girls with brothers: She knew how boys talked among themselves.

Patrick had been by far the most libidinous . . . not that she'd thought in those terms then. What she'd thought was that, of all the boys she knew, Patrick was the one who liked girls best. He found them endlessly fascinating and was indiscriminate in his admiration, finding beauty where others saw none. Whoever said that youth is wasted on the young didn't know Patrick . . . or Angel, either, for that matter. She had kept Patrick more or less in line; but no one could stop him looking and wanting . . . including his wife, apparently.

Well, he could look all he wanted now, for all the good it would do him.

"For instance," she said, "Chloe was invited to a party by the eighteen-year-old drummer in a rock band. What would you have said?"

"No fair asking me, my memory's way too good. If I had a daughter, she'd never go out. Plus, she'd have a black belt in karate."

"My feelings exactly, though there are a lot more seducers than rapists out there. So I said no; only at the same time I'm saying no, I'm seeing me and Angel shinnying down her drainpipe to party with you guys."

"A memorable occasion," he said with a wistful sigh. "Both of you in miniskirts. You'll notice I didn't tell *that* story."

She smacked his arm. "And you never will!"

"Ah," he said, dark eyes flashing. "Leverage!"

Willa drew back a little. "For what?"

"I was thinking about what you said last time, about the reunion. Would they come, you said, and I said of course they would. Afterward, though, I had some doubts."

"You think they've forgotten?" She felt a pang of disappointment as sharp as it was unexpected. Patrick's reappearance and all the stories he told had pried the lid off a Pandora's box of memories, and this in a house already lousy with them. Now she longed to see them—Caleb, Angel, and the others who had been everything to her in high school—and longed even more for her own lost self: the girl who'd slid down drainpipes, cut school, ridden on the back of a motorcycle with the wind in her face and her arms around the waist of a boy she loved with a reckless heart. What had become of that bold girl? Did any bit of her survive, trapped beneath the scar tissue?

"Not a chance they forgot," Patrick said firmly. "But they might not remember the exact date. And some of them live far away. Maybe we ought to reach out, make sure everyone's on the same page."

"Reach out where? Do we know where they are?"

"We could find out."

Willa sipped her wine. "We," he'd said, meaning her. But why not? It's not as if she were busy. For months, she'd done nothing but hunker down at home, seen no one but Chloe. Friends were put off with the excuse that she was working on a book. If only it were true. Work would have taken her out of herself, but work, in the form of another biography, was impossible. How could one so blind to her own life presume to comprehend a stranger's?

She'd do it, she told him. Patrick was delighted. So delighted that he leaned over and kissed her. Chastely at first, then less so. Against his hard lips, Willa's felt bruised, unready. She pushed him back.

"Sorry," he said penitently, but with the air of a salesman who's talked his way inside and knows he's not leaving empty-handed. "Lost my head."

Willa laughed at him. "Since when do you think with your head?"

5

On a day bright and cold enough to frost their breath, Willa and Patrick met at the Millbrook station. He took the train from the city; she drove and met him at the station. Willa was tired. Last night she'd dreamed about Angel. In her dream, they were up on Beacon Hill, just the two of them, sharing a joint. "I *did* try you," Angel said. "Many times. Your line was busy."

Patrick got into the BMW, and they headed south toward his old neighborhood, known locally, for reasons that had passed into obscurity, as Cobb's Corner. Westchester was a rich county, but someone had to pick up the garbage, clean the houses, maintain the pools, and baby-sit the children; Cobb's Corner, an unprepossessing jumble of small Capes and ranches with tiny fenced-in yards and porches full of cast-off furniture, was where those people lived.

She thought she might not remember the way, but when she came to Washington Avenue, Willa automatically turned right, then a quick left onto Hamilton and there, third from the corner, on the right, was Patrick's old house. She pulled up to the curb and turned off the engine. They looked at the house.

"They changed the roof line," Patrick said. A dormer had been added, eliminating the sloped roof where, to their peril, they used to hang out and smoke.

"And sided the house," Willa said. "I prefer the old wood shingles, myself."

"The hoop's gone."

"And the car." More a project than a car, a Tinkertoy for big boys, Patrick's red '57 Chevy had reigned over the front yard, enthroned on cement blocks. All senior year, the boys had worked on that car, scouring junkyards far and wide for spare parts to lay on its altar. They'd planned to drive it cross-country the summer after graduation, the gang's last hurrah before splitting up. By June, it was running like a charm. Then, days before they were due to set out, Vinny took the car and totaled it. Willa had been away in France when it happened, but she'd heard all about it when she came home.

"Fuckin' Vinny, man," Patrick said, shaking his head.

"Poor guy," said Willa.

"Took me forever to forgive him. I'm not sure I ever did." Patrick leaned across and opened her door, then his own. It didn't look like anyone was home in his old house. But he marched up to the front door, anyway, and rang the bell.

Willa followed. "They'll think we're Jehovah's Witnesses."

"Or encyclopedia salesmen," he said.

"Now there's a dying breed."

No one answered. A black kid eyed them from the porch next door, but when Patrick waved he went inside and shut the door. Eventually they gave up and got back in the car. As they cruised down the block, Patrick provided a running commentary. "Theresa Rizzo lived here. Her window faced mine and she never drew her shades, God bless her generous heart. There's Shake's house; sold long ago, though I think Nancy's people still live around here. The Copa twins: Tommy died in 'Nam, Jimmy went to Canada. Digger Harris, a major pest, but we put up with him for his mother. Hottest woman on the block, Millbrook's own Mrs. Robinson. Vinny did her."

"Get out!"

"She always liked him. The day he turned sixteen, she gave him a special birthday present."

"I never heard that story," Willa said indignantly.

Patrick laughed. "You think we told you everything?"

They came to Vinny's house, larger and older than its neighbors. Millbrook was an old settlement, one of many founded in the early nineteenth century along the eastern bank of the Hudson. Before the advent of fast trains transformed it into a bedroom suburb, Millbrook had been a farming community and staging point for river transport. Vinny's house was a relic of that era, a sprawling, two-story farmhouse with peeling white paint, a listing porch, and the resigned look of a house that's known better times, but not lately.

"Look at that," Willa said. The name "Delgaudio" was painted on a freestanding mailbox at the edge of the driveway. "They still live here."

"His parents left years ago. They bought an RV and they're tooling around the U.S.A., fancy-free and happy as birds. Two of Vinny's brothers bought the house off them."

"Should we knock?" she asked.

"No need. Vinny's got a garage in the Bronx. I've got the address somewhere."

They drove on. The more they rode through the old neighborhood, the more Willa remembered. They'd wandered these streets constantly as kids, with the sense of ownership that comes from knowing every house, every alley, every crack in the sidewalk. It was their turf and they'd defended it: no hardship, for the boys knew how to fight and enjoyed a good brawl now and then. Any pretext would do when they were in the mood: a crack about their hair or hippie attire, some guy hitting on one of their girls, the wrong song playing on a jukebox.

They turned a corner and suddenly they were on Caleb's street. Willa would have known it anywhere by the anxiety that gripped her, as if it had been lying in wait all these years. You never quite knew where you were with Caleb, who answered to no one.

She parked in front of his house. They got out of the car and stood on the sidewalk, looking at the house, which hadn't changed much over the years. It seemed possible that at any moment the front door would open and their friend would appear.

Then the door did open, but the figure that emerged wasn't Caleb, but rather a hard-faced young woman with a cigarette dangling from her mouth. She held a stringy German shepherd by the collar. "You lost or what?" she said.

Patrick approached slowly, one eye on the woman, the other on the dog. "An old friend of ours used to live in your house, a guy named Caleb Rhys. We're trying to find him."

"When was this?" she said. The dog growled. Willa got the feeling it was speaking for both of them.

"His parents owned the house till 1980."

"Way before my time. We bought this dump three years ago."

"Would you happen to know if any of your neighbors are long-time residents?" Willa asked from the sidewalk.

The other looked her up and down, assessing her clothes in the age-old manner of women taking each other's measure. Willa had dressed for the weather, not a tea party, but her cashmere overcoat spoke for itself. "Nobody stays around here who doesn't have to," the woman said finally. "The neighborhood's changing; anyone can see that."

"I grew up here," Patrick said. "Back then people stayed put. This was a pretty stable neighborhood."

"Too close to the Bronx," the young woman said shortly. "Try the old lady next door. She's been here since before God died." Then she went back in her house and shut the door.

They looked at each other. The light was dying, the air growing colder. Willa felt discouraged. Cobb's Corner felt strange to her now, hostile. Time had erased their tracks; now it felt as if they'd never reigned here. Patrick put his arm around her shoulder and gave her a hug.

Mrs. Blume peered at Patrick through thick glasses. Then she pointed one of her knitting needles at his face. "I remember you! Patch, they called you. What a rascal you were! You haven't changed much."

Patrick shook his head in awe. "No flies on you, Mrs. Blume."

"I might be old, but I'm not senile." She laid aside her knitting and pressed more strudel on them; it shouldn't go to waste.

They were in her overheated living room, drinking tea from china cups. Mabel Blume was a frail, birdlike woman dwarfed by her own furniture, which was large, dark, and looming. She was all willingness, no information. Hadn't seen Caleb or his sister since their mother's funeral, she should rest in peace. Didn't know where he was. Didn't know where the sister was, or what her married name was. "I know the date she married, though, if that's any help," she said. "August 6, 1967. I know because it was the day after we buried my dear mother. We couldn't go to the wedding 'cause we was sitting shiva, but we stood at that window right there, me and Mr. Blume, and watched her leave for church. She saw us and waved. What a beautiful bride she was. That whole family, a treat to look at." She sighed, myopic eyes gazing at something they could not see. "So sad," she said.

"What was so sad?" Willa asked as they drove on toward Angel's house.

Patrick shrugged. "Who knows? Life's full of sadness, most of it created by families."

True enough, she thought. Her own parents had been very affectionate . . . toward each other. They had married late, an autumn romance; her father had money, her mother breeding and taste. They delighted in each other and saw no need for children; Willa's unplanned intrusion had been greeted with a polite reserve that never quite thawed. Though her every material need was met, though she was never mistreated or abused, Willa grew up understanding that her existence was a regrettable impediment to the lives her parents had charted for themselves. The least she owed them was good behavior and respectable grades, and for a long time she provided those. Then she met Caleb and the other Beacon Hill kids and her priorities changed. By the time her parents tried to clamp down, it was too late; Willa was in love.

But her parent problems were nothing compared to those of her friends. It was one of the things they had in common, a deficit in the family department, which they'd filled through one another. Angel's mother had died years before Willa met her. Her father was a raisin of a man who spent every night in front of the TV, chugging beer in his undershirt. To get upstairs to Angel's room, it had been necessary to pass between the couch and the television. Busky used to watch Willa walk by as if she were doing it for his benefit.

As they turned onto Angel's block, Willa felt a sudden clutch of nervousness. "Do you think he still lives here?"

"He's in the phone book," Patrick said.

Then both fell silent as they rounded a bend and the house came into view. Willa parked across the street, and they got out but didn't cross. Angel's house hadn't changed a bit, except to deteriorate. Surrounded by knee-high prickly weeds, it looked as if nothing had been done to or for it in twenty years: not a coat of paint added, not a shingle fixed or a shutter repaired. The drainpipe they used to climb was still there, but it was hanging by a thread and looked as if it wouldn't bear a sparrow's weight. The bay window in the kitchen was blocked with stacks of newspapers, and the raggedy shades that covered the upstairs windows gave the house an expression of tight-lipped, slit-eyed suspicion. On a block of small but tidy homes, this dump was a cinder in the eye.

Wherever Angel was, Willa thought, she was better off. Then she shivered.

"They didn't live like this when she was here," Patrick said quietly. "This is sick."

A man came out of the house next to Busky's and lurched toward them. He was very old and very black, and he had a three-legged gait: one good leg, one bad, and one cane. "You folks come about him?" he asked, jerking his head at Busky's house.

They had, Patrick said.

"About time," the old guy grumbled. "I lost track how many times I called."

"So what's the story, what's up with that house?"

"You *see* what's up. Question is, what you gonna do about it?"

"Have you tried talking to him?"

"Now does that look like the house of a man you could talk to?"

"No, sir, it doesn't," Patrick said.

"You got that right. Place's a goddamn firetrap, and I got to live next door to it."

"Is he alone?" Willa asked.

The old man looked disgusted. "No, he's got a staff of ten. Of course he's alone! What woman's gonna live like that?"

"I was thinking of his daughter. Does she ever come around?"

"First I hear of any daughter. Nobody goes in that shithole but him." His eyes narrowed; he looked from one to the other. "You folks aren't from the health department at all, are you?"

"Sorry," Patrick said. "We're old friends of his daughter . . ." But the old man had already turned away, shaking his head and muttering as he went.

They watched him cross the street. Then Patrick held out his arm to Willa. "Shall we?"

Willa shuddered. She had the strangest feeling that the house was watching them: not someone in the house, but the house itself. "Do we have to?"

"We do if we want to find Angel."

They crossed the street. The cement path to Busky's front door was webbed with cracks and colonized by weeds and anthills. The doorbell was disconnected, wires dangling where the button used to be, and the screen door was locked. As Patrick pounded on the frame, Willa caught herself hoping no one would answer, hoping they'd hit a brick wall.

Now why was that? she wondered. Surely not that ancient quarrel. Caleb was nothing to her now, and Simon beyond temptation. The trouble with finding people was that, once found, they were liable to stay that way. Willa had loved Angel as a girl, but would she love her as a woman? What sort of person might she have grown into? Patrick seemed himself, only more so. And Willa knew that she herself, despite the best of intentions, had drifted back toward her origins. "The apple doesn't fall far from the tree," her mother used to say, but Willa had always intended to fall as far as possible from hers. She'd known exactly how her adult life would go. She would live in a great city, New York, perhaps, or London, or Paris. She would write novels, full of symbolism and deep meaning and the raw stuff of life. She would hang out in cafes and conduct passionate love affairs with brilliant young artists and writers, who would paint her or write her, thinly disguised, into their novels. All this had been as clear and certain as sunrise in the desert. Yet here she was, twenty years later, living a muted life barely distinguishable from her mother's.

Somewhere she'd read that identical twins grow more rather than less alike with age. This had struck her as odd, for surely people ought to be progressively individualized by their disparate life experiences. And yet twin studies had revealed that the opposite was true: an example, her mother might have said, of the apple rolling back toward the tree.

Through a peephole in Busky's door, a tiny glimmer of lamplight shone. Suddenly the light was obscured. Willa touched Patrick's arm; he nodded to show he'd seen it, too.

"Mr. Busky," he called, "it's Patrick and Willa, Angel's friends. Can we talk to you for a moment?"

No response, but they could feel him hovering, a small, dark presence on the other side of the door.

"One minute, Mr. Busky," Willa coaxed. "Then I promise we'll go away and leave you in peace."

Another long moment passed. Then the inner door slowly swung inward, just wide enough to reveal Busky, greatly aged and diminished, a study in gray from the tangled mat of his hair to his grimy T-shirt and bathrobe. They could smell him through the door, a stench distinct from the moldy breath of the house itself. Cigarette dangling from his mouth, he blinked hard against the sunlight. First he squinted at Willa, looking her up and down. Then he turned to Patrick, and his hard face grew harder still. "You," he rasped. "What do you want?"

"We're looking for Angel," Patrick said.

"Long gone." Busky puffed on his cigarette. "And good riddance."

"Gone where?"

The old man let out a hacking cough. A sliver of ash fell from the tip of his cigarette and landed in his patchy beard.

"Dead," he croaked, when the cough subsided.

"Oh no," Willa cried, but Patrick laid hold of the screen door as if locks meant nothing to him.

"Liar!" he shouted.

"The hell I am! She's dead to me. Stole my car, didn't she? Wrecked it, didn't she? Seven hundred bucks it cost to fix, and it still never run right, after. And her without the decency to come back and pay up for what she done."

"Come back for what," Patrick said, "more abuse?"

Busky stepped up to the screen and pressed his face to it. "Abuse from who, you little pissant?" he said. "I'm not the bastard fucked her brains out all through high school! *Now* you wanna find her? Where the fuck were you twenty years ago?" Then he stepped back and slammed the door in their faces.

6

Jeremiah's house was a solid brick colonial surrounded by mature plantings and a sweeping lawn manicured to within an inch of its life. Geographically, the Inglewood section of Mill-brook was less than a mile from Cobb's Corner; demographically, it was the other side of the world. In Inglewood, the homes were old and gracious, set back from the streets and as far apart as one-acre zoning would allow. Majestic elms canopied the roads. This was also Willa's old neighborhood; she, Jeremiah, and Travis had attended the same elementary school, though they hadn't become friends until high school. Nothing homogenous about that Beacon Hill gang. Part of their ethos had been self-definition, emancipation from outside expectations. Still, gauging the gap now with adult eyes, Willa wondered at their success, temporary though it had proved.

They'd stopped briefly at Travis's house (no one was home) and Willa had firmly declined a drive-by of her own childhood home. Now the engine was off, but she still had not unlocked her door. "Is this absolutely necessary?"

Patrick said, "His number's unlisted. We don't know who he works for. Besides, what's the worst she can do?"

"Chop off our heads and feed them to the cats?"

"She must be well into her sixties. I think we're safe if we stick together."

They were only half kidding. Back in high school, if you'd asked the Beacon Hill kids who had the scariest parent, the unanimous answer would have been Jeremiah. Marion Stafford Wright ruled her household with an iron fist in a lace glove. She had married a man much older than herself who had the good grace not to linger over-long. He'd died quietly when Jeremiah was twelve, leaving Marion free to focus all her energy and ambition on her son. The Scourge, Jeremiah called her; his friends had other names for her. President of the PTA, chairwoman of the Ladies' League, village councilwoman, meddler in a thousand pies, Marion was the reason Jeremiah had, it was generally presumed, graduated from high school a virgin. So rigid was her orchestration of her only son's overachieving life that his time was scheduled down to the quarter hour, and so excellent and varied her intelligence sources that any deviation was instantly discovered. It had taken the combined ingenuity of the Beacon Hill kids, along with Caleb's forging skills, to free him up at all.

Jeremiah's friendship with them was the one area of her son's life Marion Wright could not control; consequently she had hated them with the implacable loathing of the shepherd for the wolf.

Patrick touched Willa's shoulder. "We're all grown up now," he said. "We're respectable."

"Even you," she teased. He'd been somber since their encounter with Busky, nearly silent in the car.

He forced a smile. "Even me."

There was a camera mounted near the top of the imposing front door with its heavy brass knocker. Below it, at eye level, was the grill of an intercom, out of which spoke a young, female voice. "Yes?"

Willa said, in her plummiest voice, "We're here to call on Mrs. Wright. We're friends of her son, Jeremiah."

A long pause followed. Then a different voice spoke, an older, querulous voice. "Who are you? What are your names?"

"It's Willa Scott Durrell, Mrs. Wright, and Patrick Mulhaven." Willa raised her face to the camera and waited confidently for Mrs. Wright to recognize her. They'd been banned from this house as kids, but things were different now.

"Just a minute," the elderly voice said, but more than five passed before the door opened and a young Latina in a maid's uniform ushered them into the foyer and took their coats. "Wait in here, please. She'll be right down." She opened one of a pair of beautifully carved double doors, and they passed through. At once Willa glanced to her right, and Patrick did the same. Their eyes met, and a guilty spark flew between. "Remember . . . ?" he murmured.

"How could I forget?" It had been one of the worst moments of their collective lives. The last time they were in this room, an étagère had stood along the right wall, a display piece for Mrs. Wright's prized china collection. Why they were there at all, Willa no longer recalled. They rarely went to Jeremiah's house and never partied there; how could you party in a house that looked like a spread from *House Beautiful*? But Marion was out that day, and in a moment of mad bravado, Jeremiah had invited them over. They were hanging out in this room, listening to the Grateful Dead, when a bit of horseplay broke out between Shake and Vinny. Shove and countershove, no big deal, and nothing at all would have come of it if Shake hadn't caught his heel on a corner of the Persian rug and tumbled backward into the étagère.

There was silence as it toppled. It seemed to fall in slow motion, though no one could stop it, and then came the most appalling crash as cabinet and contents shattered on the parquet floor.

For a few moments after the last gold-rimmed plate stopped spinning, no one spoke. This was beyond words, beyond remedy. None of them could look at Jeremiah. The impact had jarred the stereo and scratched the album into a continuous loop. *Driving that train, high on cocaine.* Caleb walked over and removed the needle. Someone said, "Oh my God," and then they were all talking at once. "What do we do?" "Oh, man, we are so fucked!" "Clean it up." "And then what, asshole, hope she doesn't notice?"

Jeremiah was not among the panicked speakers. He stood where he had when the crash occurred, a tall thin boy with long arms stiff by his side. Only his dark, intelligent eyes moved. He raised a hand so pale and thin the light seemed to shine through it, and at once the others fell silent.

"Get out," he told them.

They protested, of course. No way were they leaving him to deal with this shit alone. It was their fault; they'd take the fall.

"You had nothing to do with this," he said, in the calm, persuasive voice of a practiced debater. "You were never here today. This is for my sake, not yours. I don't have time to argue or explain. Go over the backyard fence, get to the car, and split. Quietly—don't call attention to yourselves. In ten minutes I'm calling the cops. You've got to be out of the neighborhood."

They obeyed him. Jeremiah was not only the smartest kid they knew, he also had the most to lose. The amazing thing, Willa thought now, was that he had pulled it off—to this day she didn't know quite how. "What did he do," she asked Patrick now, "report a burglary?"

"Attempted." Patrick lowered his voice, hooked his arm in

hers, and led her away from the door. Among her other talents, Mrs. Wright had been an assiduous eavesdropper. "A case of bur-glarous interruptus. The story was, he walked in on it and they fled, knocking over the china cabinet in their haste."

"And the cops bought that?" Willa said, thinking like a mother. "Nobody thought, 'Hmm, big mess, kid home alone; what's Junior been up to?'"

"The back door was jimmied, they found a sack of jewelry and stuff in the garden, plus you've got Mrs. Councilwoman Wright fussing over poor Jeremiah nearly getting himself killed. I don't think they looked too hard."

"And she never found out?"

"He's still breathing, isn't he?" Patrick wandered over to exam-ine the array of photos on the mantelpiece: posed shots of Jeremiah with Governor Cuomo, Senator Apfel, and Senator Moynihan, and one candid shot of Jeremiah nose to nose with Newt Gingrich, both of them looking furious.

The door opened and Marion Wright entered. She was shorter than Willa's memory of her, and her spare frame was draped in fawn cashmere and pearls, which Willa suspected had been donned for the occasion. She had frosty blue eyes, a pointed chin, a thin red slash of a mouth. Her makeup was immaculate; her hair, black then, now salt and pepper, was perfectly coiffed. Mrs. Wright advanced briskly, in the manner of one called away from more important tasks. Willa got a firm handshake and a quick, knowing once-over. Patrick got a handshake, too, though his was at arm's length.

"Sit," she said, pointing to the sofa while she herself took a facing seat. "The girl will bring tea. Unless you prefer coffee." She said this in a voice that implied a willingness to take infinite pains, no matter how unreasonable.

"Tea is fine," they replied in unison.

Mrs. Wright nodded at the maid. Then she arranged her fea-tures in a look of sympathy, which she turned on Willa. "I was very sorry to read of your loss. It is bad enough to lose a husband so prematurely, but to have to cope with that loss in the glare of the most intrusive publicity—I can only say, my dear, that I truly felt for you."

Patrick looked at her, then quickly looked away. Willa knew it had always been a matter of time before he found out; but that didn't excuse this interfering old bitch. But Mrs. Wright didn't know who she was messing with. For one full month, after Simon's death, Willa had been besieged by reporters. Compared to them, this old woman packed as much punch as a piece of lint.

"Kind of you to say so, Mrs. Wright. But then, we have so much in common."

The smile froze on the old woman's face. She spoke around it. "Whatever do you mean?"

"Both of us widowed young, left to raise children alone. Why, what did you think I meant?"

Their eyes held. *Here I am*, Willa's said. *Take me on if you dare.* And Mrs. Wright dared not. The fulcrum had shifted over time; the balance of power had changed. Both women knew it, and even the man had an inkling. Finding herself in the unaccustomed situation of having nothing to say, Mrs. Wright turned to Patrick. "And what have you done with yourself, young Mr. Mulhaven?"

"Not so young anymore," he said. "I teach at NYU."

Willa said, "It's Dr. Mulhaven, actually, but why stand on ceremony? You knew us as Willa and Patrick; those are still our names."

The maid entered backward, trundling a tea cart. Mrs. Wright poured with a hand that trembled slightly. The maid distributed the cups and left, closing the door gently behind her.

"Not a snowbird, Mrs. Wright?" Patrick asked. "Still sticking out the long, hard winters?"

"I've never been one for lolling beside overchlorinated swimming pools. My time is divided between New York and Washington."

"Where Jeremiah's doing very well, we've heard."

Discretion warred with pride, an unequal battle. "Doing well?" Mrs. Wright said, as if tasting the words. "Well, I suppose so. If you call being the top legislative aide of a most distinguished senator 'doing well,' then yes, I should say so."

They made appropriate noises. "Which senator?" Patrick asked.

"Senator Marvin Apfel," said Mrs. Wright.

Patrick let out a low whistle. Apfel's name was much in the news these days. If the Democrats won the presidency, he was likely to be tapped for the cabinet. "So Jeremiah's Apfel's boy. Good for him!"

Mrs. Wright stared over her teacup. "His *boy*?"

"We always knew he had a brilliant career ahead of him," Willa said soothingly. (As if the poor guy had a choice, she thought, with this virago on his back.) "I can just see him working the strings and pulleys, the go-to man in the Senate. Although I must say I never saw Jeremiah as the behind-the-scenes type. He was always so front and center, I just assumed we'd end up voting for him one day."

"He is a natural," his mother agreed, resistance at an end. "Jeremiah can relate to anyone; he has my gift for that. Far be it from me to interfere in my son's life; he loves his job, and it has been a brilliant apprenticeship in the art of politics. Yet I believe the day is coming when Jeremiah will have to step out from behind the curtain and assume his place in the sun." There was something almost biblical in the way she pronounced his name.

"Well," said Patrick after a short silence, "it's a good thing we're catching him before he does. Afterward there'll be no approaching him."

"What's that?" she said sharply, cutting her eyes from one to the other.

"Could you let us have his number, Mrs. Wright?" Willa said. "We'd like to call him."

"What for?"

"There's a reunion coming up," Patrick said. "A very special one. He wouldn't want to miss it."

Mrs. Wright fussed with her pearls. "I don't think you quite realize how busy Jeremiah is."

"We're going to invite him, Mrs. Wright, not kidnap him," Willa said. Not the wisest choice of words, she realized immediately; because hadn't the boys done that once on Jeremiah's birthday, abducted him for a night on the town?

"I'm relieved to hear it," she said drily. "As for his home number, much as I would like to help, my son has given me strict instructions never to give it out. Perhaps it would be better to drop him a line. Or better yet, leave your numbers with me and I'll see that he gets them."

Willa took a card from her wallet and Patrick produced one as well. They passed them to Mrs. Wright, who held them between thumb and forefinger. Willa could see exactly where she planned to deposit them once they were gone. They stood and placed their cups carefully on the tea cart. Willa took Mrs. Wright's hand in hers. It was parchment dry and bony: a widow's hand, she thought, then pushed the thought away. "Thank you for the tea and for sharing the good news about Jeremiah. If you could remember to give him our message, that would be great. But don't go to any trouble. We can always reach him through the senator's office."

"I do not advise that," said Mrs. Wright, clearly regretting her earlier indiscretion. "I myself never call him there. It's impossible to have a conversation. He cannot talk thirty seconds without interruption."

"I'm sure it won't be necessary," Willa said sweetly. "Good-bye, Mrs. Wright. Lovely to see you again."

7

Jeremiah Wright swept through the corridors at a pace calibrated to discourage interruptions. Already he'd been delayed twice by Republican senators touting their new, improved environmental protection bill, which, while marginally better than the last draft, was still so far off the mark that Jeremiah was convinced they had no intention of making it work. He'd implied as much to the second senator, Martin Rosings, who dispensed a look of paternal disappointment and said, "Jeremiah, we all have to live in this world. Republican or Democrat, we breathe the same air."

"Actually," Jeremiah said, "we don't. That's why there are epidemics of asthma in every major city in the country. But you know that, don't you, Senator? You're on the health committee."

They parted in mutual dissatisfaction, and Jeremiah checked his watch. Allowing twenty minutes for the taxi ride through rush-hour traffic, he should just make it. Then Bobby Mazzaro appeared at the far end of the corridor, bearing down with a meaningful look. Mazzaro was Jeremiah's counterpart on the Republican side, and this latest half-assed bill had his prints all over it. Ordinarily Jeremiah would have welcomed the chance to tell Mazzaro what he thought of it, but not today. If he was late to his own birthday party, Olivia would shoot him.

He slipped through a side door and emerged into a gallery overlooking the Senate chamber, where he was surrounded by the straggle end of a tour. High school kids by the look of them, half of them playing it cool and the other half genuinely bored. None of them looked as if he felt anything remotely like what Jeremiah had on his first visit to the Capitol building: a jolt, followed by a sense of rightness, as if a dislocated joint in his brain had popped into place.

Of course, he'd been primed for it, having just won his first election. It was the first time a junior ever won the post of student council president, and in the course of running, Jeremiah had discovered that campaigning suited who he was, a person who needed to be liked. But he'd thought of it as kid stuff, résumé padding, until the field trip to Washington and the Capitol building. They'd toured the elegant old Senate chamber, peeked into the president's room, then entered the gallery over-looking the Senate chamber. Their guide droned on about the busts of the vice presidents and the ceremonial snuffboxes on the Senate floor, but Jeremiah tuned her out. The air was dense with power, not his mother's diluted domestic brand or the petty tyranny of school officials, but the real stuff, heady as wine. Like a country choirboy turned loose in the Vatican, he strained for and was rewarded by glimpses of what lay behind the scenes: actual denizens of the place, seen in passing behind half-open doors or strolling through the apses of this secular cathedral. The thought came to him—more than a thought, a premonition—that one day he would be one of those dark-suited men who walked the inner corridors, holding each other's arms and speaking in soft voices. One day the Senate would be his home.

And so it had come to pass, although, in the manner of wishes granted, not quite as he'd envisioned it. Jeremiah was not a sena-tor; he was a legislative aide. A top aide to be sure, and a fine job for a promising young man; but was he quite, at thirty-seven, a promising *young* man? Birthdays are a time for introspection, and thirty-seven was an age at which a man takes stock of his life: What have I accomplished, he asks himself, and what remains to be done? It was also an age at which a man looks around and notices that some of his peers have passed him by. Last week, Jeremiah had had the painful pleasure of watching Bill Clinton work the Senate, soliciting support for his presiden-tial bid. Pleasurable because this man from nowhere, the gover-nor of *Arkansas*, for Christ's sake, was the best natural politician Jeremiah had ever seen. Painful because Jeremiah, long accus-tomed to being the wunderkind of every political gathering, felt like a slug beside Clinton. The man was on the fast track of fast tracks: state attorney general at thirty, governor at thirty-three, and now, at forty-five, a credible if dark-horse candidate for pres-ident. Clinton had gone the electoral route, Jeremiah the legisla-tive; now Clinton was a player and he a policy wonk. But a wonk with possibilities, Jeremiah reminded himself, a wonk with skills. A wonk who knew strategy as well as policy, who loved the game and played for keeps.

Change was in the air. Election nerves jangled the Capitol.

One thing only was certain: A year from now, the entire constellation would be different.

Jeremiah left the Capitol building through the main doors,
nodding to Henry, the security guard. He knew all the guards'
names, and they knew his; for Jeremiah made a point of staying
in touch with the little people, even as he himself ascended. The
plaza was swarming with tourists and he had to hustle for a cab.
By the time he caught one, he was sweating. He gave the driver
the restaurant's address, wiped his brow with a handkerchief,
and through long habit checked the cabby's license. "Desmond
Achebe," it read; Nigerian, most likely. "Any relation to the
writer?" he asked.

Astonished eyes met his in the rearview mirror. "You know
Chinua Achebe?"

"I read *Things Fall Apart* in high school. Since then I've read
everything of his I can get my hands on. He's a world-class
writer."

"And you, sir, are an educated man."

"Just one who loves to read," Jeremiah said modestly.

"It is the same."

Then the driver turned back to the road and Jeremiah settled
back with a sigh of satisfaction. This kind of encounter was the
reason he often took cabs—that and the fact that his Mercedes
spent so much time at the mechanic's that they might as well
have had joint custody. Most D.C. cabbies were recent immi-
grants, some highly educated. A number of Jeremiah's most
informative conversations about foreign affairs had been with
cabbies, who, for their part, were so grateful for his receptive ear
and genuine interest that not infrequently he rode for free.

Fifteen minutes later the taxi pulled up in front of Papa Luigi's.
An odd choice for Olivia, Jeremiah thought as he paid the driver.
Not that he didn't like Luigi's; it was one of his favorite restaurants.
He and Olivia ate there often, on nights when both of them were
free. But it was just a small neighborhood joint, a homey Italian
restaurant with checkered tablecloths and reliable if not brilliant
food. Its chief virtues were excellent service and the fact that no one
they knew dined there, and Jeremiah rather thought they had a tacit
agreement to keep it that way; but no doubt Olivia had her reasons.

He entered the vestibule through glass doors, checked his coat but not his briefcase, and examined himself in the mirrored wall. Not bad for thirty-seven, he thought. He'd put on fifteen pounds since high school, none of it fat; he kept in shape with tennis, squash, and swimming at his club. He still had all his hair and it wasn't gray yet; his smooth, pale face was unlined. He was no Adonis—his features were too narrow and sharp for that, his limbs too long and gangly—but Jeremiah flattered himself that he was better looking now than as a kid. I'm in my prime, he thought. It's never going to be better than it is now. The thought saddened him.

He paused just outside the dining room to summon a party spirit. Jeremiah had no idea who was coming; he left that sort of thing to Olivia, who had been born and raised to it. He turned the corner and scanned the room, looking for a large party and finding none. Only when his wife waved did he notice her sitting alone at a table for two. There are women who stand out in crowded rooms, and women who disappear in empty ones. Jeremiah had married one of the latter, and it was the smartest move he'd ever made. Love, to his mind, was a much overrated commodity. All his friends had married for it and now most were divorced, while eight years into their partnership, he and Olivia were stronger than ever.

Olivia greeted him with a nervous smile. "Surprise."

He kissed her cheek. Her skin, though sallow to look at, was smooth and warm. Olivia's father had been a handsome man with a long, rugged face, a forceful chin, and a nose to match, features which, having no son, he'd passed on to his daughter. The results fell somewhere short of felicitous. Olivia was a woman of greater than average height and weight, which by Washington's unforgiving standards made her large; she had a squarish figure, lanky brown hair, expensively cut, and the sort of face often described as horsey. She was three years older than her husband, who had married her less for her fortune (which was considerable) than for her connections. Olivia knew everyone who mattered; her Rolodex was a *Who's Who* of Washington's elite.

Jeremiah sat opposite her, and a martini appeared unbidden before him. "No one came?" he said. "That's the surprise?"

"No one was invited. I took you at your word."

"What an odd thing to do. Which word?"

"I asked who you wanted to invite. You said the best birthday you could imagine would have no guests, no conversation, and no politics. So, I brought your paper and my book. I've ordered all your favorite foods. You can eat and drink and rest your elbows on the table. You can read the paper and not say a word all through dinner, if you like, and I promise I won't mind a bit. Are you disappointed?"

He was a bit, but it was just as well; they needed to talk. Jeremiah summoned up a gracious smile. "A loaf of bread, a jug of wine, and thee. What could be better?" They drank to each other. Then Olivia nodded at the waiter and the first course was served. Jeremiah leaned back and tried to let the day's tensions drain from him.

"Hard day?" asked Olivia, who could not, after all, sit in silence.

"Mazzaro shat out a new version of the environmental bill, totally bogus. But it's not that." He toyed with his pasta for a moment, then looked up and met his wife's eyes. "I'm at a cross-roads." He didn't mean to put it so dramatically; it just came out that way, surprising them both. "Apfel's finished with the Senate. If we take the White House, he figures on a cabinet seat or ambassadorship. If not, he'll serve out his term and go home."

Olivia sat without moving, deep in thought. She had a capacity for stillness that Jeremiah admired. He touched his lower lip, and she absently wiped a trace of marinara sauce from hers. "He told you?"

He nodded. "Avuncular as hell, arm slung around my shoulders." He deepened his voice, assumed a Midwestern drawl. "'You've paid your dues, Jeremiah, done a hell of a job. You can write your own ticket now.'"

"That's it?" Olivia looked scandalized. "Hail and farewell?"

"Not quite," Jeremiah said in his own voice. "He dangled a Cabinet post if we win. Undersecretary," he added quickly, as Apfel had done, lest Jeremiah get ideas above his station.

Olivia toyed with a strand of hair, wrapping it around a finger, while she considered the offer; and who better to assess it than she, who knew the relative value, weight, and status of every job in the capital?

"It's not peanuts," she said at last. "Everyone knows it's the undersecretaries who run the departments."

"Power!" he said, making a joke of it. "Prestige! Access!"

"All the above. Everyone in Washington would know your name."

"And no one outside it."

"Ah," she said. "Was there an alternative on offer?"

"Not from him. This is something I've been considering." His tone casual. "A different direction."

"What direction?"

"There's a Congressional seat opening up in New York. The district includes Wickham." They owned a house in Old Wickham, a renovated farmhouse that they used several times a year as a getaway. Olivia started to speak, but Jeremiah hurried on. "The incumbent, George Ivey, is stepping down; poor man's got serious health problems. There'll be a special election. Moynihan's as good as promised me his support if I run."

"For the House?" Olivia said with a worried frown, as if Jeremiah had suddenly started speaking in tongues or poured his wine out on the floor. Decades, generations of snobbery informed those three syllables. Her father and grandfather had been senators, and she had grown up sharing their view of the House as a tenement for transient, jumped-up local pols.

Jeremiah gazed at his wife with affection. It pleased him to think how far his marriage had carried him: from a mother whose fondest hope had been to one day say, "My son, the lawyer," to a wife who wondered if the United States Congress was good enough for him. "It would just be for a little while," he said, employing his most persuasive voice. "A term or two at most. D'Amato has all sorts of problems. He can be taken—once I'm in a position to act. Right now no one knows me outside the Beltway. I need a base. I need a track record. I need to show I'm electable."

"But the House . . ."

He laughed. "Our friends will still speak to us."

"It would mean moving to New York. And cultivating all those state and local people. And fund-raising. And campaigning. Is it worth it, do you think, Jeremiah? Assuming you win, a freshman congressman has no power at all compared to what Apfel's offering you."

Jeremiah shook his head impatiently. "Pie in the sky. He's trying to keep me on board till the end. At best his offer depends on our winning the presidency. I'm tired of back rooms, Livvy. If my future is going to hinge on an election, I'd just as soon it were my own." He noticed that he was gripping the table and let go.

His wife looked at him, her napkin to her lips. Olivia understood ambition, having grown up in its precincts, and in her own way, she shared her husband's. He wanted to be a powerful man; she wanted to be the wife of such a man. Politically a staunch feminist, in her private life Olivia preferred to keep a low profile. She was as smart as he was, but her gifts differed from his. Jeremiah was the meeter and greeter, the handshake artist, the charmer with a knack for remembering names and family details; Olivia was the one who kept the files that fed his fabled memory. Lacking beauty, she was often overlooked and had learned to turn that to her advantage. Her talents lay in assembling interesting, powerful people and carefully observing the results. Olivia's salons were a Beltway tradition, her invitation lists closely parsed by pundits, even her seating plans scrutinized.

"I can't do it without you," Jeremiah said, leaning toward her. "And it can't be done halfheartedly."

"Have I ever done anything halfheartedly?"

He apologized hastily. Olivia was as supportive a wife as any ambitious man could wish for; but she also had a solid sense of self-worth it did not pay to offend.

"But do you really understand what's entailed?" Olivia peered at him earnestly. "The press, the constant questioning, the invasion of privacy: Are you prepared for all that?"

Jeremiah spread his hands. "My life's an open book," he said.

The phone was ringing as they entered, echoing through the silent town house. Silent because they had not been blessed with children, as Jeremiah generally put it, implying disappointment when in fact he'd known going into the marriage that, due to a childhood bout with cancer, Olivia was barren. Indeed he had considered it one of her many assets, not that he would ever have been so cruel or foolish as to say so to her or anyone else. Jeremiah had nothing against other people's children; he simply begrudged the time required to raise one's own. Their childlessness pained his wife, but since the disability was hers, she had nothing with which to reproach her husband, while Jeremiah earned full marks for stoic forbearance.

Ignoring the phone, Olivia tossed her coat over a chair and went straight upstairs. Jeremiah detoured to the kitchen and picked up the cordless. "Hello?"

"Happy birthday, darling!"

"Thank you, Mother."

"Although I must say, if you keep this up, you'll soon be my age; and that would not be at all appropriate."

"Then I shall age by increments of half the difference, and Xeno's paradox will preserve your lead."

His mother laughed. She was proud of his wit and took full credit for it. Dinners at home had been verbal Ping-Pong matches between the two of them, with his father, while he lived, serving as the net. "The oddest thing happened, darling," Mrs. Wright said. "You'll never guess what."

Jeremiah took an open bottle of wine from the refrigerator and poured himself a glass. "Since I'll never guess, why don't you tell me?"

"Two of your old hoodlum friends came to call: Patrick Mulhaven and Willa Scott. Willa Scott Durrell now, if you please. You'd think she'd have gone back to her maiden name after that messy business with her husband. I'm sure I told you about that."

She had, with considerable relish. Jeremiah had put down his glass and was standing very still. "What did they want?"

"Some nonsense about a reunion. I told them how busy you are, but they insisted on talking to you personally, if you please. They seemed prepared to make a nuisance of themselves, so I thought you might want to head them off at the pass."

So they did remember. I'll be damned. Jeremiah took a pad and wrote down the names and numbers. Then he eased his mother off the phone and sank into a chair. When he looked down at the two names on the pad, half a dozen others emerged, and with them a flood of memories. Most were erotically charged, and no wonder; he'd spent his entire high school career in a state of free-floating lust, which more often than not attached itself to the Beacon Hill girls. The two hottest girls in the school for his money, and opposites to boot. For years he'd jerked off to elaborate fantasies of having them both at once, fantasies that even now possessed the power to arouse.

Lord, he thought, how purely I lusted. Where is that passion now?

Shunted elsewhere, he supposed; sublimated into a greater passion. In the old days, politicians could have their cake and eat it, too. The Kennedys probably racked up more nookie than Mick Jagger, and no one said a word. Even now you heard stories, about Clinton, for instance. Clinton looked like a guy who would run through women like junk food; but considering what happened to Gary Hart, Jeremiah found it hard to believe he would risk his whole career for a side of pussy. These days the press would flay you alive for crap like that. Jeremiah could lust with the best of them, and did; but he kept his pants zipped.

His wife entered the kitchen in a filmy black negligee. Jeremiah's heart sank, but Olivia was perfectly within her rights; they always made love on birthdays and holidays. Other times were optional.

He held out his hand, and she came and plopped herself onto his lap, a solid slab of woman. "Is that a cell phone in your pocket," she said huskily, "or are you just glad to see me?"

It was a cell phone. The pad with the names and numbers lay faceup on the table. When he saw her reading it, he said, "That was my mother just now. Some old friends turned up on her doorstep, looking for me. My 'hoodlum friends,' she calls them."

Olivia turned to look at him. "You had hoodlum friends?"

"They weren't really. Just a tad wild."

"And your mother put up with that?"

"She hated them," he said with irrepressible pride. "And there wasn't a damn thing she could do about it."

Not that she didn't try. Prep school was the Damocles sword, that and refusing to pay for him to go away to college, when she knew perfectly well he'd set his sights on Princeton or Harvard.

He'd believed her, too, thought her capable of thwarting his life if he defied her; and yet he would not give up his "hoodlum friends."

Olivia twisted herself around to stare at his face. "You were close to these people?"

Jeremiah hesitated. His wife had led a sheltered childhood. There were things about his life that she was not equipped to understand, certain stories he kept to himself, knowing they would worry her needlessly. *No*, he meant to tell her, *they were nothing much to me.*

"They were the best part of high school," he heard himself say.

Olivia caught her lower lip between her teeth. "Wild how? Drugs?"

Suddenly the kitchen was gone and Jeremiah was back on the hill, Jimi Hendrix on the radio, the air pungent with weed. They're lolling on the boulders. A fat joint comes his way and as usual he passes it on untasted. It's not the cops he fears but his mother, whose powers of detection far outshine theirs. But when the joint reaches Angel, she carries it back to Jeremiah, plops herself on his lap, takes a long toke, and fastens her lips to his. There is no way his mouth can resist hers. He opens his lips and inhales a lungful of sweet smoke.

"Got your cherry," she says, pinching his cheek.

"Jeremiah," his wife said sternly. She had removed herself from his lap and was now sitting beside him at the kitchen table. "This is no joke. You're talking about running for office. Can these people hurt you?"

"They wouldn't even if they could, which they can't."

"But I don't understand. If you were so close, how come I've never heard of them before? Didn't you stay in touch?"

"No."

"Why not?"

"We just didn't. Not enough in common, I guess. After high school, we went our separate ways," Jeremiah said, sorry now that he'd mentioned them at all. Olivia, like his mother, was relentless.

"Why would they show up now," she asked, "after so many years?"

"Because it's almost twenty. They're planning the reunion."

"A high school reunion?"

"No, our own. The night of graduation we made a pact: We swore that whatever happened, wherever we were, we'd meet again in twenty years. Kid stuff," he added with a little laugh.

"Kid stuff, but you remembered."

"Yes."

"And so did they."

"Apparently."

Olivia looked troubled. "Do you want to see them?"

A simple question, to which there was no simple answer.

8

Vinny Delgaudio was in a foul mood. The day had started badly—dirty looks from his daughter and the frosty aftermath of a fight with the wife—and he was late getting to work. He strode through the station's C-shop without a word for the cashier, threw open the door to the garage and poked his head in. Two mechanics looked up and Manny Hernandez, the foreman, called out, "Hey, Vinny." Vinny thought Frank was missing till he spotted his long legs sticking out from under a Porsche. "Send him to me when he's done under there," he told Manny, nodding toward the legs. A second door in the rear of the shop led to a short corridor, with the staff bathroom on the right and his office on the left. Last week he'd walked into the john and caught the gas attendant smoking a joint. Fired his ass on the spot. The way Vinny saw it, what a man did in his own home was his business. He didn't care if the kid shot Windex and smoked cockroach dung in his off hours. But not in Vinny's shop, and not on his time.

The sight of his office, usually so uplifting to his spirits, did nothing for him today. Unlike any garage office he'd ever known, it resembled, by design, a doctor's consulting room. Instead of metal and plastic, he had wood and leather; instead of girlie calendars pinned to the wall, he had framed posters of *New Yorker* covers. He had a solid beech desk that would not have looked out of place in a corporate office, thick-pile carpeting (whose color, charcoal gray, was the only concession to the office's surroundings), a sofa and chair upholstered in Italian leather as soft as ladies' gloves. Cost him a small fortune, but it was a smart move, worth every penny. Customers ushered into this room added an extra zero onto the checks they were mentally writing. Guided toward the sofa, they steeled themselves for the worst possible news. "Mr. Smith," Vinny would say gravely, "Mrs. Smith, I'm sorry to tell you that your Audi is critically ill."

His wife had decorated the office, and she'd done a good job, he had to give her that. He could never have pulled it off. Vinny once overheard someone describe him as a grease monkey in an Italian suit. On principle he'd clocked the guy, but in his heart he savored the description. He dressed well, even elegantly—his wife again—but he kept a set of overalls in his office closet and more days than not worked side by side with his men. In twenty years, he'd gone from a kid with nothing to a respected businessman, owner of a five-bay service station with twelve gas pumps and a convenience store. Delgaudio Repairs specialized in high-end, high-performance vehicles. The shop was in the Bronx, just off Fordham Avenue, but most of their clientele came from West-chester. Vinny was proud of how far he'd come in life, but he was also proud of the grease under his nails.

There was a tap on the door and Frank followed, holding a steaming mug. "Hey, Uncle Vinny. Got your coffee."

"How many times I gotta tell you, call me Vinny here, like the other guys." Bad enough his longtime guys had to cope with a nephew on the job; no need to rub their faces in it.

"Sorry, Vinny."

Vinny waved it off. Frankie was a good kid. Smart, too—passed the Mercedes course first time out, which was more than Vinny could say for himself. He sipped his coffee—not the C-shop's anemic brown water but the real stuff they brewed in the garage, thick enough to stand a spoon in—and studied his nephew. Frank was named after his father, Vinny's eldest brother, who'd died in Vietnam three months before the kid was born. That Frank Sr. hadn't gotten around to marrying his girlfriend made no difference to the Delgaudios, who absorbed both mother and child into their large, untidy family with barely a rip-ple. Tina became the sister and daughter they'd never had, and the boy was raised by his mother, grandparents, and four uncles. Now Frank was twenty-two, a strapping young man with his own place in the city, a good job, and a bright future. Vinny wouldn't have admitted it for anything, but the day Frank came to work for him was one of the happiest of his life. Here and there in his life, Vinny had maybe done things he wasn't proud of; so Frank turning out like he did seemed to balance the scales. It was a matter of deep satisfaction to Vinny that this fatherless child had grown up without a chip on his shoulder.

Frank placed the mug on a coaster and slid it across the desk. Didn't sit and wasn't asked to, since he was in greasy overalls, but leaned comfortably against a corner of the desk. "Wassup, Unc?" he said. "You okay?"

"Why shouldn't I be?"

"Just asking. You're never late is why."

"Women," Vinny said with a sigh, and his nephew nodded wisely, as if to say, "Tell me about it." Vinny had to laugh. Twenty-two years old and thinks he knows something. Good-looking boy, young Frank. Caught more than his share of passes from lady customers and, as far as Vinny knew, never failed to convert. But still.

"Think she'd be grateful, wouldn't you?" he said. "It's her daughter, too. But no. 'Don't interfere,' she tells me. 'The girl just wants to have fun.' The woman has no clue. It's a fuckin' jungle out there."

"Nicole's got herself a boyfriend," Frank guessed.

Nicole was Vinny's sixteen-year-old daughter. He had a son, too, twelve-year-old Vincent Jr. Easygoing kid, no *agita* there. Nicole was the one putting gray in his hair. "Take my advice," Vinny said. "When the time comes, have boys."

"What'd the kid do?"

"Arrogant little twerp, sits in his car and honks for her. Never worked a day in his life and drives a BMW—not his father's, mind you, his. Everything on a fucking platter. So I go out, have a fatherly talk with the kid. For this I am called a 'troglodyte.' What the hell's a troglodyte, anyway?"

"Some kind of prehistoric sloth, I think. What'd you say to him?"

"Nothin'. I gave him a few health tips is all."

Frank nodded. He'd been on the receiving end of some of his uncle's health tips, which generally ran along the lines of: "If you wanna stay healthy, show some respect."

Vinny had laid it out for the kid. "You want to see my daughter, you get your lazy ass out of the car and ring the bell. Lay a finger on her, I break your hand. Lay a hand on her, I break your arm. You see where this is going?"

"Full-body cast?" the boy had ventured.

Smart-ass kid. He got the message, though. Nicole was home by eleven, safe and sound and furious with her dad.

That was okay. You had to expect that. What pissed Vinny off was Theresa taking her side. His wife had no idea what eighteen-year-old boys were capable of, the casual cruelties they could inflict. Vinny did. He remembered more than he wanted to about teenage boys and their escapades.

Troglodyte his ass. When it came to his daughter, he was Tyrannosaurus Dad.

Frank stirred restlessly, anxious to get back to the Porsche. "Did you want me for something, Vinny?"

Vinny brought eyes and attention to bear on his nephew. "What'd I tell you about the C-shop, Frank?"

"You thought someone was ripping us off."

"I don't think it anymore, I know it. Spent the night going over the books, breaking down sales by shift. Certain shifts, regular as clockwork, we're down ten percent or more. What's that tell you?"

"Someone's skimming."

"Wrong." Vinny jabbed a finger at Frank's face. "It tells you one greedy bastard's skimming ten percent more than the others."

"That's cold, man."

"Yeah, well, welcome to the real world."

"So what do we do about it?"

Vinny nodded; he liked the "we." Frank worked with the men, but he was the owner's nephew. He needed to be real clear on where his loyalties lay, which made this event into what Theresa called a teaching experience.

"We're going to catch the thief. We're going to get him on film and then we're gonna bust him. I want you to call the guys who installed our security cameras and tell them we need another; tell them what for. They'll know what to do. It'll have to be at night, after the store's closed. And, Frank."

"Yeah?"

"You and me're the only ones know about this. Let's keep it that way."

"I hear you." Frank's facial repertory didn't run to rebellious; he looked troubled instead. "I just can't believe it. I can't see any of them stealing from you."

"Most natural thing in the world," Vinny said. "The tempta-tion's always there; some are bound to fall. Can't be sentimental about the workers, Frank. They're sure as hell not about us." He went on to say that nowadays no one wanted to come up the hard way, by working; nowadays everyone wanted to get rich quick; but by then Frank had quit listening. He was thinking about the Porsche, and besides, he'd heard his uncle's "No one ever gave me nothin'" speech many times before. No silver spoon in Vinny's mouth, no, sir. He'd worked his way up, broken his back, scrimped and saved, bought a failing business and turned it around. Frank was edging toward the door when the intercom buzzed. Vinny grabbed the phone. "Yeah?"

Manny's high-pitched voice was audible to both men. "Guy out here wants to see you about a car. Says to tell you he's irate."

"*Irate*, huh," Vinny said, winking at Frank. "Which car?"

"Hang on."

Vinny covered the receiver and said, "If it's that Boxster again, I swear to God I'm gonna pop that preppy asshole. Beautiful machine, and he treats it like a kid stripping wings off a fly."

Manny came back sounding pissed. "He says it's a fifty-seven Chevrolet. I told him we don't work on domestics, but he don't want to hear it from me."

"A fifty-seven Chevy?" Vinny turned away from Frank and spoke softly. "What color?"

"What's it matter what color?" Manny said.

"Shut up. Just ask him."

Manny relayed the question and then the answer: "Red." Vinny dropped the phone and strode out of his office, not hurrying, but moving with such blinkered concentration that Frank, scenting trouble, trotted after him. They entered the garage through the side door. Manny was standing just outside bay one with a dark-haired man in corduroy slacks and a tweed jacket. The man looked up at Vinny bearing down on him and didn't flinch. At the last moment before impact, Vinny spread his arms and enveloped the visitor in a bear hug.

"I knew it was you," he said.

"Who else would it be?" agreed Patrick.

"Look at you," Patrick said. "This place, those cars out there, it's a pipe dream come true. Who'da thunk it, back in the days?"

"Look who's talking, *Professor.* I always figured you'd end up bumming dimes on the street." Vinny took two Buds from the small refrigerator under his desk, carried them to the sofa, and handed one to Patrick. "So you make a living watching movies, and I make one playing with cars. I'd say we both did all right."

"I'll drink to that," Patrick said, and they did. Vinny looked at Patrick almost shyly and found him the same, only more so. The same smile, the same restless laugh bubbling just beneath the surface. *Let's go,* he heard. *There's a flick we've gotta see. A car show in the city. Three girls Caleb met, crazy chicks, into yoga and macrobiotics.* Bizarre as it seemed at first, the fact that Patrick of all people had become a college professor made a strange sort of sense. He'd been the most curious guy Vinny had ever known, and the most eager to share. Good with women, too, though Caleb had been the undisputed king of bird dogs. Caleb. Vinny asked whatever happened to that madman.

"Dunno," Patrick said. "We'll soon find out."

"How?" Vinny said, the first stirring of unease rising within him.

"Like you don't know."

"You're not talking about that crazy pact . . ."

"What else?"

Vinny shook his head. "Twenty years, man. Who's gonna remember, much less show?"

"You remembered. I did. So did Willa, who was kind enough to offer her house as reunion HQ."

"Willa Scott." Vinny whistled softly. "Jeez. Are you in touch with her?"

Patrick nodded.

"Hot as ever, right?" Vinny said.

"How did you know?"

"Saw her picture."

"On a book jacket?"

Vinny snorted. "Yeah, right. In the paper, when her husband died."

Puzzled, Patrick asked, "They ran a picture of her with the obituary?"

"No, man, in the news. Didn't you hear about it?"

"What do I got to do, feed you quarters?"

Vinny told the story, or what he remembered of it. Willa's husband, Simon Durrell, had been a hotshot lawyer who specialized in high-profile police brutality cases. His death of a heart attack at forty would have been news even if it hadn't occurred in what the papers were quick to term a "love nest." He was in the apartment, a studio on West Tenth, when he collapsed. An ambulance was summoned by a woman who gave her name only as Meredith. She was less discreet with Simon's name; consequently the press arrived just minutes after the ambulance. The first call to Willa had come, not from the hospital or police, but from a *Daily News* reporter. "It couldn't be my husband," she'd told the reporter. "Simon's in Chicago."

The woman who called for the ambulance was gone by the time it arrived, but it took less than a day for reporters to discover her identity: Her name was Meredith Eisner, and she was a municipal court judge. The subsequent scandal battened on allegations of corruption, for Judge Eisner had been so unwise as to sit in judgment on two cases in which her lover appeared for the plaintiff, and Simon had won both cases.

Now everything made sense to Patrick: Mrs. Wright's razor-edged condolences, Willa's unwillingness to talk about her husband, the sense of subterranean anger in her home, like the relentless ticking of an unexploded bomb. "Poor Willa," he said, and Vinny nodded. They sat for a moment without speaking, though not in silence, for the sounds of the garage and the street beyond it leached into the room, along with the mingled odor of oil, exhaust, and gasoline. Once, in her decorating zeal, Theresa had secreted one of those plug-in pine-scented gizmos in his office, but Vinny had rooted it out. He liked the smell of garages, always had. To him it was as alluring as the scent of horse barns to young girls.

"So," Vinny said presently, "you really think it's gonna happen?"

"We swore to it, didn't we?"

"Do you even know where they are?"

"I found you, didn't I? And we've got a line on Jeremiah."

"Yeah, right," Vinny said. "Like he's gonna show."

"Why not?"

"I heard he's some kind of hotshot Washington suit."

"So what?" Patrick said. "Imagine all of us together again—what a blast!"

"All of us being . . . ?"

"Caleb, Travis, Shake and Nancy, Jeremiah, Willa, Angel."

"You know, I actually ran into Travis Fleck," Vinny said. "Five, six years ago, we're out in Santa Fe over Christmas vacation. I walk into a bar and who's sitting there but fuckin' Travis, ponytail and all. He's wearing this Indian serape and cowboy boots, like a refugee from a hippie commune. I take the stool next to his. He looks over, does a double take. 'Jesus, Vinny, is it really you?'

"'It's me, man,' I say. 'I've come to collect that twenty you owe me.' You should of seen his face. I swear to God he thought I meant it."

Patrick laughed. "What's he doing?"

"Building houses, believe it or not, and making a decent living at it. I saw this really nice adobe house he made for himself, and he showed us pictures of others he'd built."

"Good for him," Patrick said. He copied down Travis's address and phone number, which Vinny dug out of a bulging Rolodex. Then he gave his number and Willa's to Vinny. "Last weekend in June, wives welcome but not required. Put it on your calendar."

"I'll try," Vinny said, looking away.

Patrick frowned. "Fuck *try*. Be there, man."

"June's a bad month for me." He got up, walked around the office. The kids needed to be driven to camp, he explained. The shop was always swamped before summer vacation. He'd have guys out on vacation.

Patrick heard him out. Then said, "What the fuck are you talking about, Vincent? Of course you're coming."

"Look, if it happens I'll try and drop by, say hello at least. But let me ask you something. Are you sure this is such a good idea?"

Patrick mimed astonishment.

"I'm not saying we didn't have good times," Vinny said. "But those days are long gone, so what's the point? It's like that Springsteen song, you know, about a bunch of old farts droning on about their glory days."

"You're not an old fart," Patrick said indignantly. "I'm not an old fart, and Willa's anything but. There's a reason we were friends back then. I bet you anything that reason still exists."

Vinny quit pacing and looked at Patrick, as Willa had, through grown-up eyes. "Remind me never to go to the track with you."

"Promise you'll come."

Vinny was tempted. It had never been easy saying no to Patrick, which was one of the reasons they got in so much trouble as kids. But then he thought of meeting Jeremiah again after all these years of going their own way. What would they say to each other? What would any of them say? Patrick didn't see the whole picture. "You really think a grease monkey like me has anything in common with the likes of Willa and Jeremiah? We hung together as kids, sure, but once high school ended, everyone retired to their separate corners. That's how it is."

"Doesn't have to be," Patrick said. "And what's this about 'the likes of Willa and Jeremiah'? What are you, chopped liver? Those two were born with silver spoons in their mouths. You built all this." He waved his arms expansively, as if encompassing a kingdom.

"Bet your ass," Vinny said. "Nobody ever gave me nothing."

"Fuck you, man. You're coming."

"If I can."

"Aren't you even curious?" Patrick asked. "Don't you want to see how they all turned out?"

Vinny shrugged. Curiosity wasn't his long suit; fixing things was.

9

Travis Fleck, washing his breakfast dishes, gazed out the window at the steep, snowy drive leading up to his house. It was hard-packed snow, no ice, perfectly safe driving, but what do Texans know about driving in snow? Half the time, weather like this, the client didn't even show, which in this case would be fine by him. Travis didn't get into this business to build trophy homes for Texas oilmen.

He dried the plate and put it away, washed the residue of ham and egg from the frying pan and stowed it in the cupboard under the counter. Then he wiped his hands on his jeans and looked around the kitchen, now restored to its pristine self. There had been a time in his life when Travis lived in squalor, surrounded by his own detritus, the disorganized mind made manifest. That time ended forever the day he moved into this house, which he himself had built with the help of friends. 2,860 adobe bricks, sun-dried mud, sand, and straw, went into this house. Travis had mixed the mud, scooped it into molds, laid the bricks out to dry. His back and arms knew the weight of every forty-pound brick. With his friend Victor Montoya, the master *enjarradoro*, he plastered the outer walls with mud seeded with chips of mica that glowed gold and pink in the sunlight. The lines of the house were subtly rounded, an effect especially noticeable in the living room, where two tall, deep-set windows framed unobstructed views of the Sangre de Christo Mountains. The inner walls were coated in aqua-tinted plaster flecked with granulated mica. On the terra-cotta floor of the living room there was a red-and-black Navajo rug, payment for a house he'd helped build, and on the wall above the earthen fireplace, a framed print of Georgia O'Keeffe's painting of the Ranchos de Taos church. The rug was of near museum quality, and people thought he was mad to keep it on the floor, but Travis believed that all things should serve the purpose for which they were created. He noticed some dog hair on the rug—Juan had been over recently with his shepherd, Lobo—and vacuumed it up. Until he built and inhabited this house, Travis never understood the meaning of the word "cherish." In homage to the house, tidiness had become a sacrament. Like

most converts to a cause, he was fanatical in its pursuit: one reason, though not the only one, he lived alone.

The clients arrived half an hour late. The Texan was a tall, vigorous man in his fifties, with a crushing handshake and apprais-
ing eyes. "Sorry to keep you waiting, Mr. Fleck," he drawled. "You
try getting anywhere on time with two women in tow."

They sat in his office, thumbing through photo albums of his
work while Travis studied the architect's drawings. The Texan's
wife, a second or third, was an assembly-line blonde, thirtyish,
with big headlights and a country-club smile. His teenage daughter wore a thigh-length sweater over black leggings that looked
like they were painted on. She reminded Travis of a girl he'd
known in high school. Angel had been a redhead, and this girl
was a blonde, but they had the same sultry, knowing eyes and
radiant sexuality. A doable girl, as they used to say—not that he
ever got to do Angel. Never got past first base, though she must
have fucked half their class.

It wasn't just her. There had seemed to be, in those days, a conspiracy involving all women to deny Travis sex until he exploded
with frustration. The sexual revolution was raging all around him,
and his comrades-in-arms were drowning in pussy; but Travis
couldn't get a taste. He was like a man dying of starvation in the
midst of a feast. Never did get laid till he was twenty-two, the oldest virgin in America. Since then he had done his conscientious
best to make up for lost time, only to discover, as others had before
him, that the girls you get never make up for the ones you didn't.

The Texan's daughter was sitting in Juan's chair, leaning back
with legs outstretched, heels resting on the desk. She caught him
peeking and lifted an eyebrow. Travis quickly looked back at the
blueprint. He liked them young, but not that young; not jailbait.

The office of the Santa Fe Adobe Cooperative was a simple
adobe structure behind Travis's house. Five years ago, the business having grown to the point that Travis wanted it out of his
living room, he and his partners had built the room in between
paying jobs. His partners were Victor Montoya, the best mud
plasterer in the Southwest, and Victor's cousin, Juan Aquila, the
adobero who had taught Travis the trade. The office was a single
large room with a filing cabinet, drafting table, three desks, one

for each of the partners, and an assortment of chairs. Victor and Juan rarely used their desks, preferring to leave the business side of things to Travis, who had more schooling than the two of them put together. It was a good partnership, in which each had something the others needed and all contributed equally.

Travis didn't mind running the office over the winter months, but in the spring and summer he liked to get out to the sites. There was no feeling in the world like that of raw adobe mud between his fingers. For Travis, working with adobe was a sensual experience, like sticking his hand in the warm, wet cunt of the earth. But the work had a spiritual side as well, though Juan and Victor laughed when he said it. It was godlike work creating form, function, and beauty from amorphous clay. Travis's image of God, to the extent that he had one, was of the master *adobero* of Genesis, sculpting not only earth and all its flora and fauna but also man himself, setting it all in motion and, in the same instant, turning away to the next world, the next creation.

Travis sometimes had a hard time letting go of the houses he built, finding excuses to go back again and again for finishing touches. God, he surmised from the evidence, had no such difficulty.

The Texan shut the album with a snap and said, "Fine-looking work, sir. But then you come well recommended."

"We specialize in adobe," Travis said. "We make our own bricks, we don't use the mass-produced commercial product. But the only woodwork we do is the roof. For everything else you'll need a carpenter."

The Texan nodded impatiently; he already knew this. "It seemed to me that the finish of the houses in the book is different from the finish on your own house, which we particularly admired as we drove up. Am I right?"

"You are," Travis said, with grudging respect. "Those houses are built to code, with cement plaster covering the adobe instead of the traditional mud plaster. It's a stupid regulation, because mud plaster works better with adobe, and it's cheaper, too. The code also requires a steel tie beam around the perimeter and a concrete foundation. We have to comply."

"*You* didn't."

"I built my place the way I wanted it, the way people around here have been building for centuries. How it works is, if they catch you before the house is finished, they can make you tear it down. Once it's done, there ain't nothing they can do."

The Texan gave Travis a look that took in his graying ponytail, sandaled feet, and faded flannel shirt. "I see," he said. "Guerrilla construction."

"Right. But with our clients' homes we go by the book." Which was not altogether true. Travis had another album in his desk, pictures of houses built the old way. He'd gone into this venture with the express aim of providing traditional adobes to native New Mexicans who could never afford homes built to federal code. This, Travis believed, was the very purpose of the code, to serve as one more weapon in the ongoing repression of the native peoples of America. It hurt him to see so many living in squalid trailer parks, while wealthy Anglos from out of state snatched up authentic adobes, driving prices even higher. Over the years, the Santa Fe Adobe Cooperative had built dozens of small traditional adobes for those Indian and Hispanic families. The inspectors knew what they were doing and looked the other way. They might work for the government, but they came from the people.

Not that any of this was the Texan's business. His rambling, hacienda-style monument to self-importance would be the talk of the town before the foundation was poured. If he wanted this house, he'd have to take the high road and pay full fare. Travis promised a quote within twenty-four hours and saw the clients out. The girl was the last to leave. When he shook her hand, she ran the tip of a finger along his palm. Travis had an immediate vision of himself on the job, stripped to the waist, elbow deep in steaming mud; suddenly she appears, in shorts and a cropped top, with two frosty beers and a towel for his hands . . . bullshit, he told himself, before it could go any further. Jailbait. Client's kid. Forget about it. And he tried, but she'd left him horny and disgruntled. He poured another cup of coffee and took it outside, not bothering with a jacket. The two piñon pines that framed his doorway were laced with snow, and more was coming; he could smell the storm in the wind, see it in the dark clouds obscuring the mountain peaks, feel it in the ache deep inside his scarred left hand. A lone eagle circled overhead. From his house, the last in a sparse line high in the foothills of the Sangre de Christo range, Travis saw no human dwelling, heard no conversation but the harsh colloquy of crows.

Another man would have been lonely. Not Travis. He had everything he needed here: his books and his music, useful work, tranquility, sweet highland air, and a mountain in his backyard. For sex he trolled the pool of tourists on forays into town, not an ideal solution but an equitable one; they got some local color, he got laid.

Three years ago, after a banner year for the business, Travis had indulged a longtime desire and gotten his teeth fixed. It should have been done when he was a kid, but his parents couldn't be bothered. Too expensive, they'd said, and the little gap between his teeth was cute. Besides, "Looks don't matter for boys." A decision that blighted his youth, for which he still hadn't forgiven them. Wearing braces as an adult was agonizing, not because of the braces themselves, but because they made him so self-conscious that he could not even attempt to pick up women. By the time they came off, Travis was heartily sick of his right hand. But the results were everything he'd hoped for, and well worth the cost.

He'd come a long way from the gawky kid who couldn't get laid for love or money. Hard work had honed and clarified his body, solitude his character. His only regret was that there was no one to bear witness to his transformation. No one to say, Jesus, Trav, is that really you? He longed to see it in their eyes: wonder leading to a rapid reassessment of the past. We had him wrong, they'd think. Look how he turned out. His high school buddies used to dream of buying land in California and New Mexico, but he was the one who'd actually done it. He yearned to meet those girls who'd spurned him, deemed him unworthy, rebuffed his fumbling passes with scorn or, worse yet, pity. He wanted to see it in their eyes: *What was I thinking?*

Ever since the calendar turned to 1992, Travis had been thinking of going back East for a visit, his first in two decades. Did anyone else still remember their pledge to meet again? He didn't suppose so, they were all pretty wrecked that night. And even if they did, they'd probably forget to invite him, the way they always had.

Thoughts of Angel had evoked memories of the whole Beacon Hill gang, who were never as far from his mind as they ought to be. He'd adored them; they'd tolerated him: That was the crux of the problem. They'd allowed him to hang with them, but they'd never called for him. The guys often did things without him. The girls treated him like a little brother, though he loomed over them all, and laughed when he came on to them. Kid stuff, in retrospect; penny-ante adolescent bullshit. Yet the pain of those small slights, repeated over time, had carved a permanent causeway in his psyche. Who ever forgets his first love? And he'd loved them all. Patrick, Shake, and Caleb were the coolest guys in school, Vinny the toughest, Jeremiah the smartest; and Angel and Willa had been by far the hottest girls. As for Travis, he was the geekiest. He'd paid his way with weed and perfect loyalty.

Loyalty's what got him in, that and a lucky accident. It happened in the lunchroom, early in junior year. Vinny, arguing a point with fork in hand, stabbed downward by way of emphasis and buried the fork deep in Travis's left hand. For a moment, no one reacted; they just stared at the fork standing upright in his hand, vibrating slightly as blood bubbled up around the edges of the tines. Vinny, his face white as chalk, backed away from the table. "What the fuck did you stick your hand there for?" he cried; then, face crumbling, "I'm sorry, man."

Travis didn't rat him out. Not then, not later in the hospital, not ever. And from that day on, he was under Vinny's protection. He became one of the Beacon Hill gang. Sort of. The one with his face pressed to the window. Travis used to think that when he died, "Not Quite" would be his epitaph.

He found that he was shivering. The storm was approaching quickly, the temperature dropping. He went back inside the warm house and shut the door. The scent of the women lingered in the air. Travis was in his bedroom pulling on a pair of woolen socks when the phone rang. He reached across the bed. "Santa Fe Adobe Cooperative."

A voice he hadn't heard in twenty years said, "Hello, Travis."

And Travis, as casually as if they spoke every day, said, "Hey, Patch. Where's the party?"

10

"I think I'll go tonight," Nancy called from the bedroom. No answer from Shake, just a brief pause before the piano started up again. The same phrase, over and over, the motif of a new song. She smoothed the sleeve of his white shirt over the ironing board and sprinkled it with water. Under the hot iron the cloth hissed and sent up aromatic puffs of steam. She was ironing because it was Saturday, and Nancy was a creature of habit. Weekdays she worked as a typist at the law firm of D'Addario, Francis, and Shire; Saturdays she watched tapes of her soaps and ironed. Lately, with their son away, there were fewer shirts to iron.

It was strange. She'd have thought the apartment would seem bigger with Dylan gone—and not only him but his stuff as well, the baggy clothes and size-twelve sneakers, the sports gear, not to mention his whole posse of friends, who had towered over and teased her, called her Mama Shake, and ate her out of house and home—but instead it felt smaller, hollowed out somehow. Nancy had known she would miss her son when he went off to college; she was prepared for that. What she'd failed to anticipate were the side effects of his leaving, like the mystifying silence that had set in between her and Shake, a reticence so dense it made being together feel like being alone.

It had a name, this state they were in. Nancy had read about it in the *Ladies' Home Journal,* which she'd picked up in the doctor's office. "Empty-nest syndrome" it was called, which described their situation to a T, except that most of the empty nesters in the article were in their fifties, while she and Shake were not even forty yet. "The transition from being a family back to being a couple can be a rocky one," the article said. "Your husband may not say so, but be assured that in his own way he, too, is suffering from the departure of his children and the realization that, ready or not, he has been thrust into a different stage of life. This is the time to pay your husband some extra attention. Take an interest in his work; plan a vacation; suggest a hobby you can take up together. All marriages require maintenance, and this is a particularly vulnerable passage, for it is apt to make men feel old; and we know their knee-jerk remedy for that unpleasant sensation!"

Nancy had waited till the receptionist was away from her desk to tear the page from the magazine and slip it into her purse. Along with the main article came a sidebar of practical advice, entitled "Making Lemonade out of Lemons." "Take advantage of your newfound privacy," was one of the suggestions. "Surprise your husband when he comes home: Open the door dressed in sexy lingerie or, better yet, nothing at all." And hope he hasn't brought home any friends, thought Nancy, who with all due respect for the *Journal* would not have been caught dead opening the door naked. Prudence, not prudishness, informed her modesty. She had put on thirty-five pounds since her marriage, and she hadn't been thin then. On her small frame, every ounce showed. "Matronly" was about the nicest thing you could call her figure; "dumpy" would suggest itself to the less charitable. It was no picnic being a woman who looked like her married to a guy who, Jaggerlike, grew sexier and better looking with age. There had come a turning point when the pleasure of seeing Shake's body was no longer worth the pain of exposing her own. They still had sex—it was, in a way, their one remaining mode of conversation—but now when they made love, it was in bed with the lights out.

She spread the back of the shirt over the board and ironed without looking, eyes fixed on the little TV on their dresser. Melissa had just told Jennifer, her best friend from childhood, that she suspected her husband, the handsome but tormented Dr. Devin Gray, was having an affair. Jennifer oozed sympathy in a manner so obviously phony that it proved what Nancy had suspected all along: Jennifer herself was the Other Woman. Meanwhile Melissa's so oblivious, she's sending Devin over to Jennifer's place to help the poor little divorcée rearrange her furniture. Nancy clucked derisively. She loved her soaps, but some of these women were so stupid they defied belief. What kind of moron would trust her husband around a woman like Jennifer? Catch Nancy being so careless! In the twenty years they'd been together, she'd fended off plenty of bitches who had tried to steal her husband. In Nancy's opinion, a woman who couldn't keep her man didn't deserve to have him. Eternal vigilance and lots of sex were the keys to a good marriage, or at least a long one.

The piano fell silent. Nancy heard footsteps, the *whoosh* of the refrigerator opening, the clink of a bottle cap. The walls were hollow in this apartment, a ground-floor walk-through in a part of Baltimore that urban renewal forgot. She turned off the iron and put the VCR on hold, stepped over the cord, and sidled between the bed and the board to get out. Was the room getting smaller or was she getting bigger? Both, probably.

Shake was back at the piano, scribbling notes onto a sheet of music paper. She waited for him to notice her. Shake hated being disturbed when he was working; it broke up his concentration and sent him back to square one. She wouldn't have minded just watching him, but he didn't like that, either. After some minutes, he looked up. "What?" he said.

"I thought I'd go tonight."

A flash of annoyance in his eyes, quickly masked. "Why?"

"I haven't heard you guys in ages. I need a music fix." And she smiled bravely to remind him of what she wasn't saying: how empty the house was, how long the nights, with Dylan gone.

"Could be a late night," he said with a frown of concern, as if it were for her sake he didn't want her at the club. Which told her, she who knew him much better than she knew herself, that he had something new going on, or at least something brewing. A waitress at the club, maybe, or that new singer. Nancy had met her once, when she came to the apartment to rehearse. Black girl—not that that would stop him. Nancy had opened the door and the girl had just stood there with her mouth hanging open, thinking, *This can't be Shake's wife*; Nancy read her like a primer. A wisp of a girl, size nothing, but with a voice that, even scaled down for rehearsal, rattled the glasses in the cupboard.

She hoped it wasn't the singer. Shake had a weakness for little girls with big voices that dated all the way back to Angel Busky. All the more reason for Nancy to show her face tonight.

There had been a time when she'd attended every gig Shake played, sitting proudly at the band's table, living for the moment between sets when he would come over and—in full view of everyone, especially the women who'd been ogling him all night—put his arm around her. For a while after Dylan was born, she'd kept it up. She would drop the baby at her mother's for the night, take in their show, hang with Shake and the boys till the sun rose, then go home to make love with her man. Shake was always horny after a night of playing, and if Nancy wasn't there . . . well, better she should be there.

She couldn't keep it up. Shake could afford to play all night, because he could sleep all day. Nancy had to work. She also had to care for Dylan, pay the bills, make sure there was food on the table and a clean, decent place to live. Shake had no head for practicalities, nor would she want him to. He was an artist, a free spirit; she was his base camp. Her girlfriends told her she did too much. "Make him help," they said. But Nancy knew where they were coming from. Just look at their husbands, if they even had them, and look at hers.

"Tomorrow's Sunday," she said. "I could sleep in."

"Suit yourself." Shake turned back to the piano.

Nancy returned to the bedroom, shunted the ironing board aside, and opened her closet. She ran through her clothes, rejecting one outfit after another. The thing about being with Shake was that inevitably people looked at her. She couldn't be invisible when she was with him, and it was getting harder and harder to look good. Half her clothes were tight on her; she only kept them in the closet to torment herself. Her work clothes were useless; in a conservative suit, she looked like Shake's mother. Finally she settled on a Carole Little skirt and a low-cut peasant blouse in a bold turquoise print. A woman her size was beyond slimming black. Nancy subscribed to the Janis Joplin philosophy of dress: plainness, flaunted, becomes beauty. She laid the clothes on the bed and went to take a shower.

The phone rang and rang. No one picked up. Shake slammed his pencil down. Where the hell was Nancy? He strode into Dylan's room and grabbed the cordless off the desk. "Hello?"

"Is this John Shaker?" A man's voice, pleasantly evocative. From the absence of noise in the background, Shake knew it wasn't a telemarketer.

"That's me," he said.

"Is this the John Shaker who grew up in Millbrook?"

A moment's silence. "Who is this?"

"Is this the John Shaker who skipped his own high school graduation out of misguided loyalty to an undeserving friend?"

"Fuck me," Shake cried. "Patrick!"

Patrick's laugh erased all doubt. "Took you long enough. How the hell are you, man?"

Shake stretched out on Dylan's bed while they exchanged two decades' worth of news. It blew his mind that Patrick was a fucking professor: Dr. Mulhaven, if you please! Not because Patch wasn't bright. He was one of the smartest kids Shake had ever known, on topics that interested him. The problem was that the set of things that interested Patrick, diverse as it was, barely intersected with the set of things the school wanted him to learn. Patrick cut more classes than he attended and squeezed through high school with grades so poor he never would have made it into college if it hadn't been for an amazing SAT score. Patrick a professor! What was that bit about God working in weird ways?

Nancy appeared in the doorway, swathed in Shake's terry robe, head wrapped in a towel. She gave him a questioning look.

"It's Patrick," he told her. "Mulhaven."

"Oh," she said, without noticeable enthusiasm.

"Is that Nancy?" said Patrick.

"In the flesh, bigger and better than ever," Shake said. Nancy flashed him her wounded-cow look and retreated.

"Well, put her on, man!"

"Pick up, Nance," Shake hollered.

A sullen moment later, she did. "Hello, Patrick. Long time no see." Her voice was cool. But Patrick brought her around, as Patrick always could. He asked about Dylan; in two minutes she was eating from the palm of his hand.

Good old Patch.

"The reason I'm calling," he said, "apart from the pleasure of talking to you guys, is to let you know there's been a change of venue."

"For what?" Shake said.

"Don't tell me you've forgotten. Graduation day, twenty years ago?"

"Aw, jeez. It's really happening?"

"Did you doubt it?"

"I swear to God, I'd forgotten all about it till this very moment. Has it really been twenty years?"

Nancy spoke at last. "What are you two babbling about?"

"You remember, Nancy," Patrick said. "The promise we made graduation night to meet again in twenty years on Beacon Hill. Only it's not going to be on Beacon Hill. Apparently we failed to anticipate the fact that by the time this event came around, we'd be middle-aged geezers used to our comforts. Willa has been kind enough to offer her house instead."

"Willa Scott," Shake said nostalgically. Nancy said nothing. He got up and carried the phone into their bedroom. Nancy sat cross-legged on the bed, still in his robe, which gaped intriguingly. He wondered idly if there'd be time for a quickie before they had to leave. Most wives would object if they'd just showered and washed their hair. One thing he'd say for Nancy: The old girl never said no.

"So who's coming to this shindig?" he asked.

"Travis is flying in from Santa Fe. Vinny, you and Nancy, me, Willa of course. Jeremiah hasn't admitted it yet, but he's coming, too. The only ones we haven't reached yet are Caleb and Angel."

"Slow down, Patrick," Nancy said. "We never said we're coming."

"Of course you're coming, darlin'. Last weekend in June. We're all staying at Willa's. She said to tell you she's got plenty of room."

"We'll let you know," Nancy said.

Shake scowled at her. What the hell was her problem? This was one party he wouldn't miss for the world. Well, she could stay home and sulk if she wanted to. He'd have more fun without her, if it came to that. He wondered how the others looked, if they'd changed much, what they were doing. "Count me in," he said.

11

They are playing hide-and-seek in the forest, and Willa is It. At first she cleaves to the edge of the woods, wading through a wash of dense green air. Underfoot, a shifting carpet of pine needles cushions her steps. *Angel!* she cries. *Caleb!* She hears them moving among the trees, laughing, whispering. Deeper into the woods she ventures, one hand clutching the other for comfort. *Patrick! Where are you?*

No one answers. She is frightened. Her mother has warned her about these woods. But even as she decides to turn back, Willa realizes she's lost her way. The trees close in, and the musty smell of damp earth fills her nostrils.

Over here, calls a voice close behind her.

She whirls around, sees no one. *Angel?*

Find me, Willa.

Close, so close! Willa looks behind every tree, she looks up into the branches. *Where are you, Angel?*

I'm lost, says the voice, at once distant and impossibly near. *Find me, Willa.*

Come out, come out, wherever you are, Willa chants; and a cold hand grasps her ankle.

"Mom?"

Willa opened her eyes to Angel's face bending over her. No, not Angel—Chloe. Willa was in bed. It was dark. Chloe was standing over her in the old gray T-shirt of Simon's she'd taken to sleeping in.

"Mom," Chloe said, "are you okay?"

Willa reached out to grasp her wrist, reassuringly warm and solid. "I had a dream."

"You had a nightmare."

"I woke you?"

"You were screaming."

Willa sat up and ran a hand through her hair, dank with sweat. She could smell herself. The dream was still with her, heavy as a rock.

"Do you want to tell me about it?" Chloe asked, mothering her mother.

"No."

"Do you want me to stay?"

And Willa was touched by this offer, the more so because in recent weeks her daughter had moved away from her, retreated into a secretive teenage world of clandestine phone calls and blank stares. A healthy development, perhaps, after the clinging that had followed Simon's death, but Willa had missed her.

"Yes," she said. "Please."

Chloe climbed into Simon's side of the bed, pulled the covers to her chin, and in seconds was sound asleep. When she was small and had nightmares, Willa would go to her, lie beside her in her little bed, and hold her until she slept. Willa herself rarely fell back to sleep, but she never resented the nights spent with Chloe; for in the child's proximity, in the touch of her hand and the scent of her hair, the mother took as much comfort as she gave. Now Willa unwound to the beat of her daughter's steady breathing, the warmth of her slumbering presence. For some time she lay awake thinking about the dream, where it came from, what it meant; then, as the first rays of dawn brightened the sky, she slept.

She woke late. Light was streaming through a crack in the curtains and the house was empty. Willa got up. In the kitchen she found a cereal bowl, half full, evidence of a rushed departure for school. She put up coffee, and while it was brewing slipped a jacket over her flannel nightgown and went out to collect *The New York Times*. There was, she noticed, a hint of early thaw in the air. In the kitchen, she drank her coffee and skimmed the front page. Clinton was gaining ground in the primary race, showing surprising strength in the polls. She studied his picture. He was a large man, taller than all the men around him, with a handsome, fleshy face, a country-boy smile, and clever, sensuous eyes. Strange to think that a man her age, or the age of an older brother, if she'd had one, could be running for president. It forced her to consider her own life, half spent already, and what did she have to show for it? Three slim books, one dead unfaithful husband, and a daughter who would soon be gone.

Judy would say that was depression talking. Willa's editor was convinced she was depressed, and Willa let her think so, since depressed people can hardly be expected to turn in books on time; but she didn't believe it. Willa believed she was recovering, the way a person recovers from severe head trauma. Slowly, little by little, faculties return. Things healthy people take for granted, like interest, curiosity, purposeful action.

She finished Chloe's cereal, soggy but sweet and good. She thought about the dream, which was not the first she'd had about Angel but one of a series, all of them troubling. And she remembered Angel's father, howling through the screen door. *Now you wanna find her? Where the fuck were you twenty years ago?* His words were missiles aimed at Patrick, but Willa had caught some shrapnel. She knew where she'd been: with Simon. The last thing she'd wanted when they first got together was for Angel to come calling; for she was not yet sure of Simon (*not yet*, oh that was rich) and so dreaded the inevitable day when those two would meet. In such matters, Angel had proved herself both a brilliant mentor and a ruthless competitor. "Fuck or be fucked" was her credo; she'd laughed at Willa's girlish scruples and, by laughing, eradicated them. Indeed, Angel had done as much as Caleb to talk Willa into his bed.

But freedom is a double-edged sword, and Willa had the scars to prove it. So she hadn't exactly mourned when Angel failed to show, and she didn't exactly knock herself out looking. For the sake of a man, she'd neglected her friend, and now long-buried guilt was rising in the form of noxious dreams.

Guilt . . . and mystification. So far they'd located all their old friends except Caleb and Angel. Caleb's drifting away didn't surprise her; he'd always been a don't-look-back kind of guy. But Angel's disappearance was something else, a mystery she could not solve, a puzzle with missing pieces. Even if Angel had chosen to break permanently with her father, why not contact her friends? "You guys are my family"; how many times had she said that? It was what they all felt. They used to talk about pooling their money to buy land in California or New Mexico, where they would start their own commune. Patrick would make films based on Willa's novels. Travis would design houses, which Angel would photograph for architectural magazines. Vinny would run a fleet of cars, and Shake, when he wasn't touring with his band, would help Nancy in the school, which would be patterned on Summerhill— for of course, *their* children would never be subjected to the mind-numbing, soul-deadening, regimented torpor that was public school. Jeremiah would be their ambassador to the straight world, and Caleb, who was clever about money, would handle the finances. So they had planned it, only half kidding, because, while it was clear that the plan could not be implemented immediately, they saw no reason why it should not come to pass eventually.

This was the state of things when, the day after their non-graduation, Willa flew off to Paris. By the time she returned, eight weeks later, everything had changed. Angel was gone, no one knew where. Patrick and Vinny weren't speaking. Everyone was splitting up, heading off in different directions. For a while after that, she'd stayed in touch; but after freshman year, with her own house sold and Angel away, Willa had no place to stay in Millbrook. When she did see her old friends, it was in small groups, never the whole gang together. Lately Willa had been wondering why. How it happened that such strong bonds dissolved so quickly. Were friends fungible? Did new ones supplant the old? They hadn't for Willa. She had never had such friendships, before or since.

Willa wasn't doing this for Patrick anymore. She was doing it for herself, and in a strange way she was also doing it for Angel. And now she was ready to ask for help.

Not from Patrick; he'd done all he could, without success. There was another man who could help, and probably would. Willa had been thinking of calling him for weeks but kept putting it off. She had nothing personal against this man, who alone among her husband's colleagues had dealt honestly with her; yet his doing so had caused her great pain, and so she felt toward him the complicated blend of gratitude and blame a soldier might feel toward a medic who had saved his life by amputating his leg.

Jovan Luisi was his name. He was a PI, an ex-cop, who did investigations for Simon's firm. After Simon died and the identity of his mistress came to light, the firm had snapped into damage-control mode; for not only Simon but his partners, too, had tried cases before Judge Eisner. As part of the general ass covering and to further distance themselves from Simon's unfortunate but personal failings, they hired Jovan to conduct an inquiry into the affair. Willa was kept out of the loop. After an initial flurry of condolences came a deep, dark silence. She was radioactive, contagious; no one at all wanted to talk to her. Her calls to his partners were not returned, or were returned by junior secretaries. Whatever Willa learned, she learned the same way her neighbors did, from the newspapers.

After the funeral, after the first numb shock wore off, Willa found herself in desperate straits. She'd been married to a stranger and now he was gone. She could not allow herself to remember the good times, because the good times were lies. She could not mourn her husband because he had betrayed her; she could not confront him because he was dead. In every attempt by friends to comfort her, she read secret disdain for that most pathetic of stereotypes, the deceived wife; but they could not despise her any more than she despised herself for her self-willed blindness, her complacency. The craven silence of Simon's partners and their smarmy, self-serving public statements of shock and disapprobation sickened her beyond measure. That she functioned at all was due to her daughter, who needed her. If Willa could not *be* strong, she could at least, for Chloe's sake, appear strong. But when Chloe was out of the house, when Willa was alone, despair overtook her.

One day, a week or two after the funeral, Jovan Luisi called. He asked if he could come talk to her. She asked why. He told her that the firm had charged him with investigating her husband's relationship with Judge Eisner.

"What's that to me?" she snapped. "Do you think it was a ménage à trois?"

"No, ma'am," he said.

"If you've read the papers, you know as much as I do," she said and hung up.

An hour later he was on her doorstep. She took him for a reporter and ignored the bell until he called out his name. Then she opened the door but stood blocking the entrance, mop in hand. He looked at her and blinked. Willa had been washing floors, having fired her cleaning woman for talking to reporters.

Her hair was tied back in a ponytail and she wore old gray sweat-pants and a red 49ers T-shirt. The clothing was a statement: Willa wasn't in mourning.

He said the only thing that could have gained him entrance. "I've come to tell you what I know."

"And to find out what I know."

"That's up to you."

Willa looked him over. Luisi was taller than Simon, well over six feet with a lean, athletic build. He had a hawkish face, olive skin stretched over high cheekbones, hooded eyes. His body had a used look to it. An attractive man, she'd have said, if she were still in the attraction business. He was wary of her, or pretended to be.

She put him in the living room, cold with disuse. It was the least revealing room in the house, and the most imposing. He looked around, didn't comment. There was coffee in the kitchen and beer in the fridge, but Willa offered him nothing. He was an emissary from the enemy.

"What do you want to know?" he said. He sat in the middle of the leather couch, hands on his knees. Willa sat across from him in a straight-backed chair.

"Who rented the apartment?" she asked.

"Your husband."

"How long?"

"Two years."

"How did he pay?"

"He had an account in the Citibank across from the office. Everything pertaining to the account and the apartment went to the office."

So his secretary knew. Willa had known she must, but it hurt all the same. She'd been fond of Minty, thought it was mutual. But nothing of this showed in her face, smooth and blank as alabaster. She went on asking all the questions that had piled up inside since the night Simon died. The more hurtful the answers, the more stoic her demeanor. It helped that Luisi showed no sign of pitying her. They might have been talking about politics, if neither of them cared about politics, or the weather. He gave her nothing but the facts.

But there was nothing else she wanted.

She saved the hardest for last. "How long had the affair been going on?"

"With Eisner? Eighteen months."

So there were others. It took her breath away. But why should it? Why hadn't she guessed? Was there any limit to her blindness? She would have broken down then, if it hadn't been for the stranger in her house. She would not add to her humiliation by betraying pain in his presence. Even fools have their dignity.

"How many?" she asked.

He hesitated. "Four or five, that I know of."

She slid her hands under her thighs to hide their shaking, and he pretended not to notice. Willa should have been grateful. But when she looked at him, she saw the men who had sent him here, her husband's partners, their dear friends, who had dined at her table more times than she could count, and bitterness welled up inside her.

"Quite a guy," she said. "You must think I'm a real moron."

"No, ma'am," he said, with a gentleness that nearly did her in. "I think you were played by a master."

"Doesn't say much for my powers of observation, does it?"

"Compulsive womanizers, like gamblers or drug addicts, are expert deceivers."

He meant to be kind, but he had no idea of the depths of her folly. Willa *wished* she'd suspected; it hardly seemed credible that she had not. And yet, up until the day Simon died, Willa would have said they had a good, strong marriage. It was true Simon worked long hours and traveled frequently; but so did most of the men they knew, and as his absences gave her time to work, she'd never resented them. Whatever deficits she'd felt in the relationship she'd attributed to her own stubborn inability to settle into her life. There was in her heart an inchoate yearning for something else, something different: for a life less comfortable, perhaps, in which more was demanded and more given.

A churlish sentiment, surely, in one who had been given so much.

But she confided none of this to Jovan Luisi. She did wish, though, as she saw him out, that she had offered him something to drink, after all; but by then it was too late.

At the door he gave her his card. "If you have any other questions," he said, "or if there's ever anything I can do for you, I hope you'll call me."

And now there was.

Jovan Luisi was on his way home from a meeting with a corporate client in Croton when Blanca, his secretary, called with Willa's message. He pulled his black Jeep off the Cross-Bronx and headed back north. He remembered the way, though he'd only been there once, six months ago. There were a lot of things about that day that had stuck with him. Like his first glimpse of Willa Durrell. Seeing her approaching, mop in hand, through the smoky glass of the portico, he'd taken her for a maid. Then she'd opened the door and he'd realized his mistake. Even in sweats and a T-shirt, no makeup, hair pulled back, she was a striking woman. Not pretty, though you could tell she had been and could be again; her face now was too tightly shuttered, the marks of suffering too clearly etched, for prettiness. But there was an irreducible beauty in the bones of her face, the symmetry of her features, the dark blue depths of her shadowed eyes. In his experience, women who looked like Willa Durrell didn't make their living mopping floors.

Which made Simon even more of a jerk than Jovan had thought, and he'd thought him a pretty big jerk already.

Tit for tat had been his plan. He'd soften her up by answering her questions (which no one else, apparently, had had the decency to do) and then maybe she'd answer his. But in the end he didn't ask any. He'd wondered if she knew about the others; plenty of wives did, and put up with it for reasons of their own. But it was obvious once he met her that Willa had been sandbagged. A lot of that coldness was shock; it showed in everything she said and did.

He had gone in braced for tears, but there were none. She asked for the truth and when he gave it to her, she didn't flinch, just took it on the chin and moved on to the next question. "Classy broad," he said later to Blanca, who rolled her eyes heavenward; they both knew his proclivity for gutsy dames in distress. But Jovan knew his limitations, too, and Willa Durrell was out of his league.

He reached Chappaqua and drove through the village, down streets lined with antiques shops, boutiques, and galleries. Too precious for his taste; give him the city any day, rough edges and all. Everyone he saw was white, which made him feel conspicuous. This was odd, since he himself was white, but Jovan was used to blending into a more colorful tapestry. He shared the city-dwellers' disdain for suburbanites, who tried to live their lives in a cocoon, as if that could protect them. That was one fallacy Willa Durrell had disproved the hard way.

He wondered what she wanted. Blanca had said only that she'd asked him to call. If he chose to call in person, would she think him out of line? Her house was on Mallow Road, a windy, hilly road of invisible houses set back behind hedges or thickets of trees. Massive oak trees, still bare in early March, laced skeletal fingers overhead. In summer they would canopy the road. Acre zoning put these houses in the million-plus range. Jovan recognized hers by the two stone lions guarding the entrance. Shifting to first, he drove up the steep driveway and parked in front of the large colonial. No sign of a car, but it could be in the garage. He walked up to the door and rang the bell.

A minute passed, then the door opened. She seemed amazed, not angry. "I just called you."

"I got the message, and I was in the area."

"Some service," she said, and stepped back to let him in.

This time she brought him into a home office, a much more lived-in room than the formal living room they'd sat in last time. There was a large oak desk, moderately cluttered, that looked out on the wintry remains of a flower garden; an oak filing cabinet and shelves; and a computer and printer on a movable cart. She motioned toward a sitting area with a soft leather sofa, chairs, and a coffee table. "What will you drink?"

He asked for coffee, hoping for time to explore her office. While she was gone he looked around with his hands in his pockets. Lots of framed photos scattered around. In one she was sitting behind a table in a bookstore, signing books. Another showed her with a teenage girl who by the look of her had to be her daughter, both of them on horseback. The girl wore a helmet but not the mother; Willa's windblown hair framed her face like a wimple. There were more photos, several of the daughter, others of other people he didn't recognize; none of Simon. On the top shelf of the bookcase, facing out, were three books by Willa Scott Durrell. He picked one up at random. *Family Secrets* was the title—a little close to home, he'd have thought, but of course this would have been written before. He turned it over and was studying the author photo when the original returned, carrying a tray.

"I hate that picture," she said, setting the tray onto the table. "Sugar? Milk?"

"Black. I bet it sells a lot of books."

"You sound like my editor." She handed him his cup and sat in the desk chair, swiveling around to face him. She looked different from last time, though he couldn't quite say how. More color in her face, maybe. She wore jeans and a sleek black jersey; her long blond hair was loosely braided. "I have a job for you," she said, "if you'll take it. I'm trying to locate two people, a man and a woman. Is that the kind of thing you do?"

"Sometimes. Who are these people and what do you know about them?"

"Their full names. Their birth dates. Their lives through high school; the college he went to. I do know they're still alive."

"How?"

"I checked the Social Security death index."

Jovan was impressed. Most people wouldn't know to do that. But she was a writer, he reminded himself, used to doing research. "Who are these people, and why are you looking for them?"

She told him. It was a long story, but hardly, as she seemed to think, a unique one. People who've suffered a traumatic loss often turn to the past for comfort. They start thinking about old loves, paths not taken, lives they might have lived. Willa's quest was a variation on that theme.

She showed him the files she'd worked up on each of the two missing persons. Of the two, the man was the easier prospect. Last encountered eleven years ago, at his mother's funeral. A simple matter to pull the obit, find out where he was living at the time, and take it from there. Angel Busky was a tougher nut. Twenty years is a long time; and women were apt to change their names.

Jovan took out his notebook and walked Willa through the standard questions. Full name, DOB, religion, names and ages of family members, previous addresses, schools attended, Social Security numbers (unknown), contacts, hobbies, interests. They were interrupted once by a phone call—the daughter, he gathered.

No, Willa said. Not tonight, I want you home. Patrick's coming . . . Love you, hon.

Jovan wondered who Patrick was.

Willa came back with a checkbook in hand.

"Put it away," he told her.

"This is a business proposition, Mr. Luisi, not a favor."

"It's not a favor; it's called professional courtesy."

"I can't accept that."

"Chances are I find these two friends of yours without leaving my office. I'm not charging you for that."

"Then I'll find someone else."

"Don't do that." What the hell, he thought. "It just so happens we've got a special on missing persons this week: two for the price of dinner with the detective."

Willa raised an eyebrow. "Some special. I wonder you stay solvent."

"Is it a deal?"

She smiled and held out her hand. "I just hope you're a better detective than you are a businessman."

The bell rang just as they were approaching the front door. Willa opened and a man stepped in, assured of his welcome, all smiles at the sight of her. He bent to kiss her cheek. Then he noticed Jovan and straightened.

Willa said, "Patrick Mulhaven, Jovan Luisi. Patrick's one of the old friends I was telling you about. Patrick, Jovan is going to help us find Caleb and Angel."

"Is that right," Patrick said. They shook hands with a measuring look, each one's grip a little firmer than usual. "How very kind."

12

"You asked me to help," Willa said.

"I did. It just seems a little intense, siccing this Jovan fellow on them."

They were in the kitchen. Patrick, in shirtsleeves, was concocting something he called a kitchen-sink salad out of odds and ends from the refrigerator, while Willa stood at the stove sautéing veal. It might have struck a domestic chord, except that in all the years of their marriage, Simon had never cooked a meal or washed a dish. "Why not?" she said. "Time's getting short, and we're no closer. Don't you want to find them?"

"You know I do," he said. "How do you know this guy, anyway?"

"Through Simon."

"What's he charging you?"

"Nothing. He refused; called it professional courtesy. It was very kind of him." Glancing over her shoulder, she caught the tail end of a scowl. Was Patrick jealous? Willa had not failed to notice a certain bristle in both men's aspects as they shook hands; truth be told, she'd enjoyed it. She wasn't ready for a lover, maybe never would be; it was the resurgence of her power she celebrated.

Patrick said, "I'm starting to wonder if they even want to be found. I mean, logically I realize that they don't even know we're looking, but it *feels* as if they're hiding. Know what I mean?"

Willa's dream came thudding back. Gone the gleaming kitchen. Now trees surrounded her, darkness all around, and a plaintive voice crying her name.

"Angel wants to be found," she said.

He quit chopping, looked at her. "How do you know?"

"I just feel it."

"If she wanted to find us, it wouldn't be hard."

"That's what I can't understand," Willa said. "I mean, I can see Caleb walking away. He was furious when I married Simon. But Angel? Why would she cut herself off like that?"

Patrick gave her a look she could not interpret. "Beats me," he said, and went back to the carrots. There was a moment of silence. Then Chloe blew into the room.

"I'm home," she announced. "Something smells good. What's for dinner? Hi, Professor."

"Hi, earthling," Patrick said.

"Veal piccata, pasta, and salad," Willa said. "I think we'll eat in the kitchen tonight, if Patrick doesn't mind being treated like family."

"I don't know," he said, puffing on an imaginary cigar. "Does that come with spousal privileges?"

"Ha!"

Chloe looked from one to the other with the blankness of expression that, in her, denoted furious thought.

The veal was delicious, the kitchen-sink salad a great success. "So who have we got?" Willa asked.

"Shake definitely," Patrick said, spearing another piece of veal from the platter. "And, knowing Nancy, no way she lets him come alone."

Willa smiled. Whenever she thought of Shake and Nancy, she pictured them conjoined: arms linked, legs intertwined, or hands tucked in each other's pockets. Angel used to call Nancy Shake's appendage; actually, that was one of the nicer things she called her. "How amazing is it that they've got a son in college? I still think of them as kids themselves."

"Time is a river," Patrick said, "and we are swimmers in its current."

"Who said that?"

"Me, just now. Vinny's coming, of course. Travis has already bought his plane ticket. Jeremiah's still hedging, but I've got a secret weapon."

"What's that?"

"You," he said. "If you ask him, he will come. I brought along his number, thought we'd give him a call later."

"So it's really happening," Chloe said with mock disapproval, "this hippie reunion of yours."

"You bet," Patrick said.

"Mom's misspent youth comes back to bite her on the—"

"Chloe!" Willa said.

"We could sell tickets." Chloe, Willa noticed, hadn't touched the food on her plate except to push it around. Her appetite had been off lately; she'd been edgy, brimming with secrets, prone to alternating fits of abstraction and animation. At home she kept to her room, talking on the phone or writing letters that she later tore into tiny pieces. No more long, cozy mother-and-daughter evenings in the den. Their latest jigsaw, a three-ring circus, lay abandoned, a surreal collage of one-eyed clowns, truncated elephants, and armless jugglers. Twice this week Willa had heard Chloe crying softly in her room. Other days she walked around the house singing "Tomorrow."

Willa told herself it was nerves—Chloe had tried out for the school play and been cast, not only as an orphan, but also as the understudy for Orphan Annie—but she was just kidding herself. Chloe's constellation of symptoms all pointed to the one malady her mother couldn't cure: The child was in love.

After Chloe went upstairs, Patrick suggested that Willa call Jeremiah. She balked. "What makes you think that'll make a difference?"

"Oh, please," he said. "The guy had the Grand Canyon of crushes on you."

"I don't remember that."

Patrick just shook his head. Sometimes he wondered if the intimate friendship of their youth had been anything more than illusion; for Willa had her version of the past and he had his, and they weren't the same at all.

They called from her office, where she had a speaker phone.

Patrick dialed, expecting to get Jeremiah's machine. To his amazement, Jeremiah picked up on the second ring and said his name briskly.

"Hey," she said. "It's Willa. Patrick's here, too."

He greeted them without surprise, as if he'd been expecting their call.

"We've been hearing great things about you," Willa said. "Your mother's bursting with pride."

Jeremiah laughed. "I couldn't believe you guys actually called on her. Did you deck yourselves in garlic?"

"No," she said, "but it took us twenty minutes to work up the nerve to knock. She was actually very gracious."

"She's in awe of you," Jeremiah said. "You're a famous writer."

"Hardly famous."

"I read your biography of Ivy Compton-Burnett. It was so good I kept forgetting I knew you."

High praise indeed. Willa flushed with pleasure. "Are you a fan of Compton-Burnett?"

"Never heard of her, I'm ashamed to say, till I read your book. But I think she would have loved my mother's household."

"I'm afraid you're right," she said, laughing. It was Jeremiah, all right, unseen and thus unaltered. His voice was the same, only a shade deeper. She had forgotten the pleasure of talking with him, how quick and funny he was. She'd forgotten how much she'd liked him. "You will come to the reunion, won't you, Jeremiah?"

He sighed. "I'd love to, you know that. I just don't know if it's possible. We have some obligations—"

"We all do," Patrick interrupted. "To the kids who stood on that hill twenty years ago and swore that come what may, our friendship would endure."

"But it didn't," Jeremiah said sadly. "It hasn't."

"Maybe this is its vehicle."

"Ah, Patrick. Still the romantic."

"You've got to come," Patrick said. "Everyone else is."

"Everyone?"

"Almost everyone. We're still looking for Caleb and Angel."

"If you don't come," Willa teased, "we'll talk about you all weekend."

Jeremiah didn't laugh. There was a silence. "Hang on a sec, would you?" he said.

Patrick winked at Willa and she grimaced. Her little joke had fallen flat, and no wonder. Some of their high school escapades had crossed the line in ways that might actually matter to someone in Jeremiah's position. But surely he knew they'd never tell those stories outside their own circle?

Then Jeremiah came back on the line. "Against my better judgment, and at the insistence of my wife, who has no idea what she's getting me into, I find that I can after all free up some time that weekend."

"That's great!" Willa said. "She'll join us, too, I hope?"

"Olivia sends her regrets. Nothing more boring than other

people's war stories, right, darling?" They heard a faint murmur of protest in the background. "But I'll be there with bells on."

"Excellent decision," Patrick said, beaming. "You won't regret it."

Jeremiah sighed. "I already do. Was there ever a time when you guys didn't get me in trouble?"

"Was there ever a time we didn't bail your ass out?"

"Out of the trouble *you* got me into."

"Well, *yeah*," Patrick said, shoving the hair out of his eyes. "Somebody had to."

"Told you," Patrick said as they cleaned up the kitchen. Willa washed, he dried.

"Now I'm starting to get nervous," she said. "What if we all get together and find out we have nothing to talk about?"

"No chance." He smelled the lemony scent of her skin. Some wisps of hair had pulled loose from her braid to curl damply at the nape of her neck. What would she do if he kissed her right there? Hand him a skillet to dry, most likely.

"Or what if Jeremiah does come and his mother shows up?"

Patrick shuddered. "Don't laugh. That woman had no concept of boundaries." How many times had they set the poor bastard up to get laid, only to have *her* swoop down at the last moment?

"You know," Willa said, handing him a crystal wineglass, "when I think about it now, I wonder what drew Jeremiah to us in the first place. I can see what we got out of it: He was smart and funny, and having him with us was a feather in our caps. But what did he get out of being friends with us, other than endless grief from his mother?"

"Apart from proximity to you and Angel? He got to be himself, which wasn't exactly the self he presented at school. He got to . . . transgress a little." Patrick's voice trailed off. The top button of Willa's shirt had come undone, and from where he stood he could see the curve of her breast, the edge of a lacy black bra.

"But he was always so careful. He hardly ever got high. I can't even remember him drunk."

Patrick smirked. "He was no saint. Remember the thing with the brownies and the bridge club?"

Her eyes widened. "Oh my God. That was Jeremiah?"

"No *duh*. Plus, you know, he liked to fight. He was good, too. Surprised the hell out of Vinny." Vinny had had his doubts at first. Claimed Jeremiah wouldn't carry his weight; called him Boy Scout. Patrick remembered one particular boys' night out, drinking and listening to music in a bar near Fordham. Halfway through the second set, some college boys took exception to Caleb hitting on one of their girls. Somebody threw a punch. In the ruckus that followed, Jeremiah grabbed a table lamp, knocked one guy out, and cut another one's forehead open, all without ruffling a hair on his sleek black head. After that, Vinny quit calling him Boy Scout.

The dishes done, they moved to the den. Willa kicked off her shoes and stretched out on the sofa. Patrick, at the other end, laid her ankles on his thighs and began to massage her feet. Through their soles he felt first resistance, then surrender.

Everyone needs to be touched, he thought, even Willa.

Barney claimed he was wasting his time. The four of them had gone out for dinner one night: Patrick and Willa, Barney and his lover, Frank. The next day Patrick and Barney met in their office and Barney delivered his considered opinion. "Give it up. The woman doesn't see you as you, she sees you as an eighteen-year-old kid."

"But that *is* me," Patrick replied.

"It's your classic *When Harry Met Sally* scenario. Once they have you pegged as a friend, it's hell to break out."

"Why do women make such a fuss about sex? Why is fucking such a big deal to them?"

Barney rolled his eyes. "It's their currency; naturally they hoard it. You've noticed, I trust, my restraint in the I-told-you-so department."

"I hadn't, actually," Patrick had said, "and now it's too late."

Served him right, asking a gay guy for advice on women. What Barney didn't get was that when it came to Willa, Patrick felt a sense of entitlement. He'd waited years for her. He'd been very patient. Over the past few months, they'd met half a dozen times, always on her terms. Old pals, buddies—that's all she would allow. Every advance stymied by her absolute refusal to take it, or him, seriously. When levity failed, she'd resorted to brutal frankness. "I'm not in the market," she said one night, removing his hand from her thigh. "And if I were, it wouldn't be you."

That he was married was obviously a handicap, though it oughtn't have been. There was a Puritanical streak in Willa that was not one of her more attractive features; and no doubt her husband's very public infidelities made it worse. Did she really expect him to divorce his wife for her? No way that was going to happen. Twice in a lifetime was more than enough. Patrick had explained to her the way things stood between him and Rachel. When they decided to live apart, they accepted all that went along with such a decision. He didn't inquire into her affairs, or she into his. But Willa was unmoved.

Still, he had persevered, biding his time like Mrs. Muir's captain, certain that time, nature, and proximity would wear her down. Sooner or later, he would have his just desserts: a happy ending, or at least bittersweet.

But finding her with Jovan Luisi had shaken his confidence. Professional courtesy his ass; Patrick saw the way the guy looked at her, and it brought out the worst in him, the jealous, spiteful side he preferred not to acknowledge.

There is such a thing as being too patient. What Patrick needed was home-field advantage. So far Willa had refused all invitations to his apartment, which proved, if he'd ever doubted it, that she knew perfectly well what a fine line their "friendship" straddled. This time, he had bait.

"You and I have a date Saturday night," he informed her, kneading the soft pads under her toes. "There's a band we need to hear."

"What band?" she said lazily, half asleep.

"Cyclops."

"Never heard of 'em."

"You may have heard of the sax player. Guy by the name of John Shaker."

Her eyes snapped open. "No!"

"They're playing a one-night gig in Tribeca. Vinny's coming, too. You up for it?"

"You bet. Where and when?"

"We'll meet at my place at five and go from there." He held his breath.

"I'll be there," she promised.

13

That night Willa was too wrought up to sleep. All this talking about and to old friends had stirred memories that came wrapped in their old feelings, feelings she'd packed away, along with her teddy bears and blue ribbons and childhood diaries when she married Simon.

The diaries! Willa sat bolt upright in bed. How could she have forgotten them? Actual documentary evidence: a way, perhaps, to tackle certain puzzling inconsistencies between Patrick's memory of the past and her own.

It was past one in the morning but sleep wasn't on the horizon, so she put on a pair of slippers and tiptoed up to the attic. The journals were in an old trunk, along with her high school yearbook. Willa carried the lot back to her bedroom.

Three of the diaries covered the years between '69 and '72. The bindings were cracked, the pages brittle, but the sight of them brought on a rush of nostalgia so acute it was painful. The entries were of all different lengths, spaced anywhere from a day to a week apart; and the handwriting was neat and rounded, a schoolgirlish script.

The first of the three volumes started in August 1969, the summer before tenth grade. Willa quickly skimmed the early entries: clothes shopping with her mother, battles over hemlines and sandals versus sensible shoes, a rundown of her class schedule, thumbnail sketches of her teachers and classmates. Then, turning a page, she came upon her very first mention of Caleb in an entry dated September 18. Much of the entry was devoted to a diatribe against her social studies teacher, an ardent supporter of the war in Vietnam.

> On and on he goes, practically foaming at the mouth. No one bothers to argue with him except me and this kid Caleb Rhys. Have I told you about Caleb, Di? Picture Art Garfunkel, only younger, darker, and better looking. Tall, slim but strong, with blondish curly hair, long eyelashes, and the face of an angel, not the

Hallmark variety but the real deal, as fierce as
he is beautiful.

I hardly know him, unfortunately. He
hangs out with a pretty wild crowd. I see
them at lunch, sitting together: a hood
named Vinny, who's been left back at least
once, a maniac named Patch, a beautiful but
tough-looking girl named Angel, and a kid
named Shake who's supposed to be some kind
of musical genius, but you'd never know it
from all the times he comes to school with
a black eye or a fat lip. All these guys
are fighters, Vinny especially. Not even the
seniors mess with him. The girls at my
table think they're bad news, but I kind of
like them. At least they're different.

So there they were in their first cameo appearance, with Willa
on the outside looking in. Not all of them, though. Travis was
missing, also Jeremiah and Nancy. Perhaps they'd had different
lunch periods; more likely, the group was still fluid then, not yet
fully coalesced.

The luminescent dial of her bedside clock showed 2:00. She
ought to try to sleep, Willa thought; she'd be useless tomorrow if
she didn't. Already her eyes were so bleary it was hard to read.
But she couldn't stop. She skipped ahead to a date circled in red.

October 12, 1969. Remember this date, Di. The
most amazing thing happened today. Someone
took a bullet for me. At least, I think he did
it for me. What if I'm just flattering myself,
though, mistaking a political act for a personal one? But in that case, why the wink?

I'm babbling, I know. Let me start at
the beginning. Second period, social studies. Kukach, who everyone calls Cockroach,
is rambling on about the Holocaust, how the
Nazis scapegoated not only Jews but gypsies

and homosexuals, too, because they were different. It's human nature, he says, to pick on people who deviate from the norm. Like retards, he says, or geniuses.

I sink down in my seat. I can see where this is headed. The man's like a train wreck—you can see him coming, but you can't stop him.

"Matthew here could tell us about that," Cockroach says. "Matt used to be in special ed, didn't you, Matt? Ever get teased about that?"

Everyone turns to look at Matt Sigurski. He's this really quiet kid with acne and a stutter, super nerdy but sweet. Now his face is bright red, except for his pimples, which are white. Behind those thick glasses you can see panic in his eyes.

Matt stares down at his desk. He can't answer because he's holding his breath to keep from bawling. But Cockroach is waiting.

"N-n-nobody knew," Matt finally says.

Cockroach beams at the class; he's made his point. I'm praying for the bell to ring but the clock's barely moving. Then he says, "It's not easy being super smart, either. Anyone here ever skip a grade?"

No one answers. I sure as hell don't. Cockroach's beady little eyes tour the classroom, pass over me, then come back. "You were skipped, weren't you, Willa?"

Everyone turns to look, and it's like forty suns beating down on me. I'm burning up. Ten minutes after the bell rings, this is going to be all over school.

But I'm not Matt. I look Cockroach in the eye. "So what?" I say.

"Have you found that there's a social

price to pay when you're singled out and
set above your peers?"

"I'm not above anyone," I say. "I'm
here, aren't I?"

The kids laugh. Cockroach's little insect
eyes narrow. I see the malice in them. He's
doing this on purpose.

"Don't some people resent it that you're
smarter than them?" he says.

They're waiting for me to come back at
him, but I'm so humiliated I'm afraid I'll
say something lame. The longer the silence
goes on, the worse it gets. Then a voice
calls out from the back of the classroom.

"Do *you* resent it, Cockroach?"

Di, it was Caleb Rhys, that gorgeous boy
I told you about (Sept. 18).

The kids are rolling in the aisles.
They've forgotten all about me. I emerge
from the desert into a shady oasis.

"Who said that?" Cockroach squawks over
the laughter. No one answers. They're not
about to give Caleb up; they know who he's
friends with.

Cockroach figures it out and sends Caleb
to the office. Caleb takes his time. As he
passes my desk, he winks at me.

Di, I think I'm in love.

It was the wink that did her in. If God himself had spoken, her
life could not have veered more sharply than it did that day. Even
now, the memory sends chills through her.

The following weeks and months were full of sightings and
speculation, the minutiae of young love.

He smiled at me in the hall today. At
least, I think it was at me. It could have
been at Laurie Price.

He got on line behind me in the lunchroom today. Cut ahead of three kids to do
it, not that they'd say anything. Like a
jerk I drop my fork. We both bend down to
pick it up, and when our hands touch (I
know, I know: disgustingly trite but I
swear it's true) I feel a jolt all through
my body.

Now Willa burned, she blushed for her own baby self, poor little patsy, fool for love. She thought with trepidation of Chloe and,
sighing, read on.

October 19, 1969. The most incredible thing
happened today, Di. First period, there was
a fire alarm and we all had to leave the
building. By the time we get back inside,
the bell's ringing for second. I go
upstairs to social studies. Cockroach isn't
there yet. As soon as I sit down, Caleb
comes over and takes the seat next to mine,
where Billy Hendricks always sits. Billy
comes in and stands beside Caleb, who
ignores him. After a while Billy goes back
and takes Caleb's seat.

Cockroach comes in late and pissed.
"Clear your desks," he barks. "Pop quiz."
Then he sits down—and the chair collapses!
All four legs fly right out from under him,
and Cockroach lands on his back with his
legs up in the air, like an overturned turtle, surrounded by pieces of wood.

There's a moment of amazement, followed
by howls of laughter. The only one not
laughing is Caleb, who's not even looking
at Cockroach. I feel his eyes on me.

Cockroach gets up, his face the color of
raw steak. "What is this?" he sputters,

holding up a chair leg that looks neatly sawn through. "What the hell is this?"

Caleb leans over and whispers in my ear, "Sensitivity training."

Di, he did it. He did it for me.

For the next three periods, I walk around in a total daze. I'm terrified Caleb will get in trouble. If they call me down to the office, I decide, I'll deny every-thing. They can torture me, they can pry off my fingernails or call my parents; I'll never tell a living soul what he said.

Finally, finally, lunch period comes. When I get to the cafeteria, Caleb's already there, sitting with his friends. Right away he comes over. "Join us?" he says, nodding toward his table.

I look over. All his friends are watch-ing us, waiting to see what I'll do. I turn back to Caleb. His eyes are sea green. He's even more beautiful up close.

"Okay," I say.

The girls at my old table stare and whisper all through lunch, but I don't care. They'd die to be where I am, no mat-ter what they say. I *like* Caleb's friends. People claim they're wild, but they were gentle with me. Angel is really, really cool. I want to get to know her better.

The pages blurred. Willa wiped her eyes on the sleeve of her nightgown. The house snored softly around her, grumbling deep in its throat like a dreaming dog. She hid the diaries away in her dresser and pulled out the yearbook. It opened to the page with Caleb's senior picture. Under it, in his spidery hand, he had writ-ten, "Free at last, free at last, thank God Almighty, we're free at last!" Her own picture was below Caleb's; she looked impossibly young and virginal.

She skipped back to Patrick's picture. "From the fool on the hill," he had written, "to the one who got away: someday, girl." Finally, Willa found Angel's picture. Even in black and white you could see how fiery her hair was; and her demeanor was that of a pirate queen. Angel's inscription was the shortest of all: "Forever, babe."

14

One of the surprises attendant upon Willa's marriage had been the discovery that Simon, whose political and professional work lay in the upsetting of apple carts and the creation of what he called holy chaos, could not abide disorder in his household. Unmade beds disgusted him; dishes left in the sink were open invitations to disease and contamination; clutter represented moral failure. A messy house, he had instructed Willa, was the sign of a messy mind; and while Simon was not at all a violent or abusive man (his displeasure found expression not in heat, but in coldness and a scathing politeness), Willa soon learned that it was better to keep the peace by doing things his way. Habits formed by the marriage had outlived it; thus, before going downstairs Saturday morning, she showered, made her bed, and straightened the bedroom.

After a solitary but pleasant breakfast in the kitchen, which faced east and was filled at this time of morning with a soft, lemony light, she went back upstairs. As she passed Chloe's bathroom, she heard the shower running. Willa continued down the hall to her own room, opened the door, and stopped on the threshold.

Something was different. She couldn't place it at first, but then she did. Her yearbook lay open on the bed, though she would have sworn that when she left the room, it was on her dresser. Willa approached the bed. Angel's picture smiled up at her triumphantly, bisected by the bold slash of her handwriting: "Forever, babe." A peace offering after their fight, or so Willa had assumed as they kissed and wept on the last day of school. Subsequent events had proved her wrong; for in Angel's stubborn, sustained absence, what could Willa read but reproach?

She shut the book, replaced it on the dresser, and went to sit at her vanity. It had been so long since she'd bothered to put on makeup that her mascara had dried up. She opened a fresh wand. Today Willa meant to indulge herself in a much-needed and long-overdue day of city pleasures: lunch with Judy Trumpledore, then something solitary—an exhibit, perhaps, or a film—and finally, that night, Shake's band. Vinny would be there, too. She wondered how the others looked, if they'd changed much. Patrick said Vinny had grown into his father. Pity they didn't invite Jeremiah, though he probably couldn't have come. Ever since their phone conversation, she'd been anxious to see him again, wondering if old friendship might prove a springboard for new.

When her makeup was done, Willa brushed out her long hair, then twisted it into a French knot and pinned it back. She dabbed a few drops of Chanel behind her ears and in the pit of her throat, then changed into the clothes she'd laid out the night before: a black leather skirt with a matching jacket and a white silk blouse—a flexible outfit for a complicated day. Finally she opened the door to her walk-in closet and studied herself in the full-length mirror. Not too shabby, she decided. Not too terribly suburban.

She went down the hall to her daughter's room, which, like Chloe herself, was a work in transition. Half her posters were of horses, the other half rock stars. On her dresser was a lava lamp flanked by a brace of well-worn koala bears. The books on her shelf ranged from Winnie the Pooh to Anne Rice. Chloe was not in the room, but her overnight case lay open on her bed. She was going to spend the day and night at her friend Lauren's. Willa had not inquired into the girls' plans, assuming the usual sort of night: pizza, phone calls, maybe a video. A glance into the open case shattered that assumption. Willa sat down on Chloe's bed and waited.

Chloe came in, swathed in a terry-cloth robe. By now a blind man could have seen what ailed the girl. Love had set her cheeks glowing with the heat of internal combustion. Love had also turned her wary and elusive with her mother, whose disapproval was assumed, perhaps even required, by Chloe's script.

Her eyes flickered from her mother to the open case and back again. "Excuse me? I don't believe I heard a knock."

"You weren't here," Willa said. "What's with the dress?"

The item in question, lying in the open case, was a pseudo-sophisticated slinky black number, as unsuitable for a girl Chloe's age as it was popular in her set. Invited to her first sweet sixteen, Chloe had chosen the dress herself, had laid claim to it with such determination that Willa hadn't the heart to argue—this was a month or two after Simon's death.

"I'm taking it to show Lauren," Chloe said.

"Lauren saw it at the sweet sixteen."

"Oh, yeah," said Chloe.

It broke Willa's heart to see how transparent the child was. Anyone could see she wasn't armed to go out in the world. There was so much Willa had to teach her, so many hard and painful steps she could save her if only Chloe would listen. Yet when she tried to find the words, they came to her as vapid echoes of the very things her own mother used to say, stupid platitudes ("Girls want love; boys want sex") or cautionary advice. Was this really the sum of her knowledge about men? It hardly mattered; Chloe would not listen any more than Willa had. You can't make your children's mistakes for them, Willa knew, and you can't stop them from making their own. Still, she had to try.

She patted the bed beside her. Chloe remained standing.

"I see a party dress," Willa said, "I think party."

Chloe sighed profoundly. "There's a dance at school. Lauren wants to check it out."

"Oh, she does!" said Willa, wondering why she was supposed to object—because clearly Chloe expected her to. "How are you getting there?"

"We've got a ride."

"Is Mrs. Rapaport taking you?"

"No."

"Then who is?"

"Why are you interrogating me? It's a stupid school dance, for Chrissake."

Willa used to go to school dances, too, to meet her friends. After five minutes they'd cut out and head up to Beacon Hill. It had seemed a fine idea back then. "Do you have a date?" she asked.

"People don't 'date' anymore, Mother."

"You know what I'm asking, Chloe."

"What is this, the Spanish Inquisition? I don't ask questions about you and your hippie professor."

Willa crossed her arms over her chest and stared. "What is there to ask? We're friends; that's all."

"Sure you are."

"What's that supposed to mean?"

Chloe couldn't quite hold her gaze. "I've seen the way he looks at you."

"What are you talking about?" Willa stood; she still had a few inches on her daughter and felt she needed the advantage. "He's married, in case you didn't know."

Chloe rolled her eyes.

"So she gives me this look," Willa said, as the waiter poured their wine, "like, 'So what if he's married?' Like I'm the child and she's the adult."

"Children are cynical by nature," Judy said. "Innocence comes with age."

"That's a cynical remark, and you are not that young."

"It's an observation, not a remark. It comes from having none of my own; I see children without sentimentality."

"You're just trying to let me off the hook," Willa said. "If a kid her age is cynical about marriage, you don't have to look far to know why."

Judy filled her mouth with a chunk of Italian bread. Forthright as she was by nature, she was circumspect on the subject of Willa's marriage. She had never liked Simon, and never said why.

The waiter brought their entrées and melted away. For a while they did not talk. Willa had ordered the portobello ravioli, which was delicious. But after a few bites, she reverted to her problems with Chloe. Lately she had taken to confiding these to her editor. Judy, having no children, was never tempted to counter with tales of her own; that, together with innate good sense, made her the ideal sounding board.

"Since when did I become the enemy?" she asked plaintively.

"Don't take it personally." Judy speared a piece of sausage. "How much did you tell your mother when you were her age?"

"Nothing. But I'm not my mother."

"To her you are."

And Willa, remembering her own teenage scribblings—*They can pry off my fingernails or call my parents*, equivalent tortures in the teenage mind—acknowledged the point. "I can't help worrying. A girl who's just lost her father is vulnerable to any man who pays her a bit of attention. I worry she'll get her heart broken."

"Everyone does, sooner or later. Maybe it ought to be done prophylactically, when we're young." Judy snapped a bread stick by way of illustration.

"Like having your wisdom teeth removed?"

"Or exposing little girls to German measles." They smiled with the ease of women who know each other well, and returned to their meals. The restaurant was continental, with expense-account prices and a famously temperamental chef. Judy lunched here often and knew all the waiters by name. One of them was a strikingly handsome young man of twenty-five or so, with jet-black hair, dark eyes, and a dancer's lithe body. Willa's eyes followed him once as he walked by. When she looked back at Judy, her friend was laughing.

"Married, worse luck," she said. "To that cute little coat-check girl."

"As if I cared!" Willa was indignant. "He's a baby."

"I like them young and unspoiled. Middle-aged men are depressing."

"They'd have to be criminally young to be unspoiled."

Judy leaned forward confidingly. "So what *is* going on with you and this Patrick I keep hearing about?"

"Nothing," Willa said.

Judy shot her a look over the top of her Donna Karan glasses. "Why not?"

"The man has a wife. Think about it, Judy: Do I need that?"

"You need something," Judy said ominously, "and you're not getting it."

There were times, and this was one of them, when Judy reminded Willa of Angel. When she'd first met Angel, Willa had been a virgin, a class Angel regarded with disdain. Didn't take her long to sit Willa down for a heart-to-heart. "Good girls think power comes from holding out. That's bullshit. You want power over a guy, give him a taste. He'll follow you around like a puppy dog."

Just do it was her watchword, long before it was Nike's. Judy Trumpledore had the same catch-as-catch-can attitude toward sex. She got around the dearth of single New York heterosexuals by expanding the pool to include married men. Both Judy and Angel understood the politics of sex in a manner Willa could only admire from afar. If sex were a college sport, they would have been varsity players, she a spectator in the stands. In her whole life, she had slept with only two men: Caleb and Simon.

The thought came: *What a waste.*

And perhaps Judy sensed the bleakness of that thought, for she reached across the table and squeezed Willa's hand. "Never mind, my dear. Let's talk about something else. How's the new book coming?"

"Fine," Willa said. "Great."

"Making progress?"

"You bet."

Judy nodded pleasantly. "Haven't written a goddamn word, have you?"

Willa blinked. "How did you know?"

"Please," said the editor, with a negligent wave. "After fifteen years in this racket?"

"You can cancel my contract. I'll return the advance."

"I don't think so. I think I'll wait, like Rumpelstiltskin. But what is the cause of this extended silence?"

"How can I write someone else's life when my own is such a mystery to me?"

Judy sat back. "You've finally gone into therapy!"

"God, no," Willa said with a laugh. "Unless planning a reunion is therapy."

"I suppose it could be therapeutic, provided you've done better than your classmates."

"They're all over the map. Patrick teaches at NYU, Jeremiah's a senator's aide, Vinny owns an auto-repair shop, Travis builds houses, Shake plays in a band, and Nancy's a secretary."

"I see," Judy said, in the voice of an editor presented with a hopeless proposition. "And this bunch had what in common?"

"Good question. That's one of the things I want to find out."

"And you're hosting this shindig? They're coming to you?"

Willa nodded.

"My advice?" Judy said. "Stock up on party games."

* * *

Loose in the city on a beautiful springlike day, Willa strode down Fifth Avenue, weaving effortlessly through the crowds. She'd known this city all her life but never took it for granted, never ceased to be surprised by it. Such a variety of faces, features, accents, races, religions, and languages. Such a clamor, a tapestry of sounds: the clang and thud of construction, the traffic, and, beneath them all, almost inaudible yet constant, the hum of conversation, like a grid of human voices. Though the air in Chappaqua was undoubtedly cleaner, Willa always breathed better in the city. It pleased her to feel, not quite invisible, but anonymous.

At Fifty-third she turned west, heading toward the entrance to MOMA, where a white banner proclaimed the arrival of a Georgia O'Keeffe exhibition. She went inside and bought a ticket.

The exhibit took up two halls. The first had been transformed into a hanging garden full of huge, voluptuous flowers rendered in extreme close-up, so that each flower was its own world. There were red oriental poppies, calla lilies, black irises, purple petunias, and sunflowers so vibrant they made van Gogh's seem anemic by comparison. Willa was awed by the focus and concentration necessary even to see in such a manner, let alone to capture that vision on canvas. There was a lesson here for her, something to do with eliminating distractions and preconceptions in favor of perception, which seemed to apply, not only to her work, but also to her life.

The second hall contained a selection of O'Keeffe's New Mexico paintings, and it was here that the artist seemed to have found the true palette of her soul in desert hues: ocher, burnt umber, pink and lavender, the red hills of the badlands. Her adobe dwellings were as subtly rounded and organic as the red sand hills that cradled them, and above them all stretched the majestic blue desert sky, the color of yearning.

There was one painting in particular that spoke to Willa, a work of radiant simplicity and clarity. It was a painting of the sky seen through the hole in a bleached white pelvis bone. Beside it, on the wall, was a quote from the artist. "When I started painting the pelvis bones I was most interested in . . . what I saw through them—particularly the blue from holding them up against the sky, as one is apt to do when one seems to have more sky than earth in one's world."

Willa had never visited New Mexico, but suddenly the desire seized her to go and see for herself if such landscapes existed; to see for herself a world with more sky than earth.

15

By five o'clock, Patrick had already vacuumed the floors, scrubbed the bathroom, stashed the pictures of Rachel, and, with his usual cheery optimism, changed the sheets on his bed. Now he was baking brownies, using Jeremiah's old recipe: two cups of flour, six ounces of bittersweet chocolate, a cup of sugar, one egg, and a quarter cup of minced marijuana. It was potent stuff. Patrick remembered once helping Jeremiah bake a batch for his mother's bridge club. Jeremiah had fallen asleep to the sound of the women's high-pitched laughter, and descended the next morning to a blizzard of cards in the living room. His mother never had a clue.

Phil Collins came on the radio and Patrick sang along. "Tonight's the night . . ." Then the telephone rang. He scowled at it, wiping his hands on a dish towel. If that was Willa calling to welsh, he was going to taxi up there and drag her out by the roots of her hair.

But it wasn't Willa. It was Rachel, his wife.

"Hey, Rach. What's up?" Concerned, because Sunday is their usual day to talk.

A tremulous sigh came over the line. "Patrick, you know I love you, don't you?"

Patrick's heart sank. No good ever came of a conversation that began like that; it was worse than "I've been thinking . . ."

Sure enough, none did. She wasn't cut out for long-distance relationships, Rachel said. It wasn't working. What they had wasn't a real marriage anymore, if it ever had been.

Patrick didn't have to be a weatherman. Don't say it, he begged, but of course she did: the dreaded *d* word.

Afterward, he stood shipwrecked in the center of the galley kitchen, swamped by waves of malignant déjà vu. Not again, oh not again. *Damn* women, was there not a faithful one among them? Rachel wouldn't be doing this if she didn't have someone else on hold. She'd denied it, but she had no talent for lying; he heard the truth in her voice. Besides, why else would a woman for whom recycling was a religion trash a perfectly good marriage? His own infidelities had been kept within strict bounds; in all the ways that mattered, he'd been faithful to Rachel. Couldn't she just have her damn affair and leave their marriage alone? He'd told her when they married: no more divorces. Because how could he bear, once again, losing not only a wife and a home, but a whole family, an entire constellation? Rachel was his first Jewish wife, and Patrick had loved that about her, all the perks that went with it: the ethnic food, the *mishpocheh*, the whole *mishegoss*. How could she take that from him?

"Damn you, bitch!" The phone was still in his hand. He hurled it across the room; it pocked the plaster wall and fell to the ground in pieces.

The moment she entered his apartment, Willa felt that Patrick was on a mission. Attentive, yet closed off; angry, but trying not to show it. She felt wary and looked around for Vinny, who was nowhere to be seen.

"Vinny's not here yet?"

"Running late," Patrick said curtly. "He'll meet us at the club." They went into the living room, which looked like the inside of Patrick's head, crammed with words, music, and films. A jerry-built assortment of shelves and cabinets housed a combination television/VCR, a CD player, and books and CDs that spilled over onto window ledges, floor, and coffee table. Patrick lit a joint and handed it to her. The smell evoked instant memories of Beacon Hill. Willa took a hit and broke out coughing.

He patted her back. "Out of practice?"

"Simon didn't allow it in the house." She saw the look on his face and added, "On purely practical grounds. He made his living suing the police. There's nothing they'd have loved more than busting him or his wife."

"I see. So you haven't smoked since . . . ?"

"Since I got married." She inhaled again and this time held it down.

Patrick showed his teeth. "Have a brownie," he said.

"Feels like old times," Willa said a while later, resting her heels on the coffee table. Mose Allison was playing on the CD.

"Except no one's mother is about to bust in," Patrick said. He moved closer and refilled her wineglass.

"Shouldn't we be going?" she asked uneasily.

"We have time." Hands on his thighs, body canted toward her.

Willa wanted to get up and move about, but doubted her ability. It had been a long time since she'd smoked weed, but she didn't remember it as being so powerful. Her skin tingled; she could feel the bones of her face, the passage of air, the coursing of blood through her body. It was a struggle to hold her head above water, to stay focused. The music lured her. If she closed her eyes, she would drift away on the voice of Mose Allison. But with Patrick poised like a crouching tiger, she knew what would happen if she shut her eyes.

It happened anyway. He took her by the shoulders, pushed her back against the couch, and kissed her hard. It took her by surprise, the ferocity of it. She pushed him away, but he pressed closer, trapping her arms between them. Patrick's lips descended to her neck, then the hollow of her throat; she felt them hard against her pulse and flailed out in sudden panic, as if a vampire had her in his grip. There was a moment when she felt him hesitate, weigh the situation, and consider pressing on—she was amazed that he would go so far, and frightened, though how could she be? It was only Patrick, after all—and then the moment passed; he released her. She got up and moved to an armchair.

No apologies this time; Patrick looked angry. "Why not?"

"It's not what I want," she said.

"Sex is an essential part of life. Without it we dry up and blow away like dandelion seeds."

That stung, but she didn't show it. "Thank you, Dr. Ruth."

"I know what your problem is. You're scared."

"No, I'm stoned."

"Let me show you the rest of the apartment."

"Is this the scene where we end up in your bedroom?"

"Willa," he said reproachfully. "You're spoiling the ending."

"The story may have gotten away from you. They say that happens."

Now the spell was broken; she was on to him. The wine, the weed, the music, Vinny a no-show, the fucking brownies: How hokey could he get? An awful suspicion assailed her. "Please tell me Shake's really playing tonight."

"Of course he is," Patrick said indignantly.

What a waste, Judy would have said. Prime boyfriend material: intelligent, charming, housebroken, eminently presentable; a perfectly suitable lover.

Only not for her. This realization seemed in some mysterious way to emanate from the O'Keeffe exhibit. She wasn't afraid; she just didn't want him. Willa had a heart of her own, scarred though it was, and the courage of its convictions. She would not be seduced. The hell with being chosen. It was her turn to choose.

Shake was tuning his sax onstage, the only place Nancy couldn't follow him, when his friends walked in. Willa entered first, followed by Patrick and Vinny. Seeing the three of them together was like hitting a time warp. Shake leaped from the stage, all of two feet from the floor, and hurried up to them.

Handshakes, hugs and kisses, cries of "You haven't changed a bit!" Of course they all had, each in his own way. Vinny had thickened, Patrick sharpened, Willa hardened. Shake knew he'd changed, too; he was leaner and meaner than ever; sexier, too, judging by the offers that came his way. What the hell did Nancy expect? Looking at Willa fed Shake's vexation with his wife, who had not only failed to keep herself up but had totally thrown in the towel.

He led them to the front table he'd reserved for them, summoned the waitress, and announced grandly that this table was on his tab, an order immediately countermanded by Patrick and Vinny. The men ordered beer, Willa Perrier. "Did Nancy come?" she asked.

Shake looked around nervously. "She's around somewhere." God help him if she was backstage haranguing Nikki; a teary-eyed singer was all he fucking needed. So much unpleasantness, just because Nancy happened to walk in on a perfectly innocent good-luck kiss and jumped to conclusions. That the conclusions happened to be true was irrelevant; they were wholly unwarranted by anything she had seen. But Nancy just plunged ahead, assuming what she always assumed.

Still, he felt bad. It was never part of the game plan to hurt the old girl. Not in anyone's interests to do that. Nikki was a terrific singer and a sweet little piece of ass, but Shake liked things quiet at home. His work demanded it. Now he saw her, halfway across the room and heading toward them. Nancy had a drink in her hand, and by the way she wove through the tables he knew it wasn't her first.

"Thar she blows," he said.

Willa followed his eyes but looked right past the heavyset woman tottering toward them, searching instead for some version of the girl she remembered. Nancy was on top of them before she realized her mistake, and, for just a moment, she allowed her surprise to show—a reaction not lost on Nancy, who entered it in the long ledger of slights and grievances suffered at the hands of her dear friends Willa and Angel.

Willa overcompensated. She gushed. She heard herself gushing and ordered herself to stop. Nancy wore a leopard-skin jumpsuit and gold stiletto heels, an outfit Willa wouldn't have worn for Halloween. She responded coolly to Willa's effusions and moved to the opposite side of the table. The others greeted her with hugs, and Shake pulled out a chair for her; she took it without sparing him a glance. Poor Nancy, Willa thought. The two of them together looked like Jack Sprat and his wife. Weight aside, the woman still had no idea of how to dress. God knows Willa had tried to teach her, and Angel, too, separately and in tandem, but it was useless. The problem went beyond taste; Nancy had seemed to lack a sense of her own body. Not knowing what she looked like, she could not choose clothing that suited her looks. Instead, she dressed a hockey-player's body in Barbie-doll clothes: Danskin tops and wraparound skirts that clung to every bulge, minidresses cut to the middle of chunky thighs, cut-off jeans tailored to reveal two little moons of dimpled ass. To the hints, suggestions, and exhortations of her friends, she had one standard reply: "Shake likes the way I dress." And it was true: She'd dressed like an adolescent boy's fantasy, only she didn't have the body for it and either didn't know or didn't care.

Patrick was on her right. Willa, having no desire to talk to him, turned to Vinny on her left. He met her glance with a bashful smile, then looked down.

"I hear you're a family man now," she said. "Got any pictures?"

He showed her one, a family shot of him with his wife, a hard-edged blonde with a brunette's skin and eyes, and their children, a girl about Chloe's age and a younger boy.

"Great-looking family. Your daughter's beautiful."

"Tell me about it," he said dourly. "The dogs are already sniffing around."

She laughed. "Look who's talking: Mr. Back Door Man himself! There wasn't a father in town who'd let you in the house. What goes around, comes around, my friend."

"God forbid." Vinny crossed himself. He was even larger than she remembered him, not fat but solid, with a jutting slab of a forehead that gave him a brutish look. Appearances don't always deceive; in high school he'd been a bruiser, but *their* bruiser. Like Shake's harmonica, Vinny's fists had spoken for them all. Looking at him now, Willa wondered how any boy would dare to date his daughter.

The lights dimmed and the band wandered out onto the stage. Shake rose, planting a kiss on Nancy's doughy cheek in passing, and leaped onto the stage with a bound that suggested an ability to scale far greater heights. He seized the tenor sax from the rack and stepped up to the mike. At his signal, the band launched into a full-bodied stomp, a raucous blast of old-time honky-tonk. Six musicians in all, two saxes, trumpet, guitar, bass, and drums, they played together as if they'd been doing it since birth, tossing the melody from one to the other like musical jugglers. Willa had been nervous on Shake's behalf; New York is a notoriously tough town for musicians. But when the first song ended, the audience rose to its feet and cheered.

Shake sent a gleeful look their way, and they applauded him, beaming with vicarious pride. That was *their* boy up there, their very own Shake doing them proud.

Then Shake introduced the singer, the band broke into "I've Got a Crush on You," and out she came, a beautiful black girl in a tight red dress. She had a sultry voice, and as she sang she vamped each of the band members in turn. Shake played her final conquest; the song ended with him on his knees, sax raised in supplication.

Another burst of applause. Only Nancy didn't clap. She sat

with her arms folded across her chest, glaring at Shake, who offered up a rueful shrug. Nancy sniffed and turned away. She signaled the waitress for another drink. Black Russians tonight, and to hell with the cost. Who did Shake think he was fooling? She was on to him long before she walked in on them making out in the dressing room. Shake was so goddamn predictable it was pathetic. Still, she would have waited it out as she always did, waited for the girl to get greedy, for Shake to get bored. When Dylan lived at home, she'd always felt secure. Shake had it good with them, and he knew it. But now he'd gone and shoved her nose in it. And that smug little bitch didn't bat an eye when Nancy walked in, just stared at her as if *she* were the intruder. Eighteen years of marriage and a son in college, and that slut looks at her like she's nothing. Nancy watched her cavorting onstage, so full of herself. *Well, think again, sister, 'cause that ain't gonna fly. I've squashed bigger bugs than you.*

The set went on. Shake introduced the band members. Nikki sang "Ten Cents a Dance," the guitar player sang "Troubles Soon Be Over," and then both of them sang "Please Don't Talk About Me When I'm Gone," an old chestnut that Shake had revamped as a duet. When he switched to harmonica, a dense cloud of nostalgia descended on his old friends. Willa felt a pang so sharp it hurt. She closed her eyes and she was up on Beacon Hill, listening to Shake play in the dark, listening to Angel sing. This girl's voice, like Angel's, seemed bigger than its vessel.

When the set ended, Shake came and sat with them. Awesome, they told him; beyond all expectation. Of course they'd always known he had it in him. Shake basked in their praise, and Nancy in its reflection. "It's the band," he said modestly.

"And that singer!" Patrick said. Nancy bristled at once; behind her back, Shake drew a finger across his throat. Patrick changed the subject. "Who does your arrangements?"

"Me," Shake said. "I write some of the songs, too. You'll hear them in the next set."

"Cool," said Patrick. "Recorded any?"

"He could've," Nancy said, in the tone of one resuming an old argument. "He was asked. But he wouldn't do it their way and in the end it fell apart."

"It didn't 'fall apart,'" Shake said. "I walked away. They didn't want the real thing. They wanted the fucking Kenny G of blues. Better not do it at all than put out a half-assed piece of work."

"He's waiting for the right offer," Nancy said.

"I'm waiting for a producer with some integrity."

"Isn't that like waiting for a virginal whore?" Patrick asked. "Or am I thinking of movie producers?"

They laughed. The waitress brought another round of drinks. "To us," Patrick said, raising his glass. They drank to themselves. Then Willa proposed a toast: "To absent friends."

"Funny thing about that," Shake said. "Seeing you guys here, I keep looking for the others. I keep expecting Angel to come sashaying in and plop herself down on Patrick's lap."

Nancy gave up a thin smile. "Or Travis." She put a whine in her voice. "'How come you guys didn't *call* me?'"

"Or Jeremiah," said Patrick. He got up and walked a few steps away from the table. Then he slunk back, peering over his shoulder. "'I'm not here,'" he said, in a dead-on imitation of Jeremiah's conspiracy voice. "'You never saw me.'"

More laughter, more drinks. They talked about their families, old times. Then Shake brought up the reunion. "Is everybody coming?"

"Everyone we reached," Patrick said, pushing the forelock out of his eyes. "Still haven't found Caleb or Angel."

"Not for lack of trying," Willa said. "It seems that no one's seen Angel since she ran away right after graduation. Unless one of you has?" She looked around the table. The others shook their heads. "Isn't that strange?"

No one spoke. Then Nancy said, "What's so strange about it? She had every reason to split and none to come back."

Willa stared at her. From the corner of her eye, she saw Patrick cover his face with both hands. A cold feeling crept over her.

"What reason?" she asked.

Nancy rolled her eyes. "Listen to her," she cackled. "Little Miss Innocent."

The coolness persisted in the cab. Willa wanted to go alone, but it was two o'clock in the morning and Patrick insisted on escorting her. He followed her into the backseat, and she placed her purse between them. She gave the driver the address of the garage where she'd parked her car. There was a pine-tree deodorizer dangling from the rearview mirror and the phony pine scent was suffocating. They rode the first ten blocks in silence.

Finally Willa said, "Why didn't you tell me?"

Patrick closed the partition between them and the driver. "She didn't want you to know."

"Bullshit," she cried. "I was her best friend."

"Then how come she didn't tell you herself?" Patrick waited for an answer that didn't come. "She was embarrassed, that's why. Angel admired you, you know."

Willa snorted. "She thought I was the village idiot. Which I obviously was."

"She looked up to you."

"Angel?" she said, staring across at Patrick. "Angel looked up to no one. When she prayed, she prayed laterally. And why *would* she be embarrassed? She used to say she wanted six children by six different men, each a genius of some sort or another."

"Yeah, well, when push came to shove, she was still a good Catholic girl who wanted a ring on her finger before she had the kid."

"And you wouldn't give it to her." She should have guessed. Had Busky known? Willa saw him again, that ruined face pressed to the screen door. *You little pissant—now you wanna find her?* No wonder Angel ran.

Patrick turned his head to the window. They were crossing Times Square now, and the neon lights tinted his hair in garish colors. He mumbled something.

"What?" she said.

He said it louder. "It wasn't mine."

"Oh, shame on you!"

He shot her a pleading look. "It *wasn't*. I always used protection. Some of the others weren't as careful."

Willa felt sick. That Angel had slept around she knew to her cost. No wonder Angel hadn't confided in her; Caleb could have fathered that child. He and Patrick weren't the only candidates, either. Willa remembered a party at Patrick's, Angel disappearing with Shake and turning up hours later, looking smug. She had gone mad those last few months of high school. But none of that excused Patrick.

As they entered Central Park, the driver pressed a button and locked the doors. Willa rested her forehead against the cold glass of the window. The park looked menacing and eerie at this hour of the night.

"I tried to help," Patrick said, in a tone of such mortification that Willa very nearly relented, until she recalled that he had gone twenty years without lifting a finger to find Angel. "I offered her money. I offered to pay for an abortion, but she didn't want that."

"Did she take the money?"

"No."

That was strange. Angel was proud; Willa could well imagine her throwing Patrick's money back in his face. But eventually common sense would have prevailed. If she meant to have the baby, she would have needed all the help she could get.

There was more to the story than he was telling. There were pieces missing; it's the sort of thing biographers notice. And here she'd thought they were in this together.

No wonder he'd objected to Jovan.

16

May 2, 1972. Last night we watched a meteor shower from the top of Beacon Hill. It was a warm, buttery sort of night, summer just around the corner. Shake took out his harmonica and started playing "Swing Low, Sweet Chariot"; lately he's gotten into spirituals, much to Vinny's disgust. Leaning back against Caleb's knees, I watched the night sky with my friends all around me, and suddenly, out of nowhere, the thought came to me: I might never be this happy again.

A star shot across the sky and I wished: "Let it never change." Another star fell. "Let it all change."

May 10, 1972. Slept over at Angel's last night. We didn't see the guys because she's pissed at Patrick again. Angel took all his pictures out of her treasure box and cut them up; then she taped them back together.

"I need a virgin," she declared. "Virgins are the best. They're so fucking grateful, they'll remember you till their dying day."

Big talker, our Angel. Remember, Di, when we first met and she would talk casually about guys she'd done and guys she wanted to do and guys she wouldn't do if they went down on their knees and begged, how shocked I was? In the world according to my mother, sex is something boys do to girls if girls aren't smart enough or strong enough to fend them off. If it wasn't for Angel, I'd still be living in the dark. Well, maybe Caleb had something

to do with it, too, but it was Angel who
first opened my eyes.

She still sees that as her job, only these
days she has to work harder to shock me. Earlier this year it was Mr. O'Rourke (Nov. 6).
Now it's this virgin mania. She sits down at
her desk to make a list. I look over her
shoulder.

"How do you know they're virgins?"

"Desperation," she says. "They reek of
it."

"How about Travis?" I say helpfully. "Is
he desperate enough?"

She gags. "Shut up! God, just the thought
of it makes me want to puke."

"Those teeth," I say. "That breath." Both
of us shudder. Poor Travis.

Poor Travis indeed. Willa laid the diary facedown on her night
table. Tired as she was, she could not sleep, so she'd gone back to
the diaries, not as sentimental relics this time, but as source
material to be mined with less emotion, more discernment. As a
biographer, Willa regarded diaries as a rich but dangerous trove:
rich in their unparalleled detail, their ground's-eye view of daily
life, their effortless evocation of context, and of course, the
access they provided to the diarist's inner life; dangerous in that,
by their very nature, they were skewed by the perspective, preju-
dices, and limitations of their author. The access they provided
was intimate but mediated; events emerged pre-interpreted. It
was up to the researcher to evaluate the diarist's account in light
of other data in order to arrive at the objective truth . . . if such a
thing could be held to exist. In light of her own seemingly liquid
past, Willa was beginning to wonder.

There was a certain pleasure in the reemergence of the dispassionate, thinking part of her brain; Willa had begun to fear it was
gone for good. But at the same time, it was troubling to read her
own diaries this way. She could not, after all, entirely detach herself; she could not cease to remember, and what she remembered

was disturbingly at odds with what she now perceived. The Angel of her memory was fearlessly outspoken—Our Lady of the Perpetual Mouth, Patrick used to call her—a free-spirited rebel, a pioneer of female sexuality. But the impression yielded by a more critical and informed reading was of a reckless, promiscuous, deeply troubled girl. As a child, Willa had discounted many of her friend's wilder claims, attributing allegorical truth to stories she was now inclined to take more literally.

The reference to Mr. O'Rourke was a case in point. Fighting the fatigue that blurred her vision, Willa took up the diary and turned back to the earlier entry that her younger self had so thoughtfully cited.

> Nov. 6, 1971. Angel's got the hots for Mr. O'Rourke—Tommy she calls him, though not to his face (math teacher, total hunk, fresh out of college). She swears she'll have him before graduation.
>
> "You're nuts," I tell her. "He's a teacher."
>
> Angel rolls her eyes. "That's the point, Einstein."
>
> "Like he's gonna risk his job for a piece of you."
>
> "What are you, kidding? The man's foaming at the mouth already. He can't even stand up in class when I'm in the room; he has to get someone else to write on the board for him."
>
> "Yeah, right."
>
> It's just talk, of course. At least I think it is. The brilliant thing about Angel is that you never know for sure.

Did Angel succeed? Willa wondered. Wouldn't she have told Willa? Perhaps not; it seemed there were many things that Angel never told her.

* * *

Willa slept late and woke to the scent of coffee, which she followed to the kitchen. There was fresh-brewed coffee in a pot and Chloe was at the stove making French toast. "Is it Mother's Day?" Willa asked, sinking into a chair.

"Hardly," Chloe said, pouring her a cup.

An odd response, but Willa was in no condition to look a gift cup of coffee in the mouth. She took a deep, restorative sip. "Perfect. You're ready for marriage."

"Funny you should say that," Chloe said.

Willa looked up in alarm, only to find her daughter laughing at her. "Very funny."

"Someone called. Jovan something."

"What'd he say?"

"Call him on his cell phone. Number's on the fridge. Who is he, another one of your hippie friends?"

Willa got up for more coffee. "No, just a business acquaintance. How was the dance?"

"Okay." Her all-purpose response to everything these days. Then Chloe surprised her by adding, "They had a band."

"Any good?"

"Awesome."

"Who are they?"

Chloe looked down at her plate, where bits of French toast floated like islands in a sea of maple syrup. "Just a local band."

One look at her glowing face, radioactive with love, and it all came together. Wendell's delivery boy, the Bliss kid: He hadn't gone away after all. Too old, Willa thought, too old and a musician to boot. Nothing good would come of this. But what could she do? If she lectured, Chloe would not hear. If she tried to stand in the way, Chloe would go around her, just as Willa had circumvented her own mother to get to Caleb. All she could do was try to stay close enough to pick up the pieces.

"Let's do something today," Willa proposed.

Chloe said nothing but gave her a sharp look.

"Want to catch a movie?"

"A movie?" Chloe said. Again that stare. "I don't think so."

"Why not?" Willa asked.

"Rehearsal, for one thing."

"On a Sunday?"

"Mom," Chloe sighed, with infinite patience, "this is *high* school."

Sunday morning, out running with his boy, Jovan discovered that a certain balance between them had shifted since they'd last met. They'd been running together since Sean was twelve, and during all those years Sean had striven to keep up with his father. Today, it was Jovan who had to struggle to keep pace. Sean had put on the infamous "freshman twenty," but in his case it was all muscle; those skinny legs and chest had finally filled out. Jovan kept himself in good shape, but there is a difference between nineteen and forty-five, and sooner or later, he supposed, that difference will out.

Twice around the campus they ran, then out into the town, up and down hilly residential streets. They did about five miles and Sean was all set for another circuit when Jovan's cell phone rang. It was Willa Durrell. "Hold on," he said to her, and to Sean: "Go on, I'll meet you at the dorm." He waited till Sean was out of sight before leaning over and bracing his hands on his knees.

Willa was amazed to get his message, she said. She'd been planning to call him that very day.

"I'm in Albany," he said, "visiting my son. If you're free, I thought I could stop by on the way home and fill you in on what I've got so far."

"Great," she said, "I've got some information, too." She didn't invite him back to her house, but arranged to meet him at a diner near the parkway. They hung up, and Jovan allowed himself another minute before starting a slow jog back toward Sean's dorm.

After debating all weekend, Jovan still hadn't decided how much to tell Willa. He'd turned up nothing at all on Angel Busky, which was not a good sign; but he doubted Willa would care much. From the first, he'd suspected that the whole reunion scheme was just a roundabout way for Willa to reach out to her real object, the old boyfriend. About Caleb, Jovan had turned up plenty, information that, in the normal course of events, he would have turned over in its entirety to his client.

But Willa wasn't a client, he told himself as he jogged along the path to the freshman dorms. Did the same obligation apply if she wasn't paying him?

Of course it did. She'd offered to pay; her intention was to employ him professionally. If he was dumb enough to waive his fee, that was his problem. He had to give her the information; what she did with it was no concern of his.

Except that it did concern him. It concerned him a lot.

Sean was waiting, sprawled on the lawn outside his dorm. They went up and showered; then Jovan took Sean and his roommate, another lacrosse player, out for brunch at the local IHOP. "Uh-oh," the waitress said when she saw them coming, "eaters on deck." And she was right. Jovan, watching the boys go at it, remembered the time Sean had taken his entire high school lacrosse team to an all-you-can-eat pancake breakfast, a fundraiser for the local parish. Still dripping from their run, the boys had paid their five bucks at the door and settled in for some serious eating. After a while Father Mallory sidled over to where Jovan was sitting with a couple of precinct cops. "Boys keep this up," he muttered darkly into Jovan's ear, "they'll not only eat up the profits, they'll bankrupt the parish." Jovan had taken the hint and reached for his wallet. He didn't mind. Watching Sean eat always made him feel he'd done something right.

When they were done, he drove the boys back to their dorm, refusing Sean's invitation to come up. The boy had his own routine now, his own friends, his own life here on campus. Albany hadn't been Jovan's choice. He'd pushed hard for NYU; what it cost in extra tuition they'd have saved on room and board. But Sean had set his heart on going away, and the Albany lacrosse coach made him an offer he couldn't refuse. In retrospect Jovan had to admit the boy had been right; it was time to cut the apron strings. Sean was thriving, and as for Jovan . . . well, as every father who's ever taught his kid to ride a bike knows, part of the job is learning to let go.

He palmed a folded fifty and slipped it into Sean's jacket pocket when they hugged good-bye.

"You have a son in Albany?" Willa said. She sat across from him in the booth in a silky gray shirt, blond hair tied back at the nape, and all the ambient light in the joint seemed to focus on her. An old expression came back to Jovan: She was one long, tall drink of water.

Designer water, that would be. Effervescent and expensive, served in crystal, on white linen.

"Sean," he said. "He's a freshman at SUNY Albany."

"Do you have other children?"

"Just the one." She didn't ask but he told her anyway: "My wife died when he was twelve. So I know what it's like, raising a kid on your own."

"I'm sorry," she said.

He nodded. The way she looked at him made him think maybe it wasn't hopeless after all. Not a flirtatious look—too direct for that, too considering—but a look that took him in, acknowledged him in a way she hadn't before.

The waitress approached and did a double take at the sight of Willa. "Oh, Mrs. Durrell, it's you!"

"How are you, Maggie? Long time no see."

"Long time, yeah. Jeez." A change came over her plump face, and she drew herself up. "I was awful sorry to hear what happened."

"Thanks." Willa opened the menu, but the waitress wasn't finished.

"I never believed a word they said about him. 'George,' I says to my hubby, 'I knew that man, and that man was a gentleman.'"

Willa's smile seemed glued in place. For a moment no one spoke. Then Jovan said, "I'll have some coffee and a piece of that nice-looking blueberry pie," and Willa ordered, too, and the waitress left them.

Willa followed her with her eyes. "We used to come here sometimes, when we didn't feel like going to a real restaurant."

Jovan nodded. "We" meant her and Simon, presumably. She never said his name, he'd noticed; thinking back, he couldn't remember a single time. After Katie died, he'd talked of her constantly, aware he was obsessing but unable to help himself. Of course Willa's situation was different. Different sort of marriage, for starters.

What must it be like, he wondered, living in a town where everyone not only knows your business but feels compelled to comment on it? And Willa was a proud woman; that had been clear from the moment he'd met her. Surprising she didn't move—but of course she had her daughter to consider.

Maggie came back soon with their orders. Willa's cappuccino left a fine line of frothy cream on her upper lip, which she licked off. Jovan realized he was staring and looked down at the table, where he'd laid out two buff folders, one thicker than the other. "I have some results on Caleb. Don't know how happy they're going to make you."

"Let's hear," she said.

He took out the top sheet from the thicker folder, passed it to her, and watched as she read it. It was a summary sheet; Jovan knew the contents by heart. Caleb was an old story, a type all bunco detectives get to know: guys with a lot of fresh starts on their résumés, a lot of hasty departures, maybe a name change or two along the way; guys who walk out on their whole lives as easily as most men walk away from a failed pickup. Caleb had left Florida University after his junior year. Defaulted on his student loan—never made a payment. Turned up next in Key West, grifters' and drifters' paradise, where he held a succession of short-lived jobs, all in the tourist trade. Twice evicted for nonpayment of rent; after the second eviction, he dropped off the radar screen for a while. Showed up next selling time shares in Miami; this was in 1978. In 1981 he married a client, one Felicity Schaeffer, a childless widow twelve years his senior. The couple returned to her hometown of Chicago, where she sold her Evanston house and they purchased, in both their names, a condo on Lake Shore Drive. In 1983 they divorced. He got the condo, which he promptly liquidated. No sign of him between then and June of 1986, when he reappeared in Miami, renting a bungalow in South Beach; this time the name on the lease read "Cal Reese." Rhys parlayed his experience in the time-share business into some sort of scam, apparently selling shares in apartments he didn't own. Did well at it, judging by the number of lawsuits filed the following year. The Miami-Dade prosecutor's office took an interest; but by the time they got around to looking, Cal Reese no longer existed and Caleb Rhys was in the wind.

That was four years ago. Since then there'd been no sign of Rhys; presumably he'd dumped the name for good.

Willa's face as she read grew longer and sadder, until she felt his scrutiny; then it hardened to the same adamantine mask she'd first presented him with. Jovan sighed. Say what you will, the messenger's always blamed. But she needs to know, he told himself, in case this mutt ever shows up at her door.

She read the page a second time, then looked at him with eyes that gave nothing away. "Is this it?"

Now Jovan was up against it. He forked a piece of pie and chewed it slowly. He wouldn't have minded admitting that he'd failed to find her old boyfriend. The problem was, he hadn't quite; in fact, he'd come perilously close to locating Caleb Rhys, perhaps just a phone call away. And that's what he didn't want to tell Willa.

"Would you choose to pursue it," he stalled, "given what you've just read? Would you really want to invite this guy back into your life?"

"I never planned on inviting him back into my life," she said coolly. "My life right now is a closed shop."

Duly noted. What a fool he was. Or not. That glimmer of interest he thought he'd seen before was gone, but not forgotten.

He reached into his jacket pocket and took out a folded slip of paper. "Sometimes, when you can't find a person, you look for a relative. I found his sister."

Willa looked at him. "You weren't going to tell me, were you?"

"No."

"Why not?"

Jovan said nothing.

She said, "You don't know him. Caleb's no predator."

"You knew him as a kid. Wolf cubs are cute, too."

"But you told me anyway," she said. "How come?"

He shrugged. "I figure it's your decision."

"Oh, very good!" she teased. "Definitely the A answer."

"That said," he went on stolidly, "you'd be a chump to call this guy."

Willa looked startled for a moment and then she laughed. It

was a transforming laugh, full throated and warm. "You couldn't resist."

"I know the type. He's the kind of guy who makes people want to get to know him, and by the time they do, it's too late. But it's your call. I gave you the number."

"You haven't, actually."

She was right; the piece of paper was still in his fist. He held it out. Willa took it and slipped it into her purse without looking at it. Then she asked about Angel.

Jovan signaled for more coffee. It was nearly five and the diner was starting to fill up with early birders, elderly couples for the most part. A blue-haired woman at the table beside their booth looked at Willa, then whispered in her husband's ear. If Willa noticed, she gave no sign.

"I found nothing on Angel Busky," he said. "Nothing at all." Would she understand what that meant, or would he have to spell it out?

She knew. He saw it in the sudden widening of her eyes, the quick intake of breath. Then, as before, she hid behind the curve of a smile and a quick retort. "Maybe you didn't look hard enough."

"I looked plenty hard." He told her where. It took five minutes just to list the sources, and he left out the illicit ones. Property records, voter registration, motor vehicle bureaus in all fifty states, immigration records, credit-rating organizations, federal and state court indices, parish records, all the commercial databases. When he finished, Willa wasn't smiling anymore.

"Maybe she changed her name," she said. "Started out fresh as someone else."

"Unlikely."

"Why?"

"Changing your identity isn't easy. It's not just a matter of picking a name. You need a valid Social Security number, documentation, credit history. And to have left no trail, Angel would have had to make the switch very soon after leaving. That assumes more know-how and preparation than an eighteen-year-old girl is likely to have had."

Willa bit her lower lip. "Maybe she's living abroad."

"There's no record of her having left the country."

"Or off the grid, home-schooling a passel of kids in rural Arkansas."

"Doesn't sound like Angel," Jovan said, and saw agreement in her eyes.

Then Maggie appeared with a pot of coffee. Willa waited till she was gone, then leaned across the table. "There's something you don't know. Angel was pregnant when she disappeared."

"And you didn't think to mention that?"

"I didn't know. Last night I saw some old friends, and while we were talking, it came out. Do you see what this means?" she said eagerly. "This could help us. Angel was a Catholic. Wild as she was, she still went to mass, she went to confession—we used to joke that the priest reserved an hour a week for hers. She wouldn't have an abortion. So I'm thinking maybe she went into one of those Catholic homes for unwed mothers."

"Willa," he said. "Angel's never been in a hospital. She never registered a birth. Not with the state, and not with the parish."

"I know she's not dead," Willa said. "I checked the Social Security death index myself."

"Not every death is listed," he said. "Sometimes people aren't identified, or they're misidentified. Sometimes bodies aren't found."

Her face was ashen and she had to wrap her hands around her cup to hide their shaking. Jovan watched and wondered. Here's a woman doesn't bat an eye when she finds out her old boyfriend grew up to be a scoundrel, yet goes to pieces at the possibility that some girl she'd known twenty years ago might be dead.

Well, maybe she hadn't quite gone to pieces. But she was certainly distraught, more distraught than she ought to be. Unless she'd already made the jump from wondering if Angel was dead to wondering how she'd died.

That could be upsetting.

17

Red roses in a vase on the front-hall table, and propped against the vase a note from Chloe: "Mom—these came. Went to rehearsal. I have a ride home." There was a florist's envelope among the flowers. "To err is human," the card said, "to forgive divine. Your penitent P."

Willa carried the vase into the kitchen to rearrange the flowers. Pricked her finger on a thorn and blamed Patrick. What was he apologizing for, anyway: his boorish behavior toward her, or his treatment of Angel? *There* he had more to answer for. Last night she'd seen a side of Patrick she wished she'd never seen.

The phone rang. She answered, cradling the receiver between ear and shoulder.

"So I'm nosy," Judy Trumpledore said. "How'd it go last night?"

Willa placed the roses one by one among the ferns that had accompanied them. No babies' breath, at least. "Tell me something," she said. "What's the connection in the male mind between flowers and guilt?"

"The Garden of Eden?" Judy said.

"That was an apple."

"Still, the association: garden, flowers, sin. Or maybe it's just a construct of the flower industry. Why? Who's feeling guilty?"

"Patrick."

"Oh dear. What for?"

"Any number of things," Willa said vaguely. Strange suspicions were gathering in her mind, but she was unwilling to speak them even to herself, as if thinking a thing could make it possible. Besides, they made no sense. If it hadn't been for Patrick, the reunion would have been quietly forgotten and no one would be looking for Angel.

Judy sighed down the line. "Didn't we talk about wasting men, Willa?"

"You want him, he's all yours. Maybe he's got a book in him."

"What a good little sharer you are! But my card's full at the moment. Just for the record, what exactly is this one's problem?"

"He's married," Willa said. "And even if he weren't . . . he's not the only man in the world, you know."

There was a pause, then, "Why, Willa, you sly thing, you. Who is he?"

"No one," she said hastily. Judy had it all wrong; Willa wasn't thinking of anyone in particular. Specifically, she wasn't thinking of Jovan Luisi.

Nancy, sleeves rolled up and hair tied back, was stirring the spaghetti sauce she'd made from scratch with her mother's recipe when Shake came up from behind and snaked his arms around her waist. "You're so sexy when you're cooking," he said, rubbing up against her. "My earth goddess."

She reached back and gave his ass a pat. They'd already fought and made up on the drive home, sealed the bargain in bed, and ratified it for good measure when they awoke. Nancy stirred the sauce languidly. Shake kissed the back of her neck and moved away. He took a beer from the fridge and sat at the kitchen table—a card table, really, all they had room for. He was shirtless, in jeans and bare feet.

"I've been thinking," she said.

"Uh-oh."

"I think we ought to skip the reunion. I think it's a bad idea."

There was a long silence. She kept herself from turning around.

"You're kidding me, right?" he said at last.

"Shake, it's pointless. Whatever we all had in common, it's gone now. Last night I looked around and thought, 'What in God's name are these people doing sitting around the same table?' Willa and Patrick have this nutty idea they're gonna resurrect the past; but that ain't never gonna happen." *And who the hell would want it to?* she added, but only to herself.

Shake twisted the cap off the bottle. "You were so drunk you couldn't see past your own nose. Everyone had a fine time."

"You didn't sit there; I did. Vinny hardly opened his mouth, Patrick never shut his, and Her Royal Highness just sat there like her shit didn't stink but ours sure did."

"Jesus, Nancy. Willa couldn't have been more gracious."

She sniffed. "'Nancy, darling,'" she cried, in a fair rendition of Willa's breathy social voice, "'it's so wonderful to see you!'"

"What've you got against her?" Shake asked. "I thought you two were friends."

"Her and Angel were friends. They didn't see me being in their league." The words came out crusted in bitterness. Nancy kept her back to Shake, but she could feel him staring.

Then he changed the subject, his usual tactic when they disagreed. "What's up with Patrick and Willa? They an item, you think?"

She turned around then, surprised, her face flushed pink from the heat of the sauce. "Not a chance."

"Why not? Patrick always had a hard-on for her. Caleb just got there first."

"He's not good enough for her. Not then, not now."

"Willa's not a snob."

"She's the worst kind of snob—the kind that think they're not."

"Ouch," said Shake, laughing.

Beside the stove there was a bowl of chopped meat and an array of spices. Nancy opened the garlic powder and gave it such a smack that Shake feared for his dinner. She added salt and pepper and plunged her hands into the mix, squashing the soft red meat between her thick fingers, muttering as she worked. "Sitting there in her fucking little size-six leather suit, which by the way cost more than my whole wardrobe put together; sitting there like butter wouldn't melt in her mouth. 'Stay with me, I have plenty of room!' I'll just bet she does; can't wait to show it off, either, the bitch."

"So what if she has money? Money doesn't buy happiness."

"Maybe not. But lack of it sure buys misery." There was a loaded silence. Nancy looked over her shoulder and saw Shake's face. "I didn't mean us, baby. I've got everything I need right here."

"Come here," he said.

She wiped her hands on a dish towel and went to him. Shake pulled her onto his lap, and she settled back against him.

"We're going to the reunion," he said. "And we're accepting Willa's invitation." She started to get up, but he tightened his arms around her. "Listen up. You have no reason to envy Willa. She may have a big house and money in the bank, but she got it through a miserable marriage that ended in death and public humiliation. And you've got one thing she'll never have." He nuzzled her neck, just below the ear. She smelled of garlic, musk, and bath oil.

"Oh, yeah?" she said. "What?"

"Me."

"Am I forgiven?" Patrick asked, tension striating his voice.

Willa, curled catlike on the windowseat in the library, shifted the phone to her shoulder. It was dark out, and dinner was in the oven, but Chloe had not yet returned. "For what?" she said. "Your flowers didn't specify."

"For—how should I say it?—employing unworthy means in pursuit of a worthy end."

"I like that. Much more original than 'To sin is human,' though equally self-serving."

"You *are* angry," he said.

But Willa was more disappointed than angry, like a kid who's stayed too long at a birthday party or watched a magic show from backstage. "Your apology, if that's what it was, is accepted. No harm, no foul. But enough is enough, don't you think?"

"What I think doesn't matter. It's what you think, and you've made that clear."

"Good," she said, "because we have other things to talk about. I saw Jovan Luisi today."

There was a sound like grinding teeth, then, "What did he have to say?"

"He hasn't found either of them yet. But he found Caleb's sister, Linda. She lives in Atlanta. He gave me her number."

Patrick let out a whoop. "Well done, Willa!"

"Jovan's doing, not mine. But there's a hitch, Patrick. I'm not sure I want to call him."

"No problem. Give me Linda's number and I'll call."

"That's not it. What I mean is, I'm not sure I want him to come."

In the silence that followed, she wrapped the tasseled end of the curtain sash around her fingers.

"Why not?" he said, in a voice steeled for bad news.

Willa gnawed the inside of her cheeks. She had violated
Caleb's privacy by siccing Jovan on him, with the result that she
now knew more than she wanted or had a right to know about
his life. Telling Patrick what she'd learned would be a further vio-
lation; but if she didn't, he would insist on including Caleb.

She compromised on a sanitized version. Mentioned money
problems, evictions, a drifting tendency with name changes along
the way; omitted the rich widow, the lawsuits, and the police. Still,
Patrick must have read something into the lacunae of her story, for
he was uncustomarily subdued when she finished.

"Doesn't matter," he said at last. "Come what may, we said;
good times or bad, in sickness or in health."

"You're thinking of your wedding vows," she said drily.

"It's your house, Willa. It's up to you. But let me remind you,
our pact wasn't conditional."

"He might not want to come. He might be embarrassed."

"I can imagine Caleb being many things. Embarrassed isn't
one of them."

That rang true. Of all the Beacon Hill kids, Caleb had cared
least what other people thought of him. For Willa, and she supposed for the others as well, that had been part of his attraction,
that edge of ruthlessness beneath the charm, the sense that the
usual limits didn't apply. Well, she thought, they'd all built careers
on their childhood strengths, Caleb no less than the others.

"We don't have to decide this minute," Patrick said. "What
about Angel? Did he find anything?"

"A whole lot of nothing. If she's out there, she's totally off the
grid."

"*If?*"

A pair of headlights approached, and Willa followed them
intently, but the car passed without slowing. She wound the sash
around her fingers. "You still expect her to show for the
reunion?"

"Hell, yeah," Patrick said stoutly. Then, after a beat, "I don't
know. Maybe."

"Jovan thinks she's dead."

"'Cause he can't find her. Give me a break."

"Her father said she was."

"To him," Patrick said, "not to the world."

"I've been thinking of having another talk with him."

"With Busky? Waste of time. Bastard wouldn't give us the time of day."

Willa didn't answer. It had occurred to her that Patrick had his own interests in the matter, which didn't necessarily coincide with her own. And it was Patrick whom Busky hated. If she showed up on her own, with a bottle of something good . . .

"Willa," Patrick said. "Don't even think about it."

Despite her anger, she couldn't help a surge of affection for one who knew her so well. "Why not? He's an old man. What's he going to do, eat me?"

"Ever see *Silence of the Lambs*?"

She smiled. "I wouldn't put him in a class with Anthony Hopkins. But there's something else I wanted to ask, while we're talking. Do you remember a teacher named O'Rourke, Tommy O'Rourke?"

"Jesus Christ." Patrick sounded disgusted. "Where'd you dig up that name?"

"My diary."

"You ought to burn that thing."

It didn't sound like he was kidding. Willa moved the phone away from her ear and looked at it. Then she put it back. "Angel had a thing for him. I wondered if it was ever consummated."

"Willa, Willa," he said. "Where are you going?"

"Was it?"

"What difference does that make now?"

"My mistake," she said slowly, "has been trying to make sense of the past before pinning down what actually took place. So I'm trying to rectify that; but the more I find out, the more I realize I didn't know."

"What are you looking for?"

"The truth," she said. "Will you help, or won't you?" Then she waited, resisting the urge to fill the silence. That had always been her role: bridging gaps, papering over differences with sheets of chatter, oiling the machine. A lot of good it did her. Silence, she was finding, had a clarifying effect, like the white bones framing the sky in O'Keeffe's painting.

"If she got to O'Rourke," Patrick said at last, "she didn't tell me."

"What do you think?"

She felt him shrug. "Who knows? Travis always claimed she did."

"*Travis?*" Willa said. Surely Travis was the last person in whom Angel would have confided. "How would he know?"

"He had his ways. But so what? If it did happen, we know who seduced who. The man has a life, Willa. After twenty years, there are some questions that shouldn't be asked."

On Sundays, as regularly as politicians go to church, Travis Fleck went hiking in the wilderness surrounding his home. It was not a trivial matter, he'd found, to live in the midst of such natural grandeur. The scale of a great mountain range is not the scale of a man; nor was this the sort of terrain a man could master, as he might a few acres of arable land. Travis's solution had been to forge an intimacy based on knowledge. He roamed the wilderness around his home until he knew it well, then gradually expanded outward. His goal was to one day say that all he could see was known to him.

Today he'd started off down the arroyo that crossed his dirt access road. After a few miles, he climbed the steep embankment and picked up a hiking trail that wove upward along a sage-and-scrub-covered slope. It was slow going, the trail pocked with patches of deceptively deep snow. At the crest of the mountain, standing alone with the vast blue vault of the sky above him and the snow-topped hills all around, Travis felt as close to God as he would ever feel: close enough to speak, if only they'd been on speaking terms.

It was cold up here, though, and windy enough to disperse even the most profound exultation. After a while Travis pulled the wool stocking lower over his ears and headed back down the trail. He enjoyed hiking alone; it was coming home to an empty house that sucked. That's when he wished for company, something to break the silence, someone to talk to. A dog, even. As an only child he'd longed for a dog, begged for one every birthday and Christmas for years, but never got it; his house-proud mother wouldn't tolerate an animal in her home. (One of many bones he had to pick with her, enough to make a skeleton.) A few months after moving in to the adobe, Travis had gone down to the shelter in Santa Fe and adopted a three-year-old shepherd mix with a torn ear, a scruffy coat, and a bring-it-on attitude that reminded him of his old friend Vinny. Although Travis did his best, the dog never took to him; after a month's trial it ran away.

A television would have helped, but Travis didn't own one. To the women who visited, he implied that this was a matter of choice, a preference for books and music over the industrial pap excreted by the networks and their corporate masters. To himself he admitted the real reason, which had nothing to do with political aesthetics and everything to do with poor reception and the lack of cable this deep in the woods.

Travis heard the phone ringing as he opened the door. He lunged for the cordless. "Hello?"

"Hey, Travis!" A female voice, and damned if his cock didn't recognize it first, stirring like a sleeping dog at the mailman's approach.

"Willa?" he said.

"Very good! Got a minute to talk?"

"Sure." He shrugged off his jacket, ran his hand over his hair as if she could see him. *She's calling to say the reunion's off* was his first paranoid thought, but Willa just asked him how he'd been and what he'd been doing, the usual long-time-no-see questions, to which Travis, who'd waited a long time to be asked, had his answers ready. He talked about the cooperative, the success of the business, his life in New Mexico; and as he spoke, he looked around his living room at the Navajo rug, the hand-carved blanket chest, the shelves of Indian pottery, all given in trade for his work. "I live in an adobe I built myself, with help from my partners."

"I heard it's beautiful. Bring pictures when you come."

"I will. But you should come out sometime."

"I may take you up on that," she said. "Yesterday I saw a Georgia O'Keeffe exhibit at MOMA that blew me away. I've never been to New Mexico. Is it as beautiful as she paints it?"

"Come see for yourself. Santa Fe's a great town. If you're interested in O'Keeffe, I know a lot of the places that she painted, and

of course Ghost Ranch. You could bring your daughter."
Teenaged, Patrick had said, and as beautiful as her mother. Travis
wondered if they'd stay with him. It took him out of the conversation for a moment. When he came back to it, she was talking
about Shake's band, which apparently had played in New York.
Wonderful music, she said. They'd been so proud of Shake.

"Wish I'd been there," said Travis, out of the loop yet again. An
old wound twanged. He settled into his recliner and took a
packet of tobacco and a Baggie of Mexican weed from a hidden
drawer built into the coffee table. Cradling the phone, he started
rolling a joint the way he liked them, half and half.

Seemed they'd done a lot of reminiscing. "In fact," Willa said,
getting down to it at last, "that's one reason I'm calling. Last night
I heard some stuff I never knew before. And it's hard to make it fit
into what I remember, what I thought I knew about us."

"What kind of stuff?" Travis asked, uneasy now, unsure where
this was heading. Some of the mix spilled out of the rolling paper
onto the coffee table. He licked a finger and blotted it up.

"Did you know Angel was pregnant when we graduated?"

"No," he said quickly, and lit the joint with hands that were
not quite steady. "But I'm not surprised."

"Why not?"

"Everyone was moving on, leaving her behind. She had to do
something. Who was the sperm donor, Patrick?"

"He says not. I thought you might have some idea."

She caught him with a lungful of smoke. "Me?" he sputtered.
"I'm the one guy who couldn't have done it."

"That's not what I meant," she said.

No, of course not—because neither Angel nor Willa would
have touched him with a ten-foot pole. Travis swallowed hard
against the resentment that churned deep inside. He didn't so
much mind about Willa, who as far as he knew hadn't given it up
to anyone except Caleb; but Angel was a whole other story. Angel
had spread her stuff all over town, yet couldn't spare a nickel's
worth for him.

But they'd forgotten, when they shut him out, that outsiders
have the best vantage point. People who are chronically overlooked must learn to turn this to their advantage, as Travis had.

Some might call it spying—Caleb and Patrick had worse names for it, the time they caught him outside Angel's house—but Travis didn't think of it that way. He subscribed to the iceberg theory of relationships: 90 percent is always invisible, subterranean. To the outward eye, Willa and Angel had been the queens of Beacon Hill, Travis the lowly court jester. But he knew things about them that they didn't know he knew, and those things gave him power; they balanced the friendships and made them tenable. Travis knew, for example, how Willa looked naked. His memory was excellent. He could shut his eyes and picture her still.

But not now. Now he needed to concentrate. Once again he'd lost the thread. Now she was talking about Tommy O'Rourke.

"Jeez," Travis said, laughing. "There's a blast from the past."

"Well?" she said. "Did they do it?"

"I thought so."

"Based on what?"

"Saw 'em together. School dance, senior year. We were all there, hanging out, goofin' on the whole school thing. He was a chaperone. They left together. Went out to the parking lot and sat in his car with the lights out."

"Doing what?"

"Talking. She seemed upset. He had his hand on her shoulder."

"You saw this?"

"I saw everything," Travis said with quiet pride. "I was the invisible man."

Her silence pleased him. It meant she was wondering what else he'd seen. He hoped she'd ask, so he could answer, mysteriously, "Plenty." But Willa, on a mission for sure, remained on track.

"Then what?" she said.

"Nothing. They went back inside."

"And this was when?"

"The winter before graduation."

"Are you sure?"

He ought to be; he'd frozen his ass off, lurking jacketless behind a parked van. "It was snowing."

"And that's it?" she said. "That's all you've got?"

Travis bristled. Who was she to question his expertise? He'd kept a fucking dossier on Angel, for Chrissake . . . and not just on

Angel. "Connect the dots. Did you know she used to go to him after school for 'extra help'? Like Angel gave a fuck about her grades."

"But wouldn't she have told us?" Willa's voice was subdued now, wondering. "Wouldn't she have bragged about it? Angel was never shy about kissing and telling."

"This was different, wasn't it? The guy could have lost his job, for one thing."

"Still," she said, "it's just the sort of thing she'd have told me."

"Evidently not," Travis said a trifle smugly. He took a deep toke and held it in. Excellent weed, this. Really first class.

18

Seven o'clock came, and still no sign of Chloe. A roasted chicken sat cooling on the kitchen table; Willa could not eat. At seven-thirty she drove to the high school and found it locked and dark. She raced home, calling Chloe's name as she opened the door, and was met with silence. The only message on the answering machine was for Chloe from her friend Lauren. So Lauren was home, and Chloe wasn't with her . . .

For a little while Willa sat huddled on the library windowseat, phone and Rolodex at hand, paralyzed by superstitious dread: If she didn't start making calls, she couldn't learn that her daughter was missing. At last, with shaking hands, she dialed Lauren's number.

Lauren's mother answered. "How *are* you, Willa?" Isabel Rapaport said warmly, but with that edge of concern Willa found so hard to tolerate. It came to her that the last time she'd seen Isabel was that day in the supermarket when Chloe had wandered off and Willa panicked. What would Isabel think of her now? But it couldn't be helped.

"Isabel, is Lauren home from rehearsal?"

"Hours ago," Isabel said. "Chloe's not back yet?"

"No, and she hasn't called. Do you happen to know how she was getting home?"

"I offered her a ride, but she said she had one."

"When was this?"

"Around five-thirty."

It was eight now. "Is Lauren there?" Willa asked.

"Hold on, I'll get her." Isabel was gone a long time. Willa heard voices in the background: Isabel's sharp and peremptory, Lauren's truculent. Then Isabel came back on the line. "Chloe left with one of the musicians, a kid named Roy Bliss. Do you know him?"

"I know who he is. What else did Lauren say?"

Isabel hesitated.

"Please," Willa said, with a catch in her voice.

"I gather they've become friends. Lauren says he was driving his mother's car. As far as she knows, Chloe intended to go straight home."

"Oh my God."

"I'm sure it's nothing," Isabel said quickly. "Just kids being kids. She'll waltz in any minute with some excuse or another."

"Yes," Willa said out of the bleakness that enveloped her.

"Willa—would you let me know when she comes in?"

She was looking up "Bliss" in the phone book when a car door slammed. Willa rushed to the front hall and wrenched the door open. Chloe stood on the threshold, the boy right behind her. Willa seized her daughter's arm and yanked her inside. "Where the hell have you been?"

Unasked, the boy followed and shut the door behind him. "I told you she'd be mad," he said.

"Jesus, Mom, take it easy."

"Where were you?"

"Out," Chloe said.

Willa slapped her. It would have been impossible to say which of them was more shocked. In her entire life, Chloe had never been struck. Willa reached for her, but she backed away, turned, and bolted upstairs.

Willa remained where she was, facing the wide-eyed boy. He took a step back, as if she might hit him, too, and spread his hands, black with grease. "It wasn't her fault. We blew a tire. I had a spare but no jack. Took forever till someone stopped."

She looked him over. Spiked hair dyed blond at the tips, three earrings in his left ear, two in his right; tattoos everywhere, no doubt. No wonder no one stopped, if there really was a flat tire. "How old are you?" she said.

"Eighteen."

"Do you know how old my daughter is? Fourteen years old. What you just did is a crime. You could go to jail."

"All I did was give her a ride."

"I *know* you've been seeing her."

"We're friends is all. I know how old she is."

She got right in his face, close enough to smell sweat and motor oil. "Maybe you think a girl without a father is easy pickings. Well, let me tell you something, Roy Bliss. She doesn't need a father, because she's got me. And if you touch one hair on her head, I will come after you and I will rip your fucking heart out and shove it down your throat. Am I making myself clear?"

She had no doubt, as she said this, that it was true, and he believed it, too; she could see that. But he didn't flinch.

"Excuse me," he said, "but I'm not the one who just smacked her."

She walked away, then came back. With an effort, she kept her hands at her side. "Where did you go? And don't you dare bullshit me. It doesn't take three hours to change a tire."

"Ask her," the boy said. "Ask your daughter."

Willa didn't go upstairs right away. First she called Isabel back, and the woman's relief very nearly undid her. She herself had felt none, had gone directly from terror to rage without passing relief. Then she went into the kitchen and nuked a plate of chicken and rice for Chloe. While it heated, she poured herself a glass of wine and drank most of it. But instead of calming down, she grew more agitated. All the fear she'd shut out before flooded her now. Impossible questions forced their way into consciousness. What would she have done if she'd lost Chloe? That one was easy: She would have died. Right away, if Chloe's death were accidental. If it weren't, Willa would have first gone after whoever did it. Either way, there would have been an interval between the time she learned of her loss and the relief of oblivion; and at the thought of that interval, bile mixed with wine rose in her throat. Willa clapped her hand to her mouth and rushed to the sink.

Afterward she felt better. The microwave had beeped some time ago. She washed her face, rinsed her mouth, then put the plate on a tray and carried it upstairs.

Chloe's door was closed. Willa listened and heard nothing. She knocked.

No reply.

Willa tried the door. It was locked. "Chloe, open up."

"Why?" Chloe's voice came from just inside the door. "So you can hit me again?"

"Don't be ridiculous."

After a moment the lock snapped open, but the door stayed shut. Willa let herself in. Chloe had retreated to her bed, where she sat cross-legged, clutching her old teddy bear to her chest. She glared at Willa through reddened eyes. "Child abuser!"

"I'm sorry I hit you," Willa said. She put the tray on Chloe's desk and sat in the swivel chair. "But you scared me to death. I thought something had happened to you; then you waltz in and mock me for worrying—"

"It wasn't my fault," Chloe wailed, torn between fury and grief. "And it sure as hell wasn't his. God, how could you?"

"That boy was totally irresponsible," Willa snapped. "So were you; but he's older."

"Way to go, Mom. Way to humiliate me in front of my friends."

"Chloe, you are not to accept rides from that boy or any other. Is that understood?"

"You don't even know him." Chloe nearly throttled her bear. "He's so nice to me and you treat him like shit!"

"He's lucky. I was one minute away from calling the cops."

"I told him not to come in, I knew how you'd be. But he insisted. He wanted to explain. Doesn't that tell you something about him?"

It did, in fact. So did his demeanor during their confrontation. But Willa wasn't about to tell Chloe that. "Explain what?" she said. "Where were you?"

"Where do you think?" Chloe said furiously. "Don't you even know what today is?"

And suddenly Willa did know, and realized with an electric jolt that she'd known all along, but had refused to acknowledge it. Today was six months to the day since Simon died. She looked at her daughter's mottled face, saw the answer to her own question, but still couldn't believe it. "You went to the cemetery?"

"Somebody had to," Chloe said. Willa buried her face in her hands. "And he offered to drive me, which is more than you ever did; and we would have been back before you even knew I was gone except for that fucking flat tire, and then he had the guts to come in with me to explain and you treat him like a fucking child molester—" Now came the tears, streams of them, choking her voice and wracking her body with fierce sobs. Willa moved to the bed and tried to hold her, but Chloe pushed her away.

"I would have taken you," Willa said. "Why didn't you ask me?"

Chloe wiped her cheeks with the back of a grimy hand. "Yeah, you would have taken me . . . and sat in the car."

It was true. It was what she'd done the other times: sat in the car, or wandered about reading the epitaphs of strangers. Great mother she was. Mother of the Year. "Sweetheart, I'm so sorry."

"You don't talk about him. You never even say his name." Chloe stared straight ahead. "If I died tomorrow, would you forget me, too?"

19

They're standing in a subway station, waiting for a train. Willa worries that they're on the wrong side of the tracks. "We have to cross over," she tells Angel, but Angel is busy flirting with some jocks in varsity jackets and doesn't answer.

The rumble of an approaching train fills the station. Headlights bounce off the opposite tunnel wall. "That's ours," calls Willa, looking back; but the platform is suddenly full of people milling about, and all she can see of Angel are occasional flashes of red hair when the crowd parts. The train shudders into view, slowing to a halt with a high-pitched squeal. "Beacon Express" says the sign on the engine. "Angel!" cries Willa, as she is forced toward the opening doors. Her own name comes back at her, faintly. She struggles, but the crowd's current sweeps her over the threshold and onto the train.

"Willa!" she hears: Angel's voice. Willa pushes toward the door, but it slides shut as she reaches it. And there is Angel, outside on the platform, staring back at her.

The train lurches into motion, and Angel begins to run alongside, crying Willa's name, until the train picks up speed and she is left behind.

Willa woke in a panic to the echo of Angel's voice. Covered with sweat, sheets dank, she cast an eye on her bedside clock. Only 3:25, but sleep, she knew, was out of the question.

The window was open and she felt the chill as soon as she threw off the comforter. She slipped into Simon's robe, curled up in the armchair beside the window, and looked out over the garden. There was no moon. The world was shades of black on black, nothing moving but the swaying treetops and the occasional silent ripple in the air that marked the passage of a bat. There was a feeling in the air of potential, though, of impending change; despite the chill (shivering, she drew the robe tighter around her), Willa could smell spring straining to break through.

Closing her eyes and resting her head against the upholstered back of the chair, Willa found herself on the far side of tired: a harshly lit landscape of massive boulders and razor-sharp shadows, the very opposite of sleep, which softens and obscures. In this place, not lit for illusion, she faced up to certain long-avoided truths. Denial, Simon had liked to say, ain't just a river in Egypt; that night, Willa reached its farthest shore and clambered out, a bit blue about the lips from long immersion, but none the worse for wear.

Voices jostled in her head.

Jovan: *People don't just disappear.*

Busky: *Long gone, and good riddance.*

Travis: *She had to do something.*

Patrick: *After twenty years, there are some questions that shouldn't be asked.*

She examined them in the light of her newfound, fragile lucidity; she also retrieved her conversation with Jovan, which Chloe's brief disappearance had thrust from her mind. It was clear that Jovan believed Angel to be dead. The moment she'd understood this, she'd rejected it, for reasons she could not share with Jovan: because if Angel was dead, who was reaching out to Willa? Who was invading her dreams, demanding her attention? She had posited some sort of telepathy, which was bad enough; her frazzled nerves could hardly be expected to accommodate an actual haunting.

But Willa had learned the hard way that what she could bear was not the guiding principle of the universe, not even a parameter. Angel had disappeared without a trace, had not been seen or heard from since the summer after high school. It was certainly possible she was dead. That Willa felt haunted by her was hardly evidence she lived; surely haunting is the provenance of the dead.

She did not believe in ghosts. If anything, Willa believed herself haunted by guilty thoughts of Angel, nothing more substantial. But even a metaphoric ghost must have an agenda. What, Willa wondered, did Angel want?

The answer was clear. The same dream in various guises, the same message repeated over and over: Angel wanted to be found.

And Willa would do it, or at least do her best; she owed Angel that. Certainly Angel seemed to think so, and Willa did not disagree. Intense friendships impose lasting obligations; if not, what continuity is there to life? She'd blamed Patrick for taking comfort in Angel's disappearance, but had she not done the same?

Angel would have to wait, though. Tonight there were other, more pressing truths for Willa to face. Like the fact that, despite a pretense of having moved on without a backward glance, Willa had made exactly zero emotional progress since the day Simon died. And the fact that she had left Chloe to mourn alone, had deserted her daughter at her time of greatest need.

What's done could not be undone, Willa knew, but what was undone could still be done. Tomorrow she would begin anew. She would continue her search for Angel, and to hell with what Patrick or anyone else thought. And she would talk to Chloe about Simon. She would say his name till she was blue in the face. She would take Chloe to the cemetery and go with her to his grave, and if she could not pray, at least she would move her lips.

It did not go quite as she planned. In the sort of novel Willa liked to read, Chloe's searing question—*Would you forget me, too?*— would have sparked a healing catharsis. Mother and daughter would have wept in each other's arms, talked till dawn, fallen asleep in the same bed, and wakened to a new understanding.

Real life is less forgiving, and so was Chloe. For days she barely spoke to her mother. Willa's efforts to initiate conversation met with blank looks and slammed doors. After a few days, she backed off, and an uneasy stalemate prevailed.

Patrick phoned. He wanted Caleb's sister's number, and Willa gave it to him. Why not? Forewarned is forearmed; she had nothing to fear from Caleb. Isabel Rapaport also kept in touch. After Simon died, Isabel had gone out of her way to help; many who owed more had done less. But Willa's gratitude had been mixed with resentment; for in those first agonizing days of shock and stunted bereavement, when every hour seemed to bring more bad news, she had felt like a patient strapped to a gurney in a teaching hospital, exposed to the probing eyes of dispassionate strangers.

None of which was Isabel's fault, and Willa could not help warming to anyone who cared so much about Chloe. Isabel called several times to chat, tactfully imparting whatever pellets she had gleaned from her daughter. It was through her Willa learned that Roy Bliss had not been frightened off by her banshee performance, but continued to hang out with Chloe at play rehearsal.

Willa reciprocated by telling Isabel what Isabel no doubt already knew: where Chloe had gone during those missing hours. The line stayed quiet when she finished.

"It was my fault," she added quickly, forestalling the judgment she was sure lurked behind the other's silence. "I should have taken her myself."

Isabel said, "You probably don't know this, but I had a child before Lauren. He died at five months. Willa, it took me two years before I could visit his grave. Don't be hard on yourself. Things happen, and we do what we have to to survive."

When Chloe came home that afternoon, Willa was in the den, sitting on the floor, surrounded by albums and packets of photos. Chloe paused in the doorway. Willa kept her eyes to herself, her voice casual. "Thought I'd make some order. Want to give me a hand?"

Reluctant but powerfully curious, Chloe inched closer. Willa nudged a red album toward her. "This one's from college. Check out your old man."

Chloe snatched it up and carried it to the couch. Willa heard the rustle of pages turning, then an indrawn breath. She knew which picture it had to be, and when she checked she was right. They were at the beach the day she took it. Simon lay on the sand, shirtless, head propped on one arm, a straw hat shading his eyes. Portrait of a beautiful young man. She sighed, and Chloe looked at her, made eye contact for the first time since their quarrel. "How did you two meet, anyway?"

"A dance," Willa said. "First big party of my freshman year." They called it the meat market; upperclassmen went to check out the freshman girls. Simon came late, with a couple of friends. She noticed him first for his looks, then for the way he worked the room, smooth as silk.

"I see where you're looking," Judy Trumpledore (dorm resident counselor, self-appointed guardian angel) murmured in her ear. "And I got one word for you. Fuhgedaboudit."

"Gay?" Willa asked, oh so sophisticated.

"Worse. A magician." Willa must have looked perplexed, because Judy rolled her eyes. "Now you see him," she explained, "now you don't."

So Willa *was* warned. Not that it mattered; she was in love with Caleb, wasn't she? Her heart was safe, immune to seduction. When Simon asked, she didn't hesitate to dance with him.

Foolish girl, scolded Willa, sage in hindsight. No one is immune to seduction who is not immune to flattery; and Willa was not that one. It had flattered her to be chosen, singled out by the most desirable senior on campus. It had flattered her to be pursued even after she turned him down. Indeed, the more she resisted, the more determined Simon grew: another danger sign, which Willa was too green to read. Men who want what they do not have often end up despising what they have. But just what is the point of learning from experience, she wondered now, when the lesson always comes too late? Simon smiled up at her, his eyes shadowed. God, what a waste. She would have shut the album on his face if it hadn't been for Chloe, gazing at her with those Oliver Twist eyes. *Please, sir, I want some more.*

That's what it was about, Willa reminded herself. Not what she herself wanted, but what Chloe needed.

"He was by far the most interesting guy there," she said. "I was amazed when he asked me to dance, and my friends were jealous. We hit it off from the start. But we didn't get together till the following year, when I was a sophomore and he was in law school."

"Why not?" Chloe asked.

"I was still seeing my high school boyfriend."

"So what happened to him?"

"Your father happened. When he wanted something, he didn't give up."

"Did he know you had a boyfriend?"

"That didn't bother him." On the contrary. Ousting her invisible but tenacious lover was half the fun for him. "And how is the elusive Caleb?" Simon would ask. "How is the absentee lover?" For her eighteenth birthday, he gave her eighteen perfect white roses. Caleb had sent nothing, not even a card. Not that she expected one; Caleb never met a tradition he didn't despise. He preferred giving unbirthday gifts, he'd told her once; but she didn't get many of those, either.

"So what did Dad do?" Chloe was beside her on the floor now, sopping up every word.

"He took a summer internship in the city and kept coming up to visit, asking me out. Meanwhile, my boyfriend stayed away and sent postcards." Her parents saw Simon as heaven-sent to take Willa off their hands at last. Four years older and decades more mature, charming and ambitious, with money of his own and a promising career, he was nothing like Caleb and everything they wanted in a son-in-law. But Willa had married to please herself, not them; it just so happened that the two coincided.

"So you dumped the high school boyfriend," Chloe said.

"I didn't *dump* him," Willa said. Their eyes met, and Willa smiled. "Well, maybe a little. He wasn't very happy."

"What was he like?"

"Caleb? Oh, he was a wild thing; he was a roller-coaster ride without seat belts."

"Do you have a picture?"

Willa sifted through the albums, searching for one in particular, a small leather-bound volume with an angel etched on the cover. "To remember me by," Angel had said when she gave it to Willa, the night before graduation. A peace offering, Willa understood at the time. An apology, not for what she'd done, which Angel considered her God-given right, but for the pain she'd caused Willa. Later, in view of Angel's prolonged absence, Willa had reinterpreted those words as a kiss-off.

Angel had filled the album with photos from their high school years. Chloe moved closer to Willa, and they looked through the album together. The first picture was of Willa and Angel standing on top of Beacon Hill, with the high school in the background. They posed for the camera, arms around each other's waists, Willa in a leotard top and wraparound skirt, Angel in skintight jeans, a man's shirt tied beneath her breasts, her impish face framed by torrents of red hair. Willa smiled, sighed.

"Let me guess," Chloe said. "The notorious Angel."

"Good guess."

"She was beautiful. Is she coming to the reunion?"

"I don't think so. We haven't been able to locate her." Willa turned the page and there were Patrick, Vinny, and Shake grinning up at her from Patrick's front yard. How young they looked! They had their shirts off and their caps on backward; their cheeks streaked with what looked like war paint but was probably motor oil; their arms around each other's shoulders. And there, behind them, was that red '57 Chevy, the god on whose altar they'd sacrificed so much of their youth.

The facing photo was a setup, a gag. Vinny, dressed in tight black jeans and a white T-shirt with the sleeve rolled up to accommodate a pack of Camels, stands before a blackboard covered with equations. He points at the board, earnestly explaining something to a student played by Jeremiah, a look of hopeless befuddlement on his face. Willa snorted, and Chloe gave her a questioning look. "Jeremiah," Willa said, pointing, "was actually class valedictorian, whereas Vinny here, well, let's just say Vinny's strengths were extracurricular."

"The persuader," Chloe remembered.

Very sharp, thought Willa, turning the page. And there was Caleb, sitting in an armchair with Willa on his lap, both of them laughing. Caleb wore a blue sweater, and Willa in a sudden flash recalled the roughness of its weave against her face, the autumnal scent of the wool mingled with Caleb's own odor, which she'd come to know as surely as a dog knows the scent of his master.

Her daughter was looking at her with newfound respect. "That's Caleb?"

"That's him."

"Wow," Chloe said.

Wow indeed, but most of what Caleb was didn't show in two dimensions. She looked more closely at the picture, which had been taken in Angel's bedroom. Willa recognized the dresser in the background and beside it, slightly ajar, the door to her closet. There was a time when she'd known the contents of that closet as well as she knew her own. She could still see it: in front, the approved clothes, the ones Angel was permitted to wear out of the house; on the sides, hidden from view, the clothes she changed into once she was out: miniskirts, slinky dresses, sheer blouses worn over a black bra. Angel was blatant about her sexuality, but she had an artist's eye for color and an exuberance that lifted her high above the nouveau-slut look of Shake's girlfriend, Nancy. Four shelves on the left wall of the closet held sweaters and jeans. Between the two middle shelves was a false bit of wall, a disguised panel that slid aside to open into the eaves. This was Angel's secret hiding place, where she concealed her treasures in a big old cookie tin with a picture of Santa on the lid. Photos of her mother, passport, love letters, mad money tithed over the course of years from every sum she earned or received. Several hundred dollars, as Willa recalled—a lot in those days.

Chloe removed the album from Willa's hands and paged through, amusing herself with sarcastic comments on Willa's friends' hippie attire. Particular mention was made of a purple paisley shirt.

"Oh, but that's Travis," Willa said. "You can't hold him against us."

"Excuse me?" Chloe cocked an eyebrow. "There was nothing inconsistent about that shirt. I saw tie-dye. I saw fringe, beads, headbands."

She went on in this vein for some time, but Willa, thinking hard, barely heard her. She was thinking about that treasure box. No matter how upset, no matter how hurried, Angel would never have run away without it. She wouldn't have left the pictures of her mother or the money she'd saved for just such an occasion.

Busky hadn't known about the box; that was the whole point of the hiding place. Apart from Willa, Angel herself, and Patrick, who built the panel for her, no one knew.

Willa wondered if the box was still there.

If it wasn't, it meant nothing. Angel might have taken it or her father found it ages ago. But what if it *was* there, money and all?

It would mean Angel never left town at all—or not of her own free will. And that, thought Willa, was a thing worth knowing.

20

A whiff of sweat in the air, lingering pheromones of adolescent funk. Willa, cooling her heels in the outer office, couldn't suppress a twinge of the anxiety peculiar to the waiting rooms of principals and dentists. Her nervousness was due in part to the dicey nature of her errand, in part to the deep familiarity of her surroundings. Many times before, she'd sat in this room, occupied this very bench, or a direct ancestor of it—hauled in for some infringement, real or imagined, sometimes alone, more often en masse. For the Beacon Hill kids were Principal Grievely's usual suspects, and proud of it.

Sometimes they were innocent; more often not. One prank in particular came back to her now: the fallout-shelter caper. Caleb's heist; he was the one who'd coveted the black-and-yellow sign for his bedroom door. Hijacking that particular sign was a serious offense in those paranoid times, and with every one of them on probation for something or other, it was foolhardy; but there was never any question of refusing Caleb. His plan, laid out with military precision, involved diversions, synchronized action on two fronts, sentries, and a purloined wrench; and it probably would have worked if it hadn't been for Travis Fleck. Standing guard at one end of the corridor with instructions to whistle in case of danger, Travis was so rattled by the unexpected sight of the principal bearing down on him that his mouth went utterly dry; and though he puckered and blew for all he was worth, nothing emerged but an arid hiss. Grievely barreled past him and turned the corner just as they were removing the final bolt.

Suspensions all around, except for Jeremiah, he whose back must always be protected. They kept him clear of school pranks: too valuable an asset, their mole in the establishment.

All that was a long time ago. It was silly to feel so nervous. She wasn't a teenager anymore; she was a woman of wealth and accomplishment. Willa smoothed her skirt over her knees. She had dressed with care for this meeting, in an Oleg Cassini suit of light gray silk, an unstructured jacket over a shell and a straight skirt. A power suit only in the sense that money is power.

It would have been better if she'd gone straight in. Waiting made her antsy, it forced her to consider what she was doing. O'Rourke should have moved on, as young teachers do; she wouldn't have chased him down. What were the odds he'd end up principal of the very school he'd started teaching in? Finding him had been the easy part; getting him to talk would be the hard. Could Patrick have been right? Maybe there *was* a statute of limitations on certain questions.

Her palms were damp. She wiped them surreptitiously on the vinyl bench cushion. Then the door to the principal's office opened, and Tom O'Rourke stepped out with his arm around another man's shoulders. He was a large man with an open, Irish face and blue eyes surrounded by laugh lines. A bit heavier now than from when she remembered him, just enough to leaven the leprechaun charm with gravitas. The big change was the age difference, which had shrunk to nothing. In high school, they'd stood on opposite sides of the kid/adult divide. Twenty years later they were contemporaries.

"Ms. Durrell?" he said. "Sorry to keep you waiting." He ushered her into his office. When Grievely had it, the room had been decorated with school pennants and sports trophies. O'Rourke had transformed the room into a cozy den that said headmaster rather than principal, with bookshelves on one wall, an antique oak desk, and leather club chairs. A picture of his family faced outward on the desk, O'Rourke with a pretty red-haired wife and identical twin boys, also redheads.

On the phone, Willa had identified herself only as a 1972 graduate of Beacon High. O'Rourke must have done some research, because he knew about her books. They chatted for a while. O'Rourke wondered, with just the right hint of diffidence, if there was any chance they might persuade her to address an assembly, perhaps even teach a workshop. It would be such a thrill for the students to meet an alumna who'd gone on to become a famous author. Hardly famous, Willa demurred, and steered the conversation back to him. When they first met, she said, he was a teacher. When had he switched from teaching to administration?

"I only taught one year," he said. "If you graduated in seventy-two, you witnessed my entire teaching career. After that year I went back for my M.A. in administration."

"Was it that brutal?" She smiled to make a joke of it.

"I enjoyed teaching," O'Rourke said, in the somewhat stilted tone of someone who knows he's talking to a writer and suspects his words may be taken down. "I just felt I could make more of a difference as an administrator."

"Do you remember any of your students?"

"A few," he said.

"Do you remember a girl named Angel Busky?"

"Vaguely," O'Rourke said. If he was struck with fear at the sound of that name, it didn't show on his broad, good-natured face.

"What do you remember about her?"

"Nice girl, but not much of a math student. Now I suppose you're going to tell me she grew up to be a CPA."

"I don't know what she grew up to be," Willa said. "I'm not even sure she grew up." As concisely as she could, she told him about the reunion, her search for Angel, and Angel's very thorough disappearance. The principal listened without comment till she was through. Then, glancing just perceptibly at his watch, he said, "I see; but why come to me? How can I help?"

"I thought possibly she'd stayed in touch."

"With *me*?" he said, answering the question by the tone in which he asked it.

"Did Angel ever confide in you?" Willa asked. "Ever tell you her troubles, ask for advice?"

"If she did, it's hardly likely I'd remember." He watered this with a thin smile. "Maybe you should try her family. There was a father, I believe."

His memory was improving by the minute, Willa noticed. "If Angel was in trouble, her father's the last person she'd go to."

"I'm sorry to hear that, but I have to ask again: Why come to me?"

"Angel and I were very close. She used to tell me everything. For example, did you know she had a huge crush on you?" She smiled as she said it, one adult to another, laughing over the follies of youth.

O'Rourke didn't smile back. A pulse beat in his forehead. "No," he said.

"Huge. She told me she wasn't going to leave school without doing something about it."

"You must have been a gullible child."

"It just seemed to me that if she were in trouble, she'd turn to an adult. A trusted teacher, maybe."

"What kind of trouble, Willa?" The shift to her first name not at all the friendly gesture it seemed, but rather a reminder of their former relationship: O'Rourke trying to reestablish boundaries.

She didn't answer at once. The silence seemed to disturb him. He glanced again at his watch, more openly this time, and pushed his chair back, preparatory to standing.

"She was pregnant," Willa said. Nothing but a hard stare from O'Rourke. "Did you know that?"

"How would I?" he said.

"She didn't tell you?"

Patches of color appeared in his face. He rose abruptly, and Willa drew back at his approach; but he kept going till he reached the window. Straight as a ruler he stood, hands clasped behind his back, gazing out at the football field.

"You imply some sort of relationship," he said to the window. "You say she was pregnant. Then you ask if she came to me about it." He pivoted to face her, eyes blazing with anger. "I'm not an idiot, Ms. Durrell, but I'm beginning to think you are."

"I made no accusation," she said.

"You implied one. How dare you? A man in my position can be as easily damaged by groundless speculation as by fact. I would hate for you to make the mistake of airing your speculations, whatever they are, outside this office."

"Why are my questions so threatening to you?"

"Not threatening; insulting!"

"I'm concerned about Angel. I think something may have happened to her, and I hoped you could help me find out. There was nothing adversarial in my approach to you."

But O'Rourke, hardly mollified, stared down at Willa as if she were something nasty he'd found under a microscope. "Maybe she doesn't want to be found; have you considered that possibility?"

"No."

"You should," he said. "It's not always wise to meddle in other people's lives."

* * *

"Was he threatening me?" Willa asked. Thirty yards away, in the dense undergrowth beyond the fence, a dark form moved like a shadow, low to the ground. There was a flash of sleek gray muzzle and a glint of yellow eyes, gone before she could point them out.

"Vice versa, I'd say," Jovan said. Then both of them froze as the wolf emerged into full view. It was a female, clearly pregnant. She raised her muzzle to the thin gray Bronx sky and sniffed deeply.

"Isn't she beautiful," Willa murmured. "All the years I've been coming here, I've never seen one come out in the open like this. They're always so shy."

"Do you come here often?"

"I do. We're members, and it's not far, you know. I use it as a getaway." They were whispering, watching the wolf instead of each other. His hand beside hers on the railing, shoulders almost touching. Why had she asked him here?

To see if he would come.

And to talk about Angel. Not that Jovan had much to say about Willa's conversation with O'Rourke. He hadn't liked it, though; she could read that much in his hawkish face.

The wolf evaporated, disappearing into the brush as suddenly as she had come. Willa turned to Jovan and caught him looking at her. "Want to see the gorillas?"

He smiled. "I'm dying to see the gorillas."

Along the way they stopped for lemonade. It was a sultry sort of day for May. He wore suit pants, a white shirt, a striped tie loosened at the throat. Willa wasn't dressed for the zoo either, having come straight from her meeting with O'Rourke. They sat on a shady bench to drink. Families strolled by, fathers with children on their shoulders, couples poring over zoo maps. Two little boys careened by. The smaller stumbled over Jovan's outstretched legs and would have fallen hard, but with a movement so quick Willa never saw it, Jovan reached out and caught him. "Easy there, big guy," he said as he set the boy on his feet. The boy gaped for a moment before tearing off after his brother.

"So," Willa said, "you didn't think O'Rourke's reaction was telling?"

"Only thing it tells me is he doesn't like being accused of impregnating students." Jovan squinted against the sun. "Probably could have figured that out ourselves."

She sighed. "Patrick told me not to do it."

"He was right."

"You think I should quit, don't you?"

"Well," he said, "there *is* a point of diminishing returns. What I'm wondering is why. Why invest so much energy looking back, just when you should be moving forward?"

"I want to move on," she said. "But I can't. I'm like an animal with its leg in a trap."

"What's the trap?"

Willa looked away from him. "It's Angel. She's been haunting me."

He didn't seem surprised. Maybe he knew a thing or two about being haunted. Or maybe he was just used to dealing with crazy people.

They finished their drinks and strolled on to the great apes' enclosure, where they stood for some time without speaking. Two female gorillas sat back to back, one of them nursing a tiny baby. Youngsters chased each other around a cement tree trunk and swung from braided, vine-colored ropes. A large silverback sunned himself on a flat rock as he watched over them all. The gorillas were fully involved with one another, oblivious to the crowd. They had always been Willa's favorites; she never went to the zoo without visiting them, and over the years had come to know them as individuals. They seemed so human in so many ways, and where they differed it was for the better. All peace, tranquility, and harmony seemed to her on their side of the fence, all ambition and cruelty on hers.

"My wife used to like it here, too," Jovan said. "The elephants were her favorites."

"What happened to your wife, if you don't mind my asking?"

"Breast cancer," he said. "But it took four years, and most of that time was good."

"Is that why you left the police?"

He nodded. "Once she got sick, I couldn't do the hours anymore. And afterward . . . as a single parent, I didn't see my way clear to going back."

"I'm sorry," she said.

"Life goes on."

"Or should."

He smiled behind his eyes. "Don't gnaw that leg off just yet."

They were high above the zoo now, riding the sky tram back toward the parking lot on the opposite side of the park. Far below them were the plains of Africa, rolling hills dotted with the feathery tips of acacias. Willa slipped off her heels and surreptitiously massaged her aching calves, though not so surreptitiously that Jovan failed to notice. He sat beside, not opposite, her, though they had the gondola to themselves. His hands were on the railing, and Willa found herself studying them. Half again the size of hers, nicked and scarred, ridged with sinew and vein, they were working hands, latent fists, a mix of weapon and tool. He'd fought with those hands, nursed a dying woman, plucked a child from midair and set him down so gently his hair didn't even ruffle. An image pushed into her mind, of those hands touching her, holding her; and though she thrust it away at once, it left its mark in reddened cheeks.

She was sure he'd noticed. He was a noticing sort of man. "About Angel," she said, lest anyone forget why they were there. "I've been thinking. There's a way to determine once and for all if she ran away by choice." Willa told him about Angel's treasure box, and her plan to look for it.

"Wait a minute," he said. "Hold on."

"I'm sure I can get in."

"I'm sure, too. But can you get out?"

"Oh, really," she said, laughing, "do you think I'm afraid of that old man?"

"I know you're not," he said. "That's what worries me." Then, with no particular emphasis, but merely as if it were next on a list of things to do, he bent over and kissed Willa on the lips. His mouth felt hard and strange against her own. There was no supplication to it, no softness. He kissed the way a thirsty man drank; and when he was done, he stopped.

She stared at him. There was hunger in his eyes, desire of a different magnitude from Patrick's peevish lust. Something stirred inside her, something fierce and unexpected. Struck with a fear of falling that had nothing to do with height, Willa turned her face away.

"Did you hate it?" Jovan asked. "Should I leave?"

She glanced at the ground, sixty feet below. "Let's not go over-board."

"I keep telling myself," he said. "I just don't listen."

21

In the yard the weeds were flowering, dandelion spores wafting like snowflakes on the summery breeze. The screen door was still locked, the doorbell still broken. Willa pounded on the aluminum frame until her knuckles hurt, then switched to her left hand. "Mr. Busky," she shouted. "It's Willa. Come to the door, please, Mr. Busky!" Embarrassment drove her on, Jovan waiting in a van just around the corner, hearing everything. How could she slink back now, tail between her legs, after resisting all his efforts to dissuade her? "Mr. Busky! I know you're in there." Doors up and down the street opened to her bellowing, yet his remained stubbornly shut. Finally Willa spied a gray face peering at her through the grimy panes of the kitchen window. She took the bottle of Johnny Walker from its sheath and held it up. The face withdrew. A moment later, the door opened.

It was cold in the house, despite the warmth outside. They sat at the kitchen table, Busky in sweatpants and a T-shirt that had once been white. He was barefoot, and his toenails were long and yellow, thick as turtle shells. He cleared a chair for her by placing a stack of *Penthouse*s under the table. Every surface in sight, and most of the floor, was covered with papers: newspapers, magazines, advertising flyers, junk mail, paper and plastic bags, flattened beer cartons, pizza boxes with bits of desiccated cheese still adhering to the covers. Like Busky's wasteland of a yard, the house's interior testified to years of dedicated neglect. Half the cabinets were missing doors, the stove had only one knob, and the table listed on three legs and a stump. The stench of mold and rot and mice was benign compared to the reek of the man himself, which would have emptied a subway car in rush hour.

The dimness of the kitchen, whose windows were all but obscured by stacks of refuse, and the general grayness of the man himself gave Willa the odd sense of having stepped into a black-and-white movie. Busky poured shots of scotch into two grimy tumblers and slid one across the table to Willa. "*Salut*," he said, raising his.

"*Salut*," she replied. He downed his drink in a single gulp and refilled the glass. Willa faked a sip. She would rather have dined on ground glass than eaten or drunk in this house.

"Where's your bodyguard?"

"Who?" she said warily.

"That shit Mulhaven."

"Patrick didn't come. It's just me." And Jovan, in a van just around the corner, at the other end of the transmitter taped to her stomach.

"Good," Busky said, his voice hoarse with disuse. "Guy's a bum. Always was, always will be."

"Why do you say that?"

"All those kids. Bums."

"Actually," she said, "those bums didn't turn out half bad."

Busky sniffed. "I remember you, too. Used to come slumming around in your torn jeans and hundred-dollar boots. 'Stick to your own kind,' I told her. 'What's her to you or you to her?' Like she ever listened." Busky took another long swallow and smacked his lips. From the debris on the table he unearthed a pack of Camels and a lighter shaped like a naked woman. As he inhaled, a fit of coughing seized him. He quieted it with some scotch.

"You said she was dead," Willa said. "Is that true?"

He squinted at her through pale, watery eyes. Smoke from his cigarette spiraled between them. "What's it to you?"

"I've been trying to find her."

"You! Cops tried, didn't find shit. You?" He let out a rheumy laugh.

Willa looked away. There was an uncovered pot of soup congealing on the stove. Something moved in the sink. *What am I doing?* she thought. *This is nuts.* But Angel's room was right above her head. She couldn't get this close without having a look.

"Have some more," she said, sliding the bottle toward him.

He filled the tumbler to the top. "Don't mind if I do. Very nice a you. Very nice."

"What happened the day she went away? What do you remember?"

"She smashed my car! Seven hunnert bucks to fix and afterwards it runs like shit."

"Before that," Willa said.

"Nothin'. Regular day. Went to work, came home, ate dinner."

"She was home?"

"I said I ate dinner, didn't I? Think it cooked itself?" Busky wheezed out a laugh. His breath smelled like a nest of mice had died in his gullet. Willa concentrated on breathing through her mouth.

"Then what?" she said.

"Stole my keys. I heard the car start. I get to the door, she's gone." He composed his features in a mournful look. "Last time I saw my little girl."

His little girl. Bile rose in her throat. She swallowed hard. "When was this?"

"Dunno. Nine, ten o'clock. Didn't come home till three in the morning, and me up worrying about my car."

Willa stared. "She came *back*? Why?"

"Packed a bag with clothes and stuff."

"You saw her?"

"Nah," he said. "Heard 'em upstairs. They was trying to be quiet but I heard the footsteps."

"They?"

"She had someone with her. Little tramp."

"Who?"

Busky shrugged. "They locked the door. Time I found my screwdriver and got back up, they was gone. Out the fucking window."

"You saw them go?"

He shook his head. The movement set off another fit of coughing. Busky heaved himself out of his chair and hacked his way out of the kitchen, heading toward the bathroom. Willa was up in a flash. She emptied her drink into the sink, then unbolted the front and screen doors, which Busky had locked behind her. "He went to the bathroom," she murmured. "I've unlocked the doors, but stay out. I'm fine."

A toilet flushed. Willa didn't think Busky would spend much time washing his hands. She was back in her seat when he returned, his walk unsteady now, the drink catching up with him. "Gotta eat," he said, veering toward the refrigerator. Willa averted her eyes. "Want something?"

About as much as she wanted breast cancer. "No thanks."

He wove back to the table, carrying a brick of American cheese and a small, serrated knife. "It's good stuff. Very healthy food, cheese."

"I just ate. Mr. Busky, do you know why Angel ran away?"

The old man placed the cheese directly onto the filthy table and sawed at it with the knife. "Stole my car, didn't she? Crashed it. Think she'd come home after that?"

"But why steal the car? Why go at all? Did something happen that day?"

A quick, sly glance then: Busky wondering what she knew. Maybe not so drunk after all. "Like what?" he said.

"Was Angel in some kind of trouble?"

"Angel was always in trouble. Trouble's what that girl lived for."

"Was she pregnant?"

Silence. Busky sawed away at the cheese, which seemed to have a rocklike consistency. Willa waited.

"Think she'd tell me if she was?" he said at last.

No, she wouldn't. But you knew all the same.

He could hear her heart pounding 100 yards away. Between that, the rasp of her clothes, and the old man's cough, Jovan had to strain to make out their conversation. Still, he heard enough to know she was pushing her luck. The woman had guts, all right, but no common sense. He had pointed this out at the zoo, every way he could think of. She'd smiled and nodded, didn't say a word.

"You're going anyway, aren't you?" he said at last.

She smiled and nodded.

So he'd tagged along. Someone had to watch her back. Blanca thought he was nuts and didn't scruple to say so. An avid reader of society news and the *Post*'s Page Six, she knew exactly who Willa Scott Durrell was. "Look at you, trotting after her like a little puppy," she'd said that morning as he left the office. "What you gonna do with a woman like that, take her bowling?"

"She's a client," he said.

"Uh-huh. So how come I ain't never billed this client?"

"Funny," he said, "I don't remember asking your opinion."

Blanca raised her alarming eyebrows, plucked to resemble

chalet roofs, and said, "For what you pay me, baby, you'll take my opinions and thank me for them!"

Jovan didn't bowl, but he got her point. It wasn't about money as much as class. Jovan made a good living, but he made it working for the men who women like Willa belonged to. Didn't need Blanca to tell him that. He'd figured his chances with Willa at slim to none . . . until he kissed her. She hadn't exactly kissed him back. But she hadn't slapped him, either, or tossed him overboard.

As the level of whiskey in the bottle sank, Busky progressed seamlessly from bellicose to maudlin. Now they were looking at pictures in a musty album. There was Angel in a wading pool with her mother, Angel petting a puppy, Angel at the beach, perched on the shoulders of a vigorous young man unrecognizable in the wreckage before Willa. Busky sighed damply. "Pretty little thing she was. Good, too, till those bums came buzzing around. They used her and abused her, my poor little girl." He seemed to like the sound of that, for he repeated it mournfully: "Used her and abused her."

"And you never heard from her after she left home?" Willa was just biding time, waiting for her chance to sneak upstairs. She knew the answer, or thought she did. Busky's response was unexpected.

His head jerked up, and his bleary eyes plucked at her face. He wanted to talk, she saw; this man who spoke to no one had things he needed to say. Willa channeled all the pity she could muster into her answering gaze.

He lit a cigarette and stared at the glowing tip. "Sometimes I hear her. Up in her room, late at night when I can't sleep. I hear her walking." Then, in a voice so low Willa feared Jovan would miss it: "Sometimes I hear her cry."

"You hear her walking?" Willa said.

"But I ain't never seen her," Busky said, and crossed himself. "Thank God I ain't never seen her."

She refilled his glass. Busky's hand brushed hers as he took it, and she shrank from his touch. He tilted back his head and gulped the drink like water. Then he dropped his chin to his chest and shut his eyes. A moment later, he was snoring.

Willa rose and plucked the lit cigarette from his yellow fingers and snubbed it out. It was a miracle, if miracles could be unfortunate, he hadn't burned the house down long ago. She moved toward the living room, cautiously at first, then with more confidence as Busky failed to rouse.

The living room was as cluttered as the kitchen. There was a newish color TV against the stairwell where the old black and white had stood; otherwise, nothing had changed. Willa wove through stacks of debris to the uncarpeted stairs that led to Angel's room. The steps were covered with bags of empty tin cans and beer bottles. Anyone attempting to negotiate these steps in the dark or in a hurry would make an unholy racket. Perhaps that was the idea.

Willa had to move things aside. If only she'd thought to bring gloves. Jovan would be wondering what was going on, but she didn't dare speak with Busky in the next room. She used the toe of her sneaker to nudge the bags aside just enough to squeeze by.

The higher she climbed, the more frightened she grew. She didn't want to believe Busky's lurid tale of bumps in the night. He was a drunk and quite possibly a madman, consumed by alcohol, loneliness, and guilt. Yet his story had rung true, and his face as he told it had been that of a man trapped in a waking nightmare.

She reached the landing at the top of the staircase. Angel's door was shut. Willa reached for the knob; then her hand fell to her side. Did she really need to do this? She already knew, if Busky didn't, why Angel had come back that night, and it wasn't for her clothes. The box would be gone or empty.

But she couldn't turn away now. She owed it to Angel to see for herself. Willa took a deep breath and opened the door.

Light streamed through the curtainless windows. The room's furnishings had not been touched. There was Angel's bed, sheeted with cobwebs. Her desk, her chair, her Janis Joplin poster on the wall, faded to a ghostly pallor. Willa wondered about Angel's clothes: Had they, too, been left to rot? She glanced at the closet, but the door was shut.

"I'm in her room," she said aloud. "He passed out downstairs." She could almost feel Jovan's relief. Her own was no less, for Angel's room was unaccountably free of the noxious odor down-

stairs. Willa inhaled deeply and caught the faint scent of sandalwood incense. A trick of memory, surely; as kids they used to
burn sandalwood to cover up the smell of pot. But it was obvious
from the cobwebs and the inch-deep layer of dust on every surface that no one had entered this room in ages.

Willa went to the window, cleared a patch of glass with her
handkerchief, and peered outside. A bunch of kids were shooting
hoops in the street, and their catcalls and laughter floated
upward. Someone in a house nearby was playing the drums. Just
out of sight, an ice-cream truck tinkled its honky-tonk tune, a
melody plucked straight from childhood. With her back to the
room, Willa felt transposed. She had a vision of Angel sitting on
her bed, painting her toenails, a joint dangling from her lips. A
memory; and yet the mingled scent of pot and nail polish filled
the room.

Willa spun around. The room was empty, of course. But the
closet door stood wide open.

Outside, in the van, Jovan heard Willa cry out, then a full minute
of nothing but short, choppy breaths. "Talk to me," he groaned,
running his hand through the stubble of his hair. "What's happening?" His hand was on the van's back latch when her breathy
voice stopped him.

"The closet door was closed. Now it's open. I didn't touch it.
God, that's freaky."

Should he go? Did she want him? Clever girl, unlocking the
front door; he could be with her in thirty seconds. But she'd for-
bidden him to enter unless called for.

"Stay there," she said. "I'm okay. I'm okay." But along with her
voice came her pounding heart, that fearful panting. It was like
being inside her.

"I can do this," she said, more to herself than to him.

"Don't," he wanted to shout. "Just leave. Get out!" But she
couldn't hear him, and wouldn't have heeded him if she could.

Someone had gone through Angel's closet. The hangers in the
front were empty. But the packing must have been done in haste,
for the back of the closet still contained the moldy remnants of

her secret wardrobe: the tight sheaths, miniskirts, and sheer blouses. Why leave those behind, Willa wondered, and take her school clothes? She stood just outside the closet, stalling. To reach Angel's hiding place, she would have to kneel down with her back to the room.

The closet door must have been off the latch, she reasoned, and her walking across the bare boards of the floor had jarred it open. It wasn't much of an explanation, but it would have to do. Still, she couldn't quite bring herself to kneel in that closet with her back to the room. Anyone could come up on her, Busky or . . . anyone. On one point at least, Willa found herself in agreement with that miserable old man. She didn't want to turn around and see Angel in this room.

The sooner you do it, the sooner you're out of here. She took a small flashlight from her purse and stepped into the closet. The shelves along the left wall had not been emptied out. Along with stacks of moth-eaten sweaters, there were boxes of photos, contact sheets, and photography gear. On the bottom shelf, Willa found Angel's Canon. A deep sadness came over her then, for she knew Angel would never have forgotten it. Gently she brushed the cobwebs off the old camera. There was still film inside, only seven pictures taken. Slipping her hand through the strap, Willa raised it to her eyes. As she peered through the viewfinder, the closet disappeared, and in its place came a vision of Angel, alive and beautiful, bursting out of her red flamenco dress as she rose, laughing, from her throne on the boulders of Beacon Hill. *Look at you!* she cries, holding out her arms, enfolding Willa in her fiery embrace. *Look at us!*

The camera slipped from Willa's grasp and caught at the end of the strap. She was back in the closet, and Angel was gone. Sweat was streaming down her ribs and between her breasts, so that she feared for the microphone. "I'm okay," she said. "Found her camera." She hunkered down and shined her light on the back of the bottom shelf.

Her view was obscured by cobwebs. Willa wrapped her handkerchief around her hand—damn her for forgetting gloves!—and cleared them away. The panel was hard to distinguish, the same noncolor as the wall, but when she touched it, it gave way and slid aside with little resistance. The old tin was in plain sight. Suspicious rustlings came from deeper in the eaves. Willa banged on the wall before reaching in. Holding her breath, she gripped the tin and pulled it out.

It was filthy, covered with mouse droppings and dead insects, but she could still see the faint picture of Santa and his elves on the lid. "It's here," she said, for Jovan's sake. "Her treasure box. I'm opening it now."

Easier said than done. She used her handkerchief again—after this she would throw it away. The rusty lid stuck, then gave way so suddenly that Willa rocked back on her heels.

The tin was full. On top was a photo, remarkably well preserved, that Willa knew well. It was Angel's favorite picture of her mother, taken long before her marriage, on the boardwalk at Coney Island. Though the photo was black and white, you could tell Angel's mother was a redhead, with the same impish smile as her daughter. Beneath the picture was Angel's passport, and under that a thick wallet. Willa, awkwardly balancing the flashlight on her knees, riffled through the money: maybe $300 in fives and tens.

"It's all here," she told Jovan. "Passport, photos, money. I'm putting it back." This by his instructions. She covered the tin, pushed it back in the hidden compartment, and slid the panel shut. But the camera she slipped into her purse.

She stood, wiping her hands on her jeans. As she stepped out of the closet, her eye fell upon a figure standing very still beside the bedroom door.

22

She shrieked. But it was only Busky.

"What the fuck," he said, and shut the door behind him.

"Sorry, Mr. Busky. I just had this impulse to see her room again. I'll go now."

"You'll go when I say you go." He took a step toward her and she noticed he was holding the sharp little knife in his hand. "You want a tour?" he said. "I'll give you a tour."

Willa held her ground. She had no choice; Busky stood between her and the door, and behind her was Angel's bed, with its cobwebs and rotting linen.

"Maybe you want something else," Busky said. He gave her an up-and-down look that in any other man she'd have called a leer; but to call it that in his case was to imply that the two of them existed in the same sexual universe, which Willa was quite certain they did not.

"I wanted to see her room," she said firmly. "And to find out what happened to her."

"You know what happened to her."

"No, but I think you do, and I believe it's eating at you. Why don't you tell me?"

Busky glared. "You come into my house, you invade my privacy; then you talk to me like that?"

She took a few steps toward the door. Busky moved to block her, and this time the knife came up. Willa shifted her weight to the balls of her feet and gripped her purse, heavy with the weight of flashlight and camera added to the usual paraphernalia. If he grabbed her she would bash him, but she hoped she didn't have to; it would be a shame to break Angel's camera. Then she thought of Jovan, listening in the van.

"What's the knife for, Mr. Busky?"

He bared his brown teeth. "Cheese."

"Is that what happened to Angel?" she said. "Did you take a knife to her, too?"

"Never touched her. Not me."

"Be careful what you say up here, Mr. Busky, because I think she hears every word," Willa said. "I mean, ask yourself: Are we really alone?"

The blood drained from his face, leaving his flesh the color
and consistency of day-old oatmeal. His pale eyes darted about
the room. She'd meant to scare him but wound up spooking herself as well. The scent of sandalwood was more pronounced now,
drowning out even Busky's smell. *Were* they alone?

Downstairs the front door banged, followed, a moment later,
by racing footsteps on the stairs.

"If I'd needed rescuing I'd have said so. You didn't have to come
bursting in like that."

"You mentioned a knife. Did you think I'd wait for gurgling
sounds?" Jovan was patient; he knew it was nerves talking. She'd
been shaking when he brought her out, covered with filth, cobwebs in her hair. First thing she wanted, understandably, was to
wash, so he stopped at the nearest diner. She spent fifteen minutes in the ladies' room. Jovan was about to go check on her
when she came out, hair damp, face and hands scrubbed raw. He
had coffee waiting, covered with a saucer. As she passed, she
dropped the transmitter in his lap, then sat across from him. Still
playing it cool; but the cup shook in her hands.

"Could you believe that house?" she said. "Have you ever seen
anything like it?"

He had, back when he was a cop. Dysfunctional people had
been their stock in trade. But he wasn't about to swap war stories. "Place stinks. I don't know how you stood it so long. You
were in there forever."

"I can still smell it. It's in my clothes, my hair, all over me."

A quaver in her voice told him she was near the edge. He
wanted badly to put his arms around her and hold her till she
stopped shaking. Luckily, maybe, the table was between them.
"Drink your coffee and I'll take you home."

"Not home. Jovan, we have to go to the cops."

God help him, it gave him pleasure just to see her lips shape
his name. "And tell them what?" he said.

"That Angel never left here of her own accord. That her own
father murdered her."

"We don't know that."

"He lied. He said she came back for her stuff in the middle of the night. But why would she take a bunch of clothes she hated and leave her valuables behind?"

"Doesn't prove he killed her."

"He'd found out she was pregnant."

"I didn't hear that," Jovan said.

"I saw his face. Believe me, he knew."

She was right about one thing, he thought. It was time to hand this one over. Angel's disappearance did not in itself constitute compelling evidence of foul play, but Willa's discovery of her hidden treasures tipped the balance. He'd take it to his old pal Harry Meyerhoff, formerly of the NYPD homicide task force, now head of Westchester's cold-case squad. Harry would take it on, if for no other reason than that Jovan asked him to. Willa didn't know that, though, and Jovan wasn't about to tell her before exacting some concessions.

"You realize that once the police get involved, it's out of your hands. No more interviews, no more Nancy Drew theatrics. You'll have to back off and let them do their job, whatever that entails."

"Fine by me," she said. "I've about had my fill."

"And don't expect them to keep you informed, because they won't. With these guys, the information flows one way."

"Just tell them they've got to go in right away and search the house. Busky saw me come out of the closet. If he finds Angel's treasure box, it's history."

"See," he said, "this is just what I'm talking about. If the police agree to take this case, they're going to run it how they see fit, and they won't account to either of us."

Willa looked at her purse and hesitated. Jovan noticed and said warningly, "It's all or nothing with these guys. No holding back."

"I took her camera. There's film inside, some undeveloped pictures."

Jovan thought fast. Theft, technically, but no DA would ever charge her; they'd be only too grateful for the evidence, if it turned out to be useful. She'd done it on her own, no police involvement, so that was okay. "Good," he said. "You can give it to me; I'll hand it over."

"Can't we develop the pictures first?" she asked.

Jovan just looked at her.

"Okay, okay," she said. "Who will you take it to?"

"A detective I know, guy named Harry Meyerhoff. Should be right up his alley. I'll give him a call."

"Shouldn't we see him together?"

And have her tell Meyerhoff that she was haunted by Angel? Jovan knew how that would go over. Meyerhoff was your basic bread-and-potatoes, just-the-facts-ma'am kind of detective, more dogged than imaginative, which was fine with Jovan; give him tenacity over brilliance any day for getting things done.

"Better let me set it up," he said, braced for an argument, but Willa just nodded. She looked exhausted, drained for once of the combativeness that held her erect. Later, in the van, she rested her head against the door and shut her eyes. Lean on me, he wanted to say. But a snide voice, not unlike Blanca's, jangled in his head: *What next, fool? You gonna ask her to the prom?*

Her breathing slowed and deepened, her clenched hands fell open on her lap. Jovan glanced over. For all her scrubbing, she'd missed a smudge of dirt on the side of her nose.

He kept his hands on the wheel.

23

"Give me a break," Harry Meyerhoff said on the phone. "Rae hears we did lunch and she wasn't included, I am dog meat. You want me sleeping on the couch, with my back?"

Jovan didn't ask how she would find out; he knew Meyerhoff had no secrets from his wife. Most detectives Jovan knew didn't tell their wives anything; but then, most of them were divorced. Harry and Rae Meyerhoff had been together for twenty-six years, and the marriage, as far as Jovan could tell, was still going strong.

So a lunch invitation from Jovan became a dinner invitation from Meyerhoff, and at the appointed hour Jovan found himself standing on the porch of the Meyerhoffs' modest colonial in Yonkers, holding a cake box in one hand and a thin buff file in the other. He rang the bell, not without trepidation. Rae Meyerhoff had been a great friend of Katie's, but that hadn't stopped her, in the years since Katie's death, from ambushing Jovan with a series of unattached females.

The door flew open and Rae greeted him with a hug. As she ushered him into the central hall, Jovan had a quick look around.

"Don't worry," said Rae. "Harry said it was business, which I hope means you're taking him up on his offer."

"Do I get dinner either way?" Jovan asked. The house smelled of roast chicken.

"What do you think?" She hooked her arm in his and marched him through the dining room and into the kitchen, where Meyerhoff, a flowered apron tied around his thick waist, looked up from stirring a pot. "Well, well, look what the cat dragged in."

"Jovan thought we were setting him up again," Rae said.

"Not 'we,'" said her husband, "you." Then, to Jovan: "She would've, too, if I hadn't called her off. What is it with women that they can't stand the sight of a single man?"

"Myra happens to be a lovely woman," Rae said. "Thirty-six, divorced, through no fault of her own, believe me; I know the husband, and she's a saint for putting up with him as long as she did. Smart, pretty, funny. Jewish, but that doesn't matter, does it, Jovan? Your first marriage was mixed."

"What are you talking about, woman?" Meyerhoff said. "Katie was as Catholic as he is."

She rolled her eyes. "Italian and Irish, which in my opinion is more of a stretch than Italian and Jewish."

Over dinner they talked about the kids—the Meyerhoffs had two, one married, the other in college—and mutual friends. Afterward Meyerhoff led Jovan to his den, offering a pretext of privacy they both knew would be violated the moment the front door closed behind him.

When Jovan first realized how much Meyerhoff told his wife about police business, he was shocked. Old cases were one thing, current cases another. On current cases, the need-to-know culture of secrecy among detectives was so strong that many had trouble confiding in their superiors, let alone their wives. And it wasn't as if Rae were even on the job; she was an English teacher.

But the one time they'd discussed it, back when Katie was still alive and Jovan still on the force, Meyerhoff had claimed that talking with Rae was as safe as talking to himself. "Don't get me wrong, the woman is a major yenta. But when it comes to my business, you couldn't pry her mouth open with a crowbar."

"Security aside," Jovan had said, "the kind of shit we see on the job, I wouldn't want to bring that home with me."

"You want your home to be a sanctuary, a tropical isle in a sea of chaos."

"Anything wrong with that?"

"No, except it means that you and your wife are living in separate worlds. She's cracking coconuts, you're cracking heads. Me, I go home, I tell my wife everything she wants to know and then some. Helps me blow off steam, and keeps us living in the same world."

Whatever gets you through the night, Jovan had figured, which still seemed about right. Now Meyerhoff, seated in an ersatz leather club chair, held out a box of cigars; Jovan took one and sniffed it.

"So what's up, my brother?" Meyerhoff said. "You come to your senses yet?"

"Never left 'em, Harry. I like what I do."

"The offer still stands, you know. It's a great gig. No squealers, no night shifts, and if you think busting some jerk with the blood still wet on his hands was sweet, wait till you start nailing the ones who think they got away. Not to mention benefits, pension, a paycheck every week."

Jovan leaned forward, accepting a light. "Cold-case squad still not up to speed?"

"Did I say that?"

Jovan waited, puffing on the cigar.

Meyerhoff sighed. "You know how it is. Looking over other cops' cases, checking their work—some guys just aren't up for it."

"Shades of the rat squad?"

"Which is bullshit, you realize. It's not about busting cops' balls, it's about technology we have now that they didn't have then. But I can see you haven't come to lighten my load."

"Afraid not," Jovan said. "In fact, I'm hoping to add to it."

Patrick was sound asleep when the phone rang. He fumbled for the receiver. "Hullo?"

"Patrick?" A man's voice; someone he knew, or had known.

"Yeah?"

"It's Caleb."

"Caleb, Jesus." Patrick squinted at his bedside clock. The fluorescent display showed 1:30, but suddenly he was wide awake, more awake than he'd been in a long time. "I can't believe it."

"Heard you've been looking for me."

"Hell yeah. You're not an easy man to track down."

"You managed."

"Took us a while, but we finally remembered the name of the guy your sister married. What can I say? The old gray cells ain't what they used to be."

"Not what I hear. There's a bizarre story going around about you being a professor at Columbia."

"NYU, actually; otherwise, strange but true."

"Good for you, buddy. Good for you."

This was said with such warmth that a part of Patrick melted . . . the part, perhaps, that had frozen when Caleb turned his back.

"So what are you up to?" he asked. "Where've you been?"

"This and that," said Caleb. "Here and there."

Typical Caleb answer. Patrick had to smile. "You realize what month this is," he said.

Static on the line, white noise. He could be anywhere. "May," Caleb said at last, cautiously.

"Next month it'll be twenty years from graduation."

"Fuck me. That's really happening?"

"So you remember."

"I remember everything," Caleb said simply, and there was a long silence, which Patrick broke.

"So yeah, it's happening, last weekend in June. Willa's invited everyone to stay at her place in Chappaqua."

"Didn't we say we'd meet on Beacon Hill?"

"We'll make a pilgrimage. Believe me, Willa's house is way more comfortable."

"How is she?" Caleb asked.

"All grown up. Beautiful as ever. Widowed."

"How's she handling that?" No surprise in his voice; he'd known this.

"Stiff upper lip," Patrick said, a bit stiff himself. "You know Willa." He had dangled her name as bait in his message to Caleb, so why should he object when the fish bit? But he found that he did.

"Not really," Caleb said. "Not anymore."

"People don't change much."

"I do," he said. "I change all the time." At least, that's what Patrick thought he said. The static on the line made it difficult to hear. "Who else is coming?"

"Everyone," Patrick said. "Almost everyone. Willa, me, Shake and Nancy, Vinny. Travis is coming all the way from Santa Fe, and Jeremiah from Washington. And now you."

"Can't make any promises," Caleb said, but he took Willa's number and address.

They talked for a while more, Caleb asking lots of questions but answering few, Patrick filling him in on their friends' lives and whereabouts; but not once in the course of their long conversation did either of them mention Angel.

24

Willa was writing again. This time, it wasn't someone else's life she was chronicling but her own.

The idea had come to her when she slept, or so it seemed, for when she awoke there it was, squatting in the forefront of her thoughts, as impossible to ignore as a toad on a welcome mat. In preparation for the reunion, Willa had searched for old photos, and she'd asked her friends to do the same. But Angel had been their photographer, and except for the small album Angel had given her, Willa found few pictures. Her diaries, on the other hand, contained as detailed an account of their time together as anyone could ask. Willa would have loved to share them with the others, but there was too much that was personal or embarrassing or just terribly written for that to be possible. And then, that morning, the solution had presented itself: She would not share the diaries themselves, but rather an abridged version of them, a digest.

So now she sat at her desk, window open to the scented breeze, diaries arranged in chronological order. The house was very quiet. From her office, which faced the garden, Willa heard only birdsong and the chirruping of insects. In the past she'd always written to music, carefully chosen for its appropriateness to her subject. For her book on Dorothy Parker, she'd started off with Dory Previn, but the clever lyrics were too distracting. As soon as she switched to some old delta blues, the whole tone of the book changed, and despite the odd pairing, she'd felt she'd finally gotten a handle on her subject. For Dawn Powell she'd chosen Miles Davis, for Ivy Compton-Burnett, Bartok. But for her own life she chose no distractions, no sound track or commentary, just the white sky of silence.

The first entry to make her digest was the one that marked her entrée into their group: Caleb's revenge on the odious Cockroach. Then a whole series of incidents revolving around their extra-academic activities, starting with the time Shake made them cut school to attend a blues festival in the city: first time in her life she saw B. B. King perform, as well as Mose Allison. The digest version omitted what had been, for her, the best part of the trip: the train ride home, when she and Caleb made out on the platform between cars.

An account of a sledding expedition roused warm memories but failed to make the cut, as most of it pertained to the surprising sensations of coasting downhill in a pile of bodies. Some of the best stories had to be sacrificed: the slut party, for one. Vinny, Caleb, and Patrick had been determined to get Jeremiah laid before graduation. (Travis, also a virgin, was deemed beyond help.) One weekend, when Caleb's parents were away, they had a party at his house. Apart from the Beacon Hill kids, the only other guests were six certified sluts, teenyboppers so thrilled to be hanging out with that infamous gang that they'd have fucked a rat, let alone a good-looking, high-status guy like Jeremiah.

The party started at nine. By ten they were all bombed. Jeremiah was lying on the couch, making out with one of the teenyboppers, when the doorbell rang. Caleb opened the door, then tried to slam it, but too late. In marched Jeremiah's mother, crackling with outrage. While the others stood by helplessly—for what, after all, can you do to someone's mom, however outrageous?—she plucked the girl off Jeremiah, grabbed her son by the ear, and hauled him out of the house.

Poor Jeremiah. Willa wiped her eyes, wet with laughing.

There were numerous accounts of brawls; Willa included her favorite. One day in the school cafeteria, a football player named Larry Phipps made the mistake of commenting on Angel's ass in the presence of Patrick, Vinny, and Caleb. "Patrick dumped a trayful of sloppy joes and Jello-O on Phipps's head," she'd written, "and if Phipps had half a brain it would have ended there; but he had to throw a punch, and then a bunch of his teammates jumped in, which gave Vinny and Caleb, who'd been standing around bored, something to do with their hands."

When the phone rang, she jumped as if shaken awake and shot a glance at the clock on her desk. Past noon, and she was still in her robe. Hungry, too; she must have forgotten breakfast. She answered the phone, braced for Caleb's voice—for ever since Patrick told her about last week's midnight call, she'd been waiting. But it was Chloe, shrieking. "Mom, oh my God, you won't believe what happened: Emily broke her leg!"

"Emily?" said Willa.

"Emily Madison? *Annie?* Earth to Mom: Come in please!"

"She can't do the part?"

"*Hello?* On crutches? Mom, it's all on me now. I'm Annie." This last in a voice of pure horror.

"Oh, poor Emily! But, Chloe, you'll do just fine. You know that part backward and forward."

"They're having a special rehearsal right after school. Mr. Kohegan wants you to come. Can you?"

"Of course," Willa promised, not without a regretful look at the diaries. "Chloe, this is so exciting!"

"It's a disaster," said Chloe, and hung up.

Willa had just finished dressing when the doorbell rang. She ran a comb through her wet hair and ran downstairs, peered through the portico. A burly stranger peered back at her. He held up a silver shield.

She served coffee in the living room, where they sat in facing chairs. The detective was a balding, lugubrious man in his fifties. He wore a good gray suit with dandruff on the shoulders, a white shirt, a solid red tie loosened at the throat, and the look of a man who's seen it all and stored most of it in the pouches beneath his eyes. Nothing about Harry Meyerhoff was impressive, and Willa's first thought was, *Couldn't Jovan have done better?*

"How did you know Angelica Busky?" Meyerhoff began. He had a little notebook balanced on his knee, where a napkin might have gone, and a pen in his paw; and the task of juggling cup, pad, and pen seemed beyond him.

"We were friends in high school. Best friends."

He gave her an encouraging nod. "So you knew her well."

"I thought so. Everyone called her Angel, by the way, not Angelica."

"Tell me about her. What was she like?"

Willa thought for a moment. "Beautiful, adventurous, multitalented. A good photographer; an even better singer. For a while she sang with our friend Shake's band. Janis Joplin was her idol; she modeled herself after her."

"Including the drugs?"

"Nothing heavy."

"Did she have a boyfriend?" Meyerhoff asked.

Suddenly uneasy, Willa nodded.

"What was his name?"

In high school, cops had been their enemy—"Pigs," they'd called them, great suburban gangsters that they were—and ratting out a friend the ultimate taboo. Even now it didn't feel right. Willa felt she should ask permission. She should have seen this coming; certainly Jovan had warned her. No holding back, he'd said, and she'd agreed. But when it came to naming names, she couldn't help but hesitate.

The detective gave her a hangdog look. "According to our mutual friend, you're the one who wanted this investigation. Well, *mazel tov*; you got what you wanted. But for me to do my job, I'm gonna need to talk to everyone she was close to."

"Patrick Mulhaven," Willa said resignedly. "He teaches at NYU now."

"I'll need his phone number and address. And the names of her other friends, and where they can be reached." Meyerhoff turned to a fresh page and pushed the notepad across the coffee table.

"Patrick Mulhaven," she wrote. "Vincent Delgaudio. Travis Fleck. Nancy and John Shaker. Caleb Rhys." Leaving out Jeremiah was second nature, even after all this time. He'd been, still was, their designated front-runner. Willa added phone numbers and addresses culled from her Rolodex for everyone but Caleb, who still hadn't called.

Meyerhoff took the list from her. "Good. Now, what can you tell me about the day she disappeared?"

"Not much. I wasn't here, you see; I left for Paris the day after graduation. But you must have all the details in the original missing-person report."

"There wasn't any. She was over eighteen, and there was no suggestion of force or foul play. It wasn't a police matter."

"So the police never looked for her?"

"Not as a missing person."

She looked at him. "What, then?"

"Car theft," he said.

Willa gasped. "Busky reported his car stolen, but not his daughter missing?"

"He said she stole it."

"That bastard!"

"When was the last time you saw Angel?" continued Meyer-hoff, a freight train of a man, solid and relentless.

"Graduation night. The next day—"

"You left for Paris, yes. But when you came back, you didn't try to find her?"

"I asked about her. No one knew where she'd gone. But she'd done it before, run away, I mean; no one took it for anything more than that. She'd promised to visit me at school; I figured she'd show up on campus one day."

"And when she didn't . . . ?"

Willa shrugged. "Then I thought she was still mad at me. And I didn't realize that no one else had heard from her either. My parents sold our house while I was in college, and after that I didn't see much of my high school friends."

Meyerhoff looked at her like a snake tracking a mouse. "Mad at you? What for?"

Full disclosure, Jovan had said. But Willa hadn't imagined how uncomfortable that would be. She'd had less intrusive pelvic exams. "A month before school ended," she said, "Angel slept with my boyfriend." Even now it hurt. But the words came out cool and calm.

"What was his name?"

"Caleb Rhys."

He wrote the name, then frowned at it. "I don't get it. She sleeps with your boyfriend and *she's* mad at *you?*"

"For failing the test. For being a 'small-minded possessive bour-geois American princess.' For letting a man come between us."

Meyerhoff hoisted those heavy eyes upward. "Sounds like a handful, your Angel."

A brief smile crossed her face. "Always."

"Must have pissed Patrick off, his girl doing it with his buddy."

"Patrick's not the jealous type." But even as she spoke, Willa saw Patrick glaring at Jovan that day their paths had crossed in her house.

"Was Angel pregnant when she disappeared?" No change in Meyerhoff's voice as he asked this; he might have been inquiring about the time.

"So I'm told."

"Was Patrick the father?"

Again that prickle of unease. They always suspected the boyfriend, didn't they? And Meyerhoff didn't exactly look like a font of original thought. Willa's own suspicions were thrust aside, forgotten. Surely Patrick would never have hurt Angel; but how would *they* know it?

"He was one candidate," she said.

"And Caleb another, I gather. Who else was in the running?"

Shake, but why put him in harm's way? O'Rourke came to mind as well, but Patrick was right about him: There was nothing to link Angel and her former teacher except Travis's fervid imagination, which was hardly enough to drag the man into a police investigation.

"I don't know," she said. "What's it matter, anyway? Her father's the one you should be talking to. He used to beat the crap out of her."

"How do you know? Did she tell you?"

"No. Patrick did."

Meyerhoff nodded, and though his face was inscrutable, Willa felt sure he was weighing the source.

"But I do know she was scared to death of her father," she said firmly. "And I know Busky lied. Did you hear the tape?"

"I heard it."

"He claimed she came home again that night to get her stuff. But if she really had come back, she would have taken her treasures and her money. He just said that to make it look like she ran away."

"It's the same story he told the police at the time."

"Which proves it's a lie!"

"How's that?"

"It's been twenty years," Willa said, surprised that she should need to tell him this. "People forget, they embellish, they censor. True stories evolve over time. Lies stay the same. Don't you find that in your work?"

Meyerhoff laid down his pen and studied her without hurry or self-consciousness, as if she were a painting in a gallery. "That's an interesting observation," he said presently. "I wonder how you came by it."

"I'm a biographer. One learns that any given incident can spawn a thousand stories, each one slightly different, depending not only on who's telling it but on who they're telling it to."

"Hmmph," was all the detective said, but from then until the end of the interview, his demeanor changed. He sat up straight, dropped the bumbling Columbo routine, and listened more than he wrote.

"Did Angel have any enemies?" he asked.

"Enemies?" Willa scoffed. "We're talking about an eighteen-year-old girl."

"Who slept around. Maybe some of those guys she went with had girlfriends."

"Angel wasn't a great respecter of boundaries," she conceded. "But that was small potatoes, high school stuff."

"Today, sure," Meyerhoff said mildly. "Did it seem small then, I wonder?"

And now it was Willa's turn to revise a first impression. Forget the clerkish air, the dogged note-taking, that manner of inhabiting his chair as if grateful not to be walking a beat; this guy was no dummy. When Angel had sex with Caleb, it had rocked Willa's world; it was the mother of all treacheries. And it was huge for Nancy, too, that time Shake and Angel slipped off together. Nancy had always been easygoing to the point of vacuity—about everything except her man. She'd bitch-slap a girl just for smiling his way; that night at the party, they'd had to haul her off Angel when she and Shake finally came strolling back in. No, Meyerhoff was right; there was nothing small about teenage passions.

He showed her a photo, one of the pictures from Angel's camera. It was a candid shot of the Beacon Hill kids in situ. Willa couldn't help smiling. How young they all were. Shake, shirtless, resting his head on Nancy's lap. Patrick and Caleb standing together, rapt in conversation; Vinny, Travis, and Jeremiah playing cards on the boulders. Neither Angel nor Willa appeared in the picture; Angel, presumably, because she was taking it, Willa because by then she was already in France.

"This would have been taken sometime between graduation and the day Angel disappeared," Willa said.

"How do you know?"

"She finished a roll of film during graduation. Not at the ceremony—we didn't go—but at our own private celebration on Beacon Hill, where we used to hang out. She ran out of film; so the pictures on the new roll must have been taken afterward. Where are the others?"

"Excellent." Meyerhoff beamed, ignoring the question. "What a precise memory you have, Mrs. Durrell. Comes of being a writer, no doubt. And who are these people? I like putting faces to names."

No, not dumb at all. He knew damn well she'd left one name out. "That's Shake—John Shaker—with Nancy, now his wife. That's Caleb and Patrick. The guys playing cards are Travis, Vinny, and Jeremiah."

He made a show of studying the list she'd written. "I don't see a Jeremiah."

"I forgot about him. He wasn't around much."

"What's Jeremiah's last name?"

"He wasn't close to Angel. I'm sure there's nothing he can tell you that the rest of us couldn't."

Meyerhoff just looked at her, and she felt like a child under his gaze.

"His name is Jeremiah Wright," Willa said at last. "He's an aide to Senator Apfel. I very much doubt he could help you. It really would be better if you could direct your questions to me."

"That's Wright with a *W*?"

"Yes."

"Got a number?"

"No."

"No matter; I'll track him down." Meyerhoff smiled. It wasn't a very nice smile, and Willa now found herself frightened by what she'd set into motion, astonished at its magnitude, as if she'd tossed a pebble into a pond and seen a grenade explode.

"You don't need to do that," she said. "If you really must talk to him, he'll be here for the reunion." Meyerhoff looked blank. "Didn't Jovan mention it? That's how this whole thing got started." She told him about the pact they'd made graduation night, and their plans to carry it out.

"They're all coming?" asked Meyerhoff, showing faint but alarming signs of animation. "Jeremiah, too, and the other out-of-towners?"

"Yes, except Angel, of course, and maybe Caleb; though it's possible he'll show up at the last minute. Why?" Then, making a joke of it, she said, "You're not thinking of crashing the party?"

"I'd prefer an invitation."

Willa pressed her hands to her temples. Major attack of buyer's remorse. "No offense, but I'm afraid inviting you would put a damper on the festivities."

"You don't know me," Meyerhoff said, pointing a stubby thumb at his chest. "I'm a party animal."

25

The auditorium was in that state of chaos that suggests an obscure, underlying purpose. Half a dozen kids milled about on the stage, carting furniture and props, while another bunch battled with a huge unwieldy backdrop that smelled of fresh paint. Stage lights flickered on and off. Little girls in orphans' rags and bigger girls dressed as matrons skittered about the auditorium. Rising above the cacophonic sounds of the band tuning up, the stentorian voice of Mr. Ken Kohegan, director, barked out commands.

Willa, standing in the rear, looked for Chloe and finally spotted her beside the band pit, which wasn't a pit at all but just a narrow strip of floor between the foot of the stage and the first row of seats. Chloe, still in school clothes, was standing with Mrs. Glouster, the play's musical director and longtime high school chorus teacher. Mrs. Glouster was a woman in her sixties with anarchic gray hair and thick glasses perched on a long, sharp nose. She'd had a brief but locally famous career as a concert pianist, and a much longer and more successful one as a music teacher, as evidenced by a caseful of medals in the front office. She had singled Chloe out early for special attention, assigning her one of only two solos for the winter concert. But two days before the concert, Simon died, and Chloe never sang the part.

With them was a tall boy with spiky blond hair. Though his back was to Willa, she recognized him at once. While Roy Bliss attended to Mrs. Glouster, who was speaking with great animation, Chloe gazed at Roy. In the midst of all those bodies scurrying about, she stood out by standing still, so focused on the boy beside her that it was immediately clear to Willa that for Chloe, no one else existed.

Willa sighed deeply. It might have been herself she saw, twenty-odd years ago, standing with Caleb in the school cafeteria. "Have lunch with us," he'd said, and her whole life changed. When she fell in love with Caleb—and, by extension, with the rest of the Beacon Hill kids—her parents' disapproval had been as nothing compared to the world that opened up to her. She had filtered them out; the more they objected, the less she cared.

There is, she saw, an inexorability to the progress of life that scoffs at our poor attempts to circumvent or slow it. A woman in labor cannot halt the birth process; so, too, this subsequent emergence. That Chloe would get hurt was inevitable. But Judy was right: Sooner or later, everyone's heart gets broken.

Willa started down the center aisle. Halfway to Chloe, she was intercepted by the director, a small man with a deep voice and an oversize mustache that crouched above his upper lip like a large, shaggy brown dog poised to spring. Mr. Kohegan was not much liked by the students, who made fun of his imperious manner and called him Napoleon behind his back, but he was respected.

"Hell of a thing," he said by way of greeting. "But she's up to it, no doubt about that. Now all we have to do is convince her."

"Hello, Mr. Kohegan."

"Oh. Hello." He shook her hand firmly, but Willa saw that she didn't exist for him, except as Chloe's mother.

"Poor Emily," Willa said. "What bad luck."

The mustache bristled. "Not luck at all; her own damn fault. What was she doing on a soccer field one week before the play? There's a time and a place for everything, I tell my students. At their age they need to understand there are priorities in life."

He went on. Willa smiled and nodded. Chloe's little group broke up, Roy returning to the band. Chloe waved to Willa and started toward her but was seized midway by a harried-looking woman with an armload of costumes and a pincushion Velcroed to her skirt. "Mr. Kohegan," the woman called, holding Chloe firmly by the arm, "can I have her now?"

"Not now, Mrs. Janssen," the director said. "We start in five minutes."

"But her costumes aren't ready, they all need altering."

"Then for now she will rehearse without them."

Just then the side door to the auditorium flew open and a girl on crutches, her left foot in a cast, entered the room. As she was noticed, the hubbub stilled to a chorus of whispers. Chloe shrank back, but the injured girl spotted her and propelled herself smartly across the room.

Chloe came out to meet her. "I'm so sorry, Emily. I can't believe this happened."

"Not your fault, babe." Emily's voice carried to the back of the room, as it was meant to. "I just came to tell you one thing. You are going to be a *great* Annie. If it had to happen, I'm glad it was you."

They hugged. Chloe, fighting tears, tried to hide her face, but Emily put an arm around her and swung her around. "I know," she said loudly, "that everyone in the cast and crew is going to come together behind you. The show must go on, right, guys?"

This was answered with warm applause, which Emily graciously pretended was for Chloe.

"What a lovely thing to do," Willa said to Ken Kohegan.

The director harrumphed, but made his way over to his sidelined star and shook her hand. "There were many ways you could have handled the situation," Willa, all of them, heard him say. "You chose the classiest."

The rehearsal started a few minutes later, a full run-through with no breaks except to change sets. Willa, alone in the auditorium, watched her daughter perform. Chills ran down her spine.

They'd always known Chloe could sing. Even as a toddler, her voice would make you stop and listen. God knows where she got it; Simon could barely carry a tune, and Willa's voice, though true, was thin and limited in range. But Willa had taken Chloe's voice for granted, assuming vaguely that all children could sing. It was only in grade school, when the chorus teacher began praising Chloe, that Willa started to pay attention. Even so, she never realized how good her daughter was until she heard her onstage with a band backing her up.

At first Chloe was stiff and self-conscious, but as the play progressed, she disappeared into a role that fit her like a second skin: For was she not herself a half orphan, a girl longing for a father? This identification of actor and character infused her voice with a pathos that moved everyone who heard it. Stagehands abandoned their posts; janitors gathered in the doorway; office ladies left their desks and drifted in.

In the final scene there was a surprise: Chloe appeared in full costume, her blond hair hidden by a curly red wig. The boys in the lighting booth chose this moment to discover the spot, isolating Chloe in a cone of white light and eliding her face in the contrast, so that Willa's eyes, inexplicably blurred, took in the red hair but not the features. For one searing moment it was Angel she saw, Angel's voice she heard, singing with such blind faith, such youthful certainty about the promise of tomorrow.

The illusion lasted an instant, no more, but, combined with what she knew and suspected of Angel's real tomorrow, it wrung Willa's heart. She had to get out. She slipped out of the auditorium and walked around the parking lot until she regained her composure.

By the time she returned to the auditorium, rehearsal had ended. Someone tapped her on the shoulder. Willa turned to find Roy Bliss beside her. They exchanged civil greetings.

"She did great, didn't she?" Roy said. "Told her she would. Shoulda had the part in the first place, except they wouldn't give it to a freshman."

"I'm sure Emily would have done a fine job."

"Emily's okay. Chloe's a whole other league." He hemmed and hawed a little, then said, "After the show on Saturday, this girl from the chorus is having a cast party. Her parents'll be there and all that. Okay with you if Chloe rides with me?"

Willa looked him over. The hair, tattoos, and earrings no longer impressed her; they were no different, she saw now, from the long hair and sandals of her day. He was half a head taller than she was, but he was just a boy.

"Roy," she said, "Chloe told me what happened, the night you drove her home. It's possible I jumped to the wrong conclusion about you. But if I came across as an overprotective maniac of a mother who would slit the throat of anyone who messed with her daughter, then you jumped to the right conclusion, because that is *exactly* what I am. Is that clear to you?"

"Yes, ma'am," he said.

"Good," she said. "Because if Chloe goes with you, she's your responsibility. My daughter doesn't drink, smoke, or ingest anything I wouldn't feed her. And while you're with her, neither do you."

"No, ma'am."

"In that case," Willa said, "you have my permission."

Then Mrs. Glouster came bearing down on them. "Mr. Bliss, nice work tonight. But what are those drums still doing on the floor?"

He was quick to escape. For a moment the teacher looked after him. "Nice kid," she said.

Willa glanced over, expecting sarcasm, finding none.

"Serious musician, too," Mrs. Glouster said. "Writes his own music. Did you know he made Juilliard?" Then, without waiting for an answer, she nodded toward the stage. "You saw Chloe?"

"Oh yes," Willa said.

"And?"

"She's good, isn't she?"

"Good?" Mrs. Glouster sniffed. "Good's a dime a dozen. Good I get every year. Chloe's in a different realm. Who is her teacher?"

Willa was confused. "Why, you are."

"I mean her private teacher."

"She doesn't have one."

"Oh, for heaven's sake." Mrs. Glouster peered through her glasses at Willa's face. "Mrs. Durrell, your daughter has a gift that cannot be taken for granted. Talent of that sort is meant to be developed; surely I don't have to tell you that."

There was an emphasis on the "you" that struck Willa as curious. "Why not?"

"I've read your books. Genius is your topic, isn't it? But what good is genius without craft? And craft is a thing that must be learned."

"Surely she has to want it first. Chloe's never asked for voice lessons."

Mrs. Glouster tapped the side of her nose. "The child doesn't yet know what she has, which is just as well—as long as we do."

They sat in the car while the parking lot emptied out. There was so much to say, but Willa was afraid to open her mouth. Something dangerous was welling inside her, an ectopic pregnancy of the heart.

"Well?" Chloe prompted. If Willa had suspected that her opinion no longer mattered to her daughter, the tension in that

"Well?," and the sideways look that accompanied it, put paid to that notion.

"You were wonderful," Willa said. "I was incredibly proud. I was awed."

"Really, Mom?"

"Of course really! You know, Mrs. Glouster thinks it's high time we got serious about your voice. How would you feel about private lessons?"

"Sure, I guess. So I really did okay? Because I saw you walk out before the end, and I thought you hated it."

"Oh, God, sweetheart, no. It wasn't that at all. It's just . . . I used to have this friend who sang. Angel; I think I told you about her."

"The redhead from the album."

"Right. She had a beautiful voice. And now she's gone. When I saw you up there in that red wig, for a moment it was like seeing her. That's why I stepped out. It got to me suddenly and I needed some air."

"Gone how?" Chloe said. "Dead?"

"I think so."

"I hate that!" the girl exploded. "It makes me sick the way people you care about just up and die on you."

And then the thing that had been swelling in Willa's heart burst. She felt a sudden tearing pain, followed by a sense of loss as deep and irrevocable as an amputee's. Sorrow, toxic with suppression, coursed like poison through her bloodstream. *Where is Simon, where is he, why isn't he here?* He'd always been there for Chloe; Willa saw him, in a montage of memories, cradling her in the delivery room, singing to her, walking her, sweeping her high above the waves at the beach.

Six months' worth of mourning condensed into a single convulsive flood. She covered her face and sobbed helplessly. *This is so wrong,* she was thinking in a far corner of her mind. *This is Chloe's night and I'm ruining it.* But her mind had no dominion over her body.

"Mom, oh God, what is it?" Chloe cried, eyes bright with panic, one hand on the door handle.

Choking on her tears, Willa gasped, "I'm sorry."

"But what's wrong?"

"It just hit me—I wish your father could have seen you tonight. He would have been so proud."

Chloe threw her arms around Willa, who clung to her as a drowning sailor to a buoy. "Maybe he did," Chloe whispered. "It's possible, isn't it?"

"Anything's possible," her mother said.

26

"I hate this case," Harry Meyerhoff said.

"Why's that?" said Jovan. They were sitting at a table in a Bronx bar without a name, sandwiched between a pizzeria and a dry cleaner on Fordham Avenue. Outside it was two in the afternoon, the sun was shining, and the avenue was thronged with shoppers. Inside there was perpetual twilight and all the cheer of a mortician's anteroom. The meeting was Meyerhoff's choice, as was the venue; Jovan had no idea why.

"Let me count the ways," Meyerhoff said, using his fingers. "No body. No evidence. No prior investigation. No scene of crime. No proof there even *was* a crime."

"But there was."

"Maybe. You can't leave out suicide."

"Sure. What I'm wondering, after she killed herself, how'd she dispose of the body?"

"Wise guy," Meyerhoff growled. He caught the waitress's eye and pointed at their empty glasses.

"So where are you?" Jovan asked.

"Did the preliminaries: NCIC, DMV, Lexis/Nexis, INS, all that jazz."

Jovan nodded, neither surprised nor offended that Meyerhoff would retrace his steps. The first tenet of the detective's credo is to take nothing on faith. Jovan wasn't even a cop anymore; Meyerhoff would have to cross the *t*s and dot the *i*s himself. "How'd you do?" he asked.

"Same as you. We're also looking for his car."

"Busky's, twenty years later? Good luck."

The waitress brought over a fresh round: beer for Jovan, club soda for Meyerhoff. She was a shapely Spanish girl in a black cocktail dress a size too small for her. Meyerhoff swiveled to watch her go. When he turned back, Jovan was grinning.

"What?" said Meyerhoff.

"Rae caught you looking like that, she'd stick a fork in your eye."

"Oh, yeah? Let me tell you something, pal. The secret to a long and faithful marriage is an active fantasy life."

"That go for her, too?"

Meyerhoff threw up his hands. "Like I want to know! There's limits to intimacy. Everybody's got to have some space of their own, right?"

Jovan took a sip of beer. "She'd still poke a fork in your eye."

"Speaking of eyefuls," said Meyerhoff, "I met your client."

"Oh, yeah?"

"Nice. Very nice."

"You think?"

"What, like you don't?"

"Never occurred to me."

Meyerhoff guffawed. "Now I know *you're* lying. Question is, is she?"

"What about?"

"Dunno. I just got the feeling she was holding back more than she was saying."

Jovan sighed. "I get that feeling a lot with her."

"Strange crew, those old friends of hers. Have you met any of them?"

"Just Patrick, briefly. And I saw old man Busky when I went in after Mrs. Durrell."

"What'd you make of him?"

"Crazy old coot. End-stage alcoholic."

"Dangerous? What would've happened if you hadn't gone in?"

"She'd have slapped him down herself. Even with the knife, he was no match for her. Why, you like the guy?"

Meyerhoff shrugged. "Early days."

"Mrs. Durrell puts it on him."

"That tells me nothing. She wouldn't like the alternatives."

"You heard the tape," Jovan said. "The man's carrying a load of guilt."

"I heard it. Saw the pictures, too." Meyerhoff stopped short, and a charged silence ensued. Jovan badly wanted to see the pictures from Angel's camera but couldn't ask; he'd forfeited that right. There were boundaries to his relationship with Meyerhoff, though within those boundaries it ran deep.

Meyerhoff chose not to enlighten him. "What's Patrick like?"

"Smart. Teaches at NYU."

"Gay?"

Jovan blinked. "I wouldn't think so. He's got a major hard-on for my client. Wasn't too pleased to find me in the picture."

"And are you?" Meyerhoff said, a shrewd gleam in those sleepy eyes. "In the picture?"

"Excuse me?"

"It's not that complicated a question."

"One," Jovan said, "it's none of your business. Two, she's a client. And three, does that woman look like she'd have time for me?"

Three denials, where one would have done. Meyerhoff smiled. Not for nothing, his gold shield. "Thought you didn't notice her looks."

"What are you, turning into your wife?"

"Please. Rae would have been much more subtle." Meyerhoff let it drop, though. "I've been thinking about this reunion she's hosting next weekend."

"What about it?"

"Perfect opportunity to chat with the out-of-state contingent."

"Aha," said Jovan, who'd been wondering why Meyerhoff had called him. (Clearly it wasn't to share information.)

"I fished for an invitation," Meyerhoff said. "Didn't get one. She seemed to think I'd spoil the party."

"You?" Jovan scoffed. "Didn't you tell her you're a party animal?"

"I did, as a matter of fact. Don't think she believed me. Maybe you should go instead."

"Wasn't invited."

"They'll talk about Angel," Meyerhoff said. "Bound to."

"You're not going to see them?"

"I'll catch a word before they leave. But it would be interesting to know what they say amongst themselves."

Jovan didn't answer. His attention had been captured by two young punks who'd walked in together and were now standing by the door, surveying the room. Both wore jackets, despite the weather. Meyerhoff turned, following his eyes. The young men noticed them watching, looked at each other, turned, and left the bar.

Jovan looked at Meyerhoff.

"What?" Meyerhoff said, spreading his hands. "They didn't do anything. So . . . ?"

"What makes you think she'd go for it?"

"A woman who walked into Busky's house wired? That's fairly driven."

"That's different. These are her friends she'd be setting up."

"Not if they didn't do anything."

"Please," Jovan said, by which he meant *Don't play me like a civilian.*

"Think about it," Meyerhoff said. "About this, too, while you're at it: If it wasn't her old man, chances are it was one of them."

Blinking in the sunlight, they parted on the pavement outside the bar. Jovan turned left for the subway. Meyerhoff left his car in front of the bar and set off on foot in the opposite direction. Perfect day for walking, seventy-five degrees, no humidity, air quality breathable for once. The streets were full of shoppers, women with strollers, children playing on stoops.

Vinny Delgaudio's service station was only three blocks away. Meyerhoff checked it out from across the street. It was a big station, with twelve pumps, a convenience shop, and a five-bay garage. There was a kid working the pumps, a woman minding the C-shop, and four mechanics inside the bays: one Hispanic, two black, and the fourth white, possibly Italian but too young to be Delgaudio. Meyerhoff hoped it wasn't a wasted trip. He hadn't called ahead. Not out of any particular suspicion—Delgaudio looked to be a bit player in Angel's story, and his business, as far as Meyerhoff could ascertain, was perfectly legit. Rather, it was a matter of principle. A good detective uses all the tools at his disposal, including the element of surprise.

Meyerhoff crossed the street, bypassed the C-shop, and entered the garage through an open bay. First thing he noticed were the cars: a Porsche, two Audis, a Mercedes. Not what you'd expect in this neighborhood. The bays were immaculate, no clutter, lots of high-tech oscillators and gear in evidence. The white mechanic, a dark-haired kid in his early twenties, left the Mercedes and came up to him. "Help you, sir?"

"I'd like to see Vincent Delgaudio."

"And you are . . . ?"

The kid spoke with an authority disproportionate to his youth, and he'd been quick to approach. Son of the owner, maybe? Meyerhoff flashed his shield. "Is he in?"

"I'll check," the mechanic said. He walked past an intercom on the wall, heading for a door in the back of the garage. Meyerhoff followed. Straight ahead, at the end of the corridor, was an office with a half-open door. Meyerhoff glimpsed a man sitting at a desk before the kid turned around and came back, blocking his view. "Excuse me," he said, politer than he wanted to be. "Would you mind waiting outside?"

"That's okay, son," Meyerhoff said. "I'll save you the walk back." He stepped forward. Reluctantly, the young man gave way.

"Mr. Delgaudio?" Meyerhoff entered unannounced, the mechanic hard on his heels. The man at the desk looked up from a stack of computer printouts, and for a moment Meyerhoff thought he'd made a mistake. This guy wore an Italian suit and a silk tie; his thick black hair was fashionably cut. He looked like a two-hundred-dollar-an-hour lawyer; only his hands gave him away, the fingertips stained black with old grease.

"I'm Delgaudio. Who are you?"

"He's a cop," the mechanic said.

"Detective Sergeant Harry Meyerhoff."

"Ya got me, copper!" Vinny said, holding out his hands, crossed at the wrists. He laughed; Meyerhoff smiled politely. "Have a seat. Okay, Frank."

The young mechanic left, after another hard look at Meyerhoff. Vinny called him back to shut the door.

"Good-looking kid. Your son?" asked Meyerhoff, sinking into a leather chair as comfortable as it was beautiful. Delgaudio's office was as incongruous as the man himself. The desk was beechwood, and the filing cabinets as well. There was thick carpeting, a sofa made of the same soft leather as Meyerhoff's chair, a glass coffee table. On the desk, photos of Delgaudio's family faced outward. Could have been a doctor's or lawyer's office, down to the framed diplomas on the wall.

"Nephew," Vinny said, removing his reading glasses. "What can I do for you, Sergeant? Is this about Fernando's trial?"

"Who's Fernando?"

"Guy we caught stealing from the C-shop. But if you didn't know that, that's not why you're here."

"No, sir," Meyerhoff said. In ways too subtle to pinpoint, Meyerhoff was not quite the same man who'd met with Jovan a short while ago. The cop Delgaudio saw was older, less focused, a civil servant nearing retirement, a pear-shaped desk jockey way past his pull date. "I was hoping you could help me with a different matter."

"Shoot," said Vinny. "Not literally, of course."

He was, if anything, too jovial, which interested Meyerhoff in a minor way. He took out his notebook. "I'm looking for a woman you once knew. Does the name Angel Busky ring a bell?"

Vinny's face didn't change but there was a beat before he answered. "A distant one. I knew an Angel Busky back in high school."

"That's the one. We're trying to locate her."

"Why come to me? I haven't seen the girl since high school."

"That's the problem. No one has."

"She ran away. Successfully, it seems."

"Any idea where she might have run to?"

Vinny shook his head.

"Ever hear from her afterward?" Meyerhoff asked.

"No. Didn't expect to. We weren't that close."

"Who *was* she close to?"

Vinny crossed his arms over his chest. His face was meant to be impassive, but Meyerhoff could see the wheels turning furiously. How much did they know? How little could he get away with saying? The detective didn't hold it against him. Nobody normal likes naming names to the cops.

"Let me jog your memory," he said. "The Beacon Hill gang?"

"It wasn't a gang," Vinny said quickly. "Not like they use the word nowadays."

"Was Angel part of that group?"

"I guess."

"Did she have a boyfriend?"

"Sergeant, this was twenty years ago. How am I supposed to remember who some girl's boyfriend was?"

"Was it"—Meyerhoff consulted his notebook—"Patrick Mulhaven?"

"Where are you getting this?" Vinny said. "Who gave you our

names? Because if it's her old man, he's the one you should be talking to. The man was one ugly drunk."

"Mr. Delgaudio," Meyerhoff said wearily, "these are not trick questions. You're not in any trouble here. The situation is, I can't put this thing to bed till I've talked with the people who knew her, and I can't do that till I find out who they were."

"Lots of guys *knew* her," Vinny said, with a signifying look.

"Yourself included?"

"Not that way. She was Patrick's girl."

Meyerhoff looked perplexed. "She was Patrick's girl, but she went with other guys? That couldn't have made him happy."

"He didn't care. It was a game they played. Every time he fooled around, she had to up him one, preferably with one of his buddies."

"But not you."

"He was my friend. I wouldn't go there."

"Most guys that age will go anywhere," Meyerhoff said. "And Angel was a beautiful girl."

Vinny said nothing. He straightened a stack of computer printouts, pushing them into alignment with his blunt, blackened fingertips.

"Did she have any enemies? Anyone you know have a grudge against her?"

"No."

"Was she pregnant when she ran away?"

"How would I know?" Vinny said; but he missed a beat.

"Was she depressed? Worried?"

"Not that I recall."

"Did she ever do or say anything that indicated she might harm herself?"

"Angel?" Vinny said. "Suicide?" As if they wouldn't fit in the same sentence.

Meyerhoff turned a page. "Who else was in this Beacon Hill gang?"

"It wasn't—"

"Whatever."

"Patrick," Vinny said reluctantly. "John Shaker. Caleb Rhys. Travis Fleck."

"Any girls besides Angel?"

"Willa Scott—she was Caleb's girlfriend. And Nancy, Shake's girl. I really don't see—"

Meyerhoff shrugged apologetically, as if he, too, found it ridiculous but couldn't say so. "Anyone else?"

"Not really."

The detective made a note in his laborious hand. Then, from his jacket pocket, he produced a photo and passed it across the desk. It was the same picture he'd shown Willa.

Vinny put on his glasses. "Where the hell did this come from?"

"Can you put a name to the faces for me?" the detective asked.

"I'm the handsome devil there," Vinny said. He named each of the others, ending with Jeremiah.

"Forgot about him, did you, sir?"

"He wasn't around much. The rest of us, even the smart ones like Patrick and Caleb, were fuckups. Cut school more than we went, always in trouble. Jeremiah was a good kid. President of the class, valedictorian, like that."

"Was he close to Angel?"

Vinny shook his head. "Opposite ends of the spectrum."

Meyerhoff turned to the next page in his notebook. "Do you remember when she ran away?"

"The summer of seventy-two. Early summer."

"Recall the date?"

"Nah, why would I?"

Meyerhoff paged back through the notebook till he found what he was looking for. "Her father reported his car stolen on the night of June twenty-eight. That's the night she disappeared, Mr. Delgaudio. Does that help?"

Vinny gave the sort of patient sigh that denotes the opposite. "Sergeant, it was twenty years ago."

"They found the car the next day, crashed into a tree. No blood in the car, and no sign of Angel. No sign of Angel ever again, after that night. That's the part I find strange, Mr. Delgaudio; don't you?"

"You wouldn't if you knew her old man. She used to say that car was the only thing he loved. She wouldn't dare go home after wrecking it."

"That I can understand. What puzzles me is what happened

next. A girl in that situation—she'd have called on her friends for help, wouldn't she?"

"The fact is, she didn't," Vinny said reprovingly, in the manner of a man more comfortable with facts than suppositions.

"Are you sure?"

"For sure she never contacted me. And I never heard she called anyone else, either."

"The thing is," Meyerhoff said, "her father claims she came home afterward, late that night. Packed a suitcase and lit out again. And she wasn't alone."

Vinny snorted. "Like he would know. The guy was drunk seven out of seven."

"He says she got in through her bedroom window. Had you ever known her to do that?"

"Sometimes. There was a drainpipe that ran down alongside her window, with struts holding it to the wall. She'd climb down using the struts for footholds."

"And get back in the same way?"

Vinny nodded.

"Who knew about this?" Meyerhoff asked.

"All her friends."

"I imagine other people used it, too, when they wanted to avoid her father."

"Not me," Vinny said at once. "That old drainpipe wouldn't have held my weight."

"How about Patrick?"

"You'd have to ask him."

"You see my problem, Mr. Delgaudio? The way I see it, Angel gets in a fight with her father, grabs his keys, and drives off. She's upset, crying, driving too fast . . . she crashes the car, disabling it. Now she's afraid to go home. She decides to run away. So far so good. But she's got nothing on her, not even a change of clothes. So what does she do?"

"Knowing Angel? She thumbs a ride."

"You think?" Meyerhoff said doubtfully.

"No doubt about it. Angel was a world-class hitchhiker. One flash of leg and the cars would pile up."

The detective tutted with paternal disapproval. "So dangerous.

But girls did that back then, didn't they? Didn't think twice."

"Kids," Vinny said heavily, shaking his head, one father to another.

"Tell me about it. That your daughter?" Meyerhoff nodded at the portrait on the desk.

"Yeah."

"Must be just about Angel's age when she—"

"Younger," Vinny said curtly. It was clear he didn't like the association. "Are we through? Because . . ."

"Almost done," Meyerhoff said, in the soothing tone of a proctologist. "I know you're busy. Quite a setup you've got here, Mr. Delgaudio. You specialize in foreign cars?"

"That's all we do."

"Wouldn't think you'd get a lot of those in this neighborhood."

"You'd be surprised; all that drug money's got to go somewhere. But most of my customers come from Manhattan and Westchester."

If there was a dig in the drug money remark, Meyerhoff didn't seem to notice. "How long have you had the business?"

"Seventeen years."

"Seventeen years," Meyerhoff wrote in his notebook. Vinny watched him do it.

"It was a broken-down, bankrupt property when I got it," he said as if dictating. "I built the business up from scratch; it's all sweat equity. Nobody ever gave me nothing."

"An American success story," Meyerhoff said.

"Damn straight," said Vinny.

The ripples spread outward via telephone.

"Patrick?"

"Hey, Vinny."

"Have the cops come to see you yet?"

"Cops? What for?"

"They're looking for Angel."

Patrick looked across the office at Barney Glass, who was pretending not to listen. He shifted the phone to his other ear.

"They had my name," Vinny said. "Yours, too. I didn't give it to them."

"I wouldn't have cared if you did."

"What the fuck is going on?"

Patrick had a pretty good idea. People start turning over rocks, you never know what they'll find. He could hear Vinny's breathing, harsh and low. *Willa, what have you done?*

"Beats me," he said. "Didn't you ask?"

"I did. He wouldn't say."

"Who's he?"

"Some old fart. Jewish name, Meyer something. You think it was her old man?"

"Busky? He's the last guy on earth who'd go to the cops."

"Somebody must've. They didn't pick her name out of a hat."

"Well, it wasn't me," Patrick said.

"They had our picture up on Beacon Hill. All of us; Jeremiah, too."

Patrick thought hard for a moment. "Where'd they get it?"

"No idea."

"Did they know everyone's name?"

This time it was Vinny who hesitated. "I didn't want to seem uncooperative."

"That's cool, man," Patrick said, shoving the hair out of his eyes. "Don't sweat it."

"He knew already. He was testing me."

"What else did he want to know?"

"Dates, details about when she disappeared, which I told him I don't remember; I mean, what the hell, twenty years! Then he asks was she pregnant. I say how the fuck should I know? This is weird, Patch, this guy coming out of the blue."

"Let him come," said Patrick.

That night Patrick called Willa and asked, "What have you been up to?"

She propped herself on an elbow; she'd been reading in bed. "Nothing much. Same old same old."

"I don't think so," he said. "A police detective called on Vinny today."

"Oh dear," said Willa, who'd been expecting and dreading this call. "Was he upset?" The last thing she wanted was to cause trouble for her friends, but this was something that had to be done. If Patrick asked, she'd decided, she would not lie. But he didn't ask; he assumed, and assumed correctly, that she'd brought the cops in.

"You could say that," Patrick said. "I guess he thought those days were over."

"Does he blame me?"

"He would if he knew."

"You didn't tell. Bless you, Patrick."

"Jesus, Willa," he burst out, "what were you thinking? This is way out of hand. Did you even consider Jeremiah?"

"I tried to keep his name out of it. It backfired."

"He is *not* going to be a happy camper."

"Worse yet," she said, only half-joking, "what if his mother finds out?"

"Should we warn him?" Patrick asked. "Should we give them all a heads-up?"

"If we do, some might not come."

"And we want them to," Patrick said.

Silence for a moment; both of them thinking of Caleb. Then Willa said, "Vinny might talk."

"Vinny doesn't talk to anyone. Know what he said the first time we spoke about the reunion? 'What's a guy like me got to say to the likes of Willa and Jeremiah?'"

Willa shrugged, though he couldn't see her. "Yeah, well, now he's got a topic. How come the detective talked to Vinny but not you?"

"Why do you think? I'm the boyfriend: Guess what that makes me."

"I'm sorry." She was shaken by the anger hovering just below the surface of his voice. "But it's not like you've got anything to hide."

"Darlin', everyone has something to hide."

There was a long silence. Willa was the one who finally broke it. "Is it really so awful that they're involved? Something good might come of it."

"Like what?" Patrick snorted.

"Like finding out what really happened; like catching whoever did it."

"Did what? We don't even know she's dead. And if you mean Busky, what's the point? Prison would be a step up for him."

"Don't you want to know, Patrick?" Willa said.

"I loved Angel," he said. "I'll always love her. But what you've done? Nothing good will come of this."

27

With surprise no longer an option (for if Willa hadn't tipped him, Vinny surely had), this time Meyerhoff phoned ahead. Patrick Mulhaven could not have been more accommodating. He made no pretense of surprise, and seemed, if anything, relieved. "Sure I'll see you. How about tomorrow morning?"

Meyerhoff offered to come to Mulhaven's home, but the cagey professor opted for his office instead, thus claiming home-field advantage without the inconvenience of exposing his lair. Which was fine by Meyerhoff. Wherever people felt most comfortable and secure, they were most communicative.

It took him a while to find the building on NYU's sprawling campus, and when he did, Mulhaven's office came as something of a surprise. Except for the absence of beds, the office looked like a dorm room, furnished with matching desks and chairs, movie posters—De Niro in *Taxi Driver*, Chaplin as the tramp—and shelves teeming with mismatched, well-worn, and predominantly paperback books. As for the professor himself, he had a distinctly Peter Pan aura about him, with a forelock of dark hair that kept flopping in his eyes and an air of innocent enthusiasm. You could tell he was a teacher by his tendency to lecture. Right now he was explaining his high school's social structure by way of a Venn diagram scribbled on the back of a Chinese take-out menu. "See, the whole school was divided up into various circles: jocks, freaks, brains, hoods, surfers, and politicians. The Beacon Hill kids came from the overlaps, the interstices. One of the things we had in common was that none of us fell cleanly into any of the standard categories. We were jocks with politics, freaks with fists, hoods with brains, and oh yeah, we all liked to get high. We were like an underground student council, only with a lot more power than the real one because we answered to no one."

Suppressing an urge to raise his hand, Meyerhoff interrupted. "Where did Angel fit in?"

"Combination den mother and sex goddess."

"She was your girlfriend."

"That's right."

"Only she slept around."

Patrick bristled. "I wouldn't put it like that. Angel liked sex, but she wasn't easy, she wasn't a slut. If that's what you're thinking, you're way off base."

"Set me straight, then."

"She could pick and choose, and she did. Wanting Angel got you nowhere; she had to want you or it was nothing doing."

"So you're telling me you didn't mind this picking and choosing."

"I was in no position to mind, though I sorta kinda did. But from a feminist point of view, she had every right. What's good for the goose and all that."

A remarkably candid statement, thought Meyerhoff, from a man who must know himself to be a suspect. Well delivered, too, with an air of rueful charm. Despite Patrick's helpful diagram, it was hard to see him and Vinny Delgaudio as high school buddies, they were such different types. Patrick was as chatty as Vinny had been terse; he had none of Vinny's guardedness, or none of its appearance.

"Was she pregnant at the end of high school?"

Patrick took out a pack of Camels and tapped it on the edge of the desk. "She said she was."

"Were you the father?"

"No."

"How can you be so sure?"

"I always took precautions. She said she was on the pill, but I wasn't about to trust her. I knew her, see. She wanted me home, and what Angel wanted, Angel usually got."

"So if it wasn't you, who was it?"

Patrick offered a cigarette to Meyerhoff, who declined. "I don't know," he said, lighting his own. "*She* didn't know."

"Who were the candidates?"

"Don't remember."

Meyerhoff sighed. "You're a smart guy, Professor, but you're making a dumb mistake. Let me give you a little advice. Anything you want to bring to my attention, anything you want to shine a light on, start by withholding. Say you don't remember when I know you do. Say you don't know when it's obvious you do. That'll get me wondering."

"I don't follow."

"Yes you do," said Meyerhoff. "Could Vincent Delgaudio have been the father?"

"No way."

"Travis Fleck?"

Patrick barked a laugh. "In his dreams!"

"Jeremiah, then."

"His mommy didn't let him play with girls like Angel."

Meyerhoff clucked sympathetically. "Tied to Mama's apron strings, was he?"

"Apron strings? More like a choke chain."

Meyerhoff studied his list. "So that leaves Shake and Caleb."

"What is this, twenty questions?"

Then the detective seemed to grow in his seat. He had that knack, like one of those sponge pets that expand in the bath. For a moment his true face showed, and there was nothing remotely deferential about it. "Do you really think I came here to play games, Professor?"

Patrick blinked. "No. Sorry. It's just . . . it wasn't a big deal."

"Then quit making a big deal of it."

"Caleb and Shake. Happy?"

"Did their girlfriends know about the affairs?"

"They weren't affairs," Patrick said irritably. "They were one-night stands; they were Angel acting out how pissed off she was."

"Did they know?"

"They found out; Angel made sure of that. That was half the fun, sticking it to Nancy and Willa."

"And the other half was sticking it to you?"

Patrick said nothing.

"You know what chutzpah is, Professor?" Meyerhoff asked, leaning on the desk.

"Of course I know."

"Well, not for nothing, but this girl had plenty. First she hands out free samples to your buddies, then, when she gets knocked up, she comes running to you."

"I understood why she did it," he said stiffly.

"You're a very understanding guy," Meyerhoff said. "Did she tell Shake and Caleb about her pregnancy?"

Patrick nodded. He'd lost his chattiness and looked slightly green.

"How'd that go over?"

"Caleb laughed it off," Patrick said. "Shake was upset. He offered her money for an abortion; so did I."

"Did she take it?"

He shook his head. "She didn't want an abortion."

"What did she want?"

"A father for her child. She wanted one of us to step up."

"Which none of you did," Meyerhoff said.

"No." Patrick rubbed his temples as if he felt a headache coming on.

"Did she tell her father?"

"Hell no! Keeping it from him was her first concern."

"So she must have been pretty upset. Desperate, even."

"She wasn't, actually."

"Pregnant, scared of her father, deserted by her friends—"

"We didn't desert her."

"—most girls would have been."

"Angel wasn't most girls. I guess she figured it would all work out somehow. Anyway, by graduation she'd quit talking about it and made up with us again."

Meyerhoff wrote this down, then stared at the page, perplexed. "Why?"

"I don't know. At the time I was just grateful."

"If what you say is true, if by graduation she was okay with the pregnancy and had made peace with you all, how come all of a sudden she up and runs away?"

"That always bothered me. I don't know the answer. My guess is that her old man found out and she had to get out fast."

"Was there anyone else in her life? Think carefully, Professor. Anyone she might have turned to for help? Anyone else she might have been involved with?"

A brief pause, not lost on Meyerhoff. "Not that I know of," Patrick said.

"Did Angel ever go in and out of her house through her bedroom window?"

"Lots of times."

"How did she reach it?"

"Drainpipe, anchored to the house."

"Did you ever get in and out that way?"

"We all did. Her father used to lock her in her room when he went out. But there was no lock on the window."

"Do you think she got out that way the day she ran away?"

"I have no idea."

"What do you remember about that day? Do you remember the date?"

"June 28, 1972," he said promptly, "give or take a day."

"I see it's stuck in your memory."

"Not because of her running away," Patrick said. "It was something else that happened."

"What was that?"

"Vinny wrecked our car, this fifty-seven Chevy we'd rebuilt almost from scratch. A real beauty."

"Jeez," said Meyerhoff, as wide-eyed as he could manage with the bags. "How'd that happen?"

"Drag racing. He tried to deny it. Pretended the car was stolen, but finally, when I said I was calling the cops, he came clean. Two years we worked on that car, two fucking years; finally we get it on the road, and he totals it in a night."

Twenty years later, Patrick's voice still quivered with passionate indignation, and no wonder. Next to sex, nothing means more to a teenage boy than his car. Not surprising he remembered the date, Meyerhoff thought; it was stranger that Vinny didn't. "What happened to the car?"

"It went off a cliff. Forty-foot drop, straight down into a quarry. Vinny miscalculated; barely made it out. I was so fucking pissed, I told him he should have gone down with the ship."

"You never retrieved it?"

"What for?"

"And this happened the same night Angel disappeared?"

"Within a day or two. I know because it was when I called her to tell her about it, I heard she was gone."

"Did you ever hear from her again?"

"No, never."

Meyerhoff looked up from his notebook. "So what do you think happened?"

"I think she said to hell with us assholes and went off and made a new life for herself." Patrick answered so readily it was clear he'd been waiting for the chance. "I think she's out there somewhere, off the grid: living off the land in Idaho, or singing in Rome, or taking pictures in Paris."

"You're probably right," Meyerhoff said. "Speaking of pictures . . ." He opened his briefcase, a battered but venerable old Coach bag that Rae had given him when he first made detective, and brought out a scuffed manila envelope. As he handed it across the desk, he felt a passing twinge where his conscience used to be.

Patrick opened the envelope and took out the photo. It took a moment to register. When it did, he dropped it facedown onto the desk. He stared at his hands, gripping the desk edge, and a deep flush spread over his face.

"Did she surprise the two of you?" Meyerhoff asked gently. "Is that what happened?"

Patrick got up and crossed to a window overlooking a small square. He kept his back to Meyerhoff. "No. You don't understand."

"Did she walk in on you?"

"This is none of your business."

"Everything to do with Angel is my business now."

Patrick tossed the hair out of his eyes and finally turned around. "It was her idea. Her initiative. A going-away party for her two favorite people in the world, she said."

Meyerhoff looked at him without comprehension.

Patrick rolled his eyes. "She was *with* us."

"I see. Where was this taken?"

"My bedroom."

"So you're saying she brought a camera to bed with her?"

"The camera was with her clothes. Afterward, she showered and dressed in the bathroom. By the time she came back, we . . . well, we didn't even hear her."

"She set you up," Meyerhoff said disapprovingly.

"No. She couldn't have expected . . ." His voice trailed off.

"Then why take the picture?"

Patrick shrugged. "Second nature with her."

"So then what?"

"Nothing. She split."

"And you went after her."

"No. I wasn't in a state to chase after anyone."

"Come on," the detective scoffed. "How long would it take to throw on some clothes?"

"It's not just that. We were smashed."

"Still, a broad takes a picture of you like that, and you don't even go after her?"

"It wasn't that big a deal. A couple of kids, drunk, a little youthful experimentation." Patrick let out a laugh, a poor sort of thing, but Meyerhoff gave him credit for trying. "Besides, I knew I'd get it off her eventually."

"But you didn't, did you?"

"Only because she ran away."

"What made you think she'd just hand it over? From what I gather, Angel liked having power over people."

"Not that kind of power," he said coldly. "She'd never have stooped to blackmail."

"Getting herself knocked up isn't blackmail?"

"You have a very cynical way of looking at things," Patrick said.

Meyerhoff made a show of picking up the picture and examining it closely, while Patrick squirmed. After a moment he blurted out, "Who's seen that thing?"

"Just me," Meyerhoff said serenely, "and the police-lab guy. So far."

"So far?"

"Nobody's looking to embarrass anyone here. I wouldn't need to show it to anyone else if I can get some help from you."

"What do you want?"

"I recognize you, of course—your face is turned to the camera. And I think I know who your partner is; but I need to hear it from you."

Patrick leaned his head against the windowpane and shut his eyes. A moment passed. "It was Caleb," he said finally, his voice a croak. "Caleb Rhys."

28

Jeremiah kept his cool for the duration of the short conversation—nothing to gain by killing the messenger—but when he hung up he let out a volley of curses that would have done a camel driver proud. What timing, he thought, what incredible timing. Though his informant had pled ignorance, Jeremiah's bitterness found a focus in Willa; either this was her doing or it was the mother of all coincidences. For twenty years no one had so much as thought of Angel Busky; then Willa set out to locate her and suddenly the police were involved.

Did she even spare a thought for him, what this could do to him? Where the police went, the press was sure to follow; and the truth hardly mattered when one juicy headline was all it would take to sink his nomination without a trace. Only let his supporters read his name in conjunction with the words "missing girl" and they would scuttle away like sand crabs: all this thanks to an idle woman with too much time on her hands and a sentimental attachment to the past.

He glanced at the dresser clock: 6:20. Olivia would be home any minute to change for dinner. Whatever else happened, his wife was not to be worried by this eruption of his past—his nonexistent past, as far as she was concerned.

He needed to act. Another man would have grabbed the phone and blasted Willa forthwith, but Jeremiah prided himself on circumspection and self-control. The more he felt, the less he showed; and what he lost in spontaneity he gained in strategic advantage. The pressing question was not how the police got involved, but what to do about it now that they were. To answer that he needed more information, information that Willa, having stirred up this hornets' nest, was best situated to provide.

He took a deep, cleansing breath and reached for the phone.

Her machine picked up on the fourth ring. He listened to her voice. His own, when it emerged, was gratifyingly free of anger; it was pleasant, polite, and businesslike.

"Willa, it's Jeremiah Wright. I need to talk to you; no doubt you know why. We're going out shortly, so don't bother returning this call. I'll try you again when we get home tonight. Hope to find you in. Thanks."

Hanging up, he heard the garage door open, then close. He quickly stripped and hit the shower. Olivia had her own bathroom; she wouldn't bother him in here. For a long time he stood under the shower, hot water sluicing over his upraised face. His pores opened and were cleansed; his brain thawed and regained its suppleness. When he emerged he felt ready once again to face the world.

When Jeremiah called, Willa had been driving Chloe and Lauren to the final dress rehearsal of *Annie*. Tomorrow they would perform it for the school, Friday for the community. Chloe had had to be coaxed to eat a bite or two of dinner; poor child was nervous as a cat, which in a way was good for Willa, since it overrode her own nervousness about the upcoming reunion.

It's not that she was unprepared. By now, Willa had the whole weekend mapped out, from room assignments to menus. She had opened the pool, done the shopping, stocked up on booze, cleaned the house. All that remained was to finish and print out the journal digest, her contribution to the communal memory, and that she would do tomorrow. No, what worried Willa wasn't the logistics of the gathering; it was the guests. They had all followed such divergent paths, grown into such different people; what would they find to talk about once the flow of reminiscences dried up? Judy Trumpledore's advice came back to haunt her: "Stock up on board games," her editor had said. Patrick claimed that whatever drew them together in the first place still existed, but Willa had her doubts. So much else had been lost.

When she arrived home, the house was deathly quiet. She was glad she wouldn't be spending the whole evening alone. Jovan Luisi was coming over on business he'd declined to discuss on the phone. Willa didn't mind; quite the contrary, if the truth be told. Jovan had backed off since the police stepped in; and though she hadn't made much of his presence, she did feel his absence.

The wildflowers in the front hall, picked from her own garden, were shedding petals. Willa emptied the vase, then went upstairs to change. The message light on her answering machine was blinking. Willa tossed her purse onto the bed and jabbed the play button.

Willa, it's Jeremiah Wright. I need to talk to you; no doubt you know why. We're going out shortly, so don't bother returning this call. I'll try you again when we get home tonight. Hope to find you in. Thanks.

"Ouch," she said. Not a happy camper, no, not at all. Patrick got that right. Not that Jeremiah sounded angry; on the contrary, he was achingly polite. His cool, clipped voice reminded her of the time Shake had knocked over Mrs. Wright's china cabinet, and Jeremiah ordered them all to get out and let him deal with it.

Who had told him? Vinny, perhaps? But Willa couldn't see Vinny phoning Jeremiah. Patrick might have done it, after second thoughts; or Meyerhoff himself might have reached out. How much did Jeremiah know? Did he blame her in particular for bringing in the police, or was he just generally displeased? Willa replayed the message. The phrase "no doubt you know why" seemed ominous. She hoped he wasn't calling to back out of the reunion. That would ruin everything.

She opened her closet door, started riffling through her clothes. Was she wrong to have gone to the cops, after all? She flung a pair of black silk pants onto the bed. Everyone was mad at her: Jeremiah; Patrick, though he wouldn't admit it; no doubt the others would be, too, if they found out. Even O'Rourke, the high school principal, had been furious. But so what? If it turned out she was wrong about Angel, if Angel was alive and well, living in Oshkosh or Timbuktu, then let them be as mad as they liked; she'd take the blame. But what if she was right? What if Angel really was dead? What if someone had killed her, faked it to look like she ran away, and gone on with his life as if nothing had happened? Well, then to hell with their pique and inconvenience.

She pulled out a shirt, red with black piping, then put it back; too much of an outfit. Tried and discarded a little white sweater that was tight in the bust. All clothing sends messages; Angel had taught her that. What did she want to say to Jovan? What did he have to say to her, for that matter? Was this just an excuse to see her? And if so, what had taken him so long? For there was something pending between them, though she couldn't say what it was. That kiss in the zoo sky tram had stayed with her, a subliminal irritant, like an unresolved chord.

What if Jeremiah called back while Jovan was there? Willa looked forward to that conversation like a dose of castor oil. She didn't mind so much about the others, but she felt guilty about Jeremiah. It had always been part of the deal that they watch his back. She remembered the time she'd first figured that out. The Great Assembly Bust, they'd called it ever after. Juniors and seniors had been summoned to a surprise armed forces assembly. On the auditorium stage, flanked by two huge American flags, four men in various military uniforms stood at attention behind folding chairs. Principal Grievely led the assembly in the pledge of allegiance. Then he welcomed their distinguished guests and in the same breath warned that any student who attempted to disrupt the proceedings would be subject to instant suspension.

Vinny went first, as he had every right to do. Five minutes into the army recruiter's pitch, Vinny stood up and started shouting about his brother who died in Vietnam. He was hauled out, kicking and yelling, by two male teachers.

Patrick was the next to stand up, then Caleb, then Shake: One by one they heckled and were ejected. Willa in those days had a soft voice and a fear of public speaking, but she knew what she had to do and she did it; shortly thereafter she found herself marching toward the principal's office in the custody of a female gym teacher, who gripped Willa's arm as if she were Bonnie Parker.

The atmosphere in Grievely's waiting room was celebratory. One by one they arrived, until they were all there save one. Willa kept looking at the door.

Caleb noticed. "Nervous?" he asked kindly; for it was her first suspension.

"No, I was looking for Jeremiah."

"He won't be here. Jeremiah keeps his head down in school."

"And that's okay?" Willa was amazed. Speaking out in that assembly had seemed as much a test as any she'd had in a classroom.

"It's more than okay," he told her. "We've got our full quota of fuckups. Jeremiah's good right where he is."

It explained a lot of things she'd noticed without understanding. It explained why Jeremiah hung with them outside school but not inside; why he rarely smoked weed and nobody pressed him (except Angel, that devil); why, when everyone else had to handle their own parent problems, they all conspired to elude and deceive Jeremiah's mother; and why he alone got a pass on activities likely to lead to suspension. He wasn't AWOL that day in the principal's office; he was on special assignment. Jeremiah was their secret weapon, their overworld spy; he was one of the good guys, and it was their job to keep him viable. That was the code, and Willa had adopted it, as she'd adopted everything else about them: their clothes, their slang, their drugs, their politics. And it still applied; hence her guilt.

Still, she'd tried, hadn't she? Never mentioned his name, till that detective showed up with the picture. And then her not having mentioned him looked suspicious, so she'd achieved the very opposite of what she'd meant to do.

Willa sighed. She noticed that her bed was now strewn with clothing, dozens of permutations, yet none that seemed exactly right. Perhaps she was unsure of the message. Settling at last on the black silk pants and a tailored white shirt, she was then faced with the question of how many buttons to leave open. One was crisp and businesslike; three screamed come and get me. She compromised on two.

Nancy hadn't said a word in fifty miles, and she wasn't sleeping, either. She was staring straight ahead at nothing, clutching a pillow and a box of Cheez-Its on her lap.

"Check out that sunset," Shake ventured. No reply. Sighing, he turned on the radio. A blast of country music filled the car for a moment; then Nancy switched it off.

Five more miles of silence, Shake driving, one hand on the wheel, whistling softly. Was the woman going to sulk all the way to New York? God knew she was capable of it; she'd done it once the entire length of Route 1, her most scenic if not her longest sulk. And all this just because he wanted to see his old friends, who happened also to be her old friends, though you'd never know it from the way she was carrying on. For weeks he'd had to listen to her dire warnings and prophecies, her some-things-are-better-left-alones and other cryptic utterances designed to cover up the one real reason she didn't want to go, which was shame. She was ashamed of the weight she'd put on, ashamed of the loss of looks that had never had much more than youth going for them anyway.

He'd done his best to sweeten the deal. Offered, on his own initiative, to take a few extra days and visit her parents before heading up to Willa's. A major concession, given that he was unable to breathe in her parents' house, much less work; the plastic slipcovers alone depressed him for days afterward. But Nancy had continued to argue until he'd told her once and for all to knock it off; he was going to the reunion, and she could do whatever the hell she wanted.

The sodium lights along the highway bleached color from the car. Shake glanced sideways at his wife's wan, fleshy face, the deep creases running from her nostrils to the corners of her mouth, the sagging chin. When did she get so middle-aged? He felt a moment's pity for her. She could hardly welcome the inevitable comparisons to Willa, exactly the same age but still hot. Shake thought of Patrick, and laughed aloud.

Nancy swung her head. "What?" she said.

"Patrick, still chasing Willa after all these years. Poor schmuck."

She sniffed. "She's a tease. Always was."

Shake knew better than to answer. When it came to other women, there was no pleasing Nancy. Willa was a tease, Angel was a slut; while she herself was Tammy Wynette, always standing by her man. True, she had stuck by him through some bad shit. But did she ever consider what it was like to be the object of such heroic, unflinching devotion? It was like marrying your mother, for Chrissake; you ended up with Mom squared. She had wrapped her life around his, like a vine encircling a tree until the tree suffocates for lack of light and air.

It's not as if he'd chosen to marry her. But he did the right thing when she got knocked up, and any regrets he had about that were outweighed by what he'd gotten in return: their son. Somehow, between the two of them, they'd turned out a damn good kid. And if there was one thing Shake was proud of in his life, apart from his music, it was knowing he'd been a good father to the boy. Dylan had tapped parts of him Shake never knew existed. He'd wanted more kids, but Nancy drew a line in the sand: No more, she declared, till he bought her a house. And he'd meant to, he really had. But somehow the money they put aside for a down payment kept getting used for emergencies, like the busted transmission on her Ford, his demo, a very special sax . . . so that somehow the house never did get bought, or the second child conceived. And now it was too late, not physically, perhaps, but emotionally.

Things had been better between them when Dylan lived at home. At least then there'd been someone else to sop up some of that hormonal flood. But Dylan was gone; he'd escaped while Shake remained, Nancy's sole object. So she fussed and she worried. He couldn't really blame her; poor old girl, she missed the boy as much as he did—more, because she had fewer resources. Shake could always lose himself in music, no matter how bad he felt.

Strange, he thought, that most of his old friends were still childless. Only Vinny and Willa had had kids. Maybe Caleb; no one knew. "I hope Caleb comes," he said; his wife shrugged. Shake shook two cigarettes out of his pack and lit them both with the car lighter. He put one between Nancy's lips and drew on the other. It suddenly occurred to him that Angel's baby, if she'd had it, would be older than Dylan, older than its parents when it was conceived. This thought saddened him for some reason. He turned on the radio. In a little while, he was singing along.

Travis was flying first class. He hadn't paid to fly first class, not because he couldn't afford to, but because he found the whole idea offensive and reactionary. But the airline overbooked, then offered a free round-trip ticket and an upgrade to anyone who would give up his seat on that evening's flight. Travis volunteered: Why not? No one was meeting him at the airport. He was staying at Patrick's for a few days, but Patrick wouldn't care what time he got in.

When the plane rose, banking eastward over Albuquerque, Travis had felt a lurch in the pit of his stomach; that feeling lin-

gered long after they reached cruising altitude. Gum might have
helped. He had some in the rucksack that served as his carry-on
luggage, but how tacky would that be, chewing gum in first class?
It was interesting that, as much as he disapproved of the whole
elitist concept, Travis enjoyed the experience of first class. It just
felt right. The seats were larger, the leg room downright generous; he could stretch out his legs and lean back without landing
in someone's lap. But the biggest difference was the stew-
ardesses, a difference that he, who had an eye for the breed,
noticed immediately. They were better looking in first class; and
they showered you with free champagne and slippers and sleep
masks and offers of every service imaginable except the one you
wanted most . . . and perhaps even that was not unattainable.
There was one attendant in particular, a saucy little redhead who
kept giving him the eye.

The seat beside his was empty. Travis had to believe there was
a reason for that. He'd already scoped out his fellow passengers,
mostly paunchy older men, business types in suits and ties; no
competition there. Travis was no Adonis, but he was tan and
muscular and fit, and his presence in first class said he had
money, a virtue which in women's eyes eclipsed all others. No
wonder she was looking.

Dinner was a ten-ounce sirloin with sautéed onions and mush-
rooms, salad, and a crisp baked potato. Travis had eaten many a
worse meal in restaurants. He had champagne with his meal, and
when the red-haired stewardess came around to refill his glass,
he patted the seat beside him and offered her a drink.

"Aren't you sweet?" she replied, in a Southern accent so thick
he suspected it was phony. "But you know, if the captain caught
me drinking on duty, he'd throw me right off the plane."

"He'd have to get through me first," Travis said gallantly. "Anyway, I won't tell if you won't."

She gave him one of those high-wattage stewardess smiles
that begin and end with the teeth. But Travis could see that
underneath the professional mask she liked him; and as she
walked away, there was a little wiggle to her ass that was just for
him. "I'll take a rain check," he called after her. She didn't turn
around, but some passengers did. Fucking first-class snobs. Later

he saw her standing outside the galley with another attendant, telling her something that made both of them laugh.

Bitch. She reminded him of that archetypal redhead, Angel Busky, everyone's Angel of Mercy but his. What would it have cost her, back then, to give him one little mercy fuck? He'd adored her, her and Willa both; hell, he'd adored them all, boys as well as girls. His horniness a big joke to them, a consuming torment to him. What would it have cost, and how much misery saved, if she had been kind to him?

His queasiness, which had died down over dinner, returned in full force. It wasn't the flight then; it was the destination, and no wonder. Nearly twenty years had passed since he'd been back. When he left he swore he wouldn't be back until he'd made something of his life, and he'd kept that bitter vow; but now that the time had come, he found he needed something in return. Approbation, vindication, call it what you will. It wasn't enough that he'd made a good and useful life for himself. He needed to see it reflected in their eyes, in their altered attitude. "Travis," he needed to hear, "we never really knew you. Travis, you're okay."

The cabin lights dimmed, and the movie came on, a first-run comedy, but Travis had already seen it. He switched on the overhead light and rummaged through his rucksack for the book he was reading, a collection of short stories by Ray Bradbury, but his hand fell instead on a packet of photos. He took them out. Along with pictures of his house and others he'd built were old photos, dug up at Willa's request: artless snapshots, now faded and worn, and yet even by the dim light of the overhead lamp, the faces emerged so vividly that Travis's breath caught in his throat. What a beautiful bunch they'd been. Not all equally, of course. Patrick had a funny face, all slants and angles, but so animated that even in still shots the eye was drawn to him. Nancy's face was plain, though her body was as round and abundant as Mother Earth. But Angel and Willa were to die for, delicious teenage vamps; Vinny, Shake, and Jeremiah were good looking, each in his own way; and Caleb, with his amber curls and Grecian profile, possessed an almost elfin beauty—not the cute, Disney sort of elf, but Tolkien's uncanny variety.

As for Travis, with his buck teeth and thick glasses, well, he

was the ugly duckling of the group. At least he had the satisfaction of knowing he was better looking now than then. How much
had they changed? he wondered. Patrick had sounded exactly the
same, but voices age less than faces, bodies, and hairlines. Willa's
voice retained that touch of arrogance that told him she was still
beautiful. Not surprising in her case; good bones age well. Travis
didn't even want to think about what Angel looked like now; but
then, Angel wasn't expected.

Another was coming from far away, traveling by train as he was
wont to do, not because he feared flying, but because he enjoyed
trains. He liked watching the land unfurl outside his window,
great swaths of it surprisingly unpopulated but for the occasional
Kinkaidesque lit-up country house. It was good to remember
now and then how big this country really was. If you weren't in a
hurry, and he rarely was, rail was just about the perfect mode of
travel.

There were, of course, practical reasons as well. Trains offered
more anonymity than planes, more comfort than buses, more
convenience than cars. They covered distance in real, not virtual
time; this, and the constant flux of passengers, made it possible
to embark on a train as one person and alight from it quite
another. One could set out from the West Coast as Robert Alexan-
der (a wonderfully generic name, solid yet instantly forgettable)
and arrive on the East Coast as, say, Caleb Rhys.

Now there was a name with memories. He hadn't used it in
twelve years, not counting lightning visits to his sister, and he
wasn't altogether comfortable at the prospect of reverting to it
now. Not out of fear—the actual risk was minimal, as no one who
wished him harm knew him by that name—but because, over the
years, he'd come to enjoy the freedom inherent in naming oneself. That most men clung to their original names, no matter how
unwieldy, Caleb ascribed to sentimentality and the need for a
superficial sort of continuity. Even he, the first time he changed,
chose a name foolishly close to his own.

But that was several names ago, when he was still young and
naive. Now Caleb's sense of continuity resided not in his name
but rather in the momentum of wanting, of desire that is not

focused on a stationary object but rather on the next goal, the next level. Because no matter how high you climbed, how much you acquired, there was always another level just out of reach.

And now he was going home. Home to Willa, home to Patrick, home to New York. It would have been an occasion for nostalgia in a man given to such emotions, but Caleb was not that man. His life was a series of hermetically sealed compartments, so airtight that it took work to open them. To play oneself, or rather, the man he would have been had he not been so many other men in the interim, would seem the simplest of roles, but it needed the same careful preparation as any other role.

The steady motion of the train lulled him into a state akin to hypnosis. Memories surfaced randomly, but they were desiccated things, drained of emotion. Many involved Patrick, his friend from kindergarten through high school. Yet the thought of seeing him again sparked no current in Caleb; mild curiosity was all he could muster for Patrick and his other childhood friends. It wasn't them he was going to see; it was Willa, and Willa alone.

He was a much more conscientious student now than when he was in school. He'd done his homework. He knew she was a wealthy woman, even by his standards. Upon her husband's death, she had inherited not only his entire estate, but also his parents'. The manner of his death, the circumstances surrounding it, meant that despite all her money, she was very likely vulnerable.

That she owed him went without saying. If there were women in the world who considered Caleb heartless, and there were, they had one of their own to thank for it. He was almost sure he'd had a heart once. He'd given it to Willa, who'd carelessly tossed it away.

29

Jeremiah and Olivia were dining at Le Petit Jardin, Washington's latest meet-and-greet spot, small, expensive, and cleverly laid out to allow patrons to be seen but not overheard. The chef/owner was politically savvy as well as culinarily gifted. Casual diners of the right sort were welcome; casual dress was not.

Their guests that evening were George Ivey, the incumbent U.S. congressman from Wickham, and Martha Grogan, chairperson of the Wickham Democratic Committee. Despite the informality of the setting, it was an important meeting. Ivey was committed to Jeremiah's nomination; Martha was the problem. It was no longer a secret in political circles that Ivey was going to resign; the big question was when. If he announced his intention within the next few weeks, the local Democratic committee, headed by Martha, would nominate his successor, which meant that Jeremiah would probably have to prevail in a primary. If, on the other hand, Ivey delayed his announcement and his resignation, it would be too late for potential candidates to circulate petitions, and the decision on his successor would fall to the incumbent himself. This was by far the best solution for Jeremiah, who did not doubt that he would win a primary but preferred to spend his energy and his wife's money on the election itself. Ivey was willing to delay; but taking that route left them open to accusations of having finessed the system and bypassed the voters. Martha Grogan's support could insulate them from such charges . . . if they could win her over.

On their way to the restaurant, Olivia had rehearsed him on the minutiae of the chairwoman's life and career. "We met her last year at the Kleinfeld's party. A widow with one grown son who she put through law school. Former shop steward; worked her way up the union ladder, then moved laterally into the party hierarchy. She's known as a coalition builder. When the chairmanship of the local branch opened up, she slipped in as everybody's compromise candidate. Don't let the veneer fool you. She may look like Edith Bunker, but she's one sharp cookie."

"What's she care most about?"

"Jobs, jobs, and jobs. It's the union woman in her."

"We can do jobs," Jeremiah said, a touch too gaily.

Olivia glanced sideways at him. "Are you all right?"

"Sure; why?"

"You're driving on the wrong side of the road."

He got back in the right lane.

They'd arrived early, but Martha Grogan was already there. Jeremiah remembered her as soon as he saw her; at the Kleinfeld's Christmas party he'd mistaken her for someone's mother. She was a short, plump woman with a round face, small blue eyes, thinning bouffant hair dyed an improbable auburn, and an air of benevolent dimness.

Cocktails at the bar, where they waited for George Ivey, were devoted to pleasantries and talk of mutual acquaintances. Olivia was very good at this, and Jeremiah let her take the lead while he smiled and nodded and fretted inwardly about Willa. What if she ignored his instructions and called while they were out? What message might she leave? He wouldn't lay two cents on her discretion. Better make sure he got to the answering machine first tonight.

Ivey arrived twenty minutes late. He kissed the women and shook hands with Jeremiah. "Sorry, all. One thing I won't miss: this damned D.C. traffic." His disease, whatever it was (Jeremiah had heard several variations, all with dire prognoses), was beginning to show. There was a gauntness to the congressman's face that hadn't been there before, an effortful squeeze to his handshake, intended to cover a tremor. It showed also in his tendency to get straight to the point, unlike Jeremiah, for whom the shortest distance between two points was often a winding path. "So what do you think of our boy here?" Ivey asked Martha, his hand on Jeremiah's shoulder.

"I'd say he's a big fish for our little pond," Martha said. Just then the maître d' came to seat them. Olivia and Jeremiah exchanged looks behind Martha's back. Over hors d'oeuvres, Olivia led the conversation around to her husband's deep ties to upstate New York.

"Oh really?" Martha Grogan said. "I understood that he hasn't lived in the state since he went away to Harvard." She pronounced it "Hahvahd," with a little twist to her mouth.

"Of course he has," Olivia said firmly. "We have a house in Old Wickham and we're up there every chance we get. Jeremiah grew up in New York; he's still very close to his old public school friends. In fact, just this coming weekend he's going to a class reunion, aren't you, darling?"

"Absolutely." Jeremiah smiled through gritted teeth. "Can't wait."

Over salad he brought up the job drain. Upstate had been hemorrhaging jobs for years, and Wickham County was no exception. Jeremiah spoke with great feeling about a dear friend and neighbor of theirs up in Old Wickham, fellow by the name of Gus Watson, who'd worked his entire adult life for the same manufacturing company, first as a machinist, then a foreman. Last Christmas, just weeks after his wife, Molly, was diagnosed with lymphoma, Gus's plant closed down and he lost his job. For six months he'd been looking for work, but there were no manufacturing jobs to be found, only minimum-wage service jobs with no health benefits. "Twenty years of sweat and loyalty and the man is left with nothing. No job, no income, no insurance; just three kids and a sick wife."

The others shook their heads sorrowfully. Even Olivia, who'd never heard of their good friends the Watsons, was moved by their plight.

Over the entrées they double-teamed Martha. Jeremiah asked for her support as humbly as if he needed it, while Ivey sang his praises. Martha ate stolidly, her eyes swinging from one speaker to the next while her fork continued its steady commute from plate to mouth. She didn't speak until her duck had been picked to the bone. Then she wiped her mouth daintily on a linen napkin and said, "Don't get me wrong, boys. It's always a pleasure to visit our nation's capital, and it's not that I don't appreciate a good meal; hell, you can see for yourselves I do. But I can't help wondering why you'd trouble yourselves. Past few days, I've had a dozen calls, from the governor and Senator Apfel on down, all putting in a good word for Jeremiah here. Do you really think I could withstand such an onslaught, even if I wanted to?"

"Oh, but I don't want your acquiescence, Martha," Jeremiah said quickly. "I will not be foisted on you. If I can't convince you that I'm the best person to represent you in the House, if I can't win your full and unqualified support, I won't run."

Ivey raised his eyebrows—he'd played enough poker to know what he was looking at here—while Martha smiled across the table at Olivia. "Seductive devil, your husband, isn't he?"

"Tell me about it," said Olivia.

"Full of blarney, though. He won't run without my support!" Martha brayed a laugh as she turned toward Jeremiah. "So this isn't about you wanting to wriggle out of a primary?"

Jeremiah ignored his wife's warning glance. Like Dylan, he didn't need a weatherman to know which way the wind blew. Tacking leeward, he adopted a confidential tone. "That, too, of course. Not because I wouldn't win a primary; I would. But it would cost us precious resources that could be better used in the general election."

"There are people, you know, who've paid their dues and think they have just as much right as you to put forth their candidacies."

"And very good people they are, too," George Ivey put in. "But they can't do for the district what Jeremiah can; and you know this."

Maybe Martha knew it, or maybe she just knew which end was up. By dessert she was onboard, part of the team. Jeremiah paid the bill with pleasure and added a generous tip. The others lingered over their coffee, sated and satisfied: Martha for having racked up deposits in the favor bank for doing what she would have had to do anyway, Ivey for having covered his ass. Jeremiah was wild to get home but of course showed nothing of this.

"That's it, then," Ivey said to Jeremiah with the air of one who, at some personal cost, has performed his side of a bargain. "The rest is up to you."

"I won't let you down, George."

"Better not. Nothing you need to tell us now, is there?" He winked. "No skeletons in the closet?"

"Not in mine," Jeremiah said blithely. "Olivia here's got a whole wardrobeful, haven't you, darling?"

His wife pretended to scowl at him. When the laughter died down, she laid her hand on Ivey's arm and said, in a voice a touch more Southern than usual, "Don't you worry about Jeremiah, George; 'cause, my goodness, if you think the New York press is tough on a fellow, you ought to see my daddy checkin' out potential sons-in-law."

They sat on a couch in Willa's den. Less formal than the rest of the house, the den was furnished in a pleasant mishmash of styles. There was a fireplace, a bar, an unfinished jigsaw puzzle on a small table, and the usual electronic toys: wide-screen TV, stereo equipment, a CD player. Family photos on the mantel included several of Simon Durrell. It occurred to Jovan that by now he'd seen every room in the house, except the one he wanted to see. "You promised me dinner," he said.

"Not *that* dinner," Willa said. "Wouldn't you rather do it another time, just the two of us?"

Was she flirting? Waste of energy if she was. One whole month he'd stayed away, doing his best not to think about her, and the moment she opened the door he was right back where he started.

"There's nothing I'd like more," he said. "But I need to meet these folks."

"Did Sergeant Meyerhoff put you up to this?"

"You said you wanted to find out what happened to Angel. Were you serious or not?"

She bristled. "What do you think?"

"Then let me come. I'm not talking about the whole weekend. One evening."

She rose and walked around the room. Her hair was loose about her shoulders. He wondered what her legs looked like beneath the black pants that flowed with her body. Her shirt was open just enough to tantalize. Jovan watched her move, though it gave him as much pain as pleasure. Did she know what she was doing?

"You're asking me to set them up," she said. "That's a rotten thing to do."

"Do you think one of your friends killed Angel?"

"No, of course not!"

"Then there's no problem," he said.

"There's a big problem. There are privacy issues. Maybe we did some stuff when we were young and wild that some of us might find embarrassing now."

"Come on, Willa. You think anyone gives a shit about a bunch of suburban kids smoking pot twenty years ago? That's not what this is about."

"What is it about, then? Why are you doing this? A girl you never met, a case you didn't even get paid for. . . . What do you care?"

Couldn't she see it in his eyes? It wasn't about Angel. It never was, not for him. Maybe Willa did see it; for she blushed and turned her head away.

"Willa," he said, "come here," and when she obeyed, his heart raced. He took her hand, held it between both of his. "If Angel is dead," he said, "someone killed her. Probably not a stranger. Probably someone close to her."

"Her father," she said. "As I've been saying all along."

"Maybe."

"If you knew what we were to each other, you'd know that none of us could have done it. We were each other's family."

"Murder happens in the best of families," he said with a shrug. The pulse in her wrist beat against his thumb. She wouldn't meet his eyes. But she didn't pull away, either.

"It wouldn't work anyway," she said. "They'd clam up around you."

"People talk at reunions. The problem's usually getting them to shut up."

"They're not stupid. They'll know who you are."

"Not if you don't tell them. Just introduce me as a friend."

"Patrick knows."

"I own a corporate security company that did some work for Simon's firm. That's how we met. But our relationship is personal."

"Personal," she said, looking at him, finally, with eyes a man could drown in. The windows were open, and the room smelled of honeysuckle. He could smell her scent as well, something enticing and exotic. "You know what they'll assume."

"Is that a problem?"

"Don't know; think we could pull it off?" she said, with the smile of a woman who knows exactly what she's doing.

Jovan reached for her.

* * *

Late that night, alone in her room, Willa stood naked in front of her mirror and examined herself critically. A few stretchmarks, courtesy of Chloe; definitely not the body of a nineteen-year-old anymore. But not bad, she decided. Nothing to be ashamed of.

She put on a T-shirt and got into bed, turned on the TV news. Bill Clinton was in trouble again. She watched him field a question from Connie Chung. Even as he denied having had an affair, he was running a speculative eye over the reporter. Definitely a player. Willa could spot them a mile away . . . except when it mattered.

But she couldn't focus on the news. She lay with her arm beneath her head, thinking of Jovan, knowing he was thinking about her. The taste of his kisses was still on her lips, the rasp of his stubble on her cheeks. If Chloe hadn't come home when she did . . . but perhaps it was for the best. There was pleasure in anticipation.

After Simon died and the extent of his philandering was revealed, along with the fact that the marriage she'd considered solid was actually Swiss cheese, Willa had been certain she would never have sex again. Obviously she stank at it; why else would Simon have felt the need for serial mistresses? As for her own needs, first among them was the need to protect herself. She didn't ever want to open herself up, make herself vulnerable to another man. Deceivers all, according to Shakespeare, who would know.

But Jovan was different, because Jovan was her choice. Not that she'd risked much; it had been obvious from the start that he was attracted to her. But he hadn't meant to act on it until she'd deliberately provoked him, and what a delicious rush of power she'd felt then! This is what Angel knew all along, Willa thought; this is what she tried to teach me.

The telephone rang. She muted the TV and answered. "Sorry to call so late," Jeremiah said. Street noise in the background told her he was either calling from a public phone or he was outside on a cell. "Did I wake you?"

"Not at all," Willa said. "I was just lying here watching Clinton try and wriggle his way out of trouble."

"You're talking about our next president, you realize."

"You think?"

"I'd put money on it."

"Do you know him?"

"Met him a few times, at dinners and the like. Formidable package: Southern manners, Oxford intellect, and New York City street smarts."

She smiled. "With one itsy-bitsy little problem."

"Don't know about itsy bitsy. Word is, it's sizable."

They laughed together. He sounded the same, Jeremiah, and it came back to her how talking with him had always been more like conversation with a girl than a guy. Not because there wasn't sexual tension, but because of Jeremiah's intuition, curiosity, and penchant for gossip, traits Willa associated more with her own sex.

Finally he got down to business. "I hear the cops are looking for Angel."

"True," she said.

"Why?"

"Uh . . . maybe because no one's seen her in twenty years?"

"But how would they know that? Did you go to them?"

"*They* came to *me*," she said. Technically true. She wouldn't lie, Willa had decided, but needn't volunteer. Why should she, when the full story would only spoil the weekend? "How'd you hear, anyway?"

"A little birdie told me. I was a bit surprised you didn't." More pained than angry, he sounded.

She winced. "I know, I should have. But I was afraid you'd stay away, and that would be tragic. You are still coming, aren't you?"

His answer was in the pause that followed. "I'd love to, of course. But—"

"I think," she interrupted, "it might be unwise to stay away."

The muted TV switched to a scene of carnage in the Middle East: shots of an ambulance, Orthodox men with body bags, weeping women. "Really," Jeremiah said at last, without inflection. "Unwise how?"

"Unwise," she said, "in that you'd be more conspicuous in your absence than in your presence. We all tried to keep your name out of it. But the detective had a photo of all of us, including you, and he seemed suspicious because we hadn't named you in the first place."

"He knows about the reunion?"

"He found out."

"From you," Jeremiah said.

"Jeremiah, I'm so sorry this is causing you concern. It's the last thing anyone wants."

"It's not the police who concern me, it's the press. Willa, within the next few weeks, I'm going to be making a major move. I can't get into details just yet, but you have to understand how sensitive my position is. One sensational story linking my name to a missing girl and the opportunity of a lifetime is gone."

"But there hasn't been any publicity, and I don't see why there should be."

"Sometimes the cops turn to the media for help. 'Has anyone seen this woman?'—that sort of thing."

"They haven't so far," she said. "I don't get the feeling this is a huge priority for them."

"What do they think happened to Angel?"

"The detective wouldn't say. I'll tell you what *I* think. I think she's dead, and I think her father killed her."

"Be careful what you say, Willa," Jeremiah replied. "Be very careful."

30

"Oh my God," Willa said, with perhaps a shade more surprise than was polite, "don't you look great!" She wouldn't have known Travis. Gone was the gawky, gap-toothed adolescent of her memory. He had traded in his glasses for contacts, had his teeth fixed, and lost that sour smell of adolescent desperation that used to be both his vanguard and his signature. His skin, once pale and spotty, was now deeply tanned. Even the dandruff was gone.

"Look who's talking, beautiful," he said.

Patrick pushed between them. "How about me? Don't I look great?"

Willa laughed. "Oh, you—you don't change." She put the cakes they'd brought into the kitchen, then led them upstairs to the blue guest room with twin beds.

"What," said Patrick, "no mints on the pillow?"

"No room service, either," she said. "I hope you two don't mind sharing."

"I mind," Patrick said. "He snores. Why don't I bunk with you instead?"

Willa ignored him. Travis, meanwhile, was rooting through a battered old rucksack, possibly the same one he'd had when she'd known him before. He handed her a rounded package wrapped in brown packing paper. "What's this?" she asked.

"Open it."

She did. Inside was a ceramic vase with the figure of a deer incised in aqua against an ocher background. It was a beautiful piece, delicately wrought, perfectly balanced. She thanked him sincerely and asked who had made it.

"Friend of mine," Travis said, flushed with pleasure, "a potter in Tesuque. When you come out, I'll take you to her studio. Look inside."

She peered into the narrow opening of the vase. A dozen or so thin white joints layered the bottom.

"That's for you. Party supplies are separate." He tapped his breast pocket.

"You flew with all this on you?"

"Wouldn't fly without it."

"He didn't even need a plane," Patrick cut in. He'd tested both beds and now claimed the one by the window by sprawling on it. "Where's Chloe?"

"Spending the weekend with a friend," Willa said.

"That's probably wise."

"Her play's tonight. I'll have to desert you for a while."

"Can I go, too?" Travis said eagerly. "I'd like to meet her."

Over my dead body, she thought, surprising herself.

An hour or so later, Nancy's trusty old Ford chugged up the circular drive and shuddered to a halt. Shake reached for the door handle, but Nancy didn't stir.

"Fuck," he said. "We're here. We've come. Why not enjoy yourself, instead of sitting there like a lump?"

"So I'm a lump now," Nancy said.

"Hey, I didn't bitch and moan at your parents', did I? And I had a lot more cause."

She crossed her arms over her chest and stared straight ahead. "Look at this place and tell me we belong here."

"We belong here," he said. "We're invited guests."

"It's a fucking mansion."

"When did you get so hung up on material bullshit? It never used to matter to us who had money and who didn't."

"It wasn't supposed to, but it always did. They were the slummers and we were the slummees."

Shake reached across her and popped the trunk button. "Nobody else remembers it like that."

"Well," Nancy said, "I guess that's my job."

Quite by chance, Vinny and Jeremiah arrived together. Jeremiah, dressed in gray slacks and a blue blazer, parked his Jeep behind Vinny's BMW. "Nice ride," he called out, hurrying up the driveway after Vinny.

"Bought it off a customer," Vinny said. "How's it going?"

"Long time no see, buddy." Jeremiah held out his hand; Vinny, out of habit more than necessity, wiped his own on his jeans before clasping Jeremiah's. They looked each other over. "Can you believe this is really happening?" Jeremiah said.

"Yeah," Vinny said, "like where'd the time go? Kinda surprised to see you here, big hotshot like yourself."

"Not too big to remember his oldest friends."

"Jeremiah Wright," called another voice, female and severe, "does your mother know where you are?"

Both of them turned. Willa was striding toward them from the side of the house. She wore a black sheath and a Spanish shawl.

"Let's hope not," Jeremiah said. "God, you look fantastic."

She kissed them both, linked an arm in each of theirs. "I'm so glad you guys came. Everyone's out back by the pool. Drop your stuff on the porch and come say hello."

She led them down a garden path lined with rosebushes, toward the pool on the far end of the property. The six-foot-high surrounding fence was disguised by fragrant spirea shrubs, already beginning to bloom. Just inside the fence was a pool house with a storage room, cabana, bathroom, and wet bar.

Patrick was the first to spot the newcomers. He jumped up from his lounge chair next to Nancy and Travis and hurried over. "Well, well, well, look what the cat dragged in."

Jeremiah batted away his outstretched hand and hauled him in for a bear hug. "Patch, jeez, you haven't changed a bit."

"Older, if not wiser." Then Patrick greeted Vinny with a hug. "Good to see you, man. I knew you wouldn't let us down."

Shake was in the pool. He swam to the side, hoisted himself up and out in a single fluid movement, and approached with water dripping from his long hair and outstretched arms. Jeremiah, laughing, backed away. "Hands off, maniac."

"What's the matter," Shake leered, "'fraid I'll ruin your pretty blue blazer?"

"Yeah, as a matter of fact."

"Pussy."

Jeremiah blew him a kiss. Meanwhile, Vinny was greeting Travis with a punch to the shoulder and a slap on the back, which Travis returned in kind. "Who'da thunk it," Travis said, "the wild man of Beacon Hill, all grown up and respectable."

"Grown up, anyways," Vinny said. "You don't look too bad yourself, for a middle-aged fart."

Alone beside the pool, swaddled in flesh, Nancy smoked and watched.

After the first flush of greetings and catching up, a lull descended on the gathering. Booze was bound to help, but it takes time to kick in, and other, speedier lubricants had been banned in Jeremiah's presence, apologetically but firmly, by the candidate-to-be. In the interim there were several awkward pauses, during which the dreaded words *How will I get through a whole weekend with these people?* swam into Willa's thoughts, and, she supposed, into the others' as well.

Differences that in high school had been meaningless compared to their great commonalities had widened over time. Willa, having taken a chaise beside Vinny, soon exhausted her meager command of car talk, and Vinny seemed to have no other; he had not uttered a word for twenty minutes, though he drank steadily. Meanwhile, Jeremiah was doing his charming best with Nancy Shaker. Good luck to him, thought Willa, who'd had none herself. At Shake's request, she'd given them a tour of the house when they first arrived. Nancy had tagged along, saying nothing but looking appalled at every sign of extravagance. The master bathroom, with its sauna and skylit Jacuzzi, seemed to cause particular offense. "Our living room could fit in here," she'd whispered to her husband, though not so low that Willa couldn't hear. And then there was that bit of unpleasantness over their room. Willa had given them the bedroom above the garage because it had a double bed and a private bath attached. But when she showed it to them, she made the mistake of mentioning that it had served the original owners as servants' quarters. "Oh, really?" Nancy had said, with a jackknife of a smile. "Well, just so you know, I don't do windows."

Jeremiah didn't seem to be faring much better now; monosyllabic returns were all he received for his pains. By the look on Nancy's face, you'd have thought the woman was lying on a bed of nails instead of a padded chaise lounge. Why had she come, Willa wondered, when she so obviously didn't want to be here? But it was a good thing she had, for otherwise Willa would have been the only woman at the party; and that would not have been comfortable.

She wasn't comfortable now, sitting between Vinny and an equally tongue-tied Travis who, though outwardly changed, retained the speculative gaze that had always made Willa feel she was auditioning for the starring role in that night's masturbatory fantasy. Thank God for Patrick, who never met a silence he didn't try to kill.

"I just had a brilliant idea!" he called from the bar, where he had set up shop. The others moaned in unison, those very words having prefaced certain of their more harebrained schemes, but Patrick went on, unheeding. "Tomorrow, after we hit the hill, let's shoot down to Vinny's place. You guys have got to see it to believe it: a palace of a garage. Am I right, Vinny?"

"As repair stations go," said the proprietor, "it's a pip. But it's no tourist attraction."

"He's too modest. This garage, ladies and gents, services nothing but the best foreign cars. Jags, Audis, and Beemers make it their home away from home. No domestics need apply. Chevys could expire of old age waiting for service. Fords could die of thirst at its gates."

"We drive a Ford," Nancy said.

And Vinny growled, "What are you, my press agent?"

"I'm just braggin' on you, my friend," Patrick said. "I'm proud of you."

Vinny jerked a thumb at Patrick. "Listen to him. Fucking professor here is proud of me."

"You're my hero, man. I got where I got through sheer inertia. You built something out of nothing, made it all on your own."

"Dude, it's a gas station, not the friggin' Taj Mahal."

"It's the accomplishment that matters," Jeremiah put in. "And of course doing it all on your own."

"Hey now," Vinny said, but Jeremiah plowed on, his voice a shade unctuous, Willa thought.

"You had a goal and you achieved it. That's the real measure of success."

Vinny flushed, not with pleasure. "Oh, is it, Jeremiah? Is that the fucking measure of success?"

"Yeah, it is, Vinny. Only you want to watch your language. There are ladies present."

"Well, excuse the fuck outta me, O protector of the fair sex."

Jeremiah and Patrick exchanged a look that went back twenty years. "Easy there, big guy," Patrick said. "You're among friends."

"Right," the big man said. "I forgot." Then he laid his head back on the lounge and shut his eyes.

Willa shivered and drew her shawl more tightly around her. The breeze had picked up; it skimmed lightly over the surface of the pool, roiling the water and tinkling the wind chimes. She looked at her watch. It was time to go.

The band struck up the overture and the auditorium faded to black. Willa, in her nervousness, had rolled her program into a tight cone, and now tried unsuccessfully to straighten it on her knee. She would have to get another during intermission. The curtains parted on the orphanage set, and a hum arose from the audience as parents recognized their children onstage. In the back of the room, a baby began to fuss. *Shut it up or get it out*, Willa thought uncharitably, straining to hear the dialogue. She was sitting alone in the third row. Isabel Rapaport and her husband, Dennis, had invited her to join them, but Willa was too edgy to endure small talk. Better to sit among strangers who would not notice if she needed the handkerchief clutched in her left hand.

The first song began, and suddenly Chloe, unrecognizable in her red wig and costume, emerged from the crowd of orphans. She began to sing, her voice strong and confident, and the auditorium fell silent; even the baby ceased its mewling. When Willa shut her eyes and listened, chills ran through her. Mrs. Glouster was right. Willa didn't have the expertise to know how good Chloe was or could become, but she had enough of an ear to know that the question must be asked and answered. As soon as the reunion ended, she would start looking for a teacher.

The first act passed quickly. Willa spent the intermission wandering around the lobby, eavesdropping shamelessly. The story of Emily's accident and Chloe's last-minute elevation to the starring role was common knowledge to an audience that consisted primarily of students and their families. Having come prepared to make concessions, they were pleasantly surprised to find that none were needed. Chloe was praised on all sides.

In the second act, Chloe had a duet with Daddy Warbucks, and once again Willa felt Simon's absence. The feeling no longer carried the torrential force of pent-up grief that had flooded her the first time, but it leavened her joy and pride with a sadness she had never before allowed herself to acknowledge. He ought to have been here. Nothing he'd done should have cost him this. He'd made a fool of her, true; but now Willa saw that life had played a far crueler trick on him; and she felt pity, and the first, faint stirrings of forgiveness.

Parents milled about the lobby, waiting for their children to emerge. Willa, bathed in reflected glory, was congratulated by all who knew her. Isabel sought her out and threw her arms around Willa's neck.

"You must be so proud," she said. "I am, and I'm not even her mother."

"I'm amazed," Willa said. "It's a strange thing to discover that your child has gifts you never gave her."

"She is *so* talented."

"They were all wonderful," Willa said. "Thanks so much for taking Chloe this weekend."

"No problem," Isabel said. "Have your guests arrived yet?"

Willa hadn't told her about the reunion, but supposed that Chloe had; it was the reason, after all, she was spending the weekend with Lauren. "Yes. I've deserted them for a little while."

"I'm sure they'll amuse themselves. High school friends, Chloe said. Are they very much changed?"

Willa thought about that. "Well, older, of course. But not changed essentially, no. If anything, they seem more themselves than ever."

Then the stage door opened and Chloe emerged in the center of a group that included Lauren Rapaport and Roy Bliss. She was dressed in street clothes and carried two large shopping bags full of costumes and a wig. Few parents recognized her out of costume. She spotted Willa coming toward her and they met halfway.

Willa hugged her tightly. "You were wonderful. I'm so proud of you."

Chloe hugged her, too, as best she could with the bags. She glowed; Willa had never seen her happier, and this time it had nothing to do with *that boy* (as she still thought of him), nor did it arise from the praise of others. Rather, Chloe had the stunned, *eureka!* look of sudden discovery. Willa knew it; she remembered the feeling. For her it had come the first time she completed a story, read it over, and realized with a shock that it was good. That the story had been published and praised only amplified her pleasure; the seed had already been planted. Now Willa sensed a similar process at work in Chloe.

"Thanks, Mom," Chloe said, and thrust the bags into Willa's hands. "Could you take these home for me? We're going straight to the cast party."

"With Lauren?"

"Roy's taking her, too."

"And you two will be home by what time?"

"Four o'clock," Chloe said, then giggled at the look on her mother's face. "Midnight, like Cinderella."

"Call me when you get in."

"Mom!" she cried, making two long syllables of it.

"Call," said Willa, and kissed her good-bye.

She was tossing the bags into her trunk when they drove by. Roy Bliss flashed an insouciant Boy Scout salute. She watched the car until the taillights disappeared.

The party had moved indoors while she was away. The cold buffet she'd set out in the dining room had been ravaged. Willa followed a trail of smoke, music, and laughter to the den. Though her friends were sprawled all over the room, their attention was riveted on a single point, a high-backed armchair whose occupant Willa could not see. Something about the quality of their attention raised goose bumps on her arms: It was that familiar.

Travis was the first to notice her. "Finally!" he cried, and they all looked over with identical expressions of gleeful anticipation, so that even before the occupant of the armchair stood and turned, Willa knew. And though her heart leaped uncontrollably at the sight of him, she kept her cool.

"Hello, Caleb," she said, as if he dropped by every day. "We were wondering when you'd get here."

31

Jeremiah's prohibition on illegal substances caused them to split up for a while. Travis stepped out to the patio to smoke a joint, and Shake and Nancy went with him. Willa took the opportunity to go clean up the remains of dinner. She wanted some time alone to digest the events of the day but feared she was unlikely to get it. Sure enough, no sooner had she finished stacking dishes on a tray than the dining room door opened behind her.

It was Caleb. "Can I help?"

"You could carry this out to the kitchen." She handed him the heavy tray. He wore a white shirt with the sleeves rolled up, no wedding ring, a gold Rolex on his left wrist. She gathered up the remaining platters of leftover cold cuts and baskets of rolls and followed him through the swinging doors into the kitchen.

Caleb unloaded the dishes from his tray into the sink, then joined Willa at the table where she sat making sandwiches of the leftover cold cuts.

It was hard to look at him, and harder to look away. In high school Caleb had been the best looking of the Beacon Hill guys, with choirboy looks that disguised a reckless nature. Here, too, time had widened the gap. The prettiness was gone, replaced by something deeper, more poignant. His face had accrued interesting lines. There was power in the ropy forearms, a lean, traveled look about him. His hair was shorter and lighter than it had been, a stubble of tarnished gold. He looked to Willa like he'd look to any woman: trouble, but the kind that was worth it.

She reminded herself of Jovan's findings. *Caleb's no predator,* she'd protested reflexively, though without doubting for a moment their essential truth—the connection between the boy and the man was too clear. Caleb had always had the ability to draw people to him. All the Beacon Hill kids had competed for his favor. His boldness, his disdain for authority and convention had elevated him in their eyes: traits as charming in a boy as they were dangerous in a man. They'd always known Caleb would cut a swath through the world; they'd just never imagined how.

"So you're back," she said.

He bowed his head. "The prodigal son has returned."

"Bring on the fatted calf. Though I've always wondered about that parable. What must the unprodigal sons feel?"

"Like they've wasted their time," said Patrick, appearing in the doorway. His eyes darted from Willa to Caleb. "Isn't this cozy."

Caleb shot him an unwelcoming look, which Patrick ignored. He crossed to the sink, rolled up his sleeves, and started loading the dishwasher in a manner intended to telegraph his familiarity with the surroundings.

"Professor Mulhaven," Caleb said mockingly. "Don't it just trip off the tongue?"

"Aw, shucks," said Patrick, scuffing a toe, "y'all can just call me Doc."

"I don't remember calling you at all, son."

"Tell us about you, Caleb," Patrick said. "What have you been doing all these years?"

"Real estate, mostly. Got lucky here and there." This was said with an air of modest understatement.

"And where do you live?" Willa asked, with a hostessy smile as bland as the mayonnaise she was spreading. Let the boys reenact their little games, for all the good it would do them. She was in a different place now.

"I tend to keep moving. Brazil, Mexico. Spent some time in the Keys. No place I really call home."

"And this suits you?"

Caleb seemed to consider this. He seemed to wonder how much to reveal. Turning his back on Patrick, he looked at Willa with eloquent eyes.

"It suited me fine for a long time," he said softly. "But it's getting old, or I am."

Patrick wanted to hoot. Vintage Caleb, that soulful, hurting look. He didn't have to see it to know it. The question was whether Willa was buying. He couldn't tell; the woman was a closed book. Now Caleb was telling an anecdote from his time in Rio, and Willa seemed to be lapping it up. Patrick tuned him out. That bastard Caleb. Did he ever stop to consider the possibility that Patrick might have staked a prior claim? Of course not. When it came to women, it was every man for himself; and in that competition Caleb had the edge. Patrick remembered the first time he'd recognized the precise nature of that edge. They were ten, eleven years old; it was summertime, anyway, and he and Caleb were over at Vinny's, wrestling on the front lawn with him and his brothers. Someone left a door open and their dog escaped, a little terrier named Maisie. Vinny's mom came rushing out, yelling, "Catch her, catch her!" All the boys tried, but the dog ran rings around them, zipping through their legs.

Suddenly Caleb fell to the ground and lay still, eyes closed, arms outstretched in crucifix position. The other boys stopped, looked at each other. "Caleb?" Patrick said uncertainly.

"Shhh!" Caleb hissed. He held his pose until Maisie came over and sniffed his face, then clamped his arms around her and leaped up grinning. "Always let them come to you," he told Patrick.

Turned out it worked with women, too. Unlike Patrick, who hadn't the looks and was a born chaser besides, Caleb grew into a honey trap. It wasn't just his looks, it was knowing how to use them. Caleb had always had a gift for awakening desire wherever he wanted; now it seemed as if somewhere along the line he'd turned pro. Had Willa forgotten all the dirt her detective dug up? Patrick sighed. More and more, life was coming to seem like the remake of a movie he'd already seen.

When he finally caught Willa's eye, the exchange was unsatisfactory. *We're on to him, right?* his look said; hers replied, *What a lovely time we're all having.* Underneath that lacquered sweetness was a reserve so thick you'd need a hammer and chisel to break through. At least he wasn't the only one left wondering. Watching Caleb grapple with Willa's Lucite smile was like watching a man try to scale a glass mountain.

Shake stretched his legs and leaned back in the Adirondack deck chair, gazing up at the starry sky. "Is this the life or what?"

Travis lit another joint, took a toke, and passed it to Nancy. "I feel like a kid again, being with you guys. I keep expecting Willa's parents to come home and turf us all out."

"Or Jeremiah's mother to start banging on the door," Nancy said, and they all laughed. It was good weed, homegrown by friends of Travis; the effect, on top of the booze, was warm and fuzzy. What a brilliant idea this reunion had been, the men agreed, and what a generous hostess they had in Willa.

Nancy sniffed. If this were her house you could bet she'd be as hospitable as Willa. Not that she would even want a house like this, with its cloying excess and luxury; but it was a hard thing, a hurtful thing, to see people flaunting their wealth when you yourself owned nothing, not even the roof over your head. Especially when the flaunter had been your peer in high school. She passed the joint to Shake, who inhaled deeply.

"Just like old times," he croaked on a stream of smoke.

"If this were then," Nancy said, "I'd be sharing that chair with you and we'd be making out."

"If this were then, we'd both fit." Shake looked past her at Travis. "Damn good showing, too. Caleb walking in like that— man, you could have knocked me over with a feather."

"I knew he'd come," Travis said. "I was sure he would."

"It's amazing everyone remembered, stoned as we were."

"The way we were heading, it's amazing we're all still alive."

Nancy lit a cigarette, and the flare of her lighter drew a moth. "You all talk like we were so bad," she said. "All we were was a bunch of middle-class suburban wanna-bes."

"Ouch," said Travis. "White squaw speak with sharp tongue."

"Got a file?" Shake asked, and they both cracked up, while Nancy glared. Who did he think he was, fucking Travis of all people, calling her a squaw?

"You know what I feel like?" Travis said, stretching. "A midnight swim."

"Skinny-dip," Shake said at once. "We should get the others." The men's eyes met and they exchanged a smile. Nancy saw that smile and seethed.

When Willa returned to the den, she found Vinny sitting at the bar, Jeremiah on the sofa facing him. Though they weren't talking, a residue of conversation hung in the air, like the ionization of a passing lightning storm. Vinny looked sullen, Jeremiah as if he was wondering what he was doing here. Both perked up at her entrance. Willa held the door for Patrick and Caleb, who entered carrying trays of sliced cake, coffee, sugar, and cream, then swooped ahead of them to clear the coffee table. Among the magazines she noticed two packets of photographs. "What's this?"

"You asked for photos and the troops obeyed," Patrick said. "We were looking at them earlier, while you were at Chloe's play." He helped himself to a cup of coffee and fixed her a cup as well, the way she liked it, dark and sweet.

Willa curled up beside Jeremiah. "That reminds me, I have something for you guys." She told them about the diary digest, copies of which she'd left in each of their bedrooms. "I didn't include everything, but what I did take is unexpurgated, which means as far as the writing goes it's fairly embarrassing. But I thought you might enjoy a few glimpses of yourselves."

"You kept a diary?" Jeremiah said.

"Full of lurid details, I promise you."

"Oy. How could you, Willa? It's like Nixon taping himself."

She laughed. "I think the statute of limitations has pretty much run out on anything we did back then. Besides, no one's ever going to see them but me. I'll take them to the grave."

"You never did go anywhere without a book," he quipped. "But aren't you afraid your daughter will stumble across them?"

"I keep them stashed away." Willa leafed through the photos, which though faded and brittle were wonderfully evocative. There was Shake holding Nancy in his arms in front of Caleb's house; Vinny and Caleb flanking a snowman whose carrot nose had been relocated; all of them so young and innocent looking, so pleased with themselves and one another's company. Willa came to a picture of Patrick dressed as Santa Claus, with Angel on his lap. "Oh look," she cried, "look at Angel! God, she was beautiful."

"Where is she, anyway?" Caleb asked, as if wondering for the first time. "Shouldn't she be here?"

The words fell into a little lull that no one seemed to want to fill. Finally Patrick said, "Nobody knows. None of us has seen or heard from her in twenty years. Unless you have?"

"Me?" Caleb said. "I haven't seen her since high school." Nor thought of her, his tone implied.

"People drift away," Jeremiah said with a shrug. "What's surprising isn't that one forgot, it's that so many remembered. What beats me is how the police got involved." He looked at Willa. She kept her eyes on the snapshots.

Caleb said, "The police?"

"They found her camera," Patrick said. "With film in it."

"Where?" Jeremiah asked.

"I have no idea."

Caleb said, "Film?"

"That's right." Patrick looked at him. "They have the last shots she took before she left."

Caleb held his eye for a moment, then shrugged and helped himself to coffee.

"So what?" Jeremiah said, looking from one to the other. "How does finding a camera trigger a police investigation?"

"I don't know if that triggered it," Patrick said, "but they obviously suspect something happened to her. So does Willa, for that matter."

"Willa's a writer," Jeremiah said dismissively. "Imagination is her stock in trade."

"I'm a biographer," she replied, stung by an attack from that quarter. "Facts are."

Patrick turned to her. "But you *have* no facts about Angel, only a complete lack thereof."

"A fact in itself; a mystery right there!"

"What mystery?" said Nancy, entering through the open French doors. Shake and Travis were right behind her. "Everybody knows what happened to Angel."

They all looked at her.

"What's that?" Willa asked.

"She wrecked her old man's car and ran away: end of story."

"Never to return? Never to be seen or heard from again?"

Nancy sneered. "Return to what? What did she have to come home to?"

"Shut up, Nance," Shake said wearily.

"How do we know she ran away?" Willa said. "No one ever heard from her again."

"What if we did?" said a voice from the bar. All of them turned to Vinny. He hooked his heels on the stool rail and swiveled around to face them. "What if I said *I'd* heard from her?"

In the silence that followed these words, the ringing of the phone was as loud as an explosion and had a similar effect. Willa started and clutched her heart. Impossible as it must be, she was certain at that moment that Angel was on the other end of the line. And maybe she wasn't the only one; out of the corner of her eye, she saw Vinny cross himself. Patrick was closest to the phone but deferred to Willa. She braced herself . . . but it was only Chloe, checking in as instructed.

No one spoke till Willa was off the phone. Then Patrick turned to Vinny and said, "What the hell are you talking about?"

"I got a postcard from San Francisco, couple of months after she split."

"Right, and you're just now remembering."

Vinny shrugged. "So I forgot. A fucking postcard! All this talking brought it back."

"He's lying," Travis said, pointing. "Look at him, he's making it up as he goes."

"Shut the fuck up, Travis." Vinny's growl was a sharp reminder of their prior relationship, and Travis's reaction showed that he remembered; he sat down and shut up.

"Bullshit," Patrick said. "Why would she write to you and not me?"

"Gee, I don't know. . . . Maybe because I didn't knock her up and blow her off?"

"Fuck you," Patrick said, and started toward Vinny. Jeremiah got between them, throwing an arm around Patrick's shoulders and talking him back onto the couch. Then he went and took the bar stool next to Vinny's.

"Let's hear it," Jeremiah said. "What did it say, Vinny, this postcard from Angel?"

"'Having a great time, gettin' laid every night'—something like that. 'Wish you was here.'"

"Did she mention where in San Diego she was staying?"

"Nah, she didn't say."

Jeremiah frowned. "I thought you said San Francisco."

Vinny's indignation as he registered the trick played on him struck the others as comical, and they burst into laughter that, being drunken, was prolonged. Only Jeremiah did not laugh, but

regarded Vinny with grave concern and said, when the raucous
laughter died out, "It's never a good idea to tell unnecessary lies."

"Who says it's a lie?" Vinny said. "Plus what the fuck do you
care, if it gets the cops off our asses?"

"Only it wouldn't, would it?" Caleb came and took the stool on
Vinny's other side, bracketing him. "All it would do would be to
focus their attention on you. You've got to be consistent with
cops. They are men of little minds. Change your story and they're
all over your ass." He spoke with unmistakable authority.

Vinny poured a shot of bourbon and raised his glass to Caleb,
a gesture everyone present understood as concession. They began
to talk again, with a general easing of tension, a sense of something narrowly averted.

Travis, remembering their mission, asked, "Anyone up for a
swim?"

"I don't think so," Willa replied at once. "It's getting late and
chilly. Shouldn't we wait till morning?"

"The pool's heated," Travis wheedled, "and there's the hot tub,
too." Shake pressed his hands together prayerfully. "Please, Mom,
please? We promise we'll be good," he begged, and the others
took their side, until finally Willa surrendered. But when Travis
brought up the idea of skinny dipping, she just laughed. She
could just see herself stripping in front of these six guys! Things
were charged enough already. Angel's absence had changed the
group dynamics in ways Willa had not anticipated, and now
things were happening that were not under her control. The balance had shifted, setting them all subtly at odds; and the focus of
sexual tension, once diffused between the three girls, had fallen
squarely on Willa. Now, though—and this was what she had
somehow, idiotically, failed to take into account—they were not
boys. Now they were men, and drunk men at that.

When she went up to change, she locked her door.

The pool party was in full swing by the time she got down.
They'd found the light panel, turned off the floods, and switched
on the blue fiber-optic underwater light that ran along the
perimeter of the free-form pool. Paul Butterfield was playing on
the poolside CD, softly, in deference to the hour and the neigh-

bors, and someone had mixed a pitcher of piña coladas. Willa took a small glass and sipped it as she looked around, unnoticed for the moment. Shake, Nancy, and Travis were in the hot tub. Nancy wore a leopard-skin bikini meant for someone half her age and two sizes smaller. Willa could almost hear Angel's mocking laughter. But it was sad, really, the way Nancy always made the worst of herself. Jeremiah was swimming laps in the pool with the sleek, strong strokes of long practice, while Caleb and Patrick paddled about under the diving board, talking quietly. Willa heard Vinny before she saw him, out cold, snoring on a chaise beside the pool. She would have to see that he got safely back to the house before they turned in.

"Willa," Patrick called, "come on in!"

She set her drink on a poolside table and took off her robe. Travis whistled. Upstairs she had vacillated for a long time between her most flattering suit, a blue Gottex halter top shot through with gold threads, and her most modest, a utilitarian black tank suit. Vanity had won; she'd worn the Gottex. But now, with everyone's eyes on her, she felt like a stripper on a runway. Willa took three running steps and dived smoothly into the deep end.

The water felt warm and welcoming, and it cleared her head at once. She glided the width of the pool underwater before surfacing on the far side. The three men in the pool were converging on her like boats on a harbor. She was tired of Patrick, wary of Caleb, and felt she owed Jeremiah some attention. So she turned to him and gave him a full-wattage smile. "Maybe this wasn't such a bad idea after all."

"Great pool," Jeremiah said. He was sleek as an otter, water streaming from his fine black hair. "We're thinking of putting one in up in Old Wickham, now that we'll be spending more time there."

"Have you got the room?" She ignored Caleb and Patrick, treading water nearby.

"Oh, there's plenty of space. Most of the land's hilly and wooded, but there's a flat acre just behind the house that would be perfect. It's a big project, though; I'm afraid we've already missed out for this summer."

"Why will you be spending more time there? Are you leaving Washington?"

"Not exactly. It's complicated. But all will be revealed soon."

She tilted her head back and regarded him thoughtfully. "You're running for something."

"Wild horses wouldn't drag it from me," he said with a mysterious smile.

"Wild horses never do," she said. They didn't this time, either, but Caleb and Patrick did, teasing mercilessly until Jeremiah gave in and said what he'd wanted to say all along:

"All right, all right! Willa guessed it. I'm running for office."

"I knew it!" she yelled, slapping the water.

"Which office?" Patrick asked.

Jeremiah held up his hands. "Not yet."

"Well, tell us this," Willa said. "Will we be able to vote for you?"

He grinned. "Not this time."

"But we'll campaign for you like last time," Patrick said. Then they reminisced about Jeremiah's first campaign for student council president. "Wright or Wrong" had been the slogan on his campaign posters; "Wright or Else," Vinny's more persuasive version. Between that and Angel's offer to kiss any boy who voted for Jeremiah, his election had been secured.

Jeremiah, grinning a shit-faced grin, waited till they were quite through. "Somehow," he said, "I don't think those tactics would work this time. If you really want to help, I'll tell you how. Stay away from the campaign. Be discreet. Don't talk to reporters, and if any seek you out, don't reminisce about the good old days and all the fun we had. That's how you can help." He was smiling but there was an edge to his voice that silenced them.

Patrick was the first to recover. "Hey, dude," he said. "If you can't trust us, who can you trust?"

Willa shivered, getting out of the pool. The temperature had dropped and the air felt much cooler than the water. Caleb followed her out, noticed her shivering, and put an arm around her. "You're freezing," he said. "Come warm up." He led her over to the hot tub, deserted now except for Travis. Willa stretched out in front of one of the jets and arched with pleasure as hot bubbles percolated up her spine. She hadn't used the tub in months . . . not since Simon died.

Travis looked on admiringly. "I've got to get me one of these," he said in a voice sodden with comfort. "Imagine this on a cold winter night, a million stars overhead."

"Sounds wonderful," Willa murmured.

"It'd be like having your own hot springs. When you come out—"

"Travis," Caleb said.

Reluctantly, Travis tore his eyes off Willa's cleavage and turned to Caleb. "Yeah?"

"Why don't you get us some drinks?"

He blinked a few times. "Sure, man. What do you want?"

"Doesn't matter," Caleb said. "Take your time."

Travis stalked off, swinging a towel behind him.

"That was rude," Willa said, more amused than angry.

"I'm tired of waiting for a moment alone with you."

"Why, do you have a secret to tell me?"

Caleb reared back, examined her. "You're mocking me!"

"No more than you deserve for that grand entrance."

"Sorry about that. I wasn't sure till the last minute I'd be able to make it."

Willa just looked at him.

"Okay," he said sheepishly. "I was afraid you'd tell me to stay away."

"Why would I do that?" she asked.

"Because I acted like such an ass last time we met. Is there a statute of limitations on stupidity, Willa, or would you accept a belated apology?"

"You had every right to be upset."

"No, I didn't, though it took me years to admit it. The truth is, I wasn't ready then to give you what you needed and deserved, and Simon was."

Willa was impressed. He was a clever rogue, clever enough that part of her insisted on believing him. She took refuge in politeness. "It's kind of you to say so."

"It's kind of you to let me come," he mimicked back at her. They stared at each other for a moment, then dissolved into laughter. It was, she felt, their first genuine communication since his return.

Patrick and Jeremiah returned, puffing from the effort of carrying Vinny up to the house. Patrick took a beer from the pool house refrigerator and offered it to Jeremiah, who shook his head. They joined the others beside the pool.

"Would you look at that." Patrick glowered across the water at Caleb and Willa, laughing it up in the hot tub.

"He doesn't waste time," Shake said.

"He's picking up where he left off," Travis said morosely. "So much for an even playing field."

Shake punched him in the arm. "Since when was it ever even, doofus?"

"Let him take his best shot," Patrick said. "She's too smart for him."

"You *know* it's not a matter of brains," Shake said. "Fifty bucks he gets lucky."

Nancy scowled; it was her money he was throwing away. Shake ignored her.

"You're on," Patrick said.

"How will you know?" asked Jeremiah. "They're hardly likely to announce it."

"Oh, we'll know," Shake said. "By the smirk on his face."

A burst of raucous male laughter rose in the air like tobacco smoke. It ended as Willa stood and stretched languorously. As she began climbing the steps out of the hot tub, the men fell silent. In the watery blue light of the pool, Willa's bare shoulders, haltered breasts, and endless legs evoked as much amazement as lust.

Even Nancy, coiled on her chaise beside Shake, felt a momentary admiration. Then she looked about and saw every man jack of them focused on Willa, enthralled. Nancy could strip naked, she could choke on a grape and die on the spot, and not one of them would notice, not even her husband.

That Willa, she thought. Always taking more than her share. Nancy sighed and ate another grape. She knew they shouldn't have come. Why didn't Shake ever listen to her? This was like being back in high school, only conscious. Everyone individually had changed, yet they all seemed frozen in their old relationships. Travis was still scared of Vinny; Caleb and Patrick were still competing; Jeremiah was still looking down from Mount Olympus; and Willa was still teasing the boys. Only Angel was missing; and that, as far as Nancy was concerned, was a definite change for the better.

32

Beacon Hill was deserted. The boulders they used to sit on were now upholstered in ivy, and brush rimmed the clearing where twenty years ago they'd danced to "Sympathy for the Devil." In the car, Patrick had worried over the prospect of finding the place occupied, assuming, as they all did, that rights to the hill had passed down through generations of transgressive teens. But it seemed the hill no longer served as anyone's hangout. Even the path had disappeared; they'd had to forge their own way up through dense mats of juniper.

But to Willa, the hilltop didn't feel empty. She had a sense of Angel's absence so acute it was almost a presence. A similar feeling had assailed her in Angel's bedroom, but here on the hill, in the company of their old friends, it was stronger by far. *Come what may*, they'd vowed; *come heaven or hell*. Under an overcast sky, their once beloved refuge looked forlorn, almost—the word came to mind—haunted. And Willa wasn't the only one who felt it. As they sat around the picnic lunch that she'd laid out in the clearing, the group was more subdued than even their hangovers could account for. "Anyone bring a Ouija board?" Travis asked, a remark greeted on all sides with disapproval but not incomprehension.

Patrick distributed beers from the cooler he'd lugged up the hill and proposed a toast. "To all of us, for keeping our word to each other and our faith with our younger selves."

They drank to that. Then Willa posed the question she'd been saving up for this occasion. "What was it that held us together back then? What made us friends, this particular group of people?"

"Pure chance, like most good things in life," said Shake, resting his head on Nancy's dimpled thighs while she fed him grapes. (At least, thought Willa, she didn't peel them.)

Nancy nodded. "It's random, like blood clotting. You don't ask why one particular molecule sticks to another. They've got to stick somewhere."

"I don't think it was random at all," Travis said, with such feeling that they all looked at him. He ducked his head and smiled,

and in that smile, so eager to please, so fearful of embarrassment, Willa suddenly saw the fusion of man and boy. "To me it
was a fellowship, like the fellowship in Tolkien. In fact, first time
I read *Lord of the Rings*, I cast us in the roles. I used to feel we
occupied a world apart, a place that was sharper and finer and
more adventurous than the regular world. It's like, in my memory, the scenes of us are in color, and all the others are in black
and white."

"Which characters?" Willa asked.

"You and Caleb were royal elves, Elrond and Galadriel. Patrick
was Frodo Baggins, Jeremiah was Gandalf, Vinny was the warrior
Boromir, Shake and Nancy were Tom Bombadil and his wife."

"And who were you?"

He smiled painfully. "Gollum."

"Oh no you weren't!" she cried, though in fact she thought his
casting painfully astute. Patrick did have the Baggins trait of
curiosity; and wasn't there a wizardly aura to Jeremiah, with his
pale, austere face and clever dark eyes? Vinny, sitting slightly
apart with his knees drawn up to his chest, was a perfect brood-
ing Boromir. "What do you think?" she asked, to coax him in; for
he seemed very withdrawn up there on the hill.

Vinny raised one broad shoulder and let it fall. "Can't say I've
given it much thought."

"I'll tell you what it was for me," Jeremiah volunteered. "For
me, this group was my refuge. With you guys I could do anything, say anything, make fun of the people I kowtowed to in
school, just generally be myself, and it was all cool. I loved hanging out with the most beautiful girls in the school. I loved it that
my mother hated you. I loved other kids knowing we were tight,
because it meant there was more to me than my well-scrubbed
surface. And I loved knowing that no matter what happened, we
had each other's backs."

"Ain't that sweet," Vinny said.

Jeremiah gave him a slow look.

"What's the matter?" said Patrick. "Is the big strong mechanic
too macho for a little nostalgia?"

"It just seems pointless, all this rooting around in the past. It
was what it was," Vinny said.

"But what was it?" Patrick said. "That's the question. I'll tell you my theory: We were misfits. High school is basically a tribal society. Everyone's labeled, everyone's assigned to a group. We were the kids who defied categorization."

"Mutants," Shake said.

"Exactly. Take you. As a musician you should have been part of the arty crowd; only in your spare time you liked boozing, brawling, and playing with cars. Vinny was a greaser who read *Rolling Stone* and dug Fellini. And so on: None of us fit in."

"But surely that's not all we had in common," Willa said.

"What else was there?"

"Passion," she said bravely, "allied with some sort of talent."

They thought about that. A bee landed on the potato salad; Jeremiah flicked it off with a plastic knife.

"Not me," Patrick said. "Passion for film, yeah, but no talent."

"Your talent was for teaching," Willa said. "I learned more watching movies with you than I would have from a dozen film-appreciation courses. Jeremiah had social talent, the ability to lead people, which translates perfectly into politics. Shake was a musician."

"And Vinny's passion was cars," Jeremiah said, getting into it, "and yours books. Very neat, Willa. Note how each of us has chosen fields that employ these talents."

"What was Caleb's?" Travis asked.

"He was a great forger. I wonder if that's come in useful," Nancy said, with a sly glance at Caleb. He raised his head and looked at her as if noticing her for the first time.

"His talent was for pleasing himself," Patrick said.

Caleb transferred the look but said nothing.

"And mine?" Travis bleated; he couldn't help himself.

"Loyalty," said Willa.

Patrick laughed. "We know what Travis's passion was. But I doubt he's made a career of it."

"Not unless there are professional voyeurs," Shake said.

"There are," Jeremiah said. "They're called tabloid reporters."

"I'll tell you your talent, Travis," Nancy said. "Pit-bull tenacity. You sank your teeth in us and never let go."

Willa winced. There is a line between teasing and cruelty, and they all knew Nancy had just crossed it. Travis stared at the ground, his face aflame, while silence gathered and swelled around him.

"Ignore her," Shake said, sitting up. "She's on the rag. God, you're a bitch!"

This last was addressed to his wife, who replied, "That was my talent."

"But have you made a living at it?" Willa asked. Something cold and wet touched her neck, and she started, but it was only a drop of rain. She turned her palms upward, hoping. If the weather turned foul, they could leave this place.

Vinny walked away from them all to stand among the boulders. He lit a cigarette. Willa followed him. "Feels strange being back, doesn't it?" she said.

"Yeah."

"A lot of memories." He didn't answer. "Is something wrong, Vinny?"

At last he looked at her, his eyes glowering beneath that great shelf of a forehead; his mouth opened, but before he could speak, Shake and Jeremiah joined them.

"Good old Millbrook High," Shake said cheerily, plumping himself down on the rocks. "Seems like just yesterday, don't it?"

Willa gazed down at the misty playing fields. The rain had decided to hold off after all. "We had some good times."

"The best. We should do this more often."

"Ten years from now," Patrick proposed, joining them. "We could have the next reunion in the White House, if Jeremiah permits."

"Depends what term I'm in," Jeremiah said.

Everyone laughed except Vinny, who looked from face to face. "What's this?"

"That's right," said Patrick, "you missed Jeremiah's little announcement last night. He's running for office! Don't ask what office; he won't say. But we all know the ultimate destination."

Vinny snubbed out his cigarette, flicked the butt down the hill. He winched his massive head around and gave Jeremiah the look he used on oil slicks. "Onward and upward, eh, Jeremiah?"

"Beats the hell out of backward and downward," the candidate replied. Then Shake produced a harmonica from out of nowhere and played a few bars of "Hail to the Chief." This time even Vinny laughed. But for Willa, the sound of the harmonica brought back that final night on the hill, graduation night, when Angel sang to Shake's accompaniment.

"Play 'Frankie and Johnny,'" she begged, and Shake could not refuse her. The others gathered around. It didn't sound like much without the lyrics, but no one joined in. Where Angel's voice should have gone, there was only the soft keening of the wind, the hum of insects. Shake finished the song and put the harmonica away. There was a long silence.

"Are we done?" Vinny asked. "Can we go now?"

The one great advantage to a large house is the privacy it affords. After their visit to Beacon Hill, the party split up. Shake and Nancy disappeared into their bedroom and were not seen for several hours. Vinny and Caleb took a swim, Patrick and Travis drove into town on a booze run, and Jeremiah went upstairs to call his wife.

Willa, relieved to have a moment to herself, went to the kitchen to get dinner started. She'd planned a solid meal to make up for last night's cold buffet. It was the only meal she would cook for her friends, and Jovan was coming as well, so she'd spent a long time deciding on a menu. Finally she'd settled on simple dishes she'd made many times before: honey-and-mustard-baked chicken, fettucini with a mushroom, asparagus, and toasted pignoli sauce, and a garden salad. They'd have prosciutto and melon for a starter, and for dessert there was all that cake the guys had brought.

Willa had finished steaming the asparagus and was chopping the stalks when Jeremiah, freshly showered and dressed in a white golf shirt and khaki pants, reported for KP duty.

"How are you with onions?" she asked.

"Masterful. When I cut onions, they cry."

She set him up with two onions and a cutting board, and they worked together companionably. Willa couldn't help feeling that the two of them were the only adults in a houseful of overgrown adolescents.

"I read your diary excerpts," Jeremiah told her. "Whoever said a picture's worth a thousand words never read your stuff."

She flushed with pleasure. "Thanks."

"Not to take anything away from the biographies, but for some reason I always thought you'd end up a novelist."

"I meant to be."

"What stopped you? Not lack of talent."

"Lack of guts." She hadn't meant to say this; it just slipped out, as if their old relationship had superimposed itself over the new. As a boy Jeremiah had been the most seductive of listeners: attentive, intelligent, and endlessly fascinated.

He finished dicing the first onion and moved on to the next, his large hands deft, his eyes as dry as advertised. "Fiction takes more guts than nonfiction?"

"Sure. Biographers explore other people's lives, not their own. Fiction writers have to invent their characters; they have to imagine them into being. And imagination isn't some sort of free-floating energy; it doesn't come from a muse. It springs from, and is fed by, the writer's own experiences."

"So you have to mine your own life."

"You have to stand outside a bit. You have to see clearly." You have to *want* to see, she thought. She herself had opted for ignorance, a fatal decision: For while physical blindness might not be an insurmountable obstacle to the writing of fiction, blindness of the heart surely was.

Jeremiah seemed to understand her all too well. No doubt his mother had filled him in on her history. His next words confirmed it. "We've none of us led a perfect life. What's done is done. The past is irrelevant; the future is all that matters."

"I hope you're right," she said. "Maybe there's a novel in me after all."

"Of course there is. Anyone reading those diaries could see you're a born storyteller."

"A born idiot," she said. "When I read them over, I couldn't believe how naive I was."

"Naive about what?"

Willa opened the oven door, and a warm, mustardy aroma seeped out. "Everything," she said, turning pieces of chicken with a fork. "Angel for starters. Did you know she was pregnant?"

Jeremiah's quick hands faltered for just a moment. "There were rumors."

"She didn't tell you?"

"Why would she?"

"She trusted you," Willa said. "We all did. You were our rock."

"And Vinny was our anvil," Jeremiah said. "Here's a whole new theory for your collection."

She was still laughing when Caleb wandered in, a towel slung around his neck, reporting for duty. Willa asked him to set the table for nine.

"Is your daughter joining us?" he asked.

"No, but a friend of mine is. He's heard so much about you guys, it seemed cruel not to invite him."

Jeremiah and Caleb exchanged a glance. Then Jeremiah said, "Isn't it crueler to invite him? I can't think of anything more tedious than listening to other people's childhood reminiscences, unless it's listening to their dreams."

"Lucky you're a politician, then, and not a shrink."

Jeremiah was wrong. Jovan was fascinated by their tales, couldn't get enough of them. Over dinner, with his encouragement, they vied to top each other in storytelling. By now everyone had read Willa's diary excerpts, and those stories were the first to air, embellished or contradicted by others' recollections. It struck Willa, who took a professional interest in such matters, how widely their recollections varied, and how often an event of great significance to one person rang no bells for another.

Many of the stories centered on road trips and adventures in the city, most of which took place during school hours. "Didn't you people ever go to school?" Jovan finally asked.

They consulted with each other around the large oval table, laden with food.

"More often than not," Shake said a bit doubtfully.

"Jeremiah did," Nancy said. "Jeremiah always did what he was supposed to, as well as what he wasn't."

"I cut sometimes," Jeremiah protested. "I went with you to that blues festival."

"And the school didn't come down on you?" Jovan asked.

"They never knew. We always had notes from our parents, thanks to Caleb."

"A useful talent," said Jovan, looking at Caleb.

Caleb took his time answering, wary of the stranger among them. "The school never looked very hard. I think they were relieved when we didn't show."

"That's what Angel used to say," Willa said.

"Angel?" Jovan said.

"Another of our group."

"How come he's not here?"

Patrick's fork, laden with pasta, was halfway to his mouth. He put it down and looked hard at Jovan, then at Willa.

"She," Nancy said. Her small eyes, ringed by dark eyeliner, looked like raisins in a bowl of bread pudding, and her lipstick had come off on her teeth. "No one knows and no one cares."

"Speak for yourself," Willa said. "She's been on my mind all weekend."

"Mine, too," Patrick said. "I keep wondering where she is now."

"Turning tricks in some alley?" Nancy suggested. The others stared at her. "Well, didn't Jeremiah say we'd all made careers of our talents?"

Willa put her head in her hands. *Twelve more hours. Sixteen at most.*

"Poor Nancy," Travis drawled. "Still jealous, after all these years."

Nancy wheeled on him. "Poor *you*. Never did get a taste, did you, Travis?"

"Bitch."

"What a bunch of hypocrites." She glared around the table. "When Angel split, who cared? Who looked for her? You were all too busy thanking your lucky stars."

"When we should have been thanking you, you mean?" Travis said.

"What?"

"Come on, Nancy, 'fess up."

"I don't know what you're talking about," she said, helping herself to more chicken. "Willa, this is delicious."

"You ratted her out," Travis said. "You told her old man she was pregnant."

Shake rose to his wife's defense. "The hell she did!"

"I saw them through the kitchen window. Nancy was talking, and the more she said, the madder Busky got."

"What were *you* doing there?" Shake said.

Vinny snorted. "What do you think? Peeping and lurking, as usual."

"So you saw them talking," Shake said. "So what? You don't know what she said."

"Angel ran away that night," Travis replied. "What do you think Nancy said?"

Shake looked at his wife.

"It never happened," she said. But her face was red, and she couldn't meet his eyes.

When the rest of Willa's guests moved to the den for coffee and dessert, Jovan followed Willa into the kitchen. "How goes it?" he asked.

"Great, till it turned into the reunion from hell."

"Lot of loose ends, it sounds like. How about I stay the night?"

"Why?" she asked, startled.

Jovan hesitated. "I'd feel better. I don't like leaving you here with these people."

"It's my home. And they're my friends." But even as she spoke, Willa wondered. If they were her friends, why did she feel so uneasy around them? The truth was, she hardly knew them anymore, and out of the whole bunch there wasn't one she'd care to meet again, except Jeremiah and possibly Patrick. Whatever happened to the bond they used to have?

Jovan stroked her bare arm with the back of his hand, and a deep shudder ran through her. She imagined taking him upstairs, making love to him while the others were in the house. The thought excited her. Months of sexual fasting had left her body a tinderbox, which that weekend's free-floating lust, all the erotic jostling and posturing, had stirred to near combustion. He grasped her shoulders. Then Caleb walked in.

"Got any sugar?" he said, looking from one to the other.

She took the sugar bowl from a cabinet, and the three of them returned to the den, where the atmosphere was thick with smoke and anger. They were talking about Patrick's lost car, or at least Patrick was, while Vinny glowered and finally exploded. "For Chrissake," he shouted, "it's been twenty years. When are you going to get the fuck over it?"

"Sorry," Patrick said at once, raising his hands. "You're right; water under the bridge." Yet he couldn't let it go. They started arguing over when the wreck occurred: Patrick said that it was right after graduation, Vinny insisted it was earlier, before school ended.

They appealed to Caleb, who shrugged. "What difference does it make?"

"It had to be after," Patrick explained, "because we spent graduation together up on the hill, which never would have happened if Vinny had already wrecked the car; I was too pissed off."

"Your memory's fucked, man." Vinny tapped his temple. "Too much loco weed."

"Isn't it strange," Willa said, "how differently we remember things? I'd thought that by all of us getting together and pooling our memories, we could triangulate the past, nail it down. But it doesn't seem to work like that."

"Maybe it's not our memories' fault," Travis said. "Maybe it's that we all experienced things differently to begin with."

"Some things are simply matters of fact," Jovan put in mildly. "Like dates."

"While others are subject to various interpretations," Jeremiah said, "which raises an interesting question: If memory is all that remains of the past, and memories differ, can we really say there is an objective truth to discover?"

"If there's not, I'm in trouble," Willa said. "Sifting through competing versions of events to arrive at the truth is precisely what biographers do, not to mention historians."

"But the truth itself may be a matter of interpretation," Jeremiah said. "And the further one is from an event, the harder it is to pin down. Take what Nancy said earlier, about me living by the rules, always playing it safe. My own memory of that period is of constant risk taking in support of my habit, which was you guys. Two contradictory interpretations: Which one's right? Maybe both."

"Like Schrödinger's cat," Willa said. "Dead and alive simultaneously."

Jeremiah beamed at her. "Exactly. If the uncertainty principle doesn't apply here, where does it apply?"

"Except for one thing. Memory *isn't* all that remains of the past. There are also documents and other artifacts. My diaries, for example; Angel's photographs."

"What does your diary say about our car?" Patrick asked.

"Nothing, which supports your version. Sorry, Vinny, but if that car had been wrecked before I went abroad, I would have remembered *and* I would have written about it."

Vinny shrugged and poured another drink.

33

It was like trying to sleep in a wind tunnel. Bits of conversation swirled through her head like tattered newspapers; faded images of the past clogged the grates of her mind. She saw Travis crouching in the bushes outside Angel's house; herself and Angel clambering down the drainpipe; bronze, shirtless boys bent over a cold engine; Caleb's face poised above hers, mouthing words she could not hear; Jeremiah popping a bottle of champagne on Beacon Hill; hands piled atop hands. Again and again she returned to Travis's accusation at dinner, and the guilt on Nancy's face. Did she know what she'd done, that stupid cow? If Angel was dead, if her father really did kill her, then it was Nancy who had loaded the gun and put it in his hand.

These were the people whose love had sustained her during the hardest years, whose various passions had permanently enriched her life. Now they filled her house, which should have been comforting but was strangely not. There were currents in the house Willa didn't understand, relationships that were hidden from view. Shake and Nancy in their room above the garage: What would they say to each other when they were alone? Patrick and Travis in a room just down the hall—a lucky pairing, given that her first idea had been to put Vinny and Patrick together, which would have been disastrous. Upstairs, on the third floor, Jeremiah and Vinny occupied separate guest rooms but shared a bath; while Caleb, for his tardiness, had been given the pull-out couch in her office, though not before she locked the computer with a password. Even so, he had access to her paper files; but the only alternative was Chloe's room, and the thought of Caleb sleeping in her daughter's bed made Willa queasy.

"I know these people," she'd told Jovan when she sent him away. But what did she really know of them, these intimate strangers, now that the grace and potential of youth were gone, now that they'd hardened into adults? Did she even know them when she thought she knew them?

When sleep eventually overtook her racing thoughts, it was not an easy sleep. Willa dreamed she was a kid again, desperately searching for her friends; if she didn't find them, something terrible was going to happen. She ran through the school, but the classrooms were empty. It was carnival day, and the football field was full of booths and rides and people milling about. After much searching she spotted Nancy behind a booth, bulging out of a spangled leotard and tights. A row of knives was set out on a table beside her. Travis was bound hand and foot to a large wheel. As the wheel turned, Nancy hurled knives at him.

Unable to watch, Willa ran away. Around midfield, a large crowd had gathered about a stage. Craning over their heads, she saw Caleb in a black magician's cape towering over a long, closed box. From one end of the box a pair of feet protruded; from the other, Angel's head. Caleb raised a large sword and twirled it overhead. Willa screamed, but the crowd drowned her out; she dashed forward but couldn't break through. The great sword rose and descended; Angel's head rolled to the floor. Caleb picked it up by the long red hair and tossed it to Patrick, who was juggling two others.

Suddenly Jeremiah was beside her. "The party's over," he said, taking her arm. On the way out they passed Mr. O'Rourke sitting in a dunking booth. He waved but they kept on going till they reached the parking lot. Vinny, dressed in a strongman's leopard-skin outfit, was straining to lift a red Chevrolet above his head. For a moment he succeeded; then his legs buckled, and the car came crashing down.

Willa woke in a cold sweat. Safe in her bed, she understood she'd been dreaming; yet every instinct she had still screamed danger. It was early morning, hours to go before dawn. Moonlight filtered around the edges of the curtains. The house was silent, the room empty, but she was not alone. Something had roused her, and it wasn't her dream.

Movement caught her eye: her doorknob turning slowly. Fear seized her by the throat. *Lock your door*, Jovan had said, his parting words; as if she'd needed telling. The lock caught, and for a moment the movement ceased. Then, slowly, stealthily, the knob returned to its original position. Though she strained to hear, no sound came from the corridor.

Get up and see, she ordered herself, but her body didn't obey. Whoever it was was standing outside, listening as hard as she was. It crossed her mind that something was wrong; perhaps someone had taken ill during the night. But then why not knock, why so sneaky? Was it Caleb, playing at succubus? Travis, hoping for a peek? *Thank God Chloe's not home,* she thought, and with this her courage came rushing back on a tide of indignation. Silently Willa slipped out of the bed, tiptoed across the carpeted floor, and pressed her ear to the door. Nothing. What wouldn't she have given for a peephole! She reached for the knob. Hesitated. Then gave it a twist and yanked the door open.

The hall was empty.

Willa didn't sleep again that night, but stayed in bed until the sun rose. Then she showered, dressed in shorts and a sweatshirt, and went downstairs to make coffee. *The New York Times* was waiting on the doorstep in its familiar blue wrapper. She was sitting at the table, inhaling her second cup and working blearily on the crossword when Caleb padded in from the hall, barefoot, in jeans and a T-shirt.

"You're up early," she said.

"Smelled the coffee," he said.

"Help yourself."

Caleb poured himself a cup and topped up hers. He sat across the table from her and said, "You'll be glad to have your house back."

Too tired to mount her usual defenses, she admitted that she would. "Although it's been . . . real."

He smiled as if they were allies. "A bit too real?"

"There seemed to be a lot of unfinished business. And Angel's absence loomed large."

"Not for me," Caleb said. "There's only one person I came to see, and I'm looking at her."

It wasn't yet eight in the morning. He was still on his first cup of coffee. But perhaps he felt he had to act fast. Willa smiled vaguely and addressed herself to the crossword. Twenty-four across: a six-letter word for "hustler." "Caleb" didn't fit.

"I've been thinking about your question up on the hill," he said. "You were right. There was a bond. It went very deep; for me, deeper than any I've known since."

"What kind of bond?" she asked.

"Love," he said. "In its various forms."

"Love is supposed to endure."

"We're here, aren't we? I'm here." And he gazed at her with those hypnotic eyes.

"For now," she said. "What are your plans?"

"That depends," he said meaningfully.

Willa could have laid her head down on the table and howled from sheer disappointment. As a boy, Caleb had been the least predictable person she knew. Now she was three or four lines ahead of him, and he didn't even know it.

At least it was within her power to change the script. "Depends on what?" was meant to be her next line. Instead she asked if he was hungry.

"No," he said without interest. "Willa—"

"Because I'm going out for bagels in a bit, but if you like I could make an omelet."

"Willa," he said, "stop."

"Stop what?"

"Stop treating me like a guest."

"Stop treating *me* like a mark," Willa said, and for the first time ever she succeeded in surprising Caleb. For one unguarded moment, his expression gave him away, or rather the series of expressions that passed over his face: amazement, followed by a rapid reassessment—*What must she know to say such a thing?*—followed by adaptation. He looked at her now with a degree of frankness that had not been there before, but only a degree; masks upon masks had Caleb. There was a roguish glint to this one's eye that she liked much better than the ardent swain look.

"I haven't led a perfect life," he said. "I don't think you have, either."

"I try to learn from my mistakes," she said.

At that he looked so crestfallen that Willa almost felt guilty, until she remembered the file upstairs. It gave her an advantage, but not, she felt, an unfair one. Her own sorry story was on display to anyone with access to a library, and she had no doubt Caleb had accessed it.

"So you still haven't forgiven me," he said.

"There is nothing to forgive in the way you left my life. There may be more in your coming back."

"I wouldn't say that. You did mention unfinished business."

"Oh," she said, with a look to mirror his own, "not between us. I think our account is settled." Then she went out for bagels, leaving Caleb skewered to his chair.

By the time she returned, the others were stirring. One by one they wandered into the kitchen and helped themselves to coffee, bagels, and doughnuts, which they carried out to the deck. The weather was overcast and cool, but still pleasant enough to sit outdoors. Soon only Vinny was missing from the group.

"Is he still sleeping?" Willa asked.

"Must be," Shake said. "Should I go wake him?"

"Would you?" For she wanted them out by noon, when Chloe would be coming home.

Shake returned a few minutes later. "He's not there."

"Probably in the can," Patrick said.

"I checked."

Willa's first thought was that Vinny had decamped without saying good-bye. But she'd seen his car up front. "Maybe he slept somewhere else."

"We all went up together last night," Jeremiah said. He looked at Patrick and Caleb, who nodded in confirmation.

The men went back into the house to find Vinny, leaving Willa with Nancy. The women drank their coffee in silence, while inside the house the men shouted for Vinny. Willa was annoyed. This was no time for hide-and-seek.

"Probably went for a walk," Nancy ventured. There was a spot of cream cheese on her chin and lipstick on her teeth. "A run, maybe, to sweat off some of that booze."

"Or a swim," Willa said, rising at the thought. Nancy grabbed a doughnut before following her down the path to the pool.

The gate was open but the pool was empty, except for an air mattress in the shallow end and a bundle of clothing floating in the deep end. Willa's eyes slid away, refusing to take in the details of that incongruous bundle. Only when Nancy began to scream did Willa see the dark hair, the hand protruding from a shirt-sleeve, only then understood what she was looking at.

She took a running dive and in two strokes was beside him. Vinny was floating facedown. Willa tried to flip him, but his flaccid weight, even in the water, was too much for her. She touched his hand, then recoiled from the coldness of it. Nancy was still screaming, but the sound was muted by the roaring in Willa's head. Averting her eyes from his face, Willa grabbed a fistful of shirt and towed him toward the side.

The others came pounding up. It took three of them to haul Vinny out, while Willa clung panting to the edge of the pool; then Caleb reached down and pulled her out. Her legs crumpled and she would have fallen if it hadn't been for his arm. He handed her over to Nancy and joined the huddle around Vinny.

For Willa, the next few minutes had a strobelike quality. Vivid, discontinuous images flashed before her eyes. Nancy led her to a chaise, put a towel around her shoulders, and held a cup of hot coffee to her lips. The men knelt around Vinny, hiding him from view. Jeremiah stood off to one side, speaking quietly into a cell phone. Travis stood and backed away, leaving a hole through which for the first time Willa saw Vinny's face. If the touch of his hand hadn't told her he was beyond help, his open, fixed eyes would have. They'd laid him on his back, arms by his side: that powerful body, perfect, intact, lifeless.

It was nothing like sleep.

"Shouldn't we . . . ?" Shake made a pumping motion.

"Too late," Patrick said bitterly. "Feel him." He passed a hand over Vinny's face and shut those eyes.

Nancy left Willa on the chaise and went over to Vinny. Pressed her palm tenderly to his forehead, like a mother checking for temperature. Her hand fell away. She stood and Shake rose and moved into her waiting arms.

Jeremiah took charge, cool and calm, a man suited to crises.

"I've called nine-one-one. Once the police arrive, no one will be allowed into the house, and the house will be searched. If anyone needs to use the bathroom"—he looked hard at Travis—"this would be the time."

Travis turned and sprinted toward the house. Jeremiah went on. "It's clear that this was a tragic accident, but there will almost certainly be a police investigation. It's important that we cooperate fully—without muddying the waters with irrelevant matters."

Patrick, still kneeling, rocked back on his heels and glared.

But Willa, even in her bleakness and confusion, was grateful to Jeremiah for stepping up. They were in for misery enough without turning their tragedy into other people's breakfast entertainment.

From far away they heard the wail of sirens.

"We'll need to meet afterward," Jeremiah said urgently. "Someplace we can talk." He looked at Willa.

No matter how many towels she wrapped around herself, Willa could not seem to warm up. Her teeth chattered, and her thoughts refused to cohere. But the instinct of hospitality ran deep. "Come back here," she said.

"That's very kind, but they probably won't allow that. Is there anywhere else?"

She suggested the Chinese restaurant in town. It had a small private room in the back. "Perfect," Jeremiah said.

Travis returned from the house. "Done," he said, panting. The sirens had grown louder; they were on the block. All of them had moved away from Vinny. Travis looked down, taking in that sodden and forlorn body.

"Poor Vinny," he said. "Poor bastard."

34

It was raining now, a steady gray drizzle. Willa hardly noticed. She could not get any wetter than she was.

Jeremiah had been right, as usual. The police would not allow them back inside. Instead Willa and her guests had been herded around the side of the house to the circular drive and held there separately by uniformed cops, who were terribly sympathetic and asked a great many questions. One officer wrapped his own raincoat around Willa, who still couldn't stop shaking.

Before the police separated them, Willa had used Jeremiah's phone to make two calls. The first was to Isabel Rapaport. Chloe, thank God, was still sleeping. Willa said the minimum: terrible accident, a drowning. Isabel allowed herself one gasp of shock and then, to her everlasting credit, asked not a single question. "I've got Chloe for as long as you need," she said. "Should I send Dennis over?" Her husband was an attorney. Willa declined. Her next call was to Jovan. All his phone numbers were in her house, and his home number was unlisted. She left a message on his office machine. "It's Willa. There's been an accident; Vinny's dead. Come if you can."

A couple of plainclothes policemen sought her out. One was Detective Sergeant Meyerhoff. The other was a younger man with spiked red hair. "This is Detective Flynn, Mrs. Durrell," Meyerhoff said. "We need you to go back there with us; can you do that?"

She didn't want to, but she fell into step with them. Vinny was lying just as they had left him, underneath a jury-rigged canopy. He was wearing the same clothes he'd worn last night, she noticed now, but he'd lost a loafer. There were a lot of people in the area, but little seemed to be happening. The EMS crew was packing up. One man was taking pictures of Vinny; another knelt by the pool, filling a beaker with water; a third pored over the electrical control box mounted on the pool house. Meyerhoff walked her toward the pool, keeping his bulk between her and Vinny. "I want you to point out exactly where he was when you found him."

She pointed toward the deep end and noticed something brown at the bottom of the pool: Vinny's missing shoe.

"What position was he in?"

"Floating facedown."

"Was he holding anything?"

"No."

"Was anything else in the pool?"

"Just that float." She pointed to the air mattress.

"And where was that?"

"Where it is now, in the shallow end."

"Was it left in the pool the last time you used it?"

"I don't remember."

"Could Mr. Delgaudio swim?" the other detective asked.

Willa nodded.

"Look around, Mrs. Durrell. Is anything missing? Anything out of place?"

She looked about, avoiding Vinny. Couldn't they for God's sake cover him up? "No," she said, "nothing."

"Have you had any problems with the pool? Anything with the water or the electrical service?"

"I just opened it last week," Willa said. "We used it this weekend. Everything was fine, there were no problems."

The two detectives consulted silently. "That's all we need right now, ma'am," the younger one said. "We'll talk more at the station, out of the rain."

They walked her back to the driveway. There was no sign of her friends, though their cars were still there. Meyerhoff said they'd been driven to the station house and that she would be, too. He was walking her toward an unmarked car when Willa heard her name called. She looked up. Jovan was running toward her.

He took her by the shoulders, and for the first time since diving into the pool, Willa felt grounded. "You're all wet!" he said. "Did you go in after him?"

"I found him." She was shaking again.

Jovan turned to Meyerhoff. "What the hell's wrong with you? Can't you see she's soaked to the bone?"

"Easy, tiger," Meyerhoff said. "You know we can't let her inside."

"So get her a change of clothes."

"Is that all right with you?" Meyerhoff asked Willa, who nodded. A policewoman was dispatched with instructions.

Jovan looked at Willa. "I should have stayed. I knew I should have stayed."

"He has a wife," she said, and for the first time began to cry. "He has two kids."

Willa spent the rest of the morning in the police station being questioned, gently but thoroughly, by Flynn and a female detective named Mary Lorenzo. Jovan was not allowed to stay with her, and though she occasionally glimpsed one or another of her friends, she was given no opportunity to speak to them.

Flynn did most of the questioning, which ranged far and wide. When did she last see Vinny? Why was he staying at her house? Who else was there? She had to explain about the reunion, their vow to meet in twenty years, come what may. How stupid it sounded now, how childish; and look what had come of it. She was asked to draw a layout of the bedrooms and indicate who slept where. As soon as she finished, Lorenzo took the sketch and conveyed it to someone outside the room.

On and on it went, a laundry list of questions. What prescription drugs did she keep in the house? Had she noticed any bees or wasps near the pool? Did Vinny mention any allergies? Did he seem depressed, worried about anything? Was he drinking heavily? Were there drugs at the party? All these questions Willa answered honestly, except the last. She tried to divine their thinking from the questions, but they seemed to be casting about blindly, unsure of their direction.

They took an exhaustive interest in matters of locks and keys. Had she locked up the house Saturday night? (Yes.) Were the doors locked that morning when she got up? (Both the front door and the door from the den to the deck were; she had not tried the others.) Was there an alarm system? (Turned off for the weekend.) Who had keys? (Only Willa; Chloe had her own front-door key, but she was away all weekend.) Were there spares, and where were they kept? Flynn seemed interested in the fact that she kept a spare key to the deck door behind the wet bar in the den. Soon afterward, he left the room and Meyerhoff came in, like a relay team. Now the questioning turned to the events of that weekend, and at once Willa grew wary. She wanted to help.

More than anything, she wanted to know what had happened to Vinny and why, and in that quest, the police were potent allies. But she felt an obligation to her friends as well; for it was she who had gotten them into this mess.

The reunion was great, she told them. Everyone got along fine.

Meyerhoff looked at her, disappointment writ large in those basset-hound eyes. "That's not what Jovan said. He said you called it 'the reunion from hell.'"

"He's exaggerating. Or I was."

He consulted his notebook. "There was some dispute about a car . . . ?"

"Hardly a dispute," she scoffed. "A discussion about dates."

"Who was right?"

"Not Vinny."

"Can you think of any reason he would want to obscure the date that car of theirs went missing?"

Willa hesitated. She hadn't thought of it like that. Taken together with Vinny's abortive claim to having heard from Angel after her disappearance, the question was particularly troubling. But Meyerhoff didn't know about that, and until she'd had a chance to think about it, she wasn't prepared to tell him.

He was waiting for her answer. She shrugged. "Vinny probably just forgot."

"Tell me about Vinny and Angel. What was their relationship?"

"They were friends," she said.

"Intimate friends?"

"No."

"How can you be sure?"

"Vinny wouldn't go there."

"Why not?" Meyerhoff said. "Everyone else did."

Willa sighed. "Because Vinny was all about loyalty and Patrick was his best friend. I can't prove it, but if you're asking my opinion, no way."

"Patrick and Vinny were best friends, you say. Why is it, do you think, the friendship didn't survive high school?"

"Well, Patrick was mad about the car. And then they just went their separate ways."

Meyerhoff looked troubled. "In fact, none of those relationships continued much beyond high school, did they? Isn't that strange, considering how tight you say you were? Don't you ever wonder why?"

What a clever creature he was. Of course she'd wondered. *What held us together?* she'd asked up on Beacon Hill, but Meyerhoff's question was the unspoken corollary: *What drove them apart?* Was it simply the passage of time, or had something else happened?

He was waiting for an answer.

"It's only natural," she said. "People drift apart."

"But your little crew didn't drift apart, did they? They flew apart, almost as if there were an explosion at the core."

"I think that's a little fanciful," Willa said.

"You do, do you," Meyerhoff said, with a look that showed a whole other side of him. "And that poor fellow in the pool this morning, was that fanciful, too?"

When they finally let her out, Jovan was waiting. She was pale and grim and still looked cold, though it was warm in the station. Her eyes touched on his face and slid off.

"Are you okay?" he asked.

"Could you drive me home?"

"They told you that you can't get in yet?"

She nodded. "I just need my car and my purse."

In the car she was quiet, and though he knew she was exhausted, shocked, and saddened, Jovan felt her silence as reproach. She couldn't blame him more than he blamed himself. The vibes were all wrong in that house. He should have trusted his instincts and stayed, should have kept his hands off her and made it clear that all he wanted was a spot on the sofa. If he had, none of this would have happened. But no—he had to try and mix business with pleasure, with the usual result of accomplishing neither.

The rain had ended, and a wispy fog lay over the village. He drove slowly and kept quiet, giving her time to decompress. They were halfway to her house before Willa spoke. "What happened to my friends?"

"They were released earlier and taken back to reclaim their belongings. I imagine they're gone by now."

A brief silence, then: "What do the police think happened?"

"They wouldn't tell me if they knew, which at this stage they probably don't. A lot will depend on the autopsy. What did they ask you?"

"The usual," she said. A brave little joke; it cracked his heart. Then her mouth quivered. "I'm sure they think it's my fault."

He glanced sideways at her profile. "How do you figure that?"

"My pool. My house. My responsibility."

On the phone she'd called it an accident. The alternatives did not seem to have occurred to her.

"Things aren't always what they seem," he said. "The police aren't making any assumptions. Neither should we."

"Will Meyerhoff confide in you?"

He shook his head. "Not about an active case. Especially not this one."

"Why especially?"

"He's got this idea in his head that I've gone soft on you. Which," he added hastily, seeing her face, "even if it were true, would not be relevant at this point."

They had to drive through a press gauntlet to get onto her property. Jovan expected her to flinch or cover her face, but Willa stared straight ahead, as if she didn't notice the reporters knocking at the car windows. She'd had practice, he recalled sadly.

"Can I take you to lunch?" he asked, but she was already reaching for the door handle.

"I have to pick up my daughter."

"And after that?"

She shrugged, thanked him for coming. It sounded like a kiss-off.

He pressed a card with all his numbers into her hand. "Will you at least let me know where you are?"

She looked him full in the face at last, and reached for a smile. "Haven't you got problems of your own?"

"I do," he said. "But yours are much more interesting."

It was a mournful and dispirited group Willa found waiting in the private room of Sun Ming Lotus. They were all there, which surprised her; she'd expected Caleb at least to bolt.

"Finally," Patrick said as she walked in. "We were about to storm the Bastille."

She slid into an empty seat between him and Jeremiah, who,

despite his cool head at the scene, looked badly shaken. He leaned over and gave her a hug.

"And then they were seven," Travis said. No one laughed.

They'd already ordered, and the oval table was laden with a variety of dishes. Patrick filled a plate for her and bullied her into eating. To her shame, Willa found, once she started, that she was ravenous.

While she ate, they compared notes. All of them had been questioned, not only about Vinny and the events of that weekend, but also about Angel's disappearance and especially her pregnancy. "They're trying to make a connection," Jeremiah said, "where none necessarily exists."

"Necessarily?" Willa stared. "What possible connection could there be?"

No one rushed to answer. Then Travis, with an edge of excitement in his voice that sounded almost pleasurable, said, "That's what I told them, too. 'Forget Vinny,' I said. 'If you want to know who knocked Angel up, you've got to widen your horizons.' Then I threw them O'Rourke, but I think they already knew about him."

"Who?" said Shake.

"Mr. O'Rourke, her math teacher," Nancy whispered.

"She slept with him?"

"According to Travis," Patrick said. "Poor bastard. That ain't right, man."

"All this," Jeremiah said, shaking his head, "in pursuit of a woman who clearly does not want to be found."

Willa was still puzzling over his last remark. "What did you mean, necessarily? Don't you think it was an accident?"

"Of course it was," Jeremiah said soothingly. "We all said so."

"Why wouldn't we?" She looked around the table. No one met her eyes.

"The police seem to think suicide is a possibility," Jeremiah said at last. "They asked a lot of questions about his state of mind, which between us and the lamppost was shaky at best."

"That's ridiculous," Willa said. "He could swim. Swimmers can't just will themselves to drown."

"They can get smashed and go for a solitary swim. It amounts to the same."

"Why would he?"

Jeremiah gave her a sorrowful look. "Why would he make up that story about getting a card from Angel?"

So there it was, out on the table along with the egg rolls and the spare ribs; only no one wanted to touch it.

Willa thought about Vinny up on the hill, the look in his eyes when she'd asked him what was wrong. He'd almost told her. What would he have said? Suddenly not hungry anymore, she pushed her plate away.

Two waiters came in to clear the table. When they were gone, Patrick leaned forward to look at Jeremiah. "You're forgetting something," he said. "You're forgetting who Vinny was. Not the one who showed up this weekend; I mean Vinny as we knew him back then. Think how protective he was with the girls. The guy was a fucking mastiff. No way he's connected to Angel's disappearance, no way."

"Something was eating him this weekend," Jeremiah said.

"I know. But whatever it was, it wasn't that."

"What do you think happened?"

Patrick shrugged. "Like Willa said, some kind of accident. He was drunk. Maybe he went out for some air, slipped and hit his head on the side of the pool."

"I didn't see any cuts or bruises. But I'm not arguing with you, Patch. The guy had a family. It's better for everyone if this is seen as an accident, unrelated to the occasion. As far as the police are concerned, our reunion was one big harmonious love fest." Jeremiah looked around the table. "Right?"

"A little late for that," Caleb said in a taut voice. He was sitting across from Willa but had not looked at her once since she'd come in.

"You got that right," Nancy said. "One of you passed on Travis's bullshit story about me ratting out Angel. I wonder who." Her beady eyes fixed on Travis.

"Not me!" he said indignantly. "What I said was just between us. I'm no rat."

Nancy slapped the table. "Neither am I, you prick!"

"It wasn't Travis," Caleb said. All eyes turned to him. "It was Willa's friend."

"Who?" Patrick said stupidly.

"You remember," Caleb said. "Quiet guy, big ears, chummy with the cops?" He looked up from the table and raked Willa's face with his eyes. "I saw him at the station."

So this is why he stayed, she thought with a sinking heart.

"Everything he heard, they know," Caleb said. "And he heard plenty, thanks to Willa."

"He was there for me," she said. "I called him."

"I thought I smelled pig last night. Tell me he's not a cop."

"Not anymore."

He glared at her. They were all staring, blame in every set of eyes. "You set us up," Caleb said, still building steam.

"You think I knew this was going to happen?" Willa said.

"Do you realize that they took our fingerprints? Searched our belongings; made us empty our pockets?"

Oh, to hell with him, she thought. To hell with all of them. "Do *you* realize that Vinny's dead? Do you realize that two children have lost their father because of our stupid reunion? I'm terribly sorry you were inconvenienced, Caleb. I'm sure Vinny would be devastated."

35

The last thing Willa wanted was to go home, even if that had been an option. Chloe felt the same way. Isabel urged them to stay with her, but Willa craved anonymity and some time alone with her daughter. They holed up in luxury, just the two of them, in a room in the Rye Marriott, and ordered dinner from the room-service menu. Comfort food: grilled-cheese sandwiches and tomato soup, brownies for desert. While they waited, Chloe ran a bath for Willa, who still couldn't shake the cold she'd felt since plunging into the pool. But as soon as she saw the full tub, Willa envisioned Vinny floating facedown; and then of course she couldn't get in. She let the water out and hunkered down on the cold tile floor and cried silently so Chloe wouldn't hear, but Chloe did hear; she came in and sat on the floor next to Willa. "Why do you always hide?" she asked. "Don't you think you're allowed to cry?"

Thus given permission, Willa gave way to her misery for a few minutes more, until the thought came that there was another woman with far more cause than she to weep that night; then she was ashamed of her self-indulgence and stopped.

Dinner came, along with a glass of wine for Willa and a milk shake for Chloe. They talked while they ate, and when the food was gone, they went on talking. Chloe had spent the morning in a frenzy of suspense, knowing something terrible had happened at home and unconvinced by Isabel's assurances that her mother was fine. Now nothing would calm her but to hear everything, every detail of what had happened.

One thing led to another and Willa found herself talking about Angel and the mystery of her disappearance, and then about the last time she'd seen Angel up on Beacon Hill. "She was so beautiful, Chloe. Gorgeous red hair, great waves of it, which of course she hated because the style then was straight and limp. She wore a red flamenco dress, and she looked like fire, too hot to touch."

"Why was she all dressed up?" Chloe asked. They were lying on one of the two queen beds, dressed in their pajamas, with a box of tissues and a box of chocolates between them. Willa's pajamas were borrowed from Isabel, who had also provided the chocolate. Really, she had been extraordinarily kind to them; it seemed that without even noticing, Willa had made a friend.

"It was graduation day," she said. "We were having our own private celebration up on Beacon Hill. We had music and champagne. Shake played his harmonica and Angel sang. I still remember the song: 'Frankie and Johnny.'"

"I know that song!" Chloe said. "We learned it in chorus." She sang a few bars.

"That's the one. Angel had a great voice, sort of raspy and down to earth, but tuneful. I wish you could have heard her."

"So do I." Chloe was quiet for a while. "Mom?"

"Yes, hon?"

"I'll never be able to swim in that pool again."

Willa shuddered. "Me either."

"It's hard enough living in a house where everything reminds me of Dad." There was a catch in Chloe's voice, and she bit her lip to keep from saying more.

They lay without talking for a while. Then Willa said carefully, "Chloe, how would you feel about selling our house and buying another one?"

Chloe sat bolt upright. "Are you serious?"

"Only if you like the idea."

"Where?"

The city, Willa thought wistfully. Or Paris, or London. Someplace where she could start fresh, be who she wanted to be instead of what she'd settled for being. Impossible now, but the time was coming when she would have no excuse for just dreaming.

"In town," she said, "so you could stay in your school. Something smaller but beautiful, without a pool. We could pick it out together."

Chloe's eyes filled with tears. "Oh God, I would love that."

Willa was amazed (as she of all people ought not to have been) by the blinding power of assumption. Why hadn't she just asked Chloe how she felt months ago? Why had she assumed that just because she loved her, she knew her daughter's heart?

Their plan could not be implemented at once, much as she would have liked it to be. But the sheer joy of knowing she would soon

be rid of her encumbering house carried Willa through the tribu-
lations of the next few days.

Meyerhoff had given her the number of a service that specialized
in cleaning up crime scenes. She called them from the hotel Monday
morning, and they met her at the house: three men with heavy-duty
vacuums, steamers, and industrial-strength cleansers. While they did
the heavy work, Willa and Chloe went through the house putting
things to right. Several times Willa glanced outside and was startled
to see uniformed policemen combing through her shrubbery. She
asked what they were looking for, but they wouldn't say.

The police had left their mark in every room. There was not a
shelf or drawer that had not been searched and subtly rear-
ranged. The bedroom Vinny had slept in had been dusted for fingerprints, which made some sort of sense; so had Willa's
bathroom, which made none. Every bit of medication had been
confiscated. Whatever possessions her friends had in their rooms
had been packed up and delivered to them when they came to
collect their cars, but they had left many things scattered about
the house: bathing suits, cassettes, photos, assorted bits and
pieces. Willa tossed them all in a box for later disposition. The
vase Travis had given her stood on the mantelpiece in the den,
minus the joints; she could only pray it was he and not the police
who had removed them.

Her greatest fear had been that they would confiscate her
diaries. The notion of a bunch of hardened detectives poring over
the intimate confessions of her youth, laughing at her effusions,
made her writhe with humiliation. But the diaries were where
she had hidden them, in her lingerie drawer. They'd been taken
out, handled, and replaced in the wrong order; but they were all
there.

Her answering machine was full. Many of the calls were from
journalists, and those she erased. Patrick had called twice to see
how she was, Jovan and Jeremiah once each. Judy Trumpledore
had left a message. "You poor baby, what a tragic end to your
reunion. Not to be crass, my dear, but I smell a book in all this.
Call me." There were calls from worried neighbors and old
friends. The last message was from Detective Flynn, asking her to
phone him.

She returned his call first. He was out, but when Willa gave her name she was asked to hold on; a moment later, Meyerhoff came on the line. They had a few more questions, he told her. Could she drop by the station?

Willa agreed. They set a date for three that afternoon. Then she called Jovan.

"I'm going with you," he said.

"What's the point? They'll just make you sit and wait again."

"Not this time."

They met in the station parking lot at a quarter to. Jovan wore a good suit and a grim look. "I'm going to twist their arms a little," he said. "Back me up."

Both Flynn and Meyerhoff were waiting for her. They bristled at the sight of Jovan. "Wait here," Meyerhoff told him, pointing to a row of chairs.

"I don't think so," Jovan said. "Mrs. Durrell wants me in the interview. Otherwise she's going to lawyer up."

They looked at Willa. She crossed her arms and looked back.

Meyerhoff gave Jovan a filthy look. "Now why would you want to get in the way? You know she's not a target."

"I'm not getting in the way. I'm just sitting in."

They let him in. A different room this time, larger and emptier than the last. No pictures on the wall, no windows, no furniture except the table and four folding chairs. Jovan and Willa sat on one side of the table, the detectives on the other.

Meyerhoff led off. "Yesterday, I asked you about Vinny's relationship with Angel. You said they were just friends. Are you sure about that?"

She had been. But last night, while Chloe slept, Willa had been thinking about Vinny, reliving the weekend. Something had been worrying him; almost from the start he'd been moody and alienated from the others. What had troubled him? Was it Angel after all? And why had he invented that reckless tale about hearing from her?

"Mrs. Durrell?" Meyerhoff said.

"I was when I said it," she said. "But I feel like I don't know anything anymore."

"One of your friends suspected they did have an affair."

Who would say that? Willa's thoughts, like Nancy's, turned first to Travis. He'd been obsessed with Angel, Patrick had said, convinced she was sleeping with everyone but him.

"That doesn't make it true," she said. "Why aren't you talking to her father?"

"We've talked to him," Meyerhoff said. "Searched his house, dug up his yard, came away with nothing."

"Any luck locating his old car?" Jovan asked.

Meyerhoff answered without looking at him. "As a matter of fact, we found it. Farmer upstate had it up on blocks for parts."

"And?"

"And nada." Meyerhoff turned back to Willa and asked her to walk them through the weekend. She did, starting with Vinny's arrival Friday afternoon. The detective stopped her when she got to Beacon Hill. "How did Vinny seem up there?" he asked.

She hesitated. *One big harmonious love fest*, Jeremiah had said. And the guy with the most to lose gets to call the shots— that's how they'd always played it. But what about the ones who'd already lost everything? Where did they fit in?

She looked at Meyerhoff. "He was antsy. Unhappy."

"Unhappy with who?"

"With me, for harping on the past. But just generally. He didn't want to be there."

Meyerhoff gave her an encouraging nod. "Why is that, do you think?"

"I don't know."

"Sometimes it can be painful to call up old memories. Do you think maybe that's what was happening with Vinny?"

So Jeremiah was right: They were trying to tie Vinny's death to Angel's disappearance. "I see where you're going," she said, "but believe me, it makes no sense. Vinny didn't kill Angel. He had no reason to. They were friends, and Vinny was protective of his friends. But even if he did, for some unimaginable reason, kill Angel, are we supposed to believe that he lived with it peaceably for twenty years before suddenly falling to pieces?"

"It happens," Meyerhoff said wearily. "Vinny wasn't a psycho, he was a nice guy with a conscience. They're the ones who crack in the end. Especially, the man's got kids of his own now, a girl

Angel's age. Then along comes this reunion, and suddenly it all backs up on him."

"Nonsense," she said flatly. "Vinny didn't kill himself. He couldn't have. Swimmers don't drown in pools."

The detectives exchanged a look; then, without a word passing between them, Meyerhoff sat back and let Flynn take over. "Do you take sleeping pills?" he asked.

"No."

"There was a bottle of Restoril in your medicine cabinet."

"The doctor prescribed that after my husband died. I took them for a few nights, no more. Why?"

"How many would you say you'd taken out of the bottle?"

She shrugged. "Three, four."

"Did anyone ask for a sleeping pill this weekend?"

"No."

"Anyone enter your bathroom?"

"Only me."

"Who had access to it?"

"Any of them, I guess. Why?"

Again Flynn failed to answer. "You said you went up to bed around midnight Saturday. Did you see anyone after that?"

"Not till morning."

"Hear anything?"

Willa stared. She saw a knob, turning slowly. "Someone came to my room the last night. They tried the door, but it was locked. I don't know who it was."

The detectives exchanged a quick look. "You never mentioned that," Flynn said.

"I forgot. A lot else happened."

"What time was this?"

"About three." A terrible thought struck her. What if it was Vinny seeking her out, needing to talk about something?

Flynn went on asking questions, which she answered automatically. What was Vinny drinking? Did he argue with anyone? Then a whole new course of questioning about locks and keys. It seemed the key to the French doors that she kept behind the bar had gone missing. "When's the last time you saw it?" Flynn asked.

Willa thought about that. "Friday night. I took it when we went for a swim, in case someone accidentally locked the door behind them. Afterward I put it back behind the bar."

"Who saw you?"

"Anyone who was watching."

"You didn't use it to lock up Saturday night?"

"You don't need a key to lock the door from the inside, you just turn the latch."

A few more questions and then, abruptly, they were done. Flynn thanked Willa for her help and walked her out. Jovan fell back with Meyerhoff. He waited till they were in the corridor, safe from prying eyes and ears. "Hang on a sec."

"Or what?" Meyerhoff said, but he lingered.

"What did the tox screen show?"

"You've got a fucking nerve asking me that."

"I need to know."

"Man, that broad's got you coming and going, don't she?"

"If one of her buddies killed Vinny, she'd better know it," Jovan said grimly. "Was he unconscious when he went in?"

Meyerhoff wrestled with himself and lost. "Could be."

"Any sign of a struggle?"

"Not a mark on the body."

"Which there wouldn't be, if he was drugged first."

"Man, I've said all I'm gonna say to you," Meyerhoff said. "Now why don't you go hold your girlfriend's hand and let us do our job?"

36

Time passed, and Willa felt its passage acutely, the way a burn victim feels air moving against wounded skin: a sensation so subtle as to generally pass unnoticed, but agonizing under the circumstances. The dreariness of waiting was exacerbated by the fact that once again, no one would tell her anything. The police did not call, and when she reached out to Meyerhoff, all she got were platitudes: The investigation was continuing; they were following several lines of inquiry.

Willa had reverted to siege protocol, screening all calls. Her phone number was unlisted but seemed common currency among the New York press; reporters phoned incessantly for several days, then tapered off. Isabel, too, delighted with Willa's decision to move house, called nearly every day with reports of perfect houses just on or about to go on the market. Willa was grateful but not quite ready. This was a time of waiting that had to play itself out. There had to be an end, a clear answer. Until that came, she had no patience for house hunting.

But day followed upon day, until a week had passed since the accident (as she thought of it), and still no answer came. Chloe was often out, a good thing given the atmosphere in the house, but it left Willa with a lot of empty time. Some of it she employed reading through her diaries, searching for any clue to Angel's thoughts, plans, and relationships that she might have overlooked before; but there was only so much of that she could bear. Willa wasn't sleeping well and blamed her nervousness on fatigue. Talking might have helped, but her old friends kept their distance. Willa shouldn't have been surprised. She'd seen the condemnation in their eyes and understood it, even shared it to an extent: she had committed the ultimate sin of breaking ranks. But she consoled herself with the thought that at least the press hadn't gotten hold of her guests' names, and they never would from her.

Caleb, Nancy, and Travis were no great loss; if she never saw them again, it would be soon enough. But Patrick's silence stung, and so did Jeremiah's. It made her think more than she wanted to about Meyerhoff's curious expression, "an explosion at the core." She would have asked them about it if they'd called . . . but they didn't.

Jovan was the only person Willa could talk to about the case, and she didn't like his answers. If she vacillated between accident and suicide, he was sure to hint at a third possibility. Though his hints were as subtle as a dentist's drill, she refused to take them seriously. Vinny's death was tragic enough, she told him, without resorting to melodrama. Jovan, professing concern for her safety, offered to move in for a few days. Though he made a point of mentioning the sofa, Willa suspected him of planning to worry himself right into her bed. There, too, she was grateful but unready.

Nights were the worst, for then her resistance was at its lowest ebb. Thoughts of Vinny crowded her sleep, elbowed her awake. While suicide seemed impossible, she had blamed herself for creating the circumstances for the accident. But the missing sleeping pills made it just possible to imagine Vinny taking a few, washing them down with more booze, then going to lie on the float and wait for nature to take its course.

But why do such a thing, and why do it then and there? There had to be a reason. Patrick had mentioned Vinny's reluctance to attend the reunion, and Willa had seen for herself how miserable he was up on Beacon Hill. She remembered his edginess all weekend, the stupid lie about a postcard from Angel, and how angry he'd gotten when Patrick talked about their car. Remembered, too, their conversation in the club: Vinny complaining about the boys hanging around his daughter, her teasing him about his own checkered past. "What goes around, comes around," she'd said; "God forbid," he'd replied, crossing himself.

What was it Meyerhoff said? *Man's got kids of his own now, a girl Angel's age . . . Nice guys with a conscience, they're the ones who crack in the end.* The detective made murder sound so ordinary, a momentary lapse of judgment that could happen to anyone. And maybe it did happen that way sometimes. Maybe Vinny had made a mistake, a single, irreparable mistake.

But these were night musings. In the day she dismissed them. Vinny had loved girls and loved a good fight, but he never mixed the two. To him, any man who hit a woman was a coward and a cur. She could far more easily picture Nancy striking out in rage, or Travis in frustration, than Vinny laying violent hands on Angel.

Of course, there was a long list of things Willa could not imagine that had proved to be true.

Monday morning, eight days after Vinny's death, Willa was eating breakfast when her eye fell on a small announcement in the *Times:* Funeral services for Vincent Delgaudio were to be held the following afternoon at St. Anselm's, in the Bronx. She reached for the phone.

Patrick answered on the first ring, as if he'd been waiting.

"Vinny's funeral's tomorrow," she said without preamble. "We should go."

She could hear him wince. "I don't know about that, Willa."

"How can we not?"

"How could I face his wife? And I'm certain she would hate facing me."

"I'm sure she doesn't blame you, Patrick."

"I'm sure she does! I blame myself. If I hadn't badgered Vinny into coming . . ." His voice trailed off.

"Accidents can happen any time, anyplace."

"This one felt specific to its time and place," he said grimly.

Willa didn't answer. She knew that if anyone were to blame, it was she. Drunk as they all were, she should have padlocked the damn pool.

"What are the police saying?" Patrick asked.

"Not much. I think they're still trying to tie Vinny's death in with Angel's disappearance."

"What possible connection could there be?"

"When I went in the second time, they told me that one of us said Angel and Vinny had an affair."

"Had to be Travis," Patrick said at once. "That guy always had his head up his ass about Angel."

"Did he really used to spy on her?"

"On both of you. Me and Caleb caught him once, hiding in the tree outside her bedroom."

"But could it be true, do you think?"

"I doubt it. But who knows? Anyway," Patrick said, "even if it was, I'll never believe Vinny hurt her."

"Me neither," Willa said stoutly. Then added, in a low voice, "Sometimes, though, at night, I have terrible thoughts."

"What kind of thoughts?"

"I think, what if Vinny and Angel were together, and something happened, an accident of some kind, and she was killed? And Vinny panicked and buried her body and never told anyone and wrecked the car so no one would find out?"

"Oh please," Patrick said. "And twenty years later, he's so overcome with remorse that he manages to drown himself in a swimming pool." But he said it too quickly, as if the same thought had occurred to him.

"He was scared," Willa said. "The police were sniffing around. Everything he'd built up over the years was in jeopardy."

"Do you really believe this, Willa?"

"No," she said. "It's just, I have a hard time imagining the accident scenario."

"He's drunk. He can't sleep. He goes out for a walk and falls in the pool and drowns: end of story."

"He goes out for a walk, locking the door behind him so he can't come back in. He takes a sleeping pill and goes for a stroll by the pool."

"He took a pill?" Patrick said. "On top of all the booze?"

"Several, I gathered," she said.

The line went quiet. After that there was nothing left to say, so they said good-bye and hung up.

So much for Patrick. It had never occurred to Willa that he would skip the funeral; she hadn't thought of it as optional. If it were, she'd hardly be going herself. It was bad enough imagining the bereaved family without actually witnessing their pain. But it seemed to her that the only thing worse than going to the funeral would be not going.

Oh, but to go alone! Shake might have accompanied her, but he was back in Baltimore. Travis, she assumed, was in Santa Fe, and God only knew where Caleb was, not that she'd call him if she could.

Then Willa thought of Jeremiah. Patrick had disappointed her, but surely Jeremiah was made of sterner stuff. But was it fair to involve him any further? So far his name hadn't appeared in connection to the "mystery death," as the papers called it. If he showed up at the funeral, he risked exposure.

All morning she debated the issue, until finally she decided that it wasn't her decision at all; it was Jeremiah's.

"Willa!" Jeremiah cried, with such warmth that all her misgivings melted away instantly. "I thought of calling a dozen times this week and stopped myself each time. Figured you had enough on your plate. How are you doing?"

"Hanging in there," Willa said. She leaned back and rested her bare heels on the deck railing. She had reached Jeremiah on his cell phone and consequently had no image of where he was. Somewhere quiet; could have been the moon for all she knew.

"And your daughter?" he asked. "How's she handling it?"

"Chloe's taken it hard. She's afraid to stay in the house by herself. Neither of us will go near the pool."

He sighed. "I should have called."

"Why, to thank me for a pleasant weekend?"

"To console and be consoled. You know, when it happened, I snapped right into crisis mode. Damage control. I could see how Patrick looked at me, like I was some kind of robotic son of a bitch, but I couldn't help it; it's hardwired in me, I guess. The personal impact came later. I don't mind telling you I'm having a rough time with it, Vinny dying like he did. It hit me hard."

There was no mistaking the sincerity in the disembodied voice. And Willa was not immune to the subtle flattery of a man like Jeremiah confiding in her. Perhaps some lasting friendship could emerge from the ashes after all.

"It hit us all," she said.

"But you've borne the brunt of it, between the press and the police. Are they any closer to an answer?"

"If they are, they're not telling me. And I'd so much rather know the worst than go on in the dark."

"The worst being . . . ?"

Willa lowered her voice, though she was alone. "Suicide. Not that I believe that."

"Willa," Jeremiah said firmly, "trust your instincts. You said

right away it was an accident. Suicide makes no sense. Vinny
wasn't the type, and besides, he had no reason."

"No . . ." she said. Then, in a rush, "They think Vinny and
Angel had an affair."

"Bullshit. Not that Vinny wasn't nuts about her. But he'd never
have done that to Patrick. Patch was his boy."

Willa sighed. For some reason, the more Jeremiah reassured
her, the shakier she felt. "I keep going in circles. I just wish we
knew for sure, one way or another."

"That's the awful thing, isn't it?" he said, with that ready sympathy. "The fact that we may never know."

"I can't accept that," she said, shocked. "I won't."

"What choice do you have? There's nothing you can do."

"There could be. For one thing, I'm combing through my old
diaries. Maybe Angel said something; maybe I saw something
that didn't mean anything then but would now."

"Good old Willa," Jeremiah said with a dry chuckle. "Never
say die."

"It's worth a shot. Not that it's going to change anything.
Jeremiah," she said, "the reason I called, Vinny's funeral's tomorrow. I'm planning to go."

"Is that wise, do you think?" he said, quick as Patrick though
more tactful.

"Probably not. But it seems necessary."

"It does, doesn't it? I just wonder if it's what his family would
want."

"I wrote to his wife," Willa said. "Hardest letter I ever wrote. I
included my phone number in case she wanted to know anything
about the weekend."

"Did she call?"

"No."

"There you go," he said. "I have an idea. Why don't I send a
wreath, in all our names?"

Willa stared down the path to the pool and heard a faint echo
of masculine laughter. "I think we owe Vinny more than that."

"Ah," said Jeremiah, with an effort at lightness, "but we've
seen what comes of paying one's debts. I'm determined never to
pay another."

"So much for our White House reunion," she said with a wan

smile. "I'm sure you've had enough of us for the rest of your natural life."

"Only my political life," he said politely.

"Not to worry, Jeremiah. I'll represent us all."

"What about Patrick?"

"He declined."

Jeremiah made a sound dismissive of Patrick. "I hate the idea
of you going alone," he said. "It's bound to be unpleasant."

Willa was taken aback by the choice of words, so typical of
Jeremiah. "Unpleasant"—yes, that was very likely. "It's okay," she
said.

A pause, then, brusquely: "When and where?"

She told him.

"No promises," he said. "But if you're really determined to do
this, I'll try and make it."

It rained the day of Vinny's funeral. Willa drove Chloe over to the
Rapaports'. "I'll pick you up when I get home," she said, "probably around four, four-thirty."

"Don't bother," said Chloe. "We're going to a party."

"Since when?"

"I told you. It's at Jenna's house. Lauren's going, too."

"Will Roy Bliss be there?"

Chloe met her mother's eyes. "I hope so."

Ever since their night in the hotel, Willa had adopted a new
policy with Chloe: When she had a question, she asked it. "Is Roy
your boyfriend?"

"He says I'm too young."

Willa was happy to hear it.

"But we're friends," Chloe went on with a steady look. "And
we're going to stay friends. And one of these days I won't be too
young."

"Oh, sweetie," said Willa, feeling a hundred years old, "don't
rush it."

It was a short ride to the Bronx, but the rain slowed things down
and the Cross-Bronx was crawling. By the time Willa made it to
the church, the parking lot was full. A man in a black suit came

over to her car. "There's street parking," he said, "but if I were you, I'd try the garage three blocks down."

She followed his directions and left the car with an attendant. It was already ten past two, and the rain was coming down heavily. Willa opened her umbrella and hurried back toward the church, as fast as she could in two-inch heels. The service was about to begin as she entered the church, but people were still milling around in the narthex. Willa, waiting to sign the mourners' book, glimpsed the coffin at the foot of the altar. Closed and covered with a white shroud, it looked too small to contain Vinny, who had always taken up twice as much space as anyone else. The thought of him cramped inside that little box brought on a sudden rush of tears, which Willa fought back; it was not her place to cry here.

The line inched forward. There were prayer cards on the table beside the book, and a young man in dark glasses stood nearby, greeting latecomers. The pews were crowded. Willa searched for Jeremiah, didn't see him but spotted Vinny's family in the front pew, a woman in black sitting between a boy and a girl. The three sat close together and all alone; even their backs looked heartbroken.

It was her turn now. "With deepest sympathy," she wrote, and signed her name. When she was young, Willa had despised such rote observances, but after Simon died she came to see their value. Those sympathetic platitudes disappeared into the background, evaporating harmlessly to leave a residual impression of kindness. Sometimes it was not helpful to say more.

She took a prayer card, entered the nave, and slipped into an aisle seat in the back. A priest emerged from the vestry and made the sign of the cross. As he began to pray, Willa felt a hand fall on her shoulder. She looked up with a smile of relief, expecting Jeremiah. But it was the young man in dark glasses from the narthex. He bent down and spoke softly, close to her ear. "Willa Durrell?"

"Yes?"

"Come with me."

He held her arm as he walked her out. It might have looked courteous, but it felt like having her blood pressure taken. The rain had stopped temporarily, though the sky was still gray. They stood at the top of the steps, where brides would pose with their retinues, and he let go of her arm.

"Leave," he said. "You're not wanted here."

Willa's blush went bone deep. Why had she come? What had possessed her? "I'm sorry," she stammered. "I didn't mean . . . I just came to pay my respects."

"You've got a fucking nerve. My aunt doesn't want to see you people."

He stood between her and the church, arms wrapped around himself; and she saw that it was all he could do to contain his anger. She couldn't see his eyes behind the glasses, but there was a touch of Vinny in the pugnacious brow and more in the stocky, muscular body. Suddenly Willa knew him, though the last time they'd met he was just a toddler. "Frankie!"

He drew back. "Don't say my name like you know me."

"I *do* know you. Vinny used to carry you around under his arm like a sack of potatoes. He was nuts about you." She laughed softly in amazement. "Little Frankie, all grown up."

He wanted to hear more, she could see that. He also wanted to shove her down the steps, which wouldn't be hard to do, tottering as she was on those stupid heels. They stood for a moment in silence; then the church door opened, and a man in driver's livery stepped out. With him came the sound of many voices raised in prayer. *The Lord is my shepherd; I shall not want. He maketh me to lie down in green pastures; he leadeth me beside the still waters.*

"Vinny was our shepherd," Willa said. "He took care of us. We loved him, too." Then she touched Frankie's cheek with a gloved hand, turned, and walked away with as much dignity as she could muster.

This time the rain held off until she reached Chappaqua, then broke with a vengeance. Willa drove the last few blocks at a crawl, hunched over the wheel, straining to see ten feet ahead. She rounded the pillars at the foot of her drive, swung around the circle, and nearly smashed into a car parked in front of the house, a dark sedan. Visibility was too poor for her to make out the model, but it didn't look familiar. The police, maybe? She looked up at the house. The front porch was empty. But there was a light on in the library, where she had left none burning.

Chloe? But what would she be doing here, and who had driven her? Could she have brought Roy Bliss home, expecting the house to be empty?

An uneasy feeling came over Willa. She parked her car where it stood and opened the door. Rain whipped in; she thrust out her umbrella and opened it before stepping out.

She unlocked the front door, stepped inside, and listened hard. Not a sound in the house, but she knew she was not alone. The library door was closed, and there was no light showing beneath the door. Willa shut the umbrella but held on to it. She slipped off her shoes, crossed the hall soundlessly in stockinged feet. She entered the library, eased the door shut behind her, and turned on the light.

The room was a disaster. Desk drawers had been wrenched out and upended, cabinets ripped open. Every book was on the floor, pages torn out and scattered everywhere. The air reeked of malice. But what turned Willa's blood to ice was knowing that whoever did this was still in the house. She'd made a terrible mistake coming in, she saw that now. But even as she started to retreat, she heard footsteps in the hall.

Change of direction. There was a phone on the library desk. Willa was almost there when the door latch clicked behind her. She wheeled around.

Jeremiah stood on the threshold.

"Get away from the desk," he said.

37

Jeremiah wore black from head to foot. Jeans, T-shirt, a hooded jacket: burglar chic, more fashion statement than disguise, except for the latex gloves on his hands. Willa was so shocked that her head emptied of thought. What she was seeing made no sense.

He said, "What are you doing here?"

She said, "You're asking *me* that?"

"You're supposed to be at the funeral."

"They kicked me out. How did you get in here?"

"Move away from the desk and I'll tell you."

Willa almost obeyed. It was Jeremiah, after all, and he was calm, almost smiling. But her stomach lurched, and despite her confusion she knew with certainty that something terrible was happening, and that the man who had torn this room apart hated her. She backed away from him until her hip touched the desk, then turned and lunged for the phone. It was in her hand when Jeremiah reached her. Willa raised the umbrella to hit him, but he captured her wrist in an iron grip. With his other hand, he ripped the phone from her hand and smashed it across her face.

Willa's world imploded into a black hole of pain. When it expanded once again, she was on the floor and Jeremiah was on top of her, pinning her down with a forearm across her throat. His face, clenched with rage, was unrecognizable. Her skirt was up around her waist. Feeling him grow hard against her, she heaved upward in panic and disgust. With his free hand, Jeremiah punched her twice more in the face. "It's all your fault, bitch!"

There was blood in her eyes and her mouth. Blood on her clothes, blood on the hardwood floor. The pain and blood made it real, made it irrevocable. Her head cleared; she felt a quickening inside. Pain was shelved alongside fear; her life was on the line and she knew it.

"Stop," she gasped. "I can help."

Slowly the pressure on her throat eased. His face composed itself. In a moment he looked like himself again . . . whoever that was.

"Yes," he said, "you can." He got up and hauled her to her feet. Movement made the pain worse. When she staggered, Jeremiah pushed her into the desk chair and stood over her. "Clean your-self up," he said, shoving a box of tissues toward her. "This wasn't supposed to happen. Look what you made me do."

"What do you want?" she said, her voice unrecognizable, a painful croak.

"What do you think I want, stupid? Those fucking diaries you're so fucking proud of!"

"The cops took 'em."

Jeremiah grabbed a fistful of hair and forced her head back. His right hand disappeared behind his back; when it reappeared, he was holding a gun. So much for not expecting her, Willa thought. No wonder he'd made Eagle Scout. She sent up a prayer of thanks that Chloe was out.

Jeremiah pressed the gun to her temple. "For your sake I hope you're lying. Last chance, Willa: Where are they?"

"Up in my bedroom."

"Show me."

She preceded him out of the library, her brain racing. Why didn't matter; she pushed that aside. Reasons would come later, if there was a later. Could she persuade him she'd keep quiet? He was too smart for that. But she had to try.

"Jeremiah," she said, "think it through. If anything happens to me after Vinny, the police will know it was someone from the reunion. And the press, my God! You'd defeat your own pur-pose."

"Sweet of you to worry," he said, shoving her toward the stair-case.

She started up slowly. "I won't say a word. I don't know why you're doing this, and I don't need to know. But if you hurt me, you're doomed. You think those gloves will protect you? These days all they need is a single skin cell, one hair."

"So what?" he said; she could hear the smirk in his voice. "I just spent a weekend in the house."

She risked a glance behind her. His long, pale face was focused and intent, businesslike, but far from robotic; for in his eyes there was a glint of pleasurable excitement.

"Take it easy, Willa," he said. "All I want is the diaries. Give them up and I promise I won't hurt you."

Lying. She knew it and he knew she knew it.

On the stairs he kept a wary distance. If he maintained that space, there was a chance she could run into her bedroom and lock the door before he got there. But could she call 911 before he shot out the lock? With nothing to lose, Willa decided to go for it. But as soon as they reached the landing, Jeremiah closed in behind her.

She opened her bedroom door. He followed her in. She thought about weapons. Candlesticks on her dresser. Perfume on the vanity, good for blinding. Books and boxes, all sorts of missiles. Jeremiah grabbed her hair again and yanked her head back.

"You're thinking," he said. "Don't think. Where are they?"

She pointed to her lingerie drawer.

He let go of her hair. "Get them out."

She obeyed.

"Put them on the dresser and go sit on the bed. Clasp your hands behind your neck."

She did as he said, watching, waiting. Jeremiah, holding the gun steady, glanced down just long enough to determine that the books really were diaries. He felt around in the lingerie drawer till he was satisfied that he had them all, then drew a crumpled plastic bag from his pocket and put the diaries inside. He used his left hand only, while the right aimed the gun at her chest. It was a small gun, but big enough, she supposed.

With the diaries in his possession, Jeremiah relaxed a little. He smiled at Willa, sitting on the bed with her hands behind her neck. "Alone at last," he said. "When's your daughter coming home?"

Willa stiffened. "Leave her out of this."

"I'm trying to."

"She's staying at a friend's house. But Jovan is on the way. He'll be here any minute."

"Feeble," he said, shaking his head sadly. "And you a writer. Any last wishes, Willa?"

The breath caught in her throat. "You said you wouldn't hurt me."

"It won't hurt. *Do* you have a last wish? Because if you don't, I do." His eyes, cruising over her breasts, felt like bugs crawling on naked skin. "I've always had a thing for you, Willa. Bad timing, I know, but better late than never."

"You're joking," she said, though she could see he wasn't.

"Take your clothes off."

"Come over here and make me," she said. He would never rape her. He'd have to kill her first, or she'd kill him.

Jeremiah, ever prudent, stayed where he was. His voice turned cajoling. "Don't be like that. Think of it: It'd be just like that movie, what's it called, where Jack Nicholson and Kathleen Turner play hit men married to each other."

"*Prizzi's Honor.*"

"Right. Remember that scene where they're in bed, making love, each of them planning to kill the other? God, that was sexy."

"You're a sick fuck, you know that, Jeremiah?"

"I'll have to tie your hands, of course. But you might get free. I might get careless in the throes of passion. It's a chance."

"I'll pass."

Jeremiah sighed. "Suit yourself," he said virtuously. "I'm no rapist."

Chloe was soaked. Rain dripped from her hair, sodden clothes clung to her body. The only parts of her that weren't wet were the parts pressed to Roy Bliss's back. She didn't care. If it were up to her, they'd have gone on riding forever.

He turned the motorcycle into her driveway and stopped short at the foot of the drive. Two cars were parked in front of the house, and he recognized one of them. "I thought you said your mom was out."

"She's supposed to be."

"Looks like she's got company. Jeez, wait'll she sees you. I'm a dead man."

"Like it's your fault!" Chloe said. If it was anyone's fault they'd gotten caught in the rain, it was hers; she'd begged and teased for a ride on Roy's new motorcycle until finally he'd given in. "Anyway, she doesn't have to know. Let's just go back to the party."

"And have you catch pneumonia?" he said grimly. "I don't think so." He killed the engine, got off the bike, and put the kickstand down. Chloe got off, too; what choice did she have? They started toward the house. Then she stopped.

"Something's weird," she said. "Why's her car out here? She always parks in the garage."

"Wait a sec," he told her. The lights were on in the library. Roy eased his way through the shrubbery and peeked in the window. A moment later he flattened himself against the side of the house.

"What is it?" Chloe whispered.

He slid back through the bushes, grabbed her arm, and started sprinting toward the road. Chloe yanked her arm free and stopped. "Tell me what's going on!"

"Looks like maybe she walked in on a burglary."

"Did you see her?"

"No, but the room was a holy mess. Come on, Chloe. We've got to get to a phone."

But she turned and ran toward the house. Roy caught up and grabbed her. She struggled. "Let go!"

"You can't go in there," he said.

"I have to. My mom could be in trouble."

"Which you could make worse. The best way to help her is to call the cops."

"You go call then. I'll stay here and keep watch."

"Look at me, Chloe. You think your neighbors will open the door to me?"

She saw that he was right and turned back with him. They'd just reached his motorcycle when the front door of the house opened and a man walked out, staggering under the weight of his burden. Over his shoulder he'd slung a squirming, woman-size form, wrapped in a blanket. He opened the rear door of the dark sedan and heaved the bundle onto the floor.

Chloe opened her mouth, but before she could cry out, Roy clapped his hand over it. He pushed her down behind a bush and sprinted up the drive toward the intruder. Halfway there he slipped in a puddle and went down. By the time he got up, the car was in motion. The driver never looked behind him, never saw Roy or the motorcycle as he sped out the other end of the circular drive.

"Where are you taking me?" Willa's voice was muffled by the quilt wrapped around her. She flexed her wrists and ankles, but there was no slack in the cords that bound her.

"To see Angel," he said. "Wasn't that what you wanted?"

"Not like this."

"As Mother always said, be careful what you wish for."

They were on the Taconic Parkway. Willa would have recognized its twists and turns anywhere. Every bump in the road sent daggers slicing through her head. He'd wrapped the quilt tightly around her, tucking in the ends. It was pitch black and nearly airless inside. "Jeremiah," she said, "I can't breathe."

"Get used to it."

"It's not too late to turn back."

"Oh, it's way too late, thanks to you," he said. "Just couldn't leave it alone, could you? You had to keep pushing. First Angel, then Vinny. I didn't plan on this, Willa; I didn't want it. But so help me God, you've got it coming."

Lying on her back, she drew her legs up as far as she could, then kicked downward. Each time she did it, she got more play in the blanket. The fourth time, a little light penetrated her dark cocoon, along with a saving seepage of air that she sucked in greedily. "What did Angel ever do to you?" she asked.

"Got herself knocked up and tried to pin it on me. Threatened to tell my mother."

"And for that you killed her?"

"Don't say it like it's nothing! You know what my mother was like. My whole life would have been derailed. And it's not just about me, you know. It never was. I've always known I have important work to do. Was I supposed to lose everything for some bastard brat that probably wasn't even mine?"

"Probably?" Willa said slowly. "Meaning it could have been?"

There was a long pause. "You didn't know?" Jeremiah said.

Willa was stunned. She and Angel had often talked about Jeremiah, agreeing that he was a sweet guy, great to talk with, but somehow sexless, too screwed up by his mother to be lover material. When had Angel changed her mind?

The car hit a bump and her head slammed against the floor. Willa moaned and floated off on waves of pain. She was on Angel's bed, and Angel was at her desk, making a list. *What I need is a virgin. Virgins are so damn grateful.*

Then Willa was back in the car and Jeremiah was speaking, more to himself than to her. "It's a shame," he said. "But I couldn't have known. You went on and on about how close you two were, how she told you everything. I thought you knew. I thought you were telling me you knew."

"And Vinny? What was his crime?"

"Vinny's on you," he said viciously. "Take *that* to the grave with you. Vinny was weak. But he'd still be alive if it weren't for you running to the cops, bringing that fucking detective to spy on us."

"What did you do?" she said.

"What I had to."

"You lured him out of the house somehow. One last drink, a quiet talk? You knew you couldn't take him on, even drunk as he was, so you doped his drink. And then you drowned him."

Silence from the front seat.

"Did you get in the pool with him, Jeremiah? Did you hold his head underwater?"

"You have no idea how painful that was." His voice, a rancid mix of self-pity and triumph, oozed under the quilt. "Really, Willa, you have a lot to answer for."

"Poor Jeremiah, forced to do such awful things."

"You know, for a woman in your situation, you've got a hell of an attitude."

Attitude was all she had, that and anger. Her head ached. She yearned for sleep the way a starving man yearns for bread. But she couldn't give up. For Chloe's sake, she couldn't give up.

In many of the murder mysteries Jeremiah read (and he took an interest in the genre), disposing of the body was the least of the murderer's problems. Burials, even dismemberments, were accomplished in a sentence or two, or elided altogether in the space between chapters. Some murderers didn't even bother to dispose of their victims, but simply left them where they lay, crawling with forensic evidence. Some might call that artistic license; Jeremiah called it artistic sloppiness. In his opinion—in his experience—careful disposal of the remains was the key to a successful operation.

The best murder mysteries were the ones in which the murderer and the detective were well matched, like Sherlock Holmes and Professor Moriarty. Jeremiah was well aware that modesty was not among his many excellent traits. But even allowing for that, he could not see that geezer detective Meyerhoff as a threat; and as for the young one, Flynn, he was Irish, which pretty much said it all.

Not that Jeremiah saw himself as a murderer; certainly not. When he read his mysteries, he might take a professional interest in the killer's technique, but he always identified with the good guys. The acts he himself had committed, regrettable though they were, clearly fell within the moral purview of self-defense. Angel had threatened to ruin his life; she might as well have stuck a gun to his head. He had no compunctions there. Vinny's death had cost him more, emotionally speaking; but there, too, what choice had Jeremiah had? If he hadn't taken action, Vinny's weakness and panic would have destroyed them both. As for Willa, Jeremiah hadn't planned on killing her, richly as she deserved it. She'd brought that on herself, first by taunting him with those diaries, then by bursting in on him. Thanks to her, he was once again saddled not only with the unpleasant necessity of taking a life, but also with the awkwardness of disposal.

His first wild thought had been to kill her in the house and set it on fire. A moment's reflection told him that would never work. If he killed her first, the ME would be able to determine that; if he bound her securely and let the fire kill her, she might conceivably escape or be rescued. Besides, burning alive was an agonizing death, and Jeremiah was a civilized man: determined, certainly, ruthless when he had to be, but never gratuitously cruel.

Burial, then, beside the friend she'd tried so hard to find; and on his own land, where no one could challenge him. Thank God Olivia had gone back to D.C. All Jeremiah needed to do was to dig the grave deep enough so that no marauding animals or flood would ever unearth her. This task, which TV villains accomplished during a commercial break, would in the real world take two men with shovels several hours to accomplish in the hard, rocky ground of upstate New York.

Only this time, Vinny wasn't around to help. Willa would have to pitch in. If Jeremiah could locate the exact spot where they'd laid Angel to rest, the work should go easier the second time around. He thought he could. They'd buried her in the woods beside his house, in a clearing marked by a young chestnut tree. A hell of a job it had been, breaking through the lattice of intertwined roots, but what else could he have done: plant her in his mother's flower garden? He thought he could find the spot. Over the years he'd visited her grave several times, always in daylight, and always with a propitiatory gift of wildflowers or a handful of pine cones. It seemed only right, since no one else knew where she was buried except Vinny, and he wouldn't come within ten miles of the spot.

Jeremiah slowed as he approached the Old Wickham exit off the Taconic. Willa had gone quiet: saving her strength for one last spurt of resistance, he supposed, though it was also possible she'd passed out or even died of asphyxiation, in which case he was royally screwed. He checked his rearview mirror as he exited. One car followed him off the ramp, but it turned left at the stop sign where he turned right. Nearly home free.

The rain had tapered off into an early twilight. As he turned on to the country lane that led to his house, his headlights caught the neighbors' daughter walking their Lab along the side of the road. She waved, and he waved back. Jeremiah enjoyed excellent relations with his neighbors.

The woods on his side of the road were posted with "No Hunting" signs. Jeremiah had nothing against the locals who hunted for meat, as many of his neighbors did; the signs were for the city folk who came up to hunt for sport. He turned up his driveway, stopped by the shed for a shovel, and continued on to the clearing at the edge of the woods. He could have used some coffee but dared not leave Willa alone; and though he would have loved to show her his house, it would have been criminally stupid to bring her inside.

"We're here," he said. No reply, but when he looked back he could see her breathing beneath the quilt. Thank God; otherwise he'd have been digging all night. As it was he had no doubt he'd end up doing the lion's share of the work. He killed the headlights, grabbed the shovel, and got out of the car. There was a flashlight in the glove compartment that would have been useful, but a light in the woods was too noticeable. A car approached his driveway and Jeremiah froze; but it kept on going. The plastic bag with the diaries was beside him on the seat. He considered bringing them along to bury with Willa: Hadn't she said she'd take them to the grave? But that was foolish; far safer to burn them.

Jeremiah opened the back door. "Up and at 'em."

No response. He hauled her out by her shoulders and dropped her roughly on the ground. "I'm going to take the quilt off now," he said. "If you fight me, if you make a sound, I'll pack your mouth with dirt. Don't make me do that, Willa."

He checked the safety, pocketed the gun, and unwrapped her carefully. Her face was swollen where he'd had to hit her, and her eyes were wide open. Even in the diffused moonlight he could see the fury in them. She offered no resistance, but he wasn't fooled. The Willa he'd known and loved was not one to go gentle into that dark night. He wished that for just one moment she would acknowledge her own role in this sad ending to their friendship, but he knew she wouldn't. People so rarely take responsibility for their own misdeeds; it was always easier to blame the other guy.

She had never been more attractive to him than she was at this moment, lying at his feet. What a pity she'd refused him back at her house. Jeremiah had never cheated on Olivia, not for lack of desire, but rather because what he stood to lose was greater than what he stood to gain. Fucking a woman who was about to die had no such downside, and who knew when that chance would come again? Never, he hoped piously. In Willa's case, though, it would have provided them both with a sense of closure.

When he touched her legs, he could feel the bunched energy running through them, just waiting for an outlet. But there was nothing she could do; he held all the cards. Jeremiah ran his hand up between her legs, just to show her he could. Her panties were smooth as silk, and he was tempted to linger; but the look in her eyes dissuaded him. He took his hand away.

"I'm going to loosen your ankles a bit," he said. "Then we're going to take a walk." Her eyes went to the shovel, then back to his face. He had to give her credit; there was no fear, only hatred in her look.

He loosened the cord around her ankles and untied the one

that held her bound wrists close to her body. Now her wrists were still bound, but she could move her arms in front of her. He hauled her to her feet. "Can you walk?" She took a few shuffling steps, grimacing as the rocky ground cut into her bare feet. Jeremiah slung the shovel over his shoulder and took the gun out of his pocket. "Let's go."

A thick mist filled the twilit woods. They walked in single file, her first, following his directions. Now and then as they walked, it seemed to Jeremiah that he heard footsteps behind them. It wasn't the first time he had heard strange sounds in these woods. A superstitious man might have said they were haunted. Jeremiah laid it down to a trick of acoustics . . . but he didn't like to walk in the woods at night.

"Tell me about Angel," Willa said.

Jeremiah didn't mind. In a way it was a relief to talk about it with someone so safe. "She called me that night," he said. "Up till then I'd been stalling, hoping for everyone's sake she'd let it drop. But that night she gave me an ultimatum. Her father knew about her pregnancy, she said, and if he didn't kill her for that, he'd kill her for cracking up his car. She couldn't go home again, she said, so I had to take her in; I had to provide for her. Not Patrick, who'd been fucking her blind since ninth grade, but me."

"So you killed her," Willa said.

Jeremiah snorted. Leave it to a woman to belabor the obvious.

"How?" she asked after a moment.

"Let's just say it wasn't a pleasant experience," he said grimly. He noticed Willa was limping now. The bare feet had been a mistake. He'd meant to keep her from trying to run, but she was no good to him crippled.

"How did Vinny fit in?" she went on.

"I called him afterward."

Willa turned around and stared. "Why?"

Jeremiah prodded her forward. "I needed help. I told him there'd been an accident, to bring the Chevy and meet me. He didn't ask questions. You know Vinny. A friend needs something, he's there."

"But when he saw what you'd done, when he saw it was Angel . . . ?"

"He was upset. Hell, we both were. For a minute I thought it had been a mistake, reaching out to him, but of course it wasn't. Vinny was a practical guy. Angel was beyond help; I wasn't."

"You used Patrick's car to bring her up here?"

"It was Vinny's car, too. What else could we do? The car would have to be dumped afterward; I could hardly use my mother's. Anyway, I more than paid him back once I came into my trust fund."

"Vinny took money," she said.

Jeremiah could see she didn't believe him, and it pissed him off. Maybe Vinny hadn't asked, but he hadn't refused, either. "He had his eye on a station in the Bronx. Where do you think the down payment came from?"

That shut her up. Maybe she was remembering Vinny's boast, the big self-made man. *Nobody ever gave me nothing.*

Finally they reached the clearing with the chestnut tree in the center. The glade was full of wildflowers: bluebells, lily of the valley, snapdragons, some growing right out of Angel's grave. "Pretty spot, isn't it?" he said. Willa just stared at him. Perhaps gratitude was too much to expect. He stuck the shovel in the ground, took out the gun, and backed away. "Start digging," he said.

"Fuck you."

"Fuck me?" Jeremiah laughed. It wasn't a pleasant sound, even to his own ears. "I can bury you dead, or I can bury you alive. It's entirely up to you."

Willa looked in his eyes. She reached for the shovel.

38

They were not alone in those woods. Not twenty feet from her mother, Chloe crouched behind a big old oak. Beside her was Roy Bliss. When Jeremiah had sped off in his car with Willa, Roy had turned back to his motorcycle, but Chloe had a better idea. Her mother kept a spare key to the Beemer in a magnetic box behind the license plate. They had it out in a moment; Roy drove, keeping well back but never losing sight of Jeremiah's taillights. When Jeremiah exited the parkway, Roy followed but turned right instead of left at the top of the ramp, in case the other driver was watching. Then he reversed course and got back on the trail.

They almost lost the guy once, when he turned into his small lane. Roy drove right past it, but realized and came back just in time to see taillights disappearing up a long driveway. They drove a hundred yards farther down the lane without passing another house. Roy pulled over, parked on the shoulder, and took a tire iron from the trunk. As quietly as they could, they ran back toward the driveway where the car had turned in.

There was a bleak moment when they found the empty car by the edge of the woods. But then they heard voices in the woods, Willa's and a man's, and they followed the voices. The mist was both a help and a hindrance; it hid their quarry from view, but also allowed Chloe and Roy to stay within earshot without fear of being seen. Chloe heard enough to put the pieces together, enough to understand that the man who had her mother was a stone-cold murderer.

When Jeremiah halted in the middle of a little clearing, Chloe was so close behind she nearly stumbled into open view. Roy pulled her back, and they took shelter behind a wide oak. She was shaking. They'd dried off in the car but gotten soaked again in the woods. Jeremiah was just fifteen feet away, his back to them; they could see the glint of the gun in his outstretched hand. Willa was five feet beyond, facing in their direction.

"Start digging," they heard him say.

"Fuck you," she replied.

Chloe had never been prouder of her mother. "What do we do?" she mouthed.

Roy hefted the tire iron and signed for her to wait. He started toward Jeremiah. Chloe caught his arm. "You can't," she murmured in his ear. "The gun's pointed right at her." Suddenly she had an idea.

Willa didn't know how much longer she could go on. Her head was in agony, her feet in shreds. Every muscle in her body ached. She kept waiting for a chance to bean Jeremiah with the shovel, but he never let down his guard, never took his eyes off her. Her options were rapidly closing down. Even if he gave her an opening, Willa wasn't sure she had the strength left to take it. She paused to catch her breath, leaning on the shovel.

"That's it?" Jeremiah said, with a disparaging look at her hole. "That's all you've got?"

"Just taking a breather."

"Not now, babe. Plenty of time to rest later."

"Don't call me babe." As she picked up the shovel, Willa saw a darting movement in the woods. Hard to tell in the dull greenish light, but it looked an awful lot like a couple of people flitting between the trees. She smothered an involuntary gasp.

Jeremiah smirked. "Oldest trick in the book," he said smugly. "Now I turn around to see who's behind me, and you chuck the shovel at my head."

She went back to digging, stealing a glance as she dumped a load of soil. No doubt about it now: There were two people in the woods behind Jeremiah. They were moving apart, making no particular effort to hide from her, but avoiding his line of sight.

A branch snapped. Jeremiah started but held the gun steady.

"Nervous?" Willa asked quickly. "Don't blame you. She's here, you know."

"Who's here?"

"Angel."

"Of course she is," he said. "You're standing on top of her."

"No, I mean here with us. I've felt it since we stepped into the woods, but it's much stronger here."

Jeremiah turned a paler shade of pale. "Shut up and dig."

She was talking just to keep his attention on her. Why she chose that particular line of patter Willa would never know; but what happened next seemed conjured up by her very words. A female voice, disembodied, faint yet poignant, rose from the woods. Though it seemed to rise from the mist itself, the voice was not ethereal but earthy, textured, honed on whiskey and cigarettes: a barroom voice singing an old, old song.

"'Frankie and Johnny were lovers, Oh Lordy, how they could love . . .'"

Willa dropped to the ground. Jeremiah let out a shriek and wheeled to his right, searching for the source of that voice. The moment he turned, a man leaped out of the woods and set upon him with a metal bar, connecting squarely with the back of Jeremiah's head.

Jeremiah pitched forward and lay still, his face in the dirt. The gun flew and landed at the feet of Chloe, who was rushing into the clearing. She stopped, picked it up, and went to look at Jeremiah.

"Chloe?" Willa gasped. "Roy?"

"Is he dead?" Chloe asked Roy.

"Not yet."

Chloe raised the gun and pointed it at the back of Jeremiah's head. Her finger found the trigger.

"Hang on a sec!" Roy cried; and Willa called out firmly, "Chloe, put that gun down!"

"Mom," Chloe said with a pleading look, "he threatened to bury you alive."

"And he killed two innocent people," Willa said. "That's why he needs to suffer. Shooting him would be too kind."

Chloe handed the gun to Roy. She went to her mother and kneeled before her. Willa touched her face, her arms. "You're real."

"What did you think?" Chloe said.

"A dream; delirium. I got hit in the face, you see. And I didn't see any way it could really be you. And Roy . . . ?"

"He's real, too," Chloe said.

"And it was you singing?"

A smile broke out on that dirty, tear-stained face. "I was just going to scream," Chloe said. "I just wanted him to look my way so Roy would have a chance. But then I heard what you said to him about Angel, and I remembered what you told me that night in the hotel; and it came to me that if I sang her song he would really be spooked. I didn't know if I could sing, but I tried and it worked."

"Oh my brilliant, brave girl," Willa said, kissing her.

"And what am I?" said Roy, coming over for his share of approval.

Willa looked up at him from the circle of her daughter's arms. "You, young man, are an honest-to-God knight in shining armor."

Roy tied Jeremiah hand and foot with the drapery cords Jeremiah had used on Willa. They took his keys, turned him onto his back so he wouldn't smother, and left him lying beside the grave where he'd intended to bury Willa.

Willa insisted she could walk, but Chloe wept at the sight of her feet. She held one arm and Roy held the other, and between them they carried most of her weight on the walk back. It was full dark now, and both Willa and Chloe were disoriented, but Roy guided them unerringly back to Jeremiah's car. Then Willa could go no farther. While Roy went for help, she sank down on the grassy verge, laid her head on Chloe's lap, and finally, gratefully, surrendered to sleep.

Willa woke on a hospital gurney. Chloe's face, drawn and old beyond its years, was the first thing she saw. She tried to smile, but her head hurt. Chloe took her hand. Someone said, "She's back," and a male face swam into view.

"What's wrong with me?" Willa whispered.

The doctor answered. "Lacerations, lots of contusions, and a whopping good concussion. No fractures, luckily. You'll be fine."

Willa looked at Chloe. "Roy?"

"He's good," Chloe said. "He's talking to the police."

"Jeremiah?"

"He'll live."

The gash on her forehead was deep, the ER doc told her, and could leave a scar. Did she want to see a plastic surgeon?

Willa declined. A scar seemed appropriate, a place for her inner and outer selves to meet.

When the doctors finished with her, the Wickham sheriff came in. Sheriff Stan Kuzak was a large, bearlike man with fierce eyebrows and a gentle manner. With him, to Willa's surprise, were Detectives Meyerhoff and Flynn. Meyerhoff could hardly look at her. Kuzak did the questioning, leading her slowly and methodically through the day. Willa got the impression that he knew Jeremiah, which wouldn't be surprising, as the Old Wickham house had been in the Wright family since before Jeremiah was born. The sheriff's face grew sadder and heavier as the story unfolded, but he didn't seem as surprised as Willa would have expected, given who Jeremiah was.

"I'm sorry for what you went through," Kuzak told her. "I want you to know Jeremiah's already in custody, and we intend to oppose bail."

"Will he get it?"

"That's up to the judge, but given his attack on you, it's highly unlikely."

"You have to find Angel."

"We're just waiting for daylight."

"Did you know him well, Sheriff?"

"I've known him a long time," Kuzak replied, in the tone of one making a distinction.

Willa nodded, acknowledging the difference. A line from Compton-Burnett came to mind, and she said it aloud. "'I believe that we know much less of each other than we think.'"

Willa's feet had been bandaged and she'd been ordered to stay off them, so she left the hospital in a wheelchair. She and Chloe were waiting outside emergency for Roy to bring the car around when the glass doors slid open and Jeremiah emerged, flanked by two uniformed deputies. His hands were cuffed behind his back, his head swathed in a turbanlike bandage. When he saw Willa he froze. Ten feet apart, they stared at each other. Jeremiah glowed with a volcanic hatred, but Willa was unscathed. He would answer for Angel. He would answer for Vinny. A terrible judgment was in her gaze. In the end it was Jeremiah who turned away.

* * *

Angel's body was found the next day. A few days later, Jeremiah was charged with her murder and Vinny's, in addition to kidnapping and assault. Bail was denied.

Willa and Chloe spent a week with the Rapaports in order to avoid the reporters and film crews who'd staked out their house. They kept busy. As soon as Willa was able to walk (in sneakers; no heels for a while), they went out and looked at houses, and on the sixth day of searching they found their new house: a three-bedroom contemporary, full of glass and light and open spaces. Taxes and utilities cost half those of the old house, and best of all there was no pool. The property included a separate guest house, which Willa meant to make into an office, and to Chloe's delight, it was within walking distance of the Rapaports'.

Willa offered the full asking price on the condition that the closing take place within a month. Her offer was accepted. That same day, she gave the agent an exclusive listing on her old house. Its recent notoriety, far from discouraging interest, seemed to stimulate it. Anxious to sell quickly, Willa had priced the house well. It sold in three days.

They started packing. And there were other projects as well. Willa paid a call on Roy Bliss's mother. Mrs. Bliss lived in an apartment above a tailor's shop in town with Roy and two younger children. The apartment was small but clean and tidy. They drank coffee at the kitchen table, and Mrs. Bliss glowed with pride as Willa described Roy's bravery and resourcefulness.

Later that day, Willa made a few phone calls and learned that, while Juilliard had offered Roy a substantial scholarship, the amount fell far short of full tuition, room, and board. The balance would have to be scraped together from the family's savings and through loans. She called the financial aid director, who, once told Roy's story, was as helpful as he could be. It was a simple task, then, to endow a four-year scholarship, anonymous now but someday to be named the Angelica Busky Scholarship, and to designate Roy Bliss as the first recipient.

It gave her great pleasure to do this for Roy as well as for Angel; and the actions required to accomplish it had the collateral benefit of bringing her out into the world. But for weeks, even as she healed physically, Willa suffered from flashbacks, obsessive recollections that intruded without warning: memories of the reunion, incidents that had passed almost unnoticed at the time but in hindsight seemed full of portent and hidden meaning; visions of Jeremiah's face as he threatened to bury her alive, the malice in his eyes that told her he was capable of it. She had to grapple with the realization that the people she thought she knew best in the world, she did not know at all. Perhaps it was impossible to know anyone through and through, because people weren't static; they were rivers, full of unsuspected currents and treacherous shallows, capable of swift change, forces to be reckoned with.

This time Willa did not hold back. She talked—to her daughter, to Isabel Rapaport, to Judy Trumpledore, who, after reassuring herself that Willa was safe and relatively sound, had lost no time in urging her to write a firsthand account of what the press was calling "The Beacon Hill Murders."

Willa supposed she would write about the Beacon Hill gang someday. Writing was how she processed things, and there was a good deal here that needed processing. But not yet, and not the sort of book Judy had in mind: because an honest account would have to expose Vinny's role in covering up Angel's murder, and Willa would not do that to his family. There were other ways of tackling a story; there were truths best approached through fiction.

"Then write it as fiction," Judy said, "and I will publish it. Only do it soon, because I hear there are other books in the works."

Willa knew that was true. Jeremiah's fall from the heights of Washington society to the depths of tabloid scandal was major news. Among the messages she didn't return were many from magazine and book writers eager to talk to her.

"Are we supposed to profit from the murders of two of my friends and the guilt of a third?" she asked.

"I don't mind," Judy said cheerily. "It's what publishers do. But if it bothers you, you can always donate your royalties to charity, or set up a tuition fund for Vinny's kids."

Though she talked to Jovan and Patrick on the phone, Willa

steadfastly refused to let them come to her. It seemed vital that she get through this hard time without leaning on any man.

Patrick took the whole thing very hard. Jeremiah's villainy shook the foundations of his world. "Was he always so ruthless?" he wondered aloud. "Were we always deceived, or did he change?"

Willa had been asking herself the same question. *I believe that it would go ill with many of us, if we were faced by a strong temptation,* her prophet, Compton-Burnett, had famously said; *and I suspect that with some of us it does go ill.* Jeremiah was tempted and he fell; and that fall determined his subsequent actions.

"The domino theory of evil," Patrick said, "as opposed to the bad-seed scenario. Free will trumps determinism every time." But that left him nowhere to go with Vinny. For as bad as he felt about Jeremiah, what really tore Patrick up was Vinny having been part of it. The idea of Vinny arriving on the scene, finding Angel dead, and agreeing to help Jeremiah was a betrayal he could not forgive.

Willa, who knew something about such posthumous discoveries, did not try to talk him out of his bitterness, but neither did she share it. It was too easy for her to imagine what must have happened, or could have: Vinny's horror and disgust; Jeremiah's remorseful tears, that compelling voice. *Angel's beyond our help, Vinny. I'm not. My life is in your hands.* Easy, too, to imagine Vinny's anguish every time Patrick harped on their lost Chevy.

Oh, he'd known whom to call, had Jeremiah. The wonder was that Vinny hadn't gone into the grave with Angel.

Sunday afternoon. Jovan was catching up on paperwork when the telephone rang.

"Hey," Willa said.

"Hey yourself." He was surprised to hear from her. For weeks she'd refused to see him, kept him at more than arm's length. "I have to handle it," she kept telling him. "I have to get through this." Which was maybe her tactful way of saying that he had been useless to her so far. Or maybe something else was in play. The last few times they'd met, their relationship had teetered on the brink of intimacy. Jovan couldn't help wondering, during the long, barren weeks of waiting, if Willa hadn't taken the opportunity to pull back.

He'd never felt so powerless in a relationship, never been in one that wasn't weighted in his favor. *She's got you coming and going*, Meyerhoff had said, and it was true. How painful, how humiliating, to fall in love at his age. Jovan kept telling himself to get out, call one of the women he saw occasionally; he kept meaning to and forgetting. Now, suddenly, Willa was calling him. Asking him was he busy tonight.

"What'd you have in mind?" he said. "Because if it's another missing persons case, I think I'll pass."

She laughed. "No business, I promise. I still owe you a dinner." There was something in her voice. It sounded flirtatious, sexy, even. But Jovan was through playing patty-cake with her. No more walks through the zoo.

"I'll cook. Steaks at my place," he said, and was amazed when she accepted.

She wore a black-and-white summer dress with skinny straps and buttons down the front, the sexiest thing he'd ever seen her wear. And she brought champagne. Jovan took her into the living room: hardwood floors, white walls, leather furniture, big-screen TV; tidy and comfortable but no feminine frills. Willa looked around. "Nice. It's just you and your son?"

"Just us," Jovan said, "and he's in Florida with friends." He left her and went to the kitchen for a corkscrew and glasses. No champagne flutes; she'd have to rough it with wineglasses. When he returned to the room, she was holding the small framed photo of Katie and Sean that he kept on the mantel.

"Your wife?" she asked.

He nodded. Took the picture and replaced it, handed her a glass. "To life."

She touched her glass to his. When she tilted her head back to drink, he saw a thin red scar across the left side of her forehead, close to the hairline. Willa noticed him looking and touched it. "Ugly, isn't it?"

"Jeremiah did that?"

She nodded. "It would be worse if it left no mark."

Jovan understood perfectly. For months after Katie died, he'd been unable to abide the sight of his unaltered face in the mirror.

She kicked off her sandals, folded her legs beneath her, and sank into the deep, soft leather of the sofa. He sat beside her, not too close. "My editor thinks I should write a book about what happened," she said.

"Why not? It's a hell of a story, and who better to tell it? If it hadn't been for you, Angel's murderer would have escaped justice."

"And Vinny would still be alive," she said.

"You don't know that. Jeremiah was an ambitious guy. Sooner or later, Vinny being out there, knowing what he knows, was bound to present too much of a risk."

"Were you surprised?"

"I knew one of them killed Vinny. Didn't figure on it being Jeremiah. He struck me as the only adult in the bunch."

Willa sipped her champagne and watched him over the rim.

"Are you hungry?" he asked, remembering his responsibilities. "Should I throw on the steaks?"

"Not yet. I'll have some more champagne, though."

Jovan refilled both their glasses and raised his own. "To the most resilient woman of my acquaintance."

"That's kind," she said. "Resilience is a virtue I aspire to."

He smiled. "What other virtues do you aspire to?"

"Boldness in pursuit of the things I desire."

Jovan swallowed hard.

"That day at the zoo," Willa said, "you asked me why I was looking back when I ought to be moving forward. I decided you were right. I've sold my house. Chloe has three more years of high school. After that I'm free to travel, to live anywhere I want."

"Sure," he said. "Free as a bird."

"Exactly. I've never had that, and now that I do, I mean to make the most of it. Do you know what went through my mind while I was digging my grave?"

"Chloe?"

"No. I couldn't afford to think about Chloe, I'd have lost it. My life didn't flash before my eyes, either. What I thought about were all the things I hadn't done, because I was too scared or shy or complacent. So when Chloe and Roy gave me back my life, I swore to myself that the next time I die, whatever regrets I have will be for things I've done, not things I've left undone."

What was she saying? She had to know how he felt about her. Women like her always know; they spend their lives fending off fools like him. "What sort of things did you have in mind?" he asked cautiously.

She laughed at him with her eyes. "Pretty dense for a detective, aren't you?"

Jovan reached for her then. She came willingly into his arms. Her skin was warm and smooth beneath his fingers. She smelled like a hot summer day, just before lightning strikes.

This time, there were no interruptions.

about the author

Barbara Rogan is the author of six previous novels: *Changing States, Café Nevo, Saving Grace, A Heartbeat Away, Rowing in Eden,* and *Suspicion*. She lives on Long Island with her husband and two sons and teaches fiction writing at Hofstra and SUNY Farmingdale. Barbara Rogan can be reached through her Web site, www.barbararogan.com.